"Your mind is very quick, Miss Winston, and your tongue only slightly less so. I admire that," he said. She could not see the look in his eyes, because she could not make herself meet his gaze. That his gaze was fixed intently on her face however, she could not doubt. Her pulse had gradually quickened, and now that he stood so close to her, she could almost feel it jumping at her neck.

"Ah, but I forget that you hate me. How foolish of me," he went on. His voice was caressing, and he put out a hand to gently lift a curl that had fallen over her eyes. Roxanne held herself very still under the light touch. This time she would not retreat, as it only appeared to encourage him.

He bent and pressed his mouth to hers. Roxanne, startled, would have stepped away, but he put a hand on her shoulder, and in an instant his lips were exerting a magical effect on her will, evoking such feelings as she knew would disgrace her in the eyes of the world.

Shame suffused her, but a secret wish that he would not withdraw his mouth from hers for a long time, and that he would embrace her more closely, crept into her heart . . .

DISCOVER THE MAGIC
OF ZEBRA'S REGENCY ROMANCES!

THE DUCHESS AND THE DEVIL   (2264, $2.95)
by Sydney Ann Clary
Though forced to wed Deveril St. John, the notorious "Devil Duke," lovely Byrony Balmaine swore never to be mastered by the irrepressible libertine. But she was soon to discover that the human heart — and Satan — move in very mysterious ways!

AN OFFICER'S ALLIANCE   (2239, $3.95)
by Violet Hamilton
Virginal Ariel Frazier's only comfort in marrying Captain Ian Montague was that it put her in a superb position to spy for the British. But the rakish officer was a proven master at melting a woman's reserve and breaking down her every defense!

BLUESTOCKING BRIDE   (2215, $2.95)
by Elizabeth Thornton
In the Marquis of Rutherson's narrow view, a woman's only place was in a man's bed. Well, beautiful Catherine Harland may have been just a sheltered country girl, but the astonished Marquis was about to discover that she was the equal of any man — and could give as good as she got!

A NOBLE MISTRESS   (2169, $3.95)
by Janis Laden
When her father lost the family estate in a game of piquet, practical Moriah Lanson did not hesitate to pay a visit to the winner, the notorious Viscount Roane. Struck by her beauty, Roane suggested a scandalous way for Moriah to pay off her father's debt — by becoming the Viscount's mistress!

Available wherever paperbacks are sold, or order direct from the Publisher. Send cover price plus 50¢ per copy for mailing and handling to Zebra Books, Dept. 2431, 475 Park Avenue South, New York, N.Y. 10016. Residents of New York, New Jersey and Pennsylvania must include sales tax. DO NOT SEND CASH.

Second Season

THERESE
ALDERTON

ZEBRA BOOKS
KENSINGTON PUBLISHING CORP.

ZEBRA BOOKS

are published by

Kensington Publishing Corp.
475 Park Avenue South
New York, NY 10016

First printing: August, 1988

Printed in the United States of America

Chapter One

The tall clock in the upstairs passage at Westcombe Hall struck ten in sonorous tones. In her room at the end of the passage, Roxanne Winston lay counting the strokes and staring at the ceiling, her thick blond hair spread out in waves upon the pillow beneath her restless head. She ordered sleep to come, but tonight it was a disobedient servant. Resolutely she closed her blue eyes and tried to compose her thoughts, but they tumbled about restlessly. She chided herself for being so ridiculously anxious, as if it were going to be her first season, and not her sisters'.

Finally she gave up the attempt at sleep, lit her lamp, and sat up with a book. It was a very fine book, Law's *Serious Call to a Devout and Holy Life* which had been recommended to her by her younger and more devout sisters, but she failed to find in it the comfort and instruction she was seeking, and soon put it down.

Perhaps she could not sleep because the room was so stuffy. Roxanne crept to the window and opened it wide, allowing in a blast of wind that blew back her hair and stung her eyes, but somehow satisfied her. She felt a secret guilt, because almost everyone else in the house was horrified at her unhealthy passion for fresh air. Never mind that it was plenty of fresh air, as

Miss Lynchard, her former governess, insisted, that brought that lovely sparkle to Roxanne's pink-tinted complexion, or kept those large, wide-set blue eyes so clear and lively.

Feeling a little wicked, she left the window open a bit, returned to her bed, and began to review in her mind the preparations for their journey to London the next morning. The packing, the extravagance of hiring a post chaise along with horses for the first stage of the journey, the instructions to the servants, and all last-minute concerns had been attended to. It only remained for herself, her father, and the twins, Melodie and Gemma, to set off for Aunt Maria's townhouse in Upper Brook Street.

The girls, eighteen, and of a serene but perhaps too solemn brunette beauty, were to make their debut under the aegis of Lady Camberwick, as Roxanne had done three years before, accompanied by her mother. The end of that season had brought no wealthy husband for Roxanne, but tragedy for the family.

Lady Anne Winston, who had always been delicate, had taken ill and died in July. Scarcely a month later Alfred, Roxanne's only brother, had fought a duel and fled to France, unaware that he had not killed but only wounded his opponent. His worried family did not hear from him, but by the new year there was plenty of evidence that the brief peace with France would soon end, and the Winstons finally received word that Alfred had been reported drowned in a storm, trying to return to England.

Since then Roxanne's family responsibilities had left her no time to regret that abandoned and unsuccessful season. At eighteen, she had been shy and unprepossessing in her looks, unsure of herself, and completely unready to put herself forward in the fashionable world. The knowledge of her duty to her family to make a good match had burdened her heavily, as it did still.

Few gentlemen had shown any interest in the thin, quiet Miss Winston, and she had had no idea of how to induce any of them to come to the point of offering for her. In the end, she had not been at all reluctant to leave the frivolity and noise of London.

Now it was her sisters' chance to make the matches that would save the family from penury, but she doubted that they were any more ready than she had been. Their strong religious faith was of the reforming rather than the contemplative kind, and Roxanne was very much afraid that they looked upon the task ahead of them as a sinful exercise, and the young men who might be their husbands as godless creatures in need of redemption.

Her father, Sir James, had suffered an apoplectic attack after the double tragedy of that year, and now he was a partially paralyzed but very lively invalid, who insisted on accompanying his daughters to London. But Roxanne was happy to see the spark of life return to her father's eyes at last, and encouraged him to live as normal a life as possible.

She and Miss Lynchard, governess to Elizabeth and Dorothea, who, at nine and twelve, were the youngest of the Winston brood, tried to keep him amused and to calm his fidgets, but the past three years had been difficult. The family fortunes were at a low ebb, and Westcombe Hall was falling into disrepair. Land had had to be sold to give the girls the small dowries they possessed, and everyone felt the disgrace of it.

The indoor staff, aside from Sir James's personal attendant, were reduced to cook/housekeeper, governess, nurse, footman, and maid, and Roxanne and her sisters bore much of the responsibility for the large household, which at its peak of prosperity had sheltered a staff of twenty, in addition to stableboys, coachmen, and grooms. Now one carriage and two tired horses did the duty of transportation under the eye of a single retainer. The Winstons of Westcombe Hall struggled on.

Roxanne was weary of the routine, and was almost as eager to return to the amusements of London as she had been to leave them the first time.

A rattle of wheels and the crunch of hooves on gravel intruded on her thoughts. She heard the creak of a carriage door and then footsteps. Roxanne left her bed and hurried to the window, her heartbeat quickening at the sight of a large traveling chaise pulled by four horses. What kind of visitors would appear before her door at this hour of the night?

Unaware that the light behind her left her slender body, now unmistakably that of a woman and not a girl, in its softly draped white nightrobe revealed to those below, she stood between parted curtains and gazed down as two men, one supporting the other, walked slowly from the carriage.

One man stayed leaning against the copper beech tree on the lawn, and the other ran forward. With one part of her mind Roxanne knew that the second man was pounding the knocker and shouting to rouse the house, but she was transfixed at the sight of the first man, the one beneath the beech tree, who stood reealed in a shaft of moonlight.

His face was turned up to her, a pale face framed by wildly waving dark hair. His lips were parted, his silvery eyes wide, and he looked up at her as if he had never in his life seen a female before. The banging below had stopped, and the door had been answered by one of the servants, roused at last from sleep, by the time Roxanne realized that for two very good reasons she ought to step away from the window.

One, of course, was that it was unseemly to so expose herself before a strange man. The other . . . but he was not a strange man, and it was too late. The man below smiled, and to her mind it was a crafty, wicked smile. She ducked back and drew the curtains closed, clinging to them, her breath coming quickly. But she supposed it was too late. The Duke of Rutledge had almost certainly recognized her.

At one o'clock on a May afternoon a week before, at the very start of the London Season of 1805, a curricle had pulled up smartly in Albemarle Street before the townhouse of Henrietta Malverne, Duchess of Rutledge. It was driven by a young man in a many-caped blue driving coat, smart gray pantaloons, and glossy Hessians, attended by a liveried groom.

The driver of the equipage tossed the reins to the groom as he jumped lightly down. "Walk them, Ned, I won't be more than a quarter of an hour."

The elderly butler who answered his brisk knock at the door abandoned his stern expression as soon as he recognized the caller. "Welcome, Your Grace! It is a

9

pleasure to see you," he said with a smile of genuine fondness.

"Thank you, Harkins. I hope all is well with you and Mrs. Harkins?"

It was not a mere polite form. The genuine warmth in the young man's gray eyes conveyed his real interest to the butler.

"Very well indeed, sir."

"Happy to hear it. It has been a great while since I've paid my respects, has it not? I'm afraid the Duchess must be preparing a scold." He grinned and winked conspiratorially at the servant.

Harkins did not so let his dignity desert him as to return the wink, but his smile remained warm.

"Her Grace is in the breakfast parlor," he said as he relieved the visitor of his coat, beaver hat, and yellow kid gloves, revealing a taught, masculine figure in no need of padding, dressed with attention but not slavish devotion to fashion.

"Don't bother to announce me, then." The gentleman strode confidently down the wide passage, past the imposing stairway with its carved oak balustrade, to a room at the rear of the house. He entered without knocking and greeted the sole occupant of the small octagonal chamber with a sweeping bow and a kiss on the hand.

The lady thus saluted dropped her toast and reclaimed her beringed hand with a wry smile. "Really, Harry, if you would be more consistent in showing as much elegance in your manner to the rest of the world, I daresay I should have no problem at all in finding you a suitable wife!"

The gentleman laughed, and pulled up a chair,

wherein he arranged his limbs in an elegant sprawl. "So that, my dearest mama, was the topic on which you so urgently needed to consult with me! I ought to have guessed, from the evidence of your cryptic letter, that there was really no need to race down to London from Ivywood last night."

Even in his comfortable slouch, Henry Malverne, Duke of Rutledge, displayed his graceful bearing, and his mother, though her face expressed her chagrin at being found out, observed him with pride. She herself could take no credit for his height, his broad shoulders, and pleasant manly voice, but she fancied that he owed his chiseled features, luxuriant black hair, and keen gray eyes to her side of the family.

The Malvernes ran to mousy brown hair, and flabby faces set with orbs of a blue so pale as to be almost colorless. No, the fact that Henry was so handsome was due entirely to his perspicacity in choosing Althea Larkmead, one of the famed beauties of her generation, for his mother.

His Grace the Duke of Rutledge, was, at three and thirty years of age, an impressive personage, with more than sufficient charm when he chose to exert it. Moreover, he was completely aware of it. It was, perhaps, his doting mother liked to think, one of his only faults.

Now she pouted at him across the table. "You are an odious boy to extract my secret from me so soon. But if you come to see me at this ungodly hour of the morning, it is no wonder I cannot gather my wits enough to deceive you."

"My dear mama," said her unrepentant offspring, "you look very fetching in lilac and the lace on your

11

cap becomes you immensely, as you very well know, but it is high time for you to change from your morning attire. It is a perfectly respectable hour for making calls, and I hope that I will not shock you when I inform you that I have been up since seven and have already ridden in the park, breakfasted, and looked in at my club."

His mother shuddered and clung to the delicate Sevres cup that contained her coffee. "How . . . how *countryish* of you, Harry! If you would begin spending more of the Season attending all the fashionable events to which you are invited, I'm sure you would acquire more sophisticated habits."

Lord Rutledge frowned and inspected the pattern on the porcelain breakfast service. "I doubt not I could have learned worse habits in the country, ma'am."

His mother blushed. "You are right, my dear. And I am so thankful that — " But she thought of the life she had left him to live with his rake of a father in the country, and could not continue.

"I'm a beast to mention it, Mama," he said apologetically, taking her hand in his. "Now as to this other matter . . . I wish you would not concern yourself with it."

The Duchess made a wry face. "So ungrateful of you, after I spent a long evening with a horrid flock of old biddies last night for your sake! I endured the most dreadful gossip session, all for the purpose of discovering a suitable girl for you to pay court to, before the other gentlemen snap up all the best prospects." She sniffed and pushed away her half-finished breakfast.

The Duke became graver, almost stern, but he replied gently, "I am indeed grateful, Mama, for your efforts on my behalf. But when I am ready, I shall choose a wife for myself, and so I have told you for the last ten years."

"It's all very well to talk of not being ready, Harry," said the Duchess, "but you are getting older, and you will need an heir, unless you want Rutledge and Ivywood and all the rest of it to go to those awful relations of your father's. Besides, the females with whom you are in the habit of associating, I understand, are not at all the sort from which you would wish to choose your future Duchess. And you never make the slightest push to get to know any other ladies who might be more suitable. I declare, you are impossible!"

"Mama, dear Mama," the Duke said, shaking his head in mock disapproval, "what do you know about the type of female with whom I associate? For shame! As to the ladies who may be 'suitable,' as you call it . . . well frankly, I find the prospect of inspecting all those insipid misses being pushed forward by their scheming mamas to be quite insupportable. No, ma'am," he continued as his mother gave signs of protesting, "none of them will do for me, and I had hoped that you would have realized it by now."

"But Harry, my dear," the indefatigable lady continued, "that is exactly my point! I have found someone who does not at all answer to that description. She is not a green girl just out of the schoolroom, and neither is she on the shelf . . . yet. She is not at all insipid, and she has no mama to scheme for her. I do not, of course, count her aunt, Lady Camberwick, for Maria is one of my dearest friends and one could hardly call her scheming," she concluded, confident of having justified her interference in her son's affairs.

"Now," she continued, barely pausing for breath lest her son interrupt, "the young lady I have in mind is Roxanne Winston."

The Duke rose from his chair and strolled over to the small hearth, where he appeared to be inspecting some Dresden figurines on the mantel. "Her name is, of course, familiar," he said casually, "she came out three years ago . . . must be an antidote, if she's still unmarried."

"Now, Harry, you must not jump to conclusions! She is not at all an antidote, and Maria says her looks are much improved. Poor child, she lost her mother that season, and ever since has been closeted in the country with an invalid father and four younger sisters. Maria is sponsoring the twins this year, and Roxanne is going to accompany them."

"She didn't take, and I heard she was a washed-out little thing with nothing to say for herself," commented Harry Malverne.

"Well, if you did hear it then it is very unkind of you to repeat it," said his mother indignantly. "And I thought you prided yourself on forming your own impressions! You did not get about much that season — at least among respectable females. You were always closeted in one of your clubs, or off to a race or a horrid mill with your friends."

"This girl's brother was one of those friends, as you must recall, except that the friendship unfortunately and fatally, went sour," the Duke pointed out, not looking at his mother but inspecting her scanty breakfast repast with disgust.

The Duchess waved this away as of no consequence. "Of course I recall, but what has that to say to anything? Now, it is true that Miss Winston was not known as a beauty, but she is a serious young lady, Maria tells me, intelligent and accomplished, just what you require in a wife. Her birth is eminently suitable, though her fortune . . ." She hesitated. "If you were like your great-grandfather, who married to bring yet more wealth into the family, I would hesitate to recommend her, but since you appear to have no ambitions to expand the fortunes of the Malvernes, I can assume that Roxanne's minuscule dowry is of no consequence. Maria, who has excellent taste, can be relied upon to dress her to advantage, and many girls, you know, do improve with a few years of maturity."

"I am afraid, Mother," he said with a rueful smile, "that there will be many obstacles in the way before you may wish us happy."

"Why, what obstacles could there be?"

"I have already mentioned Alfred Winston," said her son.

Her Grace looked blank.

"Come, Mama," he said with some annoyance, "the girl's brother was once, to his misfortune, my friend, and surely you do not still pretend that the duel never happened?" He gave a short laugh. "I wouldn't be at all surprised if the first time she sees me, she gives me the cut direct. And of course, there are my other well-known eccentricities—"

"Come now, Henry, nobody who is anybody in society really believes you are anything like the man

15

your father was . . ." She stopped and fidgeted with a teaspoon. "As for the Winston boy, well . . ." She glanced at her son and hesitated. ". . . to be sure, it is very sad that he was so mistaken and fled to the Continent before he could be told he *hadn't* killed you . . . but it has been three years since he died, and surely the family has realized that you weren't at fault. After all, *he* challenged you," his mother pointed out.

"Yes, he did, didn't he?" said Henry. His gaze was far away.

"As for your eccentricities . . ." the Duchess continued, her mischievous smile revealing itself as the progenitor of His Grace's own. "As your mother and a lady, I realize I am not expected to know about such things, but the tales of your gaming and the extravagance lavished on your Birds of Paradise are no doubt greatly exaggerated."

"Mother!" cried the Duke, laughing, "indeed you should not know about such things, or at any rate, pretend not to notice if you should hear them," he admonished. "Besides, I have been a model of proper behavior lately," he told her, which was, surprisingly, quite true.

Even the Duchess knew, in the way mothers invariably did, that her son no longer found much pleasure in the risqué amusements he had formerly patronized. That was another reason she thought him at last ripe for marriage.

Her Grace glanced at him with sympathy. She realized how dreadful it was for a proud man to be the subject of scandal, even though it was long forgotten. A twinge of guilt afflicted the Duchess, but only a small one, as it had been twenty-one years since she had fled her husband's estates for London, leaving her son, as the law required, in his father's possession. It made no difference to the law that the Duke had insulted his wife and all standards of propriety by establishing his latest mistress at Rutledge, the ancient family seat, flaunting the creature in her face.

Divorce, of course, was out of the question. She could not have borne the incessant talk and investigation in order for the special bill to be passed through Parliament, and the isolation that would have been her lot afterward. Besides, the other women who had suffered it had done so in order to marry again. Henrietta Malverne had no such desire. So she had remained in London while her husband enjoyed his bacchanalian revels at Rutledge, and her son, Harry, grew up in the midst of them, protected only by a few scandalized but devoted servants who stayed on for his sake.

The Duchess had maintained a loving correspondence with her child and, through his all too infrequent visits, had determined that he had the strength of character to grow up uncontaminated by his father's excesses. She found her own consolation in the social whirl of the haut ton.

When the Duke died, his end no doubt hastened by his years of dissipation, and Henry came into his inheritance, there were whispers whenever his name was mentioned, speculation as to what kind of life he had led under his father's roof, and his future course.

On the one hand he was much sought after and toadied to by ambitious flatterers, but on the other he was treated coolly and kept at a distance by the people who should have been his companions. Though his

17

inborn pride was not calculated to overcome this initial prejudice, gradually society began to realize that he was not at all the man his father was, and the talk eventually died down. But the damage had been done, and he was more reserved and aloof than his mother liked.

In his habits, he was very much like other young men of his age and class, except for his ability to foil all attempts at intimacy by a chilling reserve. He had few close friends, but the Duchess had to console herself with the fact that he was now universally respected, if not always liked.

In the years when it was still safe and a matter of course, the young Duke had visited the Continent for months at a time. He used part of his inheritance to renovate Ivywood, a large country house long in the late Duke's possession and long neglected, filling it with beautiful objects acquired on his trips, and he retreated there whenever the scandals and flattery of London became too much for him.

The Duchess thought her son's life unnatural, and she endeavored to mend it by trying to provide him with a wife who would do what, in her judgment, all his riches and good looks and freedom had failed to do. That is, to make him happy.

The only time she had seen him truly busy and content was during his brief friendship with the clever and lively Alfred Winston. For several months, three years ago, they had been seen everywhere in London together. Their mutual regard ended when the young Alfred, new to Town and generously sponsored about by the more knowledgeable Rutledge, was said to have became interested in the same female of dubious virtue who was at that moment the object of the Duke's attentions.

Her Grace recalled with pain the beginning of the quarrels, the shouting in the drawing room before shocked witnesses, the glasses smashed against the marble mantel, and then the fateful game of cards at which young Winston had accused Harry of cheating. The Duke had then requested him to name his friends.

She had not known of the duel until it was all over, and it was Geoffrey Pearson, Alfred Winston's friend and neighbor, who had brought her wounded son back to her. Oddly enough, Henry had smiled at her, as though he had accomplished some great feat, just before he fainted from loss of blood.

And before the ton could even begin to exclaim over it, Alfred Winston, terrified that he had killed his noble opponent, had fled to France. The Duchess could remember Roxanne that year, pale and shy, unable to enjoy the brief round of gaiety before her mother and brother were taken from her. But Maria Camberwick had assured her that the girl was now lovely. Her Grace did not consider that poor Mr. Winston's fate could possibly make a difference to her matrimonial plans for his sister.

Henry stood and bowed over her hand. "Mother, it has been delightful, but I must go. And please, not another word about this Miss Winston. I'll wager you my diamond stickpin that she wouldn't have me anyway." He smiled his most charming smile, but his fond parent was not deterred from her mission.

"Don't be absurd. What use should I have for your paltry diamonds? Besides, I'm sure Roxanne is much too sensible a girl to turn down an advantageous offer simply because of an unfortunate incident in the past. She has her family to think of, you know."

Rutledge frowned. "Is she on the catch for a wealthy husband then?"

The Duchess winced. "Pray don't be so vulgar, my dear. Of course she must marry well, with all those sisters to look after and no fortune. I'm sure the child has come to terms with her brother's behavior by now, and cannot blame you for his death!"

"No, I doubt she would let such a scruple stand between her and the match of the season, if she is as intelligent as you say," muttered Henry. "You make me feel like the fly in the spider's web. Pray stop spinning your web, Mother, you and Lady Camberwick and this Miss Winston, for I am a good deal cleverer than most flies, you know."

The Duchess grimaced but continued, undaunted. "Stop being nonsensical, my boy, and listen to me. I can assure you that you needn't worry about the past, because Maria tells me that there is quite a religious streak in the family now, so very likely they look upon the dead brother as a sheep gone astray and taken to the Lord's bosom, or some such thing," she said. "None of which has anything to do with the fitness of Roxanne Winston to be your wife, which is the only thing of which I am certain," she concluded.

"You are adorable," her son said with infuriating calm. He kissed her hand, and left.

Chapter Two

On a sunny but windy May afternoon, the day before the Winstons' departure for London, a ducal traveling chaise emblazoned with the arms of Rutledge was journeying toward Westcombe, a village a short distance from Salisbury, on the edge of the plain. It passed, unbeknownst to its passengers, a small alehouse set some distance off the main road. This humble structure was screened from view by a tangle of trees, the path leading to it from the road almost totally obscured by vegetation.

But from its narrow, low-pitched doorway a knowledgeable observer could keep watch over all that passed on the road. That was, in fact, just what a big bearded man was doing at the moment when the Duke of Rutledge, accompanied by former Army Lieutenant Geoffrey Pearson, was driven past.

The man's frame filled the little door of the alehouse, blocking out most of the light in the shabby room, where dirty and roughly dressed men were tossing down tankards of ale. A few amused themselves with dice, others with cards. Some were openly cleaning and checking pistols.

The bearded watcher at the door spat on the ground, squinted into the room, and allowed himself to grin in satisfaction.

"Here they are, m'lads, as expected. Look sharp on't now!" Several heads looked up from the ale, and in a surprisingly short time, three of the men were alert and ready to mount their horses, which were concealed at the back of the house.

Geoffrey Pearson, his valet, and the Duke's coachman were blithely unaware of this activity as they continued on their road, thinking only of the good dinner awaiting them at the Angel at Westcombe, and then, of their beds at Rosemark, the Pearsons' home some fourteen miles farther. But Rutledge's attention strayed from the conversation almost imperceptibly as they passed the hidden alehouse, as though he were listening for the very slight rustle of departure which he could not possibly have heard. Then they were past.

"Any regrets about selling out, Geoffrey?" Rutledge asked his companion.

Geoffrey shrugged and brushed back a strand of straight blond hair from his broad forehead. "You know I'm not the hero type, my lord. I liked soldiering well enough, and I live for the day when we beat Boney for good, but I've a feeling it won't be soon, and I'm needed at home now that father's gone. Besides," he said with a look of distaste, "I've seen too many friends die already, and I can tell you I've no stomach for it. Not to mention the business with Alfred."

The Duke's eyes flashed a warning, and Geoffrey colored and stammered for a moment. "Th—that is . . ."

Rutledge's caution was wasted, because the valet whose presence required this discretion was fast asleep. Nevertheless he thought it wise to remind his young friend not to speak of certain matters.

"I sh-shouldn't like to think of what he went through . . ." finished Geoffrey.

"Then I advise you, my friend," said the Duke dryly, "not to think of it — or speak of it." And he closed his eyes.

The bearded man and his band of cutthroats watched the equipage pass, waited a few moments, and started after them as they rounded a bend in the road. Though the thud of the hooves following them was barely noticeable under the sound of the chaise, a keen observer would have noted the Duke's slight glance backward and a fleeting smile of satisfaction. However, Geoffrey Pearson noticed none of these things.

The mounted men did not pursue their prey along the road, but used some paths and byways unknown to the more conventional traveler, emerging on the main road only to be sure of keeping the chaise in sight until they reached Westcombe. The Angel was a big, bustling place, and there the four men separated without drawing any notice to themselves, gave their horses into the care of the ostlers, and settled down in the taproom to wait.

The Duke's chaise, meanwhile, having been driven smartly between the gateposts of the inn yard and drawn up before the entrance, was received with a great deal more ceremony, and the Angel's landlord was overwhelmed at being presented to a Duke, and being able to contemplate the honor of feeding him. It was some time, owing to Mr. Muggins's awe and his inquiries about Lieutenant Pearson's health and lately ended army career, before the two men were settled in the best private parlor. But Rutledge, during this long conversation, had made a leisurely survey of the yard, as though mildly curious about all of his fellow travelers. He gave a quick glance into the open door of the taproom, all the while conversing with his companion.

"I'm sharp set, and I've a devil of a thirst," he remarked as they took possession of their parlor.

"What can you give us, Muggins?" asked Geoffrey, stretching before the lighted grate.

"A pasty of eels, sir, a beautiful joint, perhaps a fresh kilt goose, my lord, and some fine new potatoes, hmm?" murmured Mr. Muggins, examining his guests' middles as if estimating their capacity for the refreshment offered by his kitchens.

"Is there any of that famous apple tart you used to give me before I bought my colors?" Geoffrey inquired.

"To be sure, young sir, and a good cheese, and some of that fine port as your late father advised me to set down so long ago, bless his soul." And he hurried off to fulfill these commissions.

For an hour, a rather abbreviated but adequate space of time to do justice to the food, the two gentlemen devoted themselves with excellent appetites to the joint of beef, the pasty, the duck, a bit of roasted mutton thrown in for good measure, and all the accompaniments. They washed it down with a very respectable claret, and finished off with the apple tart, set off with slices of good sharp cheese.

When the remnants of this feast had been cleared away, they sat over the excellent port, reluctant to resume their journey, as the wind, by the sound of it, had picked up considerably and now that the sun was down there was no warmth to offset its power.

After a few minutes of desultory conversation, the older man said, "I'm afraid we must leave the comforts of the Angel and get back on the road. We should be at Rosemark in less than two hours, and then you will have the felicity of surprising your entire family with your belated return to the hearth. I suppose they expected you a week ago, and are now wondering what had become of you."

Geoffrey grinned a little sheepishly. "I couldn't very well go back to them in the condition in which you found me, Harry."

"It would do you good to be ashamed of yourself, young man," said Rutledge. "Although I have been found many a time suffering in the morning from the affects of a night on the town, never yet have I managed, even in my heedless youth, to frequent places of the type from which I was forced to remove you last night."

"Now you're funning me, sir! Heedless youth, indeed! Why, no one could have been more dedicated, or gone into more danger—"

"Silence, youngster! You begin to annoy me." The Duke put down his glass with ringing firmness.

"You are too modest," Geoffrey persisted. "I only wish the world could know—"

"And I wish you will wish nothing of the sort," said Henry Malverne in chilling tones. "The subject of my escapades is closed for now, because"—he leaned toward his companion and his face was deadly serious—"it isn't over yet by half. Talking's dangerous at

25

all times, but especially now. You put someone's life in danger every time you open your lips. If you haven't learned discretion by now, I'm afraid you will no longer be of use to us." He held the younger man's gaze with his own for a long moment.

Geoffrey took his rebuke well. "I'm sorry, but whenever I think of Alfred, I always . . ." He bit his lip. "I won't mention it again."

Henry relented. "You're a good fellow, Pearson, just a little wet behind the ears."

"Not wet behind the ears, my lord, surely not a man who's been to war!" protested his companion.

"But I daresay you have learned your lesson by now," continued the Duke. "Anyway, isn't it time you left off that rakish fool's play and started thinking of setting up your nursery now you're home for good?"

"Well, I like that!" cried Geoffrey. "First I'm wet behind the ears, then it's time to think of getting leg-shackled. Fine talk for a man who's still a bachelor himself. Shouldn't His Grace think of finding himself a bride?"

Rutledge stopped in mid-chuckle. "Your sister wouldn't have me, you know. It was always Alfred with her," he said quietly, "though I was foolish enough to think it was only a childish infatuation."

"I'm sorry for it, because it would be splendid to have you for a brother, but Alfred and Fanny were always thick as thieves, and probably never thought of marrying anyone else but each other," Geoffrey replied. "And you needn't worry about her talking, Harry. She's the most closemouthed female I've ever—"

"I have the greatest confidence in Miss Pearson's

discretion," said Rutledge, a slow smile creeping over his face, "although I am fast losing whatever trust I once put in yours."

Geoffrey looked sheepish.

"As for heirs . . . I have an heir," continued the Duke.

"Beg pardon, my lord, but your cousin isn't fit to clean your shoes, let alone step into them. You ought to have an heir of your own get," Geoffrey insisted.

Rutledge aimed a playful blow at his companion. "Are you in cahoots with my scheming mother, sir? Let's go, we've a late start as it is, and I want to deliver you to your family unharmed. If you keep on like this, I won't be able to guarantee it!"

Geoffrey merely grinned, and when their shot had been paid and their compliments given to Mr. Muggins, he followed his friend out of the inn.

Their carriage had been ordered with the port, and the horses and coachman were both refreshed and ready. Neither the Duke nor Geoffrey took any notice of four men who individually made their ways from the taproom and were mounting in the inn yard at the same time. That is not to say, however, that Henry Malverne was completely unaware of their presence.

After clearing the yard of the Angel, they made a slow but steady progress, their way illuminated by the rising three-quarter moon and their carriage lamps. By way of entertainment, Geoffrey brought up the subject of marriage again, and Rutledge, who had been a little distracted and sleepy since dinner, had to be spoken to twice before Geoffrey could get his attention.

"You were not far off the mark, Harry," he said,

"when you suggested that now I'm home I ought to think of the future. I have a lady in mind."

"Do you? Who is she?"

"Well, that's the rub. It's demmed awkward . . . I've known her forever, but I've never spoken of marriage. To tell the truth, I have no idea whether she'll have me or not."

"Oh?"

In the darkened carriage, the Duke felt his companion shift on the cushions and heard him sigh. "It's—it's Miss Winston," said Geoffrey.

The Duke's head came up. "Winston?"

"Yes, Roxanne. The devil of it is that though we've known each other forever, she hasn't seen me since—"

"Alfred was killed. And she is his sister. A pity." That was all Rutledge said, but in the darkness the valet sitting across from them would not have seen his hand grip Geoffrey's elbow in warning.

"I wish you luck. I suppose you'll go to her tomorrow?" the Duke asked, thinking of the disappointment in store for his mother and the girl's aunt.

"Of course, and I pray she'll have me." Geoffrey sounded miserably uncertain.

Rutledge did not know why, but he heard himself say, "Then why not wait . . . let her get to know you again? There's no hurry, I'm sure. She's remained unmarried this long . . ."

"Oh, but there is need for hurry. She's going to town this season, to bring out her younger sisters, and it'll be just my luck she'll take this time 'round," Geoffrey said gloomily.

The Duke forbore to comment, and his companion could not tell from his expression what he might think

28

of the matter. At any rate, he had lapsed into his preoccupation again, and Geoffrey had the distinct impression that his conversation was no longer required. If he had not known how ridiculous it was, he would have thought that the Duke was . . . waiting for something.

At length they turned off onto a local lane, and after this the road grew rougher.

Geoffrey fidgeted wearily. "Only two more miles. It seems as though it will take an eternity at this pace," he said as the wheels sank into another rut in the damp ground.

At that moment a sharp noise split the night, and reflexively Geoffrey threw himself to the floor of the chaise. The Duke was not dilatory in following his example, and just as he hit the floor, a second shot rang out, this time closer, the sound coming from the woods to their left. The horses were rearing and Rutledge's coachman was terrified himself, but doing his best to control them.

Two attackers became visible, emerging mounted from the woods, and in half a moment former Lieutenant Pearson had drawn his own pistol and, after a leap from the rocking carriage, returned the fire.

He wounded one man while Rutledge slipped out of the carriage and, having armed himself with two pistols which he always kept hidden in the vehicle, crouched behind it and aimed at the other man. The man eluded him and drew close enough to hit Geoffrey, who fell, clutching at his leg.

Rutledge hit the man in the arm a second later, and he and the other wounded attacker drew off, but no sooner had Rutledge called to the coachman to help him get Geoffrey back into the carriage, than the big bearded man and a companion, who had been hiding in reserve among the trees, emerged.

A choked cry from the coachman was a warning that came too late for Rutledge. The bearded man shot the Duke in the shoulder before he could reload, and the two were on him in a moment. He struggled against them, but was knocked senseless with a pistol butt, and other weapons aimed at Geoffrey, the coachman, and the terrified servant, who poked his head out of the window of the carriage, ensured their stillness.

The bearded man rummaged through the Duke's pockets. Curiously, he ignored the heavy signet ring, the silver watch, fob, and seal, though he did appropriate the diamond pin which glittered on his neckcloth. At last, with a grunt of satisfaction, he pulled from a pocket inside His Grace's coat a sealed letter. He slipped it into his own dirty coat, and gestured to his companion. Keeping pistols trained on Geoffrey, his servant, and the coachman, they backed away and remounted their horses, then turned and rode off into the woods after their wounded companions.

The heretofore paralyzed coachman and valet leaped to assist their masters. Geoffrey struggled to sit up, grimacing in pain, while the other two frantically tried to revive the Duke. "Get His Grace . . . lift him into the chaise," said Geoffrey weakly, waving away their assistance.

The two men clumsily lifted the large, unconscious form of the Duke and half dragged, half carried him into the vehicle, laying him on the seat. Then they came back for Geoffrey and performed the same office. "Drive on," he told them, before loss of blood made him lose consciousness. "Take the first turn . . . there's a house there . . . Winstons' . . . Westcombe Hall . . ." and then he collapsed.

The frightened coachman urged the horses on over the ruts. A particularly bad bump awakened Rutledge, who groaned and felt his head carefully. There was a large lump on it, but little blood. He could not lift his left arm, however, and his shoulder felt warm and sticky.

"Are you all right, Your Grace?" asked Geoffrey's valet, who had been doing his best to stanch both men's bleeding.

"Aside from the fact that my stomach is heaving, my head is in blinding pain, and I have a bullet in my shoulder, I feel perfectly well," he assured the man, closing his eyes against the moonlight that now streamed into the carriage.

"We'll be all right soon, Your Grace," the servant told him. "My master said there's a house not far away." The valet had pulled a spare shirt out of one of Geoffrey's boxes and, having ripped it in two, had inexpertly bandaged both men's wounds.

"Tighter, man . . ." The Duke pointed at his unconscious friend. "He'll bleed to death unless the bandage is made fast."

The valet fumbled with the makeshift bandage. "Take . . . take my neckcloth . . ." whispered Rutledge. "Tie it round his leg . . ."

The valet looked horrified. "But Your Grace! Your neckcloth!"

"Don't worry, the world will not end because Rutledge gets some bloodstains on his linen," he said,

31

and he would have removed the cloth himself, weak as his fingers were, had not the valet leaped to do it for him.

"Your Grace . . . your pin . . . they've stolen it."

"Stolen?" The duke's brows rose, and he felt about his coat and waistcoat, but his hand fell nervelessly at his side. He waited till the valet had secured the neckcloth tightly around Geoffrey's leg.

"If you will do me the favor of searching in my coat for a moment . . . yes, that pocket there. Is there a letter?" He waited, his eyes closed, his mouth very white.

"No, no, Your Grace, there is nothing here."

The white lips curved in what could have easily been mistaken for a smile of satisfaction, but was no doubt actually a grimace of pain.

While the servant was attending to Geoffrey, Rutledge made himself sit up on the seat and endure the bumps and jolts until they turned off the road and went through some iron gates, fortunately open, onto a gravel drive. The gravel rattled in the wheels and crunched under the horses' feet, and finally the chaise stopped. By now Geoffrey had regained consciousness, and he and the valet protested when the Duke got out, but Rutledge's head was clearing, and he insisted.

Before them was the dark bulk of a house, dimly outlined in moonlight, with only one window lit up in a corner, on the second floor. The valet left the Duke leaning against the broad trunk of a tree, while he went to raise someone within, thumping on the door and calling for help.

Rutledge's thoughts were rambling. He was very

sorry that it had all been so much more violent than expected. He had never meant for Geoffrey to be hurt. The enemy was more ruthless than he had thought. Poor Alfred. . . . But the ruse had succeeded.

He wanted to go and call for help himself but his voice would not obey him. All he could do was stare up at the window of the lighted room and hope that its inhabitant would come down and make sure that Geoffrey did not bleed to death. For himself, he had few fears. He had suffered more grievous wounds and lived.

His wish was granted, but it only caused him more confusion. White curtains parted, and a slender female figure was framed in the window. He thought, very hazily, that she was the loveliest creature he had ever beheld. She was robed in white, with hair that shone like gold in the lamplight behind her, cascading around her shoulders. The girl looked down at him with huge eyes that gleamed midnight blue, to match the sky. Or so he saw them. By this time her figure was beginning to blur. Her mouth opened in a wide "O," and Rutledge smiled, but in a moment she drew the curtains closed. That was the last thing he saw before he fell into a soft blackness.

Chapter Three

Roxanne dressed quickly, putting on the simple blue round dress she had worn that day, and hurriedly pulled her hair back, tying it with a ribbon. Male voices floated faintly up from downstairs, along with the voice of the housekeeper. It was time to face what had to be faced. Roxanne had no idea why the man responsible for her brother's death should have the temerity to present himself at Westcombe Hall late at night, but the sounds from below were anxious, and it was obvious that, aside from the oddity of the Duke's appearance, something was very wrong.

In the hall she met the cook and housekeeper, Mrs. Porter. "Oh, thank goodness you've come down, Miss Roxanne. I didn't like to wake you, but there's two wounded gentlemen come to the door, and I've put them in the rear sitting room and sent for the doctor." Before Roxanne could question her she hurried away muttering about hot water and clean cloths.

Roxanne headed for the sitting room, her heart full of trepidation. Wounded! Even if the Duke of Rutledge were the devil himself, she could not, in common charity, refuse him help. She struggled for inward as well as outward calmness, but the fact that the Duke, from the sofa where he had been placed by the Winstons' footman, met her glance immediately she entered the room rendered these efforts useless. Roxanne felt her face flush with anger. He was examining her with unabashed interest, completely unaffected by her frowns.

"What's this? Is it my fair apparition! You have lured me here by your lighted window." He laughed, but winced immediately, raising a hand to his head. "Perhaps no apparition, then, but a creation of this damnable bump on the head."

Roxanne pushed aside her anger, and went to him. She had much experience nursing the sick in the village, and till the doctor arrived she must do what she could. So involved was she in checking his bandage and feeling his pulse, all the while avoiding his sardonic silvery gaze, that it was a few moments before she remembered the presence of a second wounded man, and then only because His Grace reminded her.

"I am forever in your debt, my dear, for your kind attentions, but I wish you would see to my friend, who may be bleeding to death," he said calmly.

Flustered and annoyed with herself for allowing the mere presence of the man to distract her, she ordered the servant to give him some brandy and went across the room to where the second gentlemen lay on another sofa, attended by a valet who was holding a bloodstained cloth to his master's leg.

Roxanne drew a sharp breath. The man was Geoffrey Pearson, their near neighbor and one of their oldest friends.

On his thigh was a red-stained bandage. Through it the wound still bled sluggishly. "Geoffrey!"

Geoffrey opened his eyes. "Roxanne," he whispered. "What — how . . ."

"Hush, never mind that now. You're wounded and the doctor is coming soon."

"Fear not, my friend, this fair angel will minister to you," came a voice from across the room. "I quickly regained my own hold on life at the mere sight of her."

Roxanne turned and beheld His Grace the Duke of Rutledge struggling to lean upon his good arm, and regarding them both with a mischievous smile.

"Your Grace, I believe your head wound has made you delirious. It would be greatly to your advantage if you would stay as quiet as possible," said Roxanne with as much authority as she could muster.

Rutledge winked at Geoffrey. "Your least wish, my fair one, is mine to obey at once." Roxanne wondered if perhaps the administration of brandy had been unwise.

The housekeeper arrived at that moment with water and cloths, and Roxanne left the Duke to the other woman's attentions, while she allowed the valet to bare the wound on Geoffrey's thigh for her inspection, before instructing him to clean it.

"Will you not do it yourself, Roxanne? This fellow is a mite clumsy." Geoffrey's voice was that of a fretful child.

Roxanne smiled. "How improper of you to suggest it," she chided him. "Come now, you know very well that a sheltered creature like myself ought not even to be permitted in the room, let alone inspect the injured part!"

She managed to elicit a weak smile from Geoffrey, who, though he had not seen her in a long time, was certainly aware that she had rarely been sheltered from anything. He knew that she had never been missish, and if the wound had been in a less delicate place, she would not have hesitated to tend it.

"It does not look too bad," she told him. "But the doctor must remove the bullet." She felt Geoffrey's forehead. "You're not feverish . . . yet. Are you in much pain?"

"No . . . not much." His wince as the valet dabbed a cloth too near the wound belied his words. He smiled. "You are an angel, Roxanne. What a strange way to meet again, after all this time. . . . I was coming to see you tomorrow . . ."

"Be quiet, Geoffrey, we can talk later when your wound is tended to," she said, but she smiled back at him.

There was pain in seeing him again, since he reminded her so much of her carefree childhood and of her brother, but she was happy too that he was home. She and her family had prayed for his safety every day since he had bought his commission. How ironic that he had escaped injury in battle only to be wounded here, barely two miles from his own home! She broke her own rule of silence and asked him, "What happened? How came you and . . . and His Grace to be shot?"

But at that moment the housekeeper called to her. "Miss Roxanne! This gentleman won't lie still and let me clean his wound for him."

She reluctantly went to Rutledge's side. "What's this, my lord? You will lie very quietly and let Mrs. Porter tend to you." She stood looking down at him, arms crossed and the sternest expression she could summon up on her face.

"Why, sweet termagant, I believe for you I will lie

still. No one has spoken to me in that tone since the days of my old Nanny's reign."

"It's about time that someone did, then," Roxanne said quite without thinking, and then cried "Oh!" and colored up when she recollected to whom she was speaking. She bent over Rutledge's wound to examine it, glad that her hair, loosened from its ribbon, fell across her eyes and screened them from his caustic gaze.

"Quite all right, my dear," said the Duke in a somewhat weaker voice. "I shall allow you to take such liberties, as we are old . . . acquaintances."

"Hardly even that, Your Grace," she said with dignity, and directed her attention to his shoulder. The bullet was buried deep in the flesh, and the look of it worried her. She wished the doctor would arrive. The valet had cut off the Duke's shirt, and though a sheet now covered most of him, his wounded shoulder, large and well muscled, lay bare before her.

"It's not so very bad," she told him. "Will you now lie still and let Mrs. Porter clean it?"

"No, I will not." He fastened his gaze on her face, assessing her reaction.

Roxanne fought down annoyance. "Your Grace, if you wish your wound tended you must—"

"You seem very knowledgeable, Miss Winston. Will you not tend to it yourself? I'm sure there's nothing at all improper in a young lady as competent as yourself dressing a perfectly innocent shoulder wound." His laughing eyes told her he had overheard her conversation with Geoffrey.

Roxanne frowned. "Very well." She tried to still the sudden trembling in her hands as she began to bathe

38

the wound. His body tensed beneath her touch, gentle as it was, and she apologized, rather stiffly, for hurting him.

It was all she could do to control the anger that welled up inside her, even after three years, at the thought of how this man had led her charming, sensible brother astray until Alfred was so lost to everything as to challenge him to a duel over a disreputable female.

She deftly bandaged the wound again, and as her patient looked so white about the lips, she administered some more brandy to him, gently lifting his head a little until he could sip from the glass. His eyes met hers as he did, and she looked down, but now the sheet had slipped and more of his bare chest was exposed.

It was broad and muscular, and covered with fine dark hair. Roxanne remembered how hot and unexpectedly smooth his skin had felt beneath her fingers, and suddenly she felt very warm herself. Beneath Rutledge's flesh, the strong curved lines that marked his muscles began to move alarmingly, and just before she was recalled to the impropriety of staring at the Duke's nakedness, she felt a sense of untapped power in this injured, but very large and vital body only inches away.

She looked away hastily, and the expression on his face explained the reason for those strange movements of his chest. He was laughing at her, and trying not to laugh at the same time. She let him lie back down against the cushions, not particularly gently, and moved away, biting her lip in vexation. No doubt his amusement caused him some pain, and she could not help but feel that, under the circumstances, it was a well-deserved punishment.

Eventually the Duke's pain won out over his amusement, and the struggle not to laugh ended. "Thank you, Miss Winston," he said softly.

Roxanne, suddenly more embarrassed than angry, avoided his gaze and said, "It was nothing at all, my lord. Now do lie still till the doctor arrives."

She went to sit with Geoffrey, talking to him quietly, checking him now and again for fever. Once he put his hand over hers on his forehead and said, "Leave it, Rozzie, it feels so cool and soothing," and she smiled to hear him use her childhood nickname, but gently removed her hand.

She liked Geoffrey, but his life and hers had gone in different directions a long time ago, and it was better not to encourage him to believe his rights as an old friend also gave him permission to take liberties. Besides, she doubted he could have serious intentions toward her. The Pearsons, like the Winstons, were a large and not very prosperous family. Geoffrey's bride must bring him, if not a fortune, then at least a competence.

When they were all children together, she and Alfred, Geoffrey and his sister Fanny, she had once idolized him. He was about three years her senior, and Geoffrey had treated her with all the formality he reserved for his younger sister, which is to say, none at all.

Three years ago, Geoffrey had grieved with them over Alfred's death, but by then he had already changed. As the women in the Winston family grew more serious, Geoffrey had grown worldly. Even at her brother's loss, Roxanne thought, the old Geoffrey would have blamed himself for letting his friendship with Alfred grow cool, and in a way, driving him into the company of a man like the Duke of Rutledge. But the grown-up Geoffrey had only expressed his sorrow, and never mentioned a word about the estrangement between himself and Alfred.

In those days it was always Rutledge, and the Duke, and His Grace on her brother's lips. The older man had taken Alfred under his wing and introduced him to the most corrupting influences of London, and the already frustrated Alfred, bound by a promise to his mother not to enter the Army, which was his heart's desire, had, to Roxanne's horror, relieved his disappointment in dissipation. He had neglected his correspondence with her and his old friends, and shrugged off in a manner utterly foreign to him thier gentle remonstrances. And Rutledge, who lay here bleeding in the Winstons family's sitting room, was at the root of it all.

Roxanne felt that remembering her Christian compassion had never before been so difficult as it was at this moment. It was with a sense of the greatest relief that she saw Miss Lynchard enter the room. Good, calm, sensible Miss Lynchard would surely be able to get the troublesome Duke to behave himself.

She quickly explained the situation to her former governess, who examined the men and approved everything that had been done. "You have handled the situation admirably, Roxanne. Your Grace, Mr. Pearson, the doctor will probably be with us shortly. Until then I strongly urge you not to move, lest your bleeding start again."

Roxanne thought she even saw a grudging respect dawning in the Duke's eyes as he listened to Miss Lynchard's sensible discourse and observed her brisk and competent movements. Well, perhaps His Grace was not entirely lost to common humanity after all. Anyone who could appreciate her sterling qualities could not be all bad.

But in the next few days she was to be severely tried and almost revoked this judgment. The doctor, who removed the bullets while Geoffrey fainted and the Duke held grimly onto consciousness, white-lipped and white-knuckled, left strict instructions that they must not be removed to Rosemark for a week.

The next morning, Sir James Winston and the twins, who had, thankfully, slept through all the excitement, were told of the occurrences of the night before and packed off to Aunt Maria and Upper Brook Street without Roxanne. She regretted it deeply, but saw no other way out of the dilemma.

"No, Papa," she said when her father protested against leaving her behind. "I know the girls and the servants will attend you very well on the journey"— she planted a swift kiss on his cheek—"though you were no doubt counting on me to spoil you as I always do."

"Nonsense!" said Mr. Winston, whose broad, well-fleshed frame and ruddy complexion belied his semi-paralyzed state. "You're stricter with me than that fool of a doctor ever is. I know when I'm well off—I shall have the twins fetching and carrying and jumping at my every whim."

Roxanne shook her head at him. " 'Tis sad, but very true, I'm afraid. Those girls dote on you excessively, and haven't the slightest notion of how to control a wretched, ill-tempered invalid like yourself." Since this teasing was almost a ritual part of their daily life, Roxanne did not expect her father to respond the way he did.

"I am a cross for to you bear, aren't I?" he said anxiously, taking her hand in his right one. The other one sat limp and useless in his lap. "Not only do my daughters have to cater to a sick old man and his foolishness, but they all accept without question their duty to bring some money into this unfortunate family." His amiable face was creased with sorrow and bitterness.

"I tell you, my dear" — his voice trembled a little — "it disgusts me that I can do so little for you children, and that it is all up to you to find wealthy husbands, when you are all worth more to me than any fortune." His sigh was as deep as though it came from his soul, and Roxanne heard it with dismay. "But that is the way of the world, and I must see you all established, if not with my money, then with some other man's."

Roxanne dropped to her knees before his chair. "Papa, I wish you will not worry. Of course as many of us as can must marry well and look after the others. Now, don't go on with that silly talk about being a cross to bear. It is only when you lose your spirits like this that I lose patience with you."

She planted another kiss on his cheek, and the good humor slowly returned to his countenance as he watched her fuss about him, arranging his pillow, putting his spectacles, books, medicine glass, and newspapers to hand.

"You know I'll worry if I'm not there to see that

you're comfortable, but I can't leave poor Miss Lynchard and Mrs. Porter all alone with the two gentlemen to nurse, and the little girls and the house to look after as well." She stood up and sighed. "It will be difficult, but Geoffrey is our neighbor, and the Duke is his guest, so I cannot do less than care for them till they can be moved."

"Don't worry, child, tend to your duty. I shall muddle through without you—if Melodie and Gemma don't sicken me with psalms all the way to town." He groaned. "It's just my misfortune to be father to the two most devout young ladies in Wiltshire."

Roxanne laughed, but she knew that her father, who had once thought of making a career in the church, was pleased at the religious devotion of the twins, though it was often carried to exasperating excess.

" 'Twill do you good to be prayed over and repent your wicked ways," she told him with a laugh.

The twins, however, were upset by the change in plans and were ready with protests. "But sister," said Gemma, "will it not do damage to your reputation to be left alone with these two gentlemen, one of whom is the very Rutledge to whom we owe the loss of our brother—"

"—and in such proximity as sick-nursing necessitates," said Melodie.

"—it is certainly a most irregular and dangerous situation," finished Gemma.

Roxanne gathered her patience together, as always when dealing with her proper and pious sisters. "You make an excellent point, girls, but we have a duty to tend to those who call upon our assistance. You

44

would not have me leave Geoffrey, our old friend and neighbor, to the mercies of the servants, or to burden poor Miss Lynchard with all of this extra work? And all for the sake of an overrefined delicacy!"

The girls looked at one another for a long moment, and Roxanne had, as many times before, the eerie feeling that they were conversing together without speaking aloud. Finally they nodded, and Melodie, usually the spokesman, said, "We understand, sister, and we will do our best to free your mind from the burden of our father's care until we are reunited in London."

"And Roxanne," said Gemma, the livelier of the two, "do you not think that you might give His Grace some improving works to read, and when he is strong enough, let him come downstairs for prayers? Perhaps the stress of his injury, and the good example of you and Miss Lynchard might effect a change in his mind, and maybe even save his soul!" Her dark eyes glowed at the thought of this accomplishment.

"It is in just such crises as these," Melodie added hopefully, "that conversion finds its most fertile soil."

Roxanne suppressed a smile. How absurd it was to think that they, the very people who had been injured by him, might, with the aid of a gunshot wound and enforced convalescence, endeavor to save a soul like Rutledge's, which was no doubt as black as coal and quite content to be so.

But the twins never lost an opportunity of awakening enthusiasm in the sinful. And of course, it was the experience of that dreadful year when they had lost their mother and brother that had led to their own conversion from mere dutiful churchgoers to enthusiastic Evangelicals.

She shook her head. "I would not attempt such a thing, my dears. I fear that His Grace would not at all appreciate it. But," she continued, a mischievous light in her eye, "of course I shall see to it that he has suitable reading matter to encourage him to reflect on his past conduct." How, she wondered, a regrettable giggle welling up inside her, would the Duke enjoy perusing a book of sermons?

After her father and sisters had gone, Roxanne resumed her usual household duties, taking time to see that Geoffrey and the Duke stayed quietly in their beds, Geoffrey in Alfred's old chamber, and the Duke, at the insistence of Mrs. Porter, who was vastly impressed at having someone of so high a rank in the house, in Mr. Winston's own room.

Her task turned out to be more difficult than she had expected. That very morning, after seeing off her family, Roxanne went upstairs to visit her patients, and found the Duke struggling to get out of bed.

"May I ask what it is you think you are doing, your Grace?" she said coolly, repressing her irritation.

"Certainly, Miss Winston. I am going to get up, get dressed, and eat my breakfast like a gentleman. I'm not an invalid."

"I beg pardon for differing with Your Grace," she said, ringing for the footman, "but indeed you are, and you shall have your breakfast right here, on a tray in your bed. This movement will start your wound bleeding again, and I assure you, after the blow you sustained on the head, you will soon feel much too dizzy to — oh!"

Rutledge had been listening to her with an infuriating look of appreciation in his eyes, but toward the end of her speech those eyes had unfocused slightly, and now he had slid halfway to the floor. Roxanne rushed to help him, and luckily, the footman arrived very soon to assist her, for at the first touch of her hands around the Duke's waist, he had opened his eyes very wide, focused very clearly on her distraught face, and given her a victorious smile.

But she bit back the reproof that had risen to her lips, not only because of his elevated rank, but because she feared it would only encourage his shocking behavior. It was clear, too, that even through his bravado he was regretting his attempt to rise from bed. His face was pale again, and as the footman arranged his limbs back under the blankets, Roxanne saw the Duke wince with pain. On impulse she went to help, and there was unmistakable gratitude in Henry Malverne's gray eyes as he looked up at her.

Roxanne found herself short of breath, though she had done nothing, and she left the room hurriedly, ordering the servant to remain with His Grace while he ate.

It was with a sense of relief that she escaped into Geoffrey's room and found Miss Lynchard helping him to sit up with his tray settled before him. His eyes brightened when he saw Roxanne.

"Oh, good, you've come to keep me company while I breakfast. Miss Lynchard promised you would."

"Why yes, of course. I just went in to see how His Grace was feeling." She forced a laugh and exchanged a meaningful glance with Miss Lynchard. "I'm afraid he needs a stricter attendant than I. He's already trying to get out of bed."

Her former governess smiled reassuringly and said, "Of course, I shall attend to him myself, dear. I am in the habit of being obeyed, so I daresay he won't give me the trouble he would give a young lady like yourself."

Miss Lynchard's wise brown eyes told Roxanne that she understood the dilemma. That experienced lady was not at all lacking in imagination and foresight where her charges and their dealings with the other sex were concerned.

Geoffrey grinned. "Isn't that just like Harry? I'm sorry for bringing all this trouble down on you, and making you postpone your trip," he said, as Miss Lynchard left and Roxanne took her seat by his bed.

"Nonsense, Geoffrey, it will only be a week, the girls are perfectly able to take care of Papa. I shan't be missing very much except shopping, and Aunt Maria can accomplish that without my assistance."

He looked with disfavor upon the gruel that the cook thought proper food for invalids, but lifted the cover of the eggs and bacon that Miss Lynchard had secretly slid onto his tray, with a sigh of gratitude. "But won't you want to shop for yourself? You'll be going about a great deal, I suppose," he said between bites. Roxanne did not notice how carefully he waited for her answer.

"I suppose I shall," she said, "but of course it's *their* season, Melodie's and Gemma's, I mean, and I shall only be a sort of chaperone—"

"Surely not!" cried Geoffrey. "You're much too young and pretty to cover your hair with a cap and sit with the matrons and spinsters."

Roxanne was startled by the sudden compliment.

She could not recall Geoffrey, or anyone, in fact, ever telling her she was pretty, though her own mirror did tell her that her appearance was much improved over the last few years. She smiled.

"Now don't try to flummery me. You'll have to eat the gruel just the same, else cook will be insulted."

But Geoffrey was adamant. "Promise me you'll let Lady Camberwick buy you a new gown or two, and that you'll dance with me when I come up to town." Roxanne had never noticed how determined he could look. He put his hand on hers.

Slowly she slid it away, but laughingly promised to dance when his leg was healed. Then she diverted the conversation onto other topics.

Though she was curious about the shooting incident, Roxanne first had to listen to a paean on the Duke of Rutledge. It was uncomfortable and very inappropriate, she thought, for Geoffrey to be so full of that man's praise. Though she kept her own counsel, he could not help but realize that Roxanne did not share his feelings.

His face grew serious. "I know that it seems to you as though the Duke is a villain, Roxanne," he said, "but really, once you get to know him, you'll find that he's not a monster, but a capital fellow."

"How is it, Geoffrey, that you forget so quickly that this man killed my brother?" Her voice trembled.

"Now Roxanne, you know that isn't true—"

"True enough," she cried. "If it weren't for the Duke of Rutledge, Alfred would be with us today."

Geoffrey bit his lip and maintained his silence.

"I—I don't mean to blame you, Geoffrey, but if you and Alfred hadn't had that falling-out—"

"That could not be helped, Roxanne," he said. "I think it a very good thing that your brother came to know Harry, for poor Alfred was miserable, having promised your mama that he would not join up, and I think, a little jealous of me that I was free to do so. Your brother thought his life was going to be wasted, and the Duke tried to help him."

"How can you say that?" cried Roxanne, staring at him in amazement. "My brother is dead!"

He averted his eyes from hers and picked over the toast on his tray. "You can't . . . there are things you don't know. . . . I know you think I'm heartless, but believe me, I miss Alfred just as much as you do. He and I were like brothers."

This time Roxanne could not mistake the sincerity in Geoffrey's voice. His eyes were shining, as though with incipient tears. Then she recalled that he was injured and that it was very wrong of her to plague him for what was, after all, not his fault. It was Rutledge she was angry with, but they had not the habit of long association and easy discourse that would excuse her berating him the way she was Geoffrey. It was unjust of her to make her old friend a scapegoat.

"Oh, Geoffrey," she said, putting her hands over his, "I am truly, truly sorry for being so unkind. I hope you will forgive me?"

He smiled, and looked, Roxanne thought, not a little relieved. "Of course, Rozzie," and took one of her hands and planted a kiss on it.

She had to make an effort not to snatch it away, for old friend or not, it was most alarming behavior. But she did not want to offend Geoffrey further. "Now, go on about last night. I want to know how you came to be riddled with holes on my doorstep!"

Geoffrey gave her his version of the incident, emphasizing Rutledge's courage, and ending by characterizing it as a mere robbery.

"What did they steal?"

"Ah . . . I believe it was Harry's diamond stickpin, and some money," Geoffrey said, caught unaware.

Roxanne was not satisfied. "Pooh!" she said. "Do you think me a simpleton to believe that someone would wound two men, one of them a Duke, all for the sake of a bauble and a few pounds?"

Geoffrey met her glance innocently.

Roxanne sighed, and lifted up his ravaged breakfast tray. "Very well, then, I shan't plague you. I know you'll only say it's nothing for a delicately reared female to know about."

"Stuff! I wouldn't mouth any such nonsense, Roxanne, you know that. Only," he added, his lips turning up irrepressibly, "as I was unconscious through most of it, perhaps you ought to ask His Grace for the rest of the details."

"Indeed, I suppose I must," replied Roxanne, but she smiled at him as she left, after ordering him to rest for a while.

She hesitated to enter the Duke's sickroom again, and salved her conscience by telling herself that Miss Lynchard was probably taking excellent care of him. Still, as she went about her daily tasks, she pondered the oddity of the shooting and so-called robbery. She could not help but suspect that the Duke was involved in something strange, perhaps nefarious, and had dragged Geoffrey into it, as he had once dragged Alfred into his frivolous and wasteful life.

But she could not keep away from Rutledge forever. The Duke must be cared for, fed, and amused, as any other guest, and she could not leave it all to Miss Lynchard, who had the little girls to look after.

When the governess appeared with her charges and announced their intention of taking a walk, Roxanne knew that it was her turn to sit by Rutledge's bedside, as Geoffrey, the housekeeper had told her, had fallen asleep and had no need of her. In truth, she did not know which gentleman made her more uncomfortable. Geoffrey did look at her so strangely sometimes.

"Roxanne," said blond, blue-eyed Elizabeth, who, at nine, resembled her eldest sister except for her propensity for mischief-making, "when can we see the men who got shot? Were there highwaymen? Maybe they have followed them to the Hall," she suggested, looking around and shivering in delight at the thought of such an adventure occurring at their placid home.

"No, silly," said chubby, sensible Dorothea, who was twelve, and looked much as the dark-haired, brown-eyed twins had looked at that age, "it was on the road, and the men ran away, and Mr. Pearson and the Duke came here afterwards."

"How did you discover so much about it?" Roxanne asked, surprised.

Miss Lynchard looked at her apologetically. "I'm afraid it was I who told them the story. Now go ahead, girls, and I shall join you in a moment." As the two strolled sedately away, only to break into a happy trot when they thought they were out of her sight, she said, "It is always better for children to know the truth, dear, and I'm sure they would come to wonder very soon why two sick gentlemen were staying in the house. I thought I'd let them see Geoffrey tomorrow, when he feels a little better. After all, they know him, and are insatiably curious to see him with all his bandages and sickroom paraphernalia. It's tremendously exciting to them, poor dears," she said very seriously.

But Roxanne knew the humor that lurked beneath that serene expression, and having once been a very curious child herself, she made no objection, hoping that the girls' chatter might entertain her bored, bedridden guests.

She could put off the courtesy of a visit to the Duke no longer. Armed with a selection of books and the newspaper, she trudged up to her father's room, scolding herself for the little flurry of apprehension in her chest. She knocked.

"Enter," said a bored, but very hearty voice.

The Duke was sitting up against the pillows, shaven, brushed, and arranged by Geoffrey's valet, who was thrilled at the opportunity to practice his skills on someone of rank. The color had returned to his face, but his eyes looked tired. Though covered in blankets, he wore one of Mr. Winston's dressing gowns, and Roxanne told herself, it was perfectly respectable for her to sit with him alone in his sickroom. But the closer she drew to him, the more anxious she became, as he fixed her with a speculative gaze the moment she walked through the door.

"Well, 'tis my sweet rescuer, come to tend the sick and, no doubt, urge the wicked to forgo their ways. You are most welcome. Do sit down." He indicated a chair very close to his bedside.

"Thank you, my lord," said Roxanne, ignoring his bantering tone and taking another seat at the bed's foot. She was not fool enough to sit that close to him. It would be difficult enough to hide her contempt and dislike for him without having him a foot away, gazing into her face.

"I hope you are feeling better?" she inquired.

"Much better . . . now . . ." he said with a lazy smile.

Oh, why must he torment her? He must know how she felt about him. . . . Any sensible man would realize it without even speaking to her. . . . Surely he could not regard himself as innocent? But she was beginning to think that the Duke of Rutledge was not at all a sensible man. He seemed totally unaware of his crimes. She wanted to ask him about the shooting, but found that she could not.

Nevertheless, she replied serenely, "I am glad to hear it. Shall I read to you from the newspaper?" She unfolded it.

He nodded. "Please."

She began to read, but in a moment the Duke interrupted her. "I'm sorry, I didn't catch that word . . . was it cucumber? Surely not."

Roxanne cleared her throat and regarded him over the paper. "It was 'Cumberland,' my lord. I was reading about the Duke of Cumberland."

He stared back at her with a troubled face. "I beg your pardon. I didn't hear it well."

"Then I will speak louder, my lord." And she raised her voice as she read the paragraphs pertaining to the movements of the royal family.

"Excuse me, Miss Winston," he interrupted once again. "But perhaps I have mistaken you . . . did you read that the Regent will host a ball in a charnel house?"

She looked at him sharply, but his face was perfectly serious, except for a little crinkling about the eyes. She was about to accuse him of mocking her attempts to entertain him, when she realized that perhaps his head injury had caused a temporary loss in hearing.

"Certainly not, Your Grace. The Prince Regent is to host a ball at Carlton House."

"Thank heavens! All those unfleshed bones would contrast so unfortunately with His Royal Highness's very well-fleshed figure, would they not?"

Roxanne suppressed the desire to giggle at this ghastly but ridiculous picture. Instead she forced herself to look at him blankly.

Rutledge regarded her for a moment and sighed. "I apologize for being so stupid today, Miss Winston. Perhaps . . . could you do me the great favor of sitting a little closer? I'm afraid I do not hear you very well from so far away."

She subdued a frown, and warily moved herself to the chair at the head of his bed.

He turned slightly to lean on his good shoulder and settled back into the pillows. "There," he said, "now I shall be able to hear you quite well, I expect," and fixed his glance on her face.

To her discomfort, he did not look away from her for quite some minutes, and appeared to take no interest in what she read to him, so intent was he on studying her physiognomy.

Under this scrutiny Roxanne began to blush and stammer and miss a word here and there, but His Grace did not appear to notice until finally, covered in confusion, she stopped reading. He said nothing, but sighed and closed his eyes.

Relieved to be spared from his gaze, Roxanne got up briskly and said, "There! That is sufficient for today. Now I think you will sleep, or do you need some of that laudanum the doctor left for you?"

"No, thank you, my dear Miss Winston. Your lovely soothing voice has relieved enough pain to send me into a restful sleep. However"—and now his eyes opened—"will you oblige me by raising me on the pillows? I shall sleep better that way . . . a touch of fever . . ." His eyes were wide and innocent of any intention at all.

"I shall ring for the servant—"

"No, don't trouble yourself. I am sure between us we can manage without him . . . so kind of you . . ." His voice had weakened to a whisper.

Roxanne edged nearer, uncertainly, and began to slide another pillow beneath his shoulders. Warmth emanated from him strongly, as if he really had the fever he spoke of. She avoided his eyes, staring instead at his dark, unruly hair. She tried to ignore the flutter in her chest, part of her acknowledging that he was quite handsome while part of her trembled with anger at this enforced intimacy. She tried not to touch him but it was quite impossible. He did little to help her, and Roxanne had perforce to take a firmer grip on his body to move the pillows beneath him. His borrowed nightshirt and dressing gown did little to protect her from the feel of his firm, warm flesh under her fingers. The Duke's smile grew bigger while she grew more flustered.

"There!" she said with artificial brightness, straightening up, away from the disturbing bulk of him beneath the blankets. "You will be comfortable now. Is there anything else you wish before I leave?"

"Yes." Roxanne was overcome with surprise as she found her hands caught in his. He held them gently, but she had the distinct impression that if she attempted to withdraw them he would only hold them tighter.

She drew breath quickly. "Wh-what is it, my lord?"

"I would like you to stop hating me."

"But I don't—"

"You are a little hypocrite, Miss Winston. I know that you do hate me. You think I am the murderer of your brother. Well, I am not. Alfred knew exactly what he was doing—"

Now Roxanne did pull her hands away. As she had expected, he tried to retain them but her anger lent her strength. "He did until you beguiled him, and led him into dissipation. Before he met you, my lord, he would not have thought of dueling, or of gambling, or . . ." but the other things she could not mention.

His Grace's demeanor had turned icy. "You are mistaken, Miss Winston. Your brother was a good man, but an ordinary one, not the saint you seem to have made him. He wanted above all to serve his country, and when he could not, in honor, do this he had to find some outlet for his natural high spirits." His lips tightened in disapproval at the thought of the vow Lady Anne Winston had extracted from her son, who would have made an excellent officer. "It was this that I gave him." He looked as though he wanted to say more, but did not.

"I — I do not know why you are telling me this," said Roxanne, not at all mollified. "It is absurd to even speak of it."

The Duke nodded. "I understand you, but I thought that I would give you a chance to think better of your determination to hate me, and forgive me instead . . . forgive your enemy." He was watching her closely, and Roxanne felt two patches of heat on her cheeks.

"Perhaps I am not as good as I ought to be, because I find I cannot forgive so easily. And now . . ." She cleared her throat, and gathered up her books and newspaper. "Let us not speak of it again."

"Very well," said His Grace. "But may I ask one thing of you before you go?"

Roxanne hesitated. He ignored this and smiled, as if nothing had passed between them.

"I should like some books to read. It is a dead bore, you know, lying in bed, and I cannot always fall asleep so easily." His gray eyes gazed up at her innocently.

Roxanne smiled now too, seeing her chance for revenge. "Ah, no doubt it is because your conscience troubles you, my lord. I have just the remedy." Whereupon she handed him Venn's *Duty of Man* and a wrinkled copy of one of Hannah More's famous penny tracts.

The Duke examined them curiously. He seemed not at all insulted by her remark on his guilty conscience. In fact, he looked amused. *The Dairyman's Daughter,* he read, holding the tract. "This sounds promising. Is it amusing?"

"I am sure you will find it so," said Roxanne blandly. Then bidding him good day, she left the room, choking back a sudden fit of laughter.

That night as she prepared for sleep, she examined her own conscience, and her conduct during that day, as had become her habit. Toward Geoffrey, she thought, she had behaved quite properly, except for that regrettable scold, but she had apologized, and felt that no harm was done.

But where Rutledge was concerned . . . she was saddened to think that she had allowed herself the weakness of giving way to her feelings in the Duke's presence. She had no business in bringing him to judgment for his crimes. He would have to account for them at the end of his life, whether he believed himself guilty or not.

But she chuckled at the thought of Rutledge poring over *The Dairyman's Daughter* in search of amusement. That maudlin tale of sickbed conversion, she thought, was as close as she could come to carrying out the twins' suggestion for the Duke's salvation. She was sure he would not at all appreciate her efforts, and went to sleep with a regrettably complacent smile on her face.

Chapter Four

His Grace the Duke of Rutledge struggled against the painful laughter that shook his broad frame, and at last put down the penny tract that Miss Winston had left him. Its blatant warning to sinners and its dramatic deathbed conversion had not had the desired effect, either of saving his soul or making him angry. In fact, the Duke planned to thank Miss Winston solemnly for her thoughtfulness in providing him with such entertaining reading matter.

Now that he had met Roxanne Winston again, Rutledge remembered her as she had been in her first season three years ago. He had seen her here and there about town, where she had been pointed out to him as the sister of his friend Winston, and though she had not been as striking as she was now, even then there had been a simplicity something like beauty in her slender form and wide-set deep blue eyes.

Of course, it had not impressed him very much at the time, but the memory was there. Now, though he was wary of his mother's matchmaking scheme, the Duke thought Miss Winston had developed into something quite exquisite, and determined that at the next opportunity he would provoke her again, if only to see that serene expression disappear under the onslaught of emotion. But he could not, of course, marry her, even if he wanted to marry, which he still felt no inclination to do, he told himself.

Since he was not longing to become a husband, Henry Malverne was very glad that it was this particular girl his mother had chosen for him, for it was an impossible match, he with his connection to her lost brother, she with her barely concealed hatred of him. Above all, he did not want to wed someone who so obviously needed to marry for fortune's sake.

When the time came, he would marry a woman who would be guided only her feelings for him, and not her pocketbook or anything else, in accepting his offer. Not, Rutledge reminded himself wryly, that there was any chance of Miss Winston's suddenly being overcome by tender feelings for him.

He closed his eyes and relaxed into a sort of invalidish daydream. In other circumstances, if Alfred were happily reunited to his family, if Roxanne had not hated him, if he had the inclination toward marriage . . . But of course, none of these necessary ingredients were as yet present. And then there was Geoffrey and his hopes . . . but he would rather not become his friend's confidant in that matter.

As the week progressed, the two invalids were allowed to sit up downstairs for an hour or two each day. During one of these periods the younger man had tried to discuss with Rutledge his uncertainty about Roxanne's feelings toward him, but the Duke had cut him off swiftly.

"I'm afraid you shouldn't look to me for advice on the subject, my friend. Miss Winston gives the impression that she regrets the bullet did not finish me. But about that night . . . I have something to tell you."

Geoffrey looked up at him, grinning. "My valet mentioned the stolen letter. I've solved the mystery myself, you see."

"Have you?" Rutledge raised his eyebrows. "Then I won't trouble you with any further details . . ."

But Geoffrey eagerly demanded to be let in on the secret.

"Very simply, my friend, it was a decoy, and I expect that it will throw some curious people off the scent, and make it that much easier to arrange a certain event in a few months."

"Then it's really going to happen," cried Geoffrey. "He's coming home!"

"Quietly, my friend. It will be best if only the three of us know about it."

"Three?"

"The two of us and Fanny, of course," replied the Duke. "It's only fair to tell her."

"Yes, of course . . . but Roxanne, surely she should be told?"

"No," said the Duke decisively. "We have not the authority to do so, and it is much too dangerous for the family to know anything, especially since they will be in London. Eyes and ears are everywhere."

Geoffrey sighed. "I suppose you are right."

When Roxanne came in, her conscience telling her that she ought to sit with the invalids for a little while, they were playing piquet and were involved in an amicable dispute over the cards. The sight of it reminded her so forcefully of Alfred and his fateful card game with Rutledge, that she stood in the doorway, breathing quickly, for a few moments before they noticed her. Finally Geoffrey looked up.

"Thank heavens you've come, Rozzie. Deliver me, I beg you, from this ferocious fellow, and say you'll play a peaceful game of backgammon with me."

"Gladly. But what will His Grace do?" She tried to speak casually, though she found herself shooting little anxious glances at the Duke. He was seated in a chair, dressed in fitted green pantaloons and an open-necked shirt with no cravat, his bandage lumped underneath, looking completely at home.

"Oh, I must be getting on with my reading," he said, picking up Adams's *Private Thoughts on Religion*. "What wonderful books you have, Miss Winston. Such a comfort at a time like this."

Roxanne had a disturbing impulse to laugh at the solemn expression he had assumed, and only wished the twins could be there to witness the apparent fulfillment of their wishes. But all the absurdity and cozening in the would would not change her opinion of him. Resolutely she turned to Geoffrey and set out the backgammon.

In the past few days she had dreaded a repetition of her disturbing scene with Rutledge and, without revealing her fears to Miss Lynchard, had managed to convey that she did not feel comfortable attending on the Duke. But Miss Lynchard was often busy, and Roxanne frequently found herself in his room, especially as the alternative, keeping Geoffrey company, was becoming equally uncomfortable.

Only yesterday she had gently forestalled an outright declaration of love from her old friend. She still had trouble accepting the fact that Geoffrey no longer thought of her as only a friend, and that he could even consider damaging his prospects and her own by offering for her. As for her own feelings, she had not let them progress beyond what was permissible. The absolute impossibility of their marriage, no matter how much affection they had for each other or how happy they could be, forbade any romantic speculation.

So Roxanne sought refuge in Rutledge's room and found it not so unpleasant as she had expected, feeling quite a lot safer in his company than in Geoffrey's. She sat by the Duke's bed with her sewing and, since he had made such a difficult audience, listened to *him* reading the newspaper in his warm even baritone. She even, maintaining her gravity with difficulty, heard him read from some "improving works" in an earnest but puzzled tone, as if he were truly trying to understand the concepts of man's depravity and the sanctification of the regenerate soul but could not quite grasp them.

Roxanne refused, however, to oblige him with a laugh, and in fact chided herself for finding his antics amusing at all. She wished wholeheartedly that it was the twins, and not she, who must assume the burden of caring for this particular sinner. They, she was sure, would swiftly repress any tendency toward levity in His Grace. Their double glances of disappointment and censure, from which even Roxanne herself was not exempt, would have summarily dispatched his amusement.

Now she applied herself to beating Geoffrey at backgammon, because in spite of his plea for peace she knew he enjoyed a stimulating game, but was very aware of the Duke's presence. Indeed, she had the feeling that he was not reading at all, but staring very hard at her back. She restrained herself, with difficulty, from looking around to confirm this, and was so successful in involving herself in the game that she quite forgot him for a quarter of an hour, till the maid brought in tea. It was the longest period she had spent with her mind unsullied by thoughts of Rutledge since his arrival.

Miss Lynchard joined them, and her presence somewhat eased Roxanne's tension. The governess quickly assumed much of the burden of conversation with the Duke, leaving Roxanne and Geoffrey to discuss the twins' prospects in London.

"I haven't seen them since they were in the schoolroom," said Geoffrey, "but they were clever, pretty girls. I'm sure they'll take."

Roxanne sighed. "I'm not so sanguine about their chances, Geoffrey. They've lately become imbued with Evangelicalism, and I'm afraid they are very much more inclined to lecture than to flirt."

Geoffrey shook his head. "That's too bad. Enthusiasts don't generally find a warm welcome among the ton. They make everyone feel so guilty, you know. Look at Hannah More. She managed to insult more people of consequence than she converted. Better advise your sisters to keep their ideas to themselves."

"Impossible." Roxanne winced, imagining her sisters' reaction to such a request. "They only agreed to go because they saw a chance to improve the morals of the ton, and because Papa impressed on them how it was their duty to find husbands and relieve him of the burden of their upkeep and to help the rest of us —"

"He didn't!" cried Geoffrey, highly amused.

"Oh, yes, I assure you that such plain talk, or a sentimental appeal, is far more effective than a promise of new clothes and parties and beaux, which was how I was induced to go through with it," she said, recalling her unprosperous season. "But I'm sure they fully intend to convert every unprincipled rake and modish miss they meet, and if that does not suit they will perhaps shun the sinners altogether."

"Lady Camberwick will talk sense to them," he said confidently, "I'm sure you can rely on her."

"I was hoping that myself," Roxanne said, remembering her aunt's practical approach to life and the all-important business of marriage.

"I saw Fanny when I passed through town," said Geoffrey, with a cautious glance at Roxanne. "She sends her best love and looks forward to seeing you. You know she has been living in the North to help my eldest sister with her brood, and now she is staying in London with my sister Margaret and her respectable Mr. Broughton."

Roxanne's face grew stern, then pensive. She had put her friend Fanny out of her life after her brother's death, and for good reason. "I had hoped so much to have Fanny for a sister. We aren't the only ones who've suffered by Alfred's death." She cast a glance at the Duke, and said quietly, "What I cannot understand is how Fanny ever managed to become entangled with Rutledge. I was very angry, you know, when it was put about that they were engaged, so soon after we lost Alfred."

Geoffrey avoided her glance and loaded a slice of bread with butter. "It wasn't true, you know," he said in a low voice. "They were friends . . . he was some-one to talk with about . . . about Alfred. She wouldn't have married him."

"But if she wanted someone to talk to she could have come to me!" Roxanne felt, once more, all the pain of those difficult days, when she had lost not only brother, but her mother, and then her best friend, to a quarrel that had not yet been healed. But here was Fanny offering an olive branch.

Geoffrey drank off the last of his tea. "She was afraid to intrude on your grief, and she didn't . . ." He, too, glanced at the Duke, but His Grace was deep in conversation with Miss Lynchard. ". . . she didn't blame the Duke the way you do, Roxanne."

Roxanne could not understand this, but felt that it behooved her to be reconciled to her old friend. Fanny and Alfred had been in love, and although the Pearsons had refused to give their daughter permis-sion to marry Alfred, because she was only sixteen at the time and they hoped for a better match for her, Roxanne was sure that her brother and her best friend would have married someday.

After Alfred's death had come startling rumors, in Aunt Maria's letters from London, that Fanny was seen a great deal with Rutledge, who had returned to town the season after his duel with Alfred, and that the beau monde was awaiting the announcement of their betrothal. Nothing had come of it, but Roxanne had been hurt at what she saw as her friend's defec-tion.

But perhaps it was time to mend the break in their friendship. "Please tell Fanny when you write to her that I am eager to see her again," she said, and Geoffrey smiled.

"That's our old Rozzie!" he said.

But though her talk with Geoffrey was pleasant and absorbing, Roxanne felt her attention straying to Rutledge and Miss Lynchard. She was amazed at how respectfully he addressed her former governess, and how intelligently he discussed the current political situation and the war with Miss Lynchard, who, regrettably, had failed to interest either Roxanne or the twins in her pet subjects, and seemed happy to find a like-minded individual in the wicked Duke.

Roxanne was surprised, too, at how much Rutledge seemed to know about the war, and how decidedly, though modestly, he expressed his opinions, and even more, how often Miss Lynchard agreed with him. Finally even Geoffrey noticed her abstraction, and he was the first to join in the others' conversation.

"His Grace is right, you know, Miss Lynchard. We ought to have known the peace wouldn't last. Ought to have learned enough about Boney by then not to trust it."

"And I also agree with Your Grace about the importance of the Navy," said Miss Lynchard. "I hope Lord Nelson will justify the confidence we've place in him."

"He will," said the Duke optimistically. "He knows what he's about, and he's well informed."

Miss Lynchard looked pensive. "Is it true, I wonder, that we have an extensive network of spies on the Continent?"

Rutledge reached for a slice of plum cake. "I'm sure it is true that if we do, Boney has an organization to equal it here."

Geoffrey was silent, but he took too large a bite of bread and had to be pounded on the back by Roxanne before he could stop choking.

The week moved slowly along amid scenes like these, and by the time the doctor gave his approval for the gentlemen to be removed to Rosemark, Roxanne was bursting with impatience and restless energy. She had had letters from her father and Aunt Maria, and it sounded as though they badly needed her help with the twins. Geoffrey had become increasingly importunate about his feelings for her, until she had to be sharp with him, at which he had turned unexpectedly sullen. Rutledge, surprisingly, gave her much less trouble than she had expected, except for the morning of his departure.

They were left alone in the hall for a moment, while Geoffrey was carried out to the chaise. The Duke seized this opportunity to take Roxanne's hand, and holding it all the while, thanked her solemnly for all her tender nursing, with that infuriating look in his eye that told her he thought the situation extremely amusing.

His hand, she noted, was perfectly warm and dry, and she was almost sure she could feel a strong pulse beating in his wrist. A good sign of recovery, she told herself.

"You are very welcome, my lord. We could do no less," was all she said, averting her gaze from his.

"Indeed, you could do no more. You saw to my every need quite expertly," he went on, blithely ignoring her discomfort. "I am most grateful for your attention and care. "Most ladies would think themselves too fine or delicate to trouble themselves over an invalid . . . let alone one on whom they could not allow themselves to look with favor." He smiled, and Roxanne noticed an expectant air about him. Did he expect her to fly up at him?

"I could never think myself too fine to aid someone in need, my lord," she said, and in a moment realized how self-righteous this sounded. Why couldn't she ever express herself properly in his presence? She must stop allowing herself to be so befuddled by this man.

"I hope I may be permitted to call upon you in London, Miss Winston, when I am fully recovered, so that you might view the end results of your nursing."

Roxanne's eyes flew open wide. It had not occurred to her that she might have to see him again. What would Papa and Aunt Maria think? It had been difficult enough to keep her composure in the presence of her wounded enemy, but the thought of him invading Aunt Maria's drawing room, hale and hearty, terrified her.

She did not give him the slightest hint of encouragement, only smiled stonily and said she hoped that he would recover without further incident. At that he let go of her hand, his expression telling her plainly that he knew exactly what she was thinking, and allowed himself to be helped into the carriage.

When he had gone, Roxanne set out to convince herself that she need not worry about a visit from Rutledge. She considered how different was his way of life from hers, and realized that she was almost certainly safe from being called upon by him in town. Surely, she thought, he would be too involved in his debaucheries to spare a moment for the Winstons. She was soon certain that he had mentioned the possibility of a visit only to annoy her.

The next day Roxanne traveled to town alone for the first time, taking inside seats on the coach from the Angel for herself and the housemaid as her attendant. She had so looked forward to traveling post, but it would be a wicked extravagance for only herself. Upon reaching Upper Brook Street she had little time to congratulate herself on successfully completing the journey before the family descended upon her full of welcome and problems.

"At last, my child, you've come to rescue me from the attentions of these eagle-eyed females," cried her papa, in real happiness at seeing her again. "They've driven me to distraction among 'em," he said, indicating the twins and Lady Camberwick, who had left off hovering about his Bath chair to embrace Roxanne.

She bent first to kiss Sir James's cheek. "Now Papa, don't pretend you didn't enjoy having them coddle you. Now that I've arrived, you know you shall be on your strict regimen again."

"So, my dear, I've heard that you have had some unexpected visitors this week. You shall tell me all about it," said Aunt Maria in a decided tone that meant she was not merely making idle conversation. "But first the girls will bring you to your room so that you may take off your bonnet."

Lady Maria Camberwick, a childless widow and once a great beauty, had finely lined fair skin, and slightly faded blond hair, but her blue eyes were undimmed and, her niece knew, keener than anyone else's. Roxanne was sure that her aunt would not let her rest till she had extracted from her the entire story

71

of the two wounded men and any interesting romantic possibilities. But poor Aunt Maria looked a little more worn than Roxanne remembered her, and as the twins led the way to the door, she glanced at her elder niece and rolled her eyes expressively.

When they were alone in her room, Roxanne sternly eyed her sisters. "Have you two been impossible to Aunt Maria?"

"Why, what could you mean?" asked Melodie innocently. "We have tried not to be a burden to her . . ."

"But of course," added Gemma, "we must make her see the importance of saving her soul, and the possible degradation into which she might, in the course of the season, be unwittingly leading us."

"Of course," murmured Roxanne, suppressing a smile. Lady Maria was universally renowned as a very good sort of woman, kind and sincere, but the intricate implications of sin and salvation were totally alien to her thoroughly practical nature, and this transformation of her nieces was not to her taste at all, as she had expressed in her letters to Roxanne. What had religion to do, she wanted to know, with the real business of a well-born but poor female—making a good match?

"Sinners there may be in the world, and souls for the saving," she had written, "but young ladies without fortunes need husbands, and I'm sure that a respectable female can go about finding them for her nieces without trampling on any of the commandments or bringing down the wrath of the Lord."

Pondering this, Roxanne took off her bonnet, washed her face and hands, and changed out of her dusty traveling gown into a demure afternoon dress of peach muslin. It was a little out of date, having been made during her ill-fated debut, but fortunately it had large seams and she had been able to let it out sufficiently to accommodate her more womanly figure. Geoffrey was right, she thought ruefully, she must get some new clothes herself, even if she were only to chaperone the girls. It would do nothing to attract wealthy men to the twins if their sister looked like a shabby dowd.

"Now," she said while she rearranged her hair, "tell me what you have been doing, and who you have met, and what invitations you have."

The twins looked at each other, and then, perhaps a little sheepishly, at Roxanne. Though they were actually quite pretty, with delicate pink lips, fine dark eyes, and dimples, there was usually a lack of animation about their faces that did not set off their looks. Now they were dressed quite plainly, in high-necked kerseymere gowns of a brownish hue, decked with only one small ruffle at the bodice, and if these were a sample of their London wardrobes, Roxanne could fully understand Aunt Maria's rolling of the eyes.

"Well, sister," Gemma began, "I'm afraid that Aunt Maria *is* perhaps a bit displeased with us. You, see—"

"—we did not like to use the new gowns she ordered for us, and the bonnets and fans and other such frivolous trinkets," added Melodie. "And Aunt's friends whom we have met have only convinced us that we are indeed landed in a den of sinners and that it is unworthy of us to bestow our friendship upon such people. Even the ladies play cards for money!"

"And Roxanne, they are in such danger of eternal damnation!" cried Gemma, with a real look of sorrow at the torments awaiting these unfortunates. "The gentlemen especially . . ." She glanced at her twin.

"But you know, sister," said Melodie, "that we would not shirk our duty to you and Papa, and have decided that, rather than be swallowed in a whirlpool of evil dissipation, as it is obvious all innocent females drawn to London by the promise of society and gaiety and romance must eventually be—"

"—we will make it our particular mission," continued Gemma, "to inspire by our example and our eloquence these unfortunate ones who have forgotten their own duty in this endless and sinful quest for pleasure."

Roxanne sat down on her bed very suddenly, for at the revelation of these detailed plans her doubts and suspicions had been confirmed, and she saw how awful a task was before her. Why, it would very likely be easier to find herself a husband, as old as she was, than to marry off these two solemn sisters of hers!

"I fear, my loves, that such intentions, noble as they are, will do you no service here in London, and indeed, in the majority of cases, you will be wasting your breath and perhaps even bringing ridicule and censure upon yourselves."

"We do not mind, Roxanne," said Gemma stoutly. "The true Christian is always persecuted, and it is his duty to go on, head unbowed, though the fallen ones rain arrows of vituperation upon his head." Melodie nodded her agreement. The brown eyes of both girls gleamed, and their neat, small faces were solemn.

They were, Roxanne thought wryly, positively eager to be persecuted. Martyrdom would no doubt suit them admirably.

Roxanne patted the bed on either side of her, and they sat down. She put an arm about each of their shoulders and said gently, "All of this is very brave and laudable, and you know that I share your faith, though not, perhaps, your vehemence. Of course, I have not your objection to all worldly pleasures. But do you not see, my dears, that all of this will render your presence in London and Aunt Maria's kindness and exertion on your part completely useless?"

"Oh, no, Roxanne, you do not understand us. Certainly we are grateful to Aunt Maria and mean to do everything she asks of us. We will even," Melodie offered, "go to routs and balls where gambling is present —"

"— though we will not, as we agreed," Gemma added, "engage in card playing."

"And of course we cannot indulge in dancing —"

"— a most sinful exercise. Or the theater. But some rational conversation, and perhaps a concert of sacred music or a public reading of some serious work, would not be amiss." The girls nodded, completely satisfied with their plans for the season.

Roxanne stifled a sharp reply. Obviously it would take more than a sisterly chat to dissuade the twins from this fixed idea of London as the den of sin. How ironic that not so long ago, she had been thinking of it in the very same terms, regarding Alfred and the Duke of Rutledge.

She pushed that disturbing thought to the back of her mind and accompanied her sisters to the drawing room. There the reunited Winstons exchanged all their news, and Roxanne told them how well Geoffrey's wound was mending, and that he expected to see them in London as soon as he was recovered, and in answer to the twins' inquiries, assured them that she had done all in her power to urge the Duke to examine his conscience and repent of his sins.

Lady Maria raised her eyebrows at this, and Sir James chuckled as he raised the cup to his lips with his good hand. Roxanne shot them both an expressive glance, and turning to the twins, she said, "Before he left he had read through the whole of the *Duty of Man* and assured me he was quite touched by *The Dairyman's Daughter.*"

"Yes!" cried Gemma. "How appropriate, and how happy we are, aren't we, Mel, that Roxanne had this opportunity to induce someone of such high rank and abandoned morals to turn his thoughts to serious matters, if only for a sennight."

Lady Maria had had quite enough by now, and directed the conversation to other topics.

"We have quite an avalance of invitations already, Roxanne, and I have only taken the girls on a single round of morning calls, and left cards at a few houses. And of course we shall give a rout presently, and you can meet everyone—many friends of mine have eligible sons . . ."

The speculative look she fixed on her elder niece was sure to mean that she had a plan for the arrangement of *her* future as well as that of the twins, but Roxanne ignored it. She and Aunt Maria were good friends, and she was sure she could make her understand that this season should be devoted to the twins, that she had had her chance, and that Gemma and Melodie, as she would soon find out if she didn't know already, would require so much of her attention that there would be no time to find a husband for Roxanne.

The next morning after breakfast, Sir James was transported by his manservant, Bath chair and all, to Boodle's, his favorite club, where he would visit with his old friends, read the newspapers, and hear all the gentlemanly gossip without having to leave his seat. He was a popular man, and his town friends had missed his presence since his illness and retirement. Now that he was among them once more, they eagerly sought to entertain him, so Roxanne felt she could lessen her habitual attendance on him for a while.

Roxanne, Lady Maria, and the twins had some shopping to do. Lady Maria had run an expert eye over Roxanne's scanty wardrobe, and hinted that some new gowns for both day and evening would not come amiss. So, with only a token resistance, Roxanne allowed her aunt to make her a present of one walking dress of aquamarine sarsenet, tight fitting in the bodice and sweeping down to a broad flounce at the hem, and an evening toilette of cream silk and almond taffeta, trimmed with ruching and tiny satin love-knots, made by a fashionable dressmaker. At the last moment she was pressed to take a ball dress as well.

The rest of her new wardrobe she shopped for very carefully in the warehouses, buying fine muslins for gowns which she would make herself, and gloves, stockings, fans, reticules, petticoats, and other necessities, until she was satisfied that she would disgrace neither her fashionable aunt nor the marital chances of her sisters.

The girls were disappointingly blasé over the enticements of the dressmakers and the drapers. When after several days of frenzied activity, all the shopping and sewing was finally finished, their new wardrobes were complete, with everything in the latest mode, but still the twins clung to their old gowns and dowdy bonnets. It took a great deal of tact for Roxanne to convince them that they must put off their plain bombazine and put on something gayer.

She even offered, in desperation, permission to remove the ribbons and ruffles on some of the muslin gowns their aunt had bought them, that they could retain their own stout, plain shifts beneath them, rather than don the soft embroidered chemises Aunt Maria preferred, and that they might wear fichus over any evening décolletage to which they objected on moral grounds.

In case they had any inclination to demur, she added, "And your aunt, I am sure, will be very hurt if you do not agree to put aside your scruples enough to dress appropriately for London society, after all the care she has taken over this season."

The girls stated that they had no desire to hurt their aunt, but one morning when they were to make calls with Lady Camberwick, their sister found them dressed in their old plain gowns.

Roxanne sighed in frustration, and tried a new tactic.

"Think how much more attention you will attract to yourselves from frivolous-minded people if you stand out in any way by your dress! People will feel themselves rebuked by your plainness of attire, and it would be very rude of you to make anyone feel uncomfortable, as you are newcomers here and must bow to the dictates of society in all matters that do not immediately concern your immortal souls."

Since this was very much like Mr. Driggs, the pastor of their church, had told them upon their leaving, the twins at last reluctantly agreed. Mr. Driggs had brought Evanglicalism to the village of Westcombe, raised money for a chapel, which attracted like-minded people from several nearby villages, and awakened a small part of the local parish to the dangerous state of their souls.

He organized classes and readings and hymn singings, and the members of his flock encouraged each other in struggling against their failings and confessed their weaknesses, striving always for perfection of spirit and conduct. So far this perfection had eluded Roxanne, but until recently she had attended dutifully with her sisters, searching for some meaning in life after the tragedies that had befallen them.

Roxanne knew that Mr. Driggs was a very worthy man, but she secretly found him rather dull. Most of all, she had not appreciated his confession, as if he were admitting a sin, of his admiration for her, which she had feared might lead to an offer of marriage.

Then too, he was constantly setting up some missionary scheme that required many hours of time and many donations from his congregation. Whether it was a society to distribute Bibles to the heathens, to end slavery, or to convert prisoners, Mr. Driggs was always ready to canvass for assistance, the twins at his side, extorting pennies to be used not, to Roxanne's annoyance, for the physical relief of the unfortunate, but for tending to their souls.

All of her sisters' other absurdities were no more

than that to her, but this devotion to Driggs and the continual begging for donations offended Roxanne's sense of right. Certainly, souls were important, but the bodies which they inhabited were obviously in more immediate need of assistance. Mr. Driggs could not seem to understand this, and was visibly annoyed when Roxanne began to dissociate herself from his group.

The twins would not listen to reason on this subject, however, and even now, as they dutifully attired themselves as she instructed, they regaled her with a letter they had had from Mr. Driggs, and with the prospect of visiting prisons and almshouses in London, as though it were an outing of the most delightful kind.

Roxanne strongly suspected her sisters of sending him their pin money for donations, for they had not bought so much as a hair ribbon or bootlace, Lady Maria told her, since they arrived, and had begged her to spend only a very little on their wardrobes and donate the rest to their favorite causes. It was Roxanne's hope that once caught up in the season, her sisters would gradually shake off the influence of the clergyman.

Finally, suitably though plainly attired, the ladies set forth in Lady Maria's barouche to make their calls. At some houses they only left cards, but at others they all alighted to ascend to a drawing room and chat, stiffly, on the twins' part, to one of their aunt's cronies, and to sip lemonade or ratafia and eat biscuits and cake. Their aunt's friends were cordial and several promised them cards to routs and drums, while another assured them of the arrival of vouchers from Almack's very soon, for the Winstons, though not wealthy, were a quite unexceptionable family, well-connected in the ton.

Their last stop was at a townhouse in Albemarle Street. "This, girls," said Lady Maria, "is the home of one of my oldest friends. She is charming, and I am sure you will like her excessively."

"Who is it, Aunt?" asked Gemma.

"My dear friend Althea Malverne, the Duchess of Rutledge," she said.

The wicked Duke's own mother! Roxanne entered the house with trepidation, but to her intense relief, they found that the Duchess was at leisure and quite alone. The Duke, of course, must still have been at Rosemark, recovering from his wounds. He could not have been allowed to travel after only a fortnight. Roxanne drew a long breath and let her eyes stop darting about the exquisitely furnished room, allowing them to rest on the Duchess herself.

She was petite and fashionably dressed, and she looked younger than her years. Her smile was warm with welcome, and Roxanne could see that between Her Grace and Lady Camberwick there existed a firm friendship. The Duchess greeted all three girls cordially, but she held Roxanne's hand for a second longer and, Roxanne thought, examined her more carefully.

"My dear," the Duchess said, "I have not caught sight of you since your first season, and I hope you won't be offended if, as an old family friend, I say that you have become quite a beauty!"

She turned to Lady Camberwick as Roxanne fought back a blush. "Maria, do you think that within no time at all your niece will be termed an Incomparable? I am certain that all the young gentlemen of my acquaintance will be enthralled with her. Those magnificent eyes! That lustrous hair! Such a delicate complexion!"

"I daresay," replied Lady Maria absently, for she had noticed the twins' alarming reaction to these compliments. They had put their heads together to confer, shooting anxious glances at their sister.

Melodie and Gemma ceased whispering to one another, and Melodie spoke while her twin looked on approvingly.

"Pardon our forwardness, Your Grace, but if what you say is true, we fear it might only encourage a dangerous vanity in our sister, though ordinarily, you know, she is perfectly humble."

Roxanne nearly sputtered with laughter at the amazement on the Duchess's face and the mortification on her Aunt Maria's, but Melodie continued, "I am not sure Roxanne would care to try it, but perhaps if her beauty could be employed to direct young men to higher and more serious thought—"

Gemma added, "Yes, to bring them to God . . . then it might not be amiss for her to called an Incomparable, and to attract many beaux." They nodded solemnly.

Roxanne knew that the Duchess was looking at her. She was afraid to meet her glance, but found, to her astonishment, that her Grace's eyes had a disconcertingly familiar twinkle, and that her expression was full of amusement and sympathy. The twinkle reminded her of the Duke's attempts to make her laugh, and she found it very odd that this delightful lady could be the mother of the same gentleman who had caused so much grief to the Winston family. But Roxanne could not help feeling a strong and immediate liking for her.

"My dear girls, I should not be at all surprised if some gentlemen declare themselves converted at first sight! Now, sit down, and you shall tell me about your plans. Oh, and you must promise to save Thursday evening for me—just a small dinner, you know, with a little music afterwards, if the young ladies would oblige?" She cast an inquisitive glance at the twins.

Roxanne looked sternly at her sisters, fully expecting a lecture on the frivolity of musical entertainments, but they surprised her.

"Of course, Your Grace," Gemma replied. "We have, thanks to Papa's encouragement, received excellent musical training."

"Yes, we take turns playing the organ at our chapel, you know."

The two identical heads leaned together and they conferred. "Perhaps a selection of hymns? I do like "Amazing Grace," or perhaps "God Moves in a Mysterious Way.""

"Hymns! What nonsense." Lady Camberwick had had enough. "Listen well, girls. You do not, when invited to display your talent on the pianoforte after dinner, offer to put your listeners to sleep with hymns!" She turned to the Duchess in despair.

"Do you see with what folly I have to contend? Oh, Althea, how shall I ever bring these girls to be creditably married? You see how I am frustrated at every turn by this most inappropriate Enthusiasm!"

The Duchess comforted her. "We shall go along

very well, Maria. They are sweet and rather . . . refreshing, as well as pretty. I am sure they will take, though they are, in truth, a bit too earnest for the comfort of the average young man."

"My dearest mama, do not despair. Perhaps the average young man, being average, is not so very particular about his comfort as you believe."

The five females in the room looked up as one, as unannounced and without ceremony, the Duke of Rutledge strolled in and bowed over his mother's hand.

The emotions in the breasts of five ladies were various, but indifference was not among them. Indeed, His Grace's mother looked quite vexed at his appearance. If she had been twenty years younger, she could be said to have pouted. Lady Camberwick, on the other hand, was all agog with curiosity to see her nieces' reaction to this model of masculine perfection.

She was not disappointed. The twins were openmouthed, for once forgetting to share their impressions with one another, as they took in the quiet splendor of His Grace's appointments, from the curly-brimmed beaver he negligently threw on a side table, to the glossy Hessians that encased his lower limbs. Roxanne, for her part, was struggling with a queer fluttering just below the breastbone, and a sudden inability to fix her glance anywhere but on the Duke's handsome visage.

The Duchess accepted his filial salute, but began to reprove him at once. "My dear boy, you illustrate quite clearly that your habits, at least, are not those of the average young man. You are rather extraordinary in your comings and goings. I had no idea you were in town again and did not look for you for at least another fortnight. I thought you were staying with Mr. Pearson in Wiltshire."

Roxanne ran her glance over the Duke's figure and only her knowledge of his wound revealed the small irregularity in the fit of his tailored blue coat and the slight awkwardness with which he held his arm. His mother very plainly did not know the history of his encounter with the highwaymen. His glance met Roxanne's for a bare instant in warning.

She flushed. Certainly, she had had no intention of alarming his mother with tales of his recent danger, or of even mentioning his name for that matter, unless Her Grace brought the subject up first.

But her sisters had no such scruples and, when presented to His Grace, immediately inquired after his wound.

The Duchess went white, and the Duke himself frowned in annoyance. "Harry! A wound . . . are you all right, my dear boy . . . oh, tell me what has happened!" She put a hand to her forehead and swayed in her seat.

Lady Camberwick rang for Her Grace's maid, and the Duke, with a suppressed exclamation, quickly poured his mother a glass of brandy from a silver decanter that stood on a little mahogany stand.

"Mother . . ." His Grace knelt beside her chair, his arm supporting her shoulders as he held the glass to her lips. "I am perfectly all right . . . all in one piece as you see."

Under his care, she soon recovered, and while she drank the brandy, he turned slowly about before her, smiling tenderly. "Observe. I assure you I am perfectly whole now. It was only a highwayman—winged me. And our little wager is off—he got away with my diamond stickpin."

"Wager?" Her Grace asked. Then she glanced at Roxanne, smiled uncertainly, and said, "Oh, I had forgotten. But who cared for you, my poor boy?"

"Fortunately, I was practically on the Winstons' doorstep, and thanks to Miss Winston's careful nursing, I am already well, as you see." He flexed his wounded shoulder for his mother's benefit, and returned to her side. "It was of no importance, Mama. Nothing for you to come over so ill about."

Roxanne was touched and rather amazed at his attentiveness and his genuine anxiety for his mother, and amused at his having had a wager with her, whatever it might have been about. But she was sorry for her hostess's agitation. She frowned at her sisters. "That was not well done, girls. Could you not see that Her Grace knew nothing of the wound?"

The twins looked repentant, and immediately begged the Duchess to forgive them for being so thoughtless as to give her such a shock. But Her Grace was not angry, only curious.

"You say Miss Winston nursed you to health, Harry?" Her glance was bright once again and darted from one to the other. "How can this be?"

Lady Maria explained the whole circumstance, and her friend gently scolded her for keeping the tale from her.

"Nonsense, Althea," said Lady Camberwick. "I knew you would only make yourself ill with worry, and Roxanne and Miss Lynchard wrote and assured me that His Grace was in no danger."

86

Roxanne could not restrain her own curiosity any longer. "I confess I am surprised to see you so soon in town, my lord. I had thought you would stay with Mr. Pearson at Rosemark. Or has his own recovery progressed so rapidly that he was eager to get back to London himself?"

"I am happy to say that my friend Pearson is regaining the use of his leg very quickly, but unfortunately he was not yet ready to return to town. No, it was my own idea. I confess that your part of the country, though charming, is not precisely filled with activity at this season, and as my host was still recovering, I excused myself after a few days to attend to some business here."

"We are so happy to hear that you are recovered, sir," offered Gemma.

"And we hear from our sister that your stay at our home brought some comfort to the soul as well as the body," added Melodie.

"Oh, she has told you then of the improving works I have read?" The Duke cast a wicked glance at Roxanne, but his tone to the twins was empty of sarcasm.

"Of course. And if there is any way in which we can advise you, Your Grace . . ."

". . . or if you wish to be directed to some other useful books . . ."

"Thank you, but I am quite at peace with what I have already learned," the Duke said quite decidedly.

Fortunately, the twins took this in the most positive way. "At peace! How happy we are for you, my lord!"

Lady Camberwick, had, with growing impatience, been attempting to introduce another subject of conversation, and at last succeeded. "I hope you are recovered enough for some society, my lord. We should be glad to see you at any time in Upper Brook Street."

The Duke raised an inquiring eyebrow at Roxanne, who pretended not to have heard this invitation. Silently she prayed that he would announce a swift departure from London.

The Duke bowed. "Yes, I should be most happy. I will remain in town for the rest of the season, and it will be a pleasure to continue my acquaintance with your charming nieces."

"And I am sure they would welcome the chance to become better acquainted with you, will you not, my dears?" Lady Camberwick pressed.

Melodie and Gemma added polite encouragements, and Roxanne was forced to say, "Indeed."

A broad smile transformed the Duke's face. Roxanne could not tell if it was a smile of triumph, satisfaction, or merely amusement, but immediately His Grace turned to his mother once more. There was no mistaking the expression on *her* face. The Duchess glowed.

"I'll bid you good day then, Mama. I only wanted to let you know I was in town, and I shall call again when you are at leisure."

He took his leave of his proud mother, an admiring Lady Camberwick, and the chastened twins. Roxanne did not look at him, but allowed him to take her hand. The feel of his warm handclasp, and the certainly that he was looking down at her made her heart flutter with annoyance and discomfort. To her relief, he left without addressing any private words to her.

"I am so grateful for the Duke's kind interest in us," said Lady Camberwick when he had gone. "It is sure to be beneficial to the girls this season."

"Although he is my son, I am not boasting when I say that young ladies who attract his notice are bound to attract other favorable attention in society," replied the Duchess.

"And I have a suspicion that Roxanne has certainty attracted his notice," said Lady Camberwick slyly, while her friend smiled.

"I am not here to attract anyone's notice, my lady. I am here to chaperone my sisters, and see them established," Roxanne protested.

"Don't be so foolish, dear," said Aunt Maria. "Do you not see how the Duke's friendship will assist us in attracting suitors to the twins?"

Roxanne knew immediately that her aunt was right. For her sisters' sakes, she must suffer the Duke of Rutledge's patronage.

Though she knew his real character, the rest of society must be blinded to his faults by his wealth, good looks, and position. She only hoped that the necessity of accepting his acquaintance would bring no dishonor to Alfred's memory.

Roxanne was by now very glad of the hours she had spent in prayer, self-examination, and contemplation, for they had made her aware of her own unimportance and of the need for suppression of her pride. She would have many opportunities to practice that, she supposed. It was going to be a very long season.

Chapter Five

On the day of the Duchess of Rutledge's dinner, Roxanne and Lady Camberwick sat after breakfast in the morning room, the former with some work, the latter perusing a fashionable journal. She rattled the pages and at length put it down.

"You must help me, Roxanne. Those girls are driving me to distraction. This"—she pointed to the dog-eared journal—"is the only enjoyable reading matter they have left me, and only because I happened to take it up to my room with me the night before they swept my house clean of everything amusing."

Roxanne shook her head, trying not to smile. In spite of her own frustration with her sisters' single-mindedness, she could not help but be a little diverted by their attempts to convert Lady Camberwick to their way of life. "I have tried, Aunt Maria, but they will not tell me what they have done with your novels and magazines." She put down her sewing, stood up, and began, for the tenth time, to search the tables, cabinets, and shelves of the room, hoping to find some remnant of her aunt's literary tastes. Instead she found several serious works, a Bible, the *Christian Observer,* and a copy of *The Missionary Register.*

She sighed and sat down with it, paging through its sentimental, heart-rending tales of missionaries and their work, interspersed with engravings of exotic people and places. "I am so sorry, Aunt Maria. I had no notion that they would prove to be so stubborn. And there is no way to punish them! Even to send them back home would only reward them."

Lady Camberwick laughed, though she was plainly not amused. "Yes, and to tell them that they may not go out with us is exactly what they wish to hear. Although, to be quite honest, after their behavior last night, I am not so sure that they will be welcome in society for very long."

The evening before, the ladies had attended a rout at the home of the widowed Countess of Culverton, who was a prominent hostess. It had been a great crush, with almost a hundred elegantly dressed people thronging the reception rooms, drinking champagne, sitting down to cards, and gossiping. The twins had seen their mission at once.

Roxanne had been a bit overwhelmed at first, as this was the first large party she had attended in so long, and so had not kept a close enough watch upon her sisters. Before she could make her way out of the hall and into the drawing room, she had lost them. She and Lady Camberwick had spent the rest of the evening, after greeting their hostess, in pushing through the fashionable crowd, looking for the two girls.

Unfortunately, finding them, Roxanne soon discovered, was even more embarrassing than losing them had been. Leaving her aunt to search the ground-floor reception rooms, Roxanne took the first floor, and was drawn by the sound of raised voices and breaking glass to a chamber near the head of the stairs. Her heart thumped uncomfortably as a dread conviction began to take hold of her. Heedless of the crowd, almost forgetting her manners in her anxiety, she worked her way to the doorway of the room and stood there, watching helplessly.

In the room were two very fashionably dressed young gentlemen, with elaborate waistcoats, intricately tied neckcloths, and collars so high that they could not possibly turn their heads with any degree of ease or comfort. Their flushed faces and glittering eyes told Roxanne that they had imbibed more wine than was good for them.

One gentleman was fair-haired and wore blue, the other was dark and wore black. These fashion plates stood glaring at each other across an overturned card table, underneath which was a smashed bottle and glasses. Not far from them stood the twins, hands clasped before them, heads bowed, either meekly awaiting the reproaches of the young exquisites or, more likely, Roxanne thought, praying for their souls.

She knew a moment of fear, and tremendous mortification, as those in the doorway of the room giggled and pointed. Guests were beginning to enter behind her to discover the cause of the noise. She could not hesitate any longer.

She went quickly to her sisters. "Whatever have you been doing?"

"Nothing but our duty, sister," said Gemma.

Roxanne glanced at the young men. The fair one in the blue coat had now fallen to his knees, not, as the twins might have thought, in repentance, but mourning the split wine, muttering, "Demmed fine claret! Ought not to have lost your temper, Tony. Ain't the thing to overturn tables and spill the wine, even if it is your own."

The dark-haired gentleman did not moderate his anger after this gentle reproach. "Never mind the wine, idiot! The cards! How could you serve me such a scurvy trick, and blame it on this pair of prosing females?"

His companion looked up. "Told you, the cards were good. A fresh, sealed pack. Can't call me out over it, Tony, I won't accept your challenge. The cards ain't mine, but theirs." He shrugged a shoulder toward the girls. "Said so, didn't they?" Carefully lifting an unbroken wineglass that still retained a drop of red liquid, he raised it to his lips, while the other gentleman turned a wrathful glance upon the twins.

Roxanne was torn between dismay and laughter, but took hold of her sisters. "Whatever you may have done to anger them, girls, I fear these gentlemen are not in a mood to hear an explanation. We had best leave at once."

In reply they only shook their heads.

"We must not go yet, Roxanne." Melodie stood firm. "These poor sinners must recognize the error of their ways. We thought that our intervention would help them see the evils of gambling."

The dark young man cried, "Take them away, ma'am, take these impertinent chits out of our sight, if you please. Damme, I've never in my life been so shabbily treated, and in my own house!"

"Come," whispered Roxanne, taking both of them by the arm, wishing that she had never heard the noise that led her to the room. The scene was shocking enough, but it was obvious by now that the aggrieved young man in black was the master of the house, son of their hostess, and therefore the Earl of Culverton.

But the twins were immovable objects, deaf to her pleas. The young Earl approached them, his expression boding no good. All thought of good manners had obviously flown from his head.

"Perhaps you would care to know, ma'am, just what these two young ladies stand accused of, before we drive them out of the house?"

"Yes, out of the house," echoed the fair gentleman, who was now off his knees and examining the twins through a quizzing glass with great interest.

Roxanne had no doubt that the girls had offended in some way, but nevertheless she could now allow herself to be treated so insolently. "These young ladies are my sisters, sir, and I would be most interested to hear any accusations; however, I must beg you and your friend not to forget yourselves."

"Your sisters, madam, appear to have forgotten themselves very thoroughly," he retorted, "or at least to have forgotten the duties of a guest."

"Yes, guests, you know," added his friend mildly. "No business interfering in a friendly game of cards." He moved a little closer and examined the twins' luxuriant brown hair and long-lashed eyes with appreciation. "Not at all the thing," he said, apparently having made a choice, and directing his words to Gemma, who merely blushed and avoided his gaze.

"But sir, as we have tried to tell you, we meant no harm," said Melodie, "It is our duty as Christians to awaken your hearts to the prospect of eternal suffering if you continue in your wickedness."

"Wickedness, is it? What about tampering with an honest man's cards and causing a row with his best friend?" demanded the Earl. "Ain't that wickedness?" His anger, however, appeared to have flown, now that he had calmed enough to observe his fair tormentors more closely. He ended with a crooked smile, and now it was Melodie's turn to blush.

The room was now full of interested listeners, laughing and enjoying the show, and servants were already coming in to clean up the destruction beneath the card table, keeping one ear on the conversation.

Roxanne was relieved to see the gentlemen apparently impressed by her sisters' beauty, but the distraction they had caused was still a source of mortification. She desperately wanted to take counsel with Aunt Maria, and leave without insulting either the Earl or his friend. Once more she tried to induce her sisters to come away, but they continued to ignore her pleas.

What on earth was she to do? Not for the first time, she wished that her father was a whole man once more and could deal with his difficult daughters himself. But it was her responsibility. She must find a graceful way out.

"If you will not leave," she whispered to the girls, "then you must apologize to these gentlemen, because obviously your meddling has caused a great deal of trouble."

Gemma spoke after a shy glance at the young man in blue, who, dispensing with the affectation of the quizzing glass, was observing her with unconcealed admiration at closer range.

95

"We will apologize for causing you distress, Roxanne, but we have done nothing wrong. We simply tried . . . that is, before the game started, we took their cards away, and replaced them—"

"—with these." Melodie bent and picked up a card. It was not a playing card, but Roxanne recognized it right away as a scripture card, or "draw card," popular among the girls' church friends. On one side was a scripture verse, on the other a hymn verse. Roxanne had often attended gatherings of the faithful where these cards were employed to stimulate serious conversation and to prevent idle gossiping. Sometimes, though this was disapproved of by Mr. Driggs, they were employed in prophecy as well. Roxanne burned with shame at her sisters' impertinence.

"You did not—how could you be so rude and so foolish!"

"Foolish indeed," said the young master of the house, who had by now completely regained his temper and could be seen to have a good-natured countenance and a ready smile. "Nearly sent me into an apoplexy—had me accusing poor Cyril of doctoring the cards! I am only thankful that these young ladies did not cause a duel." He tried to look stern, but did not entirely succeed.

This did not relieve a bit of Roxanne's vexation, and worse still, she could no longer ignore the whispers behind her. She burned with shame at what the spectators were saying.

"What's to do?"

"Winston's girls . . . shocking!"

"An unfortunate family . . . and now this!"

"Rich meat for tomorrow's scandal broth . . ."

Roxanne knew that she and her sisters were surrounded by the inquisitive and delighted faces of
strangers savoring the scene. Her patience was at an
end and scandal was already foretold, so she replied
witheringly to the Earl, "If you were not so befuddled
with liquor, my lord, you would have seen that these
were not playing cards before you sat down to play!"

"I don't think you've any call to say something like
that, madam," the Earl replied, looking hurt. "After
all, my friend and I are the injured parties."

Roxanne was sorry she had lost her temper, for the
crowd behind her loudly signified its amusement, and
now perhaps there would be even more unpleasant-
ness. Oh, if only the stupid girls had gone away with
her at once! She didn't know where to turn.

Quite suddenly, she became aware that the buzz of
conversation and laughter was beginning to fade, the
room was beginning to empty, and the door to the
corridor was soon shut. The two young men looked
abashed, and the twins were staring wide-eyed over
Roxanne's shoulder as if they had seen the Savior
himself.

"I am acquainted with these young ladies, Culverton, so if you will allow me to intervene . . ."

"Rutledge! Of course, sir . . . we did not
know . . ." Suddenly the young men were bowing and
moving aside to make room for the Duke.

Roxanne had not known, nor had she expected,
that he would be at the rout, and she sent up a small
prayer of gratitude before she permitted herself to be
annoyed at his turning up at this moment.

She tried to stand proud and tall as he bid her a
casual good evening, as though there were nothing at

all odd about their manner or place of meeting. His gaze did no more than flicker over her, and in a moment he was strolling over to evaluate the damage to the card table, and to address the twins and the young men. He speared each of them with a glance as he stood completely at his ease among the chaos.

"Ladies, I don't believe you are acquainted with the Earl of Culverton?" He indicated the red-faced young man whose impeccable evening dress and dark curls were by now both rumpled.

Numbly the twins shook their heads, while Roxanne watched, puzzled.

"Culverton, this is Miss Winston"—he took Roxanne's arm and drew her irresistibly into the circle— "Miss Melodie Winston, Miss Gemma Winston." Amazingly, the young man bowed, and after him, that other sprig of fashion, whom the Duke introduced as Mr. Cyril Bentley, followed suit.

Roxanne could not find a word to say. How could the man be so infuriatingly self-possessed? He had even introduced the twins in correct order of birth! A lucky guess. But he was going on.

"I understand there has been some difficulty over the cards."

"Yes, Your Grace," said Melodie, all shyness gone. "My sister and I, for the moral benefit of these gentlemen, tried to introduce some good in the place of the evil habit of gambling." She held out the card she had picked up, and Rutledge examined it.

"Let every soul be subject unto the higher powers: for there is no power but of God," he read. "Excellent advice, ladies, but perhaps misdirected. The only power gamesters recognize, at least for the moment, is that of Chance. Come, you can't really expect to change a man's lifetime habits with a childish trick like this," he chided them gently.

"Exactly, Your Grace! And so I would have told them," said the Earl. Mr. Bentley, however, looked completely cowed by the Duke's presence and did not raise his eyes, except to sneak a look at Gemma.

"Would you have, indeed?" Rutledge fixed the Earl with a glance.

The young man stepped back, abashed. But the twins were not discouraged.

"Oh, we are not so foolish as to believe that our act would bring about an instant change, but it is our duty to leave no opportunity untried to exhort others," said Gemma as her sister nodded her approval.

Roxanne realized that she must speak, before the Duke took entire command of the situation. "I think that it is time for us to take our leave. Gentlemen, I sincerely apologize for the way my sisters disrupted your game, and I assure you"—she looked sternly at the twins—"it will never happen again. My lord"—she turned to the young Earl—"I hope that you will apologize to your mother for us. I will take my sisters home now, until they learn how to behave in a gentleman's home. Come, girls." The Duke nodded his approval, which gave Roxanne not the slightest bit of comfort.

But under Rutledge's watchful eye, the twins went with her, chastened. The Duke took a few languid steps, reaching the door in time to open it for them, upon Lady Maria's startled and worried face.

"What—" she began.

But Roxanne's mind was all on the Duke. As she ushered the twins out before her, letting them deal with Lady Camberwick's curiosity, Roxanne knew that she owed him her thanks, but it was difficult. How was it that, with very little effort, he had managed to restore order where she had only made things worse? Nevertheless, it had to be said.

"Thank you, my lord. I — we are very grateful for your kind intervention. I — we shall endeavor not to trouble you again." And then she hurried away, but not before she heard his warm chuckle behind her.

Now, the morning after the disagreeable scene, Roxanne could not but agree with her aunt that if the twins were not controlled somehow, they would soon not be welcome in any respectable London house and their season would be in vain.

"I have given them a good scolding," she told her aunt, "and have even quoted that odious Mr. Driggs to them, who, for all his faults, I am sure would not have condoned such behavior. No," Roxanne mused, "he is far too careful of courting the good opinion of the wealthy and powerful, that he might extract donations from them. He would never have offended the Earl of Culverton."

"The Countess, I am quite sure, will cut me the next time we meet," moaned Lady Maria. "And I was not even present when it all happened! Well, we shall have to see that they behave properly tonight at dear Althea's dinner."

"As there will be neither cards nor dancing, nor anything the girls could object to, I don't suppose we need worry too much," said Roxanne hopefully. "But I am not at all looking forward to it." Then she bit her tongue, because she realized she could not tell her aunt the reason. It was, of course, because the Duke would be present, and she was loath to face him after last night. He would be bound to refer to her dilemma and to make her feel foolish over it, and probably had not been satisfied with her cold thanks for his rescue. Oh, why couldn't the man just ignore her, knowing as he must how she felt about him?

Just then the two miscreants of the night before entered the morning room. They always appropriated the half hour after breakfast for their prayers, and since Roxanne preferred to pray alone and Lady Camberwick would not consent to having her servants called away from their work and assembled for this daily ceremony, as the twins had urged her to do, the girls always retired to their room. Roxanne hoped that they had been praying for forgiveness, as she had prayed for patience.

They were dressed, as usual, in a plain style, but their sister was coming to believe that it suited their particular kind of beauty very well. Their long, thick hair, instead of being fashionably cut and curled by Lady Maria's maid, as she had offered, was drawn back simply by day, or put up by night, and their oval faces, large eyes, and chiseled mouths showed to advantage. Their skins were clear, their color excellent, their figures graceful, and Roxanne knew that could she only cure them of their meddling habits, and perhaps give them a few hundred pounds' dowry, they would be off her hands in a matter of weeks. But it appeared, she sighed to herself, that it was not to be.

The girls sat and took up their work without referring to last night's escapade. They had taken their scolding very well, with a few tears, gratitude that Roxanne had promised not to tell their father, and promises that they would behave more circumspectly in future.

But Aunt Maria felt no qualms about bringing up the matter once again. "It is simply too bad, girls, that you had to choose Lady Culverton's rout to make such exhibitions of yourselves. Why, had you made a good impression, I am sure we could have aroused the interest of the young Earl in one of you. He is known to be on the lookout for a suitable wife, and fortune, although of course always desirable, need not guide him in his choice. And his friend, Mr. Bentley, was present at that disgraceful scene as well . . ." She sighed at yet another lost opportunity. "I know his mother, and she positively pines for him to marry some respectable young lady. He is to have a baronetcy one day, you know. You two have done a great deal to hurt your chances, perhaps the best chances you will ever get."

"We are sorry, Aunt Maria, but we cannot sacrifice our principles merely to attract these worldly and unworthy gentlemen," said Melodie with some of her old firmness.

"Would you really have us marry such . . . such . . . libertines?" asked Gemma sadly.

"Come now," said Roxanne briskly, "you must not label every fashionable young man a libertine, simply because he drinks wine and plays cards. You must do people the justice of discovering their good qualities. Just because you disapprove of certain superficial aspects of their lives does not mean that they are evil men."

"Well, I can remember you calling the Duke of Rutledge a libertine when Alfred met him, simply because he was known to indulge in all the fashionable diversions," said Gemma with a sly glance at her twin.

Roxanne blushed, as she saw Aunt Maria's amused gaze on her. "That was different. He was older, more experience. . . . and I'm sure it was not only cards and drinking. And after all, ensuing events proved that I was right."

"I thought that the Duke, although he scolded us last night, seemed much improved since he turned his mind to serious matters. You did him a great service, Roxanne, in encouraging him to think of his soul while you nursed his body," offered Melodie.

"Yes." Gemma nodded. "I think that he is on the way to being saved."

At that moment, the subject of their conversation was announced, and the footman was urged by Lady Camberwick to show His Grace into the morning room at once.

Roxanne, suppressing an anxious quickening of her heartbeat, looked sternly at her sisters. "I do not wish to hear you importune the Duke regarding the state of his soul, and I think that later today we should call upon the Countess of Culverton to give her our apologies in person."

But this plan was rendered unnecessary, for no sooner had Rutledge been properly greeted, seated, and plied with refreshment, Roxanne attempting to control her usual uncomfortable reaction to his presence, than the Earl of Culverton and his friend Mr. Bentley were announced as well.

Gemma and Melodie, for once, looked to their sister for guidance, apparently perturbed at having to face the victims of last night's abortive plan.

Roxanne took pity on them. She leaned toward them and whispered, "Be calm, girls, and remember what I have told you. Apologize, and then Aunt Maria and I will endeavor to introduce another subject."

"An excellent plan, Miss Winston," said Rutledge, sotto voce, his eyes full of amusement at her discomfiture.

"Thank you, my lord," she replied coolly, and turned from him to greet the new visitors.

The Earl and Mr. Bentley were rather neater and soberer than they had appeared the evening before, and Lady Maria was charmed with them, beginning her apologies for her nieces' behavior even before the twins could get a word out.

"So impulsive, the dear girls, yet they mean well. . . . I intend to call on your mama, Lord Culverton, and beg her to forgive—"

But the Earl and his friend seemed even more disturbed at the mention of last night's trouble than were the perpetrators of it.

"Not at all, please do not trouble to mention it to Mama . . ." The Earl glanced, almost shyly, at the twins. "We must apologize ourselves, for our rudeness . . ."

"Had been drinking, you know," offered Mr. Bentley, "wouldn't have talked so to ladies if we hadn't." He seemed to recall something and stuck his hand into his coat pocket, where Roxanne had noticed an unsightly bulge disrupting the elegant lines of his tailoring.

"Your cards." He offered the pack of scripture cards to Gemma with a disarming smile. She took them shyly, with an uncertain glance at her twin, and thanked him. Roxanne was impressed with the behavior of both, and began to have hopes not very different from those of her Aunt Maria.

The two parties mutually forgave one another and, under the guidance of Lady Camberwick, entered into careful conversation, in which the twins strove not to mention their pet preoccupation and the gentlemen were models of masculine propriety.

All of which Roxanne looked on with pleasure, except for the fact that it left His Grace the Duke of Rutledge's attention free for conversation with herself. She strove to control her outrage at this turn of events, and girded herself for a struggle.

She was disconcerted, however, when His Grace did not at once refer to the events of the night before, but instead inquired about the health of her father, her younger sisters, and Miss Lynchard, recalling and once again thanking her for her family's kindness to him during his convalescence, and expressing the wish that she and her sisters would enjoy the season.

Roxanne was too shocked at this sudden civility to do more than reply politely and noncommittally, and she was almost relieved when he said, in something like his accustomed manner, "I fear, however, Miss Winston, that your season will not be entirely made up of pleasure parties. Your sisters' propensity for mischief will no doubt keep you busy for weeks to come."

He was certainly correct, but Roxanne felt she could not permit him to criticize her sisters, though the criticism was a mild one and he himself had, by dispersing the crowd, saved them from the unfortunate results of their behavior the night before.

"What you mistakenly call mischief, my lord, is only the result of a praiseworthy enthusiasm. My sisters merely seek to improve the state of a dissipated society, beginning with—"

"—beginning with two of its most harmless, innocent members? I am surprised that Miss Melodie and Miss Gemma did not begin with hardened rakes—they seem brave enough for it." The amusement was back in his voice, and he was watching carefully for Roxanne's reaction. She lost no time in giving it to him.

"I daresay that to you gambling and drinking to excess are harmless enough pastimes—no doubt you have indulged in them often. But to my sisters—as well as to me—they are but symptoms of a malaise that leads to the death of the immortal soul to salvation."

Roxanne knew she was being unnecessarily vehement, but as usual, in the presence of that knowing smile and those laughing gray eyes, she could not control the surge of annoyance that made her say more than she had meant to say.

If she hadn't known better she would have thought that he flinched a little, but after a tiny pause he smiled. "Indeed. I meant no disrespect to your beliefs, Miss Winston. From my course of reading at your home, I should have been more familiar with your sisters' motives, and the result of such a combustible combination as the two of them and the wicked city of London."

He laughed, and Roxanne recalled those absurd moments of his "improving" readings. A pang struck her. It would be so easy, and even pleasant, to give in and laugh with him, but she could not. There was a life between them, Alfred's life, and she could not allow him to think that she, like her brother, was so easily led astray.

"As for those two young gentlemen being harmless, my lord," she went on before her resolve could falter, "I cannot offer you any argument, not being fully acquainted with their characters, but I assure you that you could never convince my sisters of their innocence, once they had seen them overindulge in wine and play cards for money."

His laugh was more of a snort this time, and he leaned a little closer, keeping his voice low. "Tony Culverton and Cyril Bentley are two of the most innocent boys that ever graced the drawing rooms of London society. They've been friends since they were in leading strings, they are not a penny in debt, except to each other, which I assure you they hardly count, they have no extravagances except perhaps, on Cyril's part, his wardrobe, and on Tony's part, his stables, and they neither of them, forgive my vulgarity, have been known to be much in the petticoat line. In short, Miss Winston, they are the most respectable youngsters, among the group now on the town, that anyone has ever seen. Of course, they do occasionally need the guidance of an older man," he conceded, "and they count on me to give it to them."

Roxanne, though conscious of being wrong, could not stop herself. "Of course, my lord, as you are so experienced in that line. I only hope that your guidance does not prove as fateful as it did in your last effort at advising an innocent young man in his first season on the town."

At that his face went dark with anger, though his eyes showed something very much like hurt surprise. Was it surprise, she wondered, that she should remind him of his sins against her family? Had he really thought that she could forgive him so easily? But his next words made her certain that hurt played no part in his emotions, except perhaps for hurt pride.

"If you are referring to the unfortunate affair with your brother, Miss Winston, then I must ask you not to mention it to me again," he said bluntly, in a hard, tight voice which contrasted sharply with his accustomed drawl. "I fear we shall never agree on that matter, and I am certain that it is useless for me to discuss it with you."

Roxanne nodded, feeling as though ice water had been thrown over her. She had a sudden urge to cry, but kept her tone as unemotional as his. "Certainly, sir. It shall be as you wish, and I agree, discussion would be useless."

"Roxanne, dear, the Earl and Mr. Bentley wish to take the girls for a drive this afternoon." Aunt Maria's voice penetrated the haze of misery that surrounded Roxanne. For a few minutes she had quite forgotten that there was another soul in the room besides the Duke and herself.

"How kind of them." She smiled determinedly on the Earl and his friend. She must cease her silly, useless brangling with the Duke and attend to her sisters' needs. After exchanging a few pleasantries with the young men, she wished the visitors would go because she knew it was her duty to instruct the twins minutely in how they were to behave in the gentlemen's company.

Luckily, their mission accomplished, the two young men stood up to leave shortly after, and the Duke left with them. He had said not another word to Roxanne, but devoted himself for a few minutes to the twins, and to Lady Maria, who smiled incessantly at him while she darted a series of knowing glances at her eldest niece.

When all the callers had gone—the Duke unsmiling, his gaze fixed briefly on Roxanne's face, the young men more cheerily—the relieved ladies had a brief respite to discuss the recent visitation.

"Girls, I'm very proud of you; you behaved charmingly. Did they not, Roxanne?"

"I must take your word for it, Aunt, as the Duke unfortunately engaged all of my attention. But I'm pleased that they seem to have made something other than a bad impression on the Earl and Mr. Bentley."

Melodie shrugged. "They are well enough, though they are much too dissipated to be interesting to us as potential husbands. But since it is our duty to accept suitors, we will drive in the park with them," she said in tones of resignation.

"Oh, certainly," said Gemma. "And you needn't worry, Roxanne, we shall not lecture them. Or at least," she added with a little smile, "not as long as we can help it."

"Oh, girls, just think!" cried Lady Camberwick, clasping her hands before her. "Last night we were in the midst of disaster, and this morning, as if by magic, all is settled to our satisfaction."

Before Roxanne could warn her aunt that the question of the twins' future was not likely to be settled so easily, Melodie said, "I believe it was all due to the Duke. He was so kind, and he made everything all right between us and the gentlemen last night."

"Yes, and I believe it was he who convinced Mr. Bentley and the Earl to call on us, and ask us to drive," added Gemma.

"Perhaps," said Lady Camberwick with a sly glance at Roxanne, "that is because he has a particular interest in the well-being of the Winston family."

"You are mistaken," Roxanne replied, knowing she blushed and hating it. "He is already familiar with the consequences of taking an interest in the Winston family, and I doubt he would be tempted to try again, lest there be another unfortunate result."

That silenced the other ladies for a while, as their thoughts turned to the absent Alfred, though Lady Camberwick frowned at her eldest niece. But Roxanne was unrepentant, and glad when other visitors were announced so that her aunt had no opportunity to scold her.

Chapter Six

The fashionable hour of four in the afternoon saw the twins safely taken up in two flashy curricles driven by those dashing, but now certified respectable young bloods, Lord Culverton and Mr. Bentley, attended by liveried grooms clinging to the the rear of the carriages.

Roxanne had fully impressed upon the girls that they were to discuss nothing of a religious nature, and that they were to behave with the utmost discretion. She spent the rest of the day at home, and was glad that she did, because she received a call she had not wanted to miss.

Fanny Pearson, formerly Roxanne's bosom friend, whom she had not seen since the events of three years ago, came to Upper Brook Street that afternoon. The two girls had quarreled over the rumors of Fanny's involvement with the author of Alfred Winston's disgrace and demise, and had neither spoken nor written since, although Roxanne had cherished a secret wish that the rift might be mended. Even her most stringent self-examination had not humbled her enough to make the first move toward peace.

Roxanne was glad that Geoffrey had given her the message from his sister, and that she had spoken to him of her willingness to see Fanny. It was high time to make up the quarrel. Now the two ladies greeted one other with embraces and tears.

Fanny was slender and rather tall. Her wispy auburn hair resisted all attempts to dress it neatly and always made her appear as if she had just been caught in a violent wind without her hat, but nevertheless it suited her. Her face was a pretty triangle, set with large dark eyes contrasting pleasantly with her fair skin and auburn hair. Alfred Winston had not been the only gentleman enamored of her piquant charms, merely the first, and the only one whose affections were returned.

Roxanne had always assumed that Fanny would one day be Alfred's wife, and her sense of betrayal when she heard the rumors about Fanny and Rutledge had been sharp indeed. Now, she told herself as she embraced her long-lost friend again, all that was to be forgotten. She would not mention it. But to her surprise, Fanny did.

"Oh, Roxanne, my dear, I am sorry it has taken me so long to swallow my stupid pride! It was just that I was so hurt that you thought I had betrayed Alfred's memory, when really I was suffering so, and the Duke . . ." She stopped, startled by the sudden change of expression on Roxanne's face.

"Why, you still blame him, don't you?" she asked.

"And do you not?" demanded Roxanne.

"I have good reason not to," said Fanny mysteriously. Then, more gently, "You know, I would not have married Harry—the Duke. He did not quite understand the strength of my feelings for Alfred. He said he would not want a wife who loved another, even if that other was . . . lost to her."

It was Roxanne's turn to be startled now, startled that Rutledge should have such a delicate sensibility where marriage was concerned.

Fanny saw her friend's reaction and smiled. "You still think he is a monster, do you not? You are wrong, yet I can hardly blame you when I think of what you have suffered. Can we not forget? And can you forgive me?"

Roxanne melted. "Of course, Fanny. I can never forget . . . but I can forgive, you at least. Come, sit down, and you shall tell me what you have been doing, and I shall tell you about my trials with the twins."

So the friends settled down to a cosy gossip, aided by tea and cakes, and soon Fanny was laughing delightedly at the tales of the twins' misdemeanors and Roxanne's efforts to present them as suitable marriage material. They made plans to shop together one afternoon, and found that they had several engagements in common in the following week.

Roxanne was delighted at the prospect of seeing her friend at most of the events of the season. She would have someone sympathetic to talk to while she played chaperone for her sisters, a task Fanny told her she did not envy her.

"But you, Fanny, have you not . . . that is . . ." Roxanne tried to put the question delicately, though a few years ago there would have been nothing she could not have asked her friend. "Have there not been other gentlemen, other suitors, offers of marriage? I confess that I expected you would be married by now."

113

Now it was Fanny who was hurt. "Did you think I could so quickly forget your brother?" Her face paled and what had been a light dusting of freckles stood out as a cluster of golden specks across the bridge of her nose.

"I'm sorry, my dear. I did not mean that I thought you had forgotten him, but after all, it has been three years, and you are not . . . that is, we are past the age where many women are already married. You are so lovely, and you were so popular in our first season, that I assumed . . ."

Fanny sighed, and pressed Roxanne's hand. "No, I should not have snapped at you. You are right to think that I might have accepted another offer. But I . . ." Now her cheeks were pink again, and there was an odd dreaminess in her eyes that made Roxanne suspect her next words. "I cannot forget Alfred so easily. I could not bring myself to accept any of the offers made me. Perhaps someday . . ."

Roxanne, though wondering if despite her words there *was* another man, knew better than to press her friend, and quickly changed the subject. The two parted like the almost-sisters that they had once been, and Roxanne knew the peace of a clear conscience again.

That evening, as they prepared to attend the Duchess's dinner, Lady Camberwick knocked and entered Roxanne's chamber. She inspected her niece's appearance and frowned. ·

"Roxanne dear, why do you not wear one of your new gowns? Do you, too, wish to disgrace me?"

"Certainly not, Aunt Maria," Roxanne assured her, taking another look in the mirror. The gown that offended her aunt was, in truth, not new, but the very best of her old gowns, let out and newly trimmed, a jonquil satin that was quite becoming to her. "I only thought . . . that is, this is a simple occasion, and there is, after all, no need for me to call attention to myself. It is the twins' toilette you should be over-seeing, dear Aunt."

"I have just come from their chamber, and though we had a bit of a struggle with Gemma over her décolletage, and Melodie objected to her entire toilette, I have managed to see them suitably dressed. But you! Come now, put on the sky blue sarsenet we made up. I recall it made you look a perfect angel."

Aunt Maria stood stubbornly, her arms folded across her violet silk-robed chest, and waited.

Roxanne sighed and submitted, but realized that her aunt was right. To wear a truly fashionable gown gave her confidence, and she would have need of that, to deal both with her wayward sisters' public behavior and with the Duke, were he to grace his mother's dinner that evening. Not, she told herself, that she felt any need to impress him with her appearance . . . but he would see that she was a person to be reckoned with, and not a country schoolgirl he could torment for his amusement.

There were eighteen to dine at the Duchess's long table that evening, and the guests assembled first in the drawing room, where introductions were made and the ladies' toilettes admired. The Duchess glided among her guests, few of whom, it turned out, were acquainted with one another, and made everyone feel welcome and at ease, with a word, a touch, or a gentle steering toward an introduction.

She flirted delightfully with Sir James Winston, giving him her hand, smiling when he impulsively kissed it, making him feel, his daughter knew, as though his inability to rise and bow to her was naught, at the same time as she discreetly detailed one of her footmen to push his Bath chair and assist him at table. It was not only civility on Her Grace's part, but seemed a genuine interest in her guest. Roxanne could not help admiring her poise, and thought she had discovered the source from which sprung the Duke's insufferable aplomb.

When Roxanne had met all the other guests, she was disappointed to find that the Earl of Culverton and Mr. Bentley were not among them. Perhaps it was just as well, though, she reflected. She doubted her sisters could have controlled themselves for an entire day *and* night in the presence of two sinners who seemed to need saving so urgently.

Although Sir James had accompanied them to the dinner, Roxanne and Lady Camberwick had agreed that they would not worry him with their apprehensions of the twins' public behavior. They did agree, however, that tonight they would keep a closer eye on their charges, and before dinner was announced this was a simple enough matter. They were conducting themselves admirably, their sister thought, although they did lapse into a brief religious discussion with one of the other guests, a Lady Allenbrook.

"Do you know that lady, Aunt Maria?" asked Roxanne, indicating the twins' new acquaintance.

"Indeed, she is some connection or other. . . . Althea told me she hardly ever travels in our set, but that for some reason the Duke begged her to invite Lady

Allenbrook tonight."

They stood at a distance and regarded the plump, grandmotherly-looking lady whose solemn expressions were interspersed with glowing smiles as she talked to Gemma and Melodie.

"All I know of her," continued Lady Camberwick, "is that she is said to be most kind, though rather eccentric — buying Bibles to be distributed to the heathens, doing much work for the poor, even visiting prisons. She does not seem to be a likely friend of a young man like the Duke, but apparently she is."

Roxanne looked across the room and saw the Duke, who had apparently just entered, approach her sisters and Lady Allenbrook. She was suddenly glad Lady Camberwick had persuaded her to change her gown, for she foresaw a difficult evening ahead. Could he have persuaded his mother to invite this aristocratic enthusiast in order to provoke more disgraceful public behavior from the twins, because she, their sister, had not shown herself sufficiently grateful for his rescue? Wicked as she thought him, she could not quite believe he would be so vindictive, but she doubted that he had interfered with his mother's guest list for anything other than his own amusement.

But she had no chance to test her suspicion, for with admirable restraint, the Duchess had seated Roxanne and the Duke too far apart for dinner conversation. Roxanne went into the dining room on the arm of a handsome but boring young man, who paid much attention to his food and little to the lady beside him. At her other side was an older man who attempted to flirt with her, and was delighted with her shy smiles at his blunt, old-fashioned gallantries.

So occupied was she with the endless courses of dinner and the attentions of her aged beau, that it was not until it was almost time for the Duchess to lead her female guests away that Roxanne realized her sisters were behaving suspiciously. She had known a moment's uneasiness when she saw them seated on either side of a very young, very fashionably dressed gentleman, who, her aunt had whispered to her, was the heir to a great fortune.

Perhaps, she had thought, the Duchess had meant well by putting the girls in proximity to this eligible parti, but her observation told her that the fellow must be quite dissipated indeed, for he drank two glasses of wine for every one the other gentlemen drank, and his conversation, loud enough to be heard by Roxanne several places away, contained many a description of wagers lost and won, horses raced, carriages overturned, punctuated now and then by a "damme" or "the devil!"

At first the twins had borne with all of this meekly, only looking at each other sadly across the sinner, or turning to the gentlemen at their other sides, but there must, Roxanne thought now, as she noticed the young man suddenly flush bright red and draw himself up in his chair, have come a point when the girls could no longer contain themselves. Roxanne could not hear what they said to him, but its effect was dramatic.

"I'll be demmed if I'll be lectured to by a pair of simpering chits! You can both go to the—"

At that point Roxanne became aware that the Duke, fortuitously seated across from the offender, had risen slightly in his seat and was staring very hard at him. "I beg your pardon, Lord Wynne," was all he

118

said.

The young man sputtered to a stop and then closed his mouth. The Duchess rose, seemingly unperturbed, said a few words to the gentlemen about enjoying their port, and gracefully led the ladies away.

Roxanne, on her way out, caught a glimpse of the Duke's face, and shivered. She would not care to be in the shoes of the twins' late dinner partner, not for any consideration. She was sure there was quite a set-down in store for him, and for a moment she almost pitied him, especially as it had been her sisters who had somehow provoked his outburst, though no doubt much provoked themselves. But when she reached the drawing room, ready to lecture the girls about patience and self-restraint, she found that they had not yet arrived, apparently stopping in whatever haven of comfort had been set aside for the female guests.

The Duchess beckoned to her, and when Roxanne reached her side she immediately began to apologize to her hostess. Indeed, she was becoming quite practiced at apologies.

"I am so sorry for that dreadful scene, Your Grace. Of course the young man was wrong to speak so rudely, but I am certain that my sisters were behind it all."

"Nonsense, my dear. I was about to apologize to you, for not having the foresight to see that something of the sort could happen. I have known Lord Wynne since he was a boy, but I never realized he had grown into such a lout! I only thought . . . that is, your aunt Maria has asked me to help introduce the twins to eligible young men, and he is that, if nothing else. But of course he will not do, not at all . . ." She shook her head, and fell into thought. "Never mind. Next time I shall examine the prospects more carefully before I present them to your sisters."

"You are too kind, Your Grace, but we have no right to burden you with our problems—"

"Not a word more, my dear. I'm glad to do it. I have no daughters of my own, you see, and it's a challenging and enjoyable business to see three lovely young ladies well established in life."

"Three—" Roxanne knew she should express gratitude for the Duchess's including herself in her concern, but she wished to make her position perfectly clear. "Again, you are very kind, but I have no ambitions along that line for myself. I have had my chance. It is my sisters who are to be launched this season," she said firmly. "And heaven knows, they are surely challenge enough!"

The Duchess smiled and was about to reply when the gentle murmur of feminine conversation was interrupted by a shocked silence. Roxanne turned to see that her sisters had entered the drawing room, taken up positions at its center, and when all attention was focused on them, begun to pray loudly.

"What on earth—" The Duchess looked as horrified as Roxanne felt. For a minute the ladies listened silently as the twins called down the Lord's mercy upon this collection of sinners and asked that they be brought to mend their ways before it was too late. Then, as Gemma went on alone, Melodie broke away and ranged around the room, extending her hands to the other guests. "Won't you join us? Please, join us in prayer." But the only reaction was nervous tittering.

Then the whispering began, and Roxanne knew she could hesitate no more. Fortunately, Lady Camberwick, who had been equally horrified by her nieces' activities, went into action at the same moment. They each gathered a twin and, after whispering sharp admonitions, led them to the door of the drawing room. Roxanne's face was flaming with embarrassment, and she wished with all her heart that she was safely back at home in Wiltshire, where no one but the family servants ever had to witness such scenes.

She and Lady Camberwick had little trouble bringing the twins away, for the girls had already begun to notice that their earnest appeal was bringing them nothing but spiteful laughter from most of the ladies. Even Lady Allenbrook, who out of all the guests must feel the most sympathy for them, remained silent and only shook her head sadly. Suddenly all talk and laughter ceased.

Roxanne, holding Gemma by the arm, had just turned to leave the drawing room when she found that the door was open already and she was face to face with the Duke, who was escorting a more sober-looking Lord Wynne.

"Oh!" she gasped before she could stop herself. She had no idea how long they had been there, but from the expression on Rutledge's face she knew instantly that he had witnessed at least some of the distressing scene in the drawing room. He appeared to be struggling against laughter, and the struggle was finally successful, evidently because he did not wish the offending Lord Wynne to see his mirth. Finally he fixed his gaze on Roxanne. His eyes were still laughing but his mouth was straight and serious.

"Come." It was only one word but it was plainly a command and Roxanne, in any case eager to remove her sisters from the scene of their disgrace, preceded him and Lord Wynne out through the hall and into a smaller room nearby. Lady Camberwick, keeping a firm hold on Melodie, followed grimly.

The Duke saw all of his charges into the room and shut the door upon them. Then he took Roxanne aside, out of hearing of the others.

"Could you not, my dear Miss Winston, have controlled your sisters this evening, after failing to control them last night? I thought you had learned your lesson, and had no further need of my intervention." Although his words were severe, his face was alight with laughter. "However entertaining they are, you really must make them behave, my dear."

Roxanne grew angrier with every word, and barely waited for him to finish before she cried, "I am in no need of your intervention, Your Grace. As you saw, I was on the point of removing my sisters from the room when you arrived."

"But not before they had already caused a most diverting scene," he pointed out. "I only hope I shall be able to settle all the ruffled female feathers in the drawing room, so that the impromptu prayer meeting might not be talked of for the rest of the season. Even Lady Allenbrook would not—"

Roxanne knew that her suspicion had been correct. "So you admit to having planted her among the guests to induce my sisters to continue their inappropriate behavior! And then to blame me for not being able to control them! You are . . . you are . . ." She stopped, unable in her rage to think of a suitable term to apply to a creature who would practice such cruelty upon her.

"I am what, my dear Miss Winston?" The Duke seemed unperturbed by her words. However, he was no longer laughing at her. No, he simply watched her with an infuriating calm.

"You are despicable! And you will, if you please, cease to address me as your dear!"

Rutledge murmured, "Have I done so? How forgetful of me. I promise not to do so again, my dear. But you prove once again unappreciative of my efforts on your behalf. You misunderstand my motives. I asked my mother to invite Lady Allenbrook here tonight not, as you suspect, to cause more havoc, but to acquaint your sisters with an older lady who, though she is just as devout as they, knows better than to try to convert the ton single-handedly. I thought perhaps she would take them under her wing and direct their energies to something more productive, but alas, I fear their latest escapade may have been too much for her."

Roxanne took all of this in without saying a word. She found it difficult to believe his smooth explanation that Lady Allenbrook was there for the reason he claimed, but contradicting him, she saw, would be of no use. His unconcern was imperturbable. Besides, the twins and Lady Camberwick had been left too long alone with the boorish Lord Wynne.

"Now," continued Rutledge, "as to the other distressing occurrence your charming sisters have instigated tonight, I have spoken with Lord Wynne and impressed upon him the seriousness of his offense.

He is now ready to apologize to Miss Gemma and Miss Melodie for his ungentlemanly outburst. And I think, my dear—that is, Miss Winston—that your sisters owe him an apology as well. They should know better than to lecture a gentleman, and a stranger at that, on his faults before a room full of other people."

But even as he spoke, the twins were already making amends, as Roxanne saw when she turned anxiously to look at them. Lady Camberwick, roused from embarrassment to anger at the folly of her nieces, had given them a scorching scold and they now stood, meek as lambs, assuring Lord Wynne that they were completely wrong in having publicly branded him a sinner.

"Quite all right, then," he said gruffly. "All forgiven. Daresay Rutledge was right. Had no business using such language before ladies. I apologize, and I hope you won't hold it against me." He flashed a glance at the Duke, who nodded, satisfied.

The twins, subdued, gave him their hands in turn and assured him that they were quite as sorry as he was, and begged him to forget all about it, as they had decided to do.

"For you know, my lord," said Melodie, regaining some of her confidence, "that it was only our concern for your soul that led us to—"

"That will do very well, girls," said Lady Camberwick. "And now let us go to back to the drawing room and face down all those biddies who will, no doubt, be eager to make us the laughingstocks of London for the next month."

But before they could do so the door opened and plump Lady Allenbrook, a worried frown creasing her benevolent brow, entered the room. "Oh, you poor dear girls. If only you had consulted me first . . ." She hurried to the twins. "I could have told you that in my experience it does little good to cast pearls before swine, no offense, my dear Duchess, meant to your guests, of course, but only figuratively speaking. . . . Dear girls, I have been talking to the others in the drawing room and trying to convince them that it is only your youth and inexperience that led you to make such idiots of yourselves — no offense meant, of course, Lady Camberwick, to your nieces . . . and since they have known me for ages and know the principles for which I stand, they are becoming reconciled to it, and perhaps all the talk will die down very soon . . . and I hope you will call on me tomorrow and let me help you learn how to get along in this difficult world . . ."

She stopped to take a long breath. By now it was plain to Roxanne that she had misjudged the Duke's actions, and yet one more apology was owed. She felt his glance on her and met his eyes, but they held no censure. Rather they begged her to join him in enjoying the kindly rattling of Lady Allenbrook's tongue. She looked away quickly, lest he induce her to smile.

The twins were somewhat revived at this good ladys' words, and Lady Maria thanked her for her assistance. Then, accompanied by their new mentor, she marched her repentant charges off, and Lord Wynne, after a moment, hurried to open the door for them, following them to await his own ordeal in the drawing room, for by now the rest of the gentlemen had no doubt rejoined the ladies, as it was well known that the Duchess would not tolerate them lingering too long over their port.

Once again, Roxanne found herself alone with the Duke, and once again, found herself indebted to him. Patience, she reminded herself, patience and humility were the two virtues of which she had the most grievous lack. She must steady herself, submerge her pride, and practice them.

What better occasion than now? Yet it was hard, so hard, to be a proper Christian woman in the presence of a man like the Duke, not only because of his capacity for causing her intense annoyance and discomfort, and of his irritating tendency to be right, but as ever, because of the past events that hung between them, whether he acknowledged his guilt in them or not.

She took a long breath, and managed to compose herself sufficiently to face him with a serene expression, hoping to hide the fact that her face did not at all accord with her feelings. That, she knew, could only come with time, but at least she could make the effort to appear forbearing.

Rutledge watched her and grinned. "Admirable, admirable, Miss Winston. I must remember the efficacy of prayer and contemplation in controlling a wayward temper. You provide an excellent example for me."

Roxanne exercised all the restraint at her command. "Oh, do you count yourself among those who possess a wayward temper, Your Grace? I would never have guessed your secret."

The Duke chuckled, and the sound was so contagious that Roxanne was tempted to join him, but refrained. Her next problem was how to thank him without appearing either ungracious or unduly submissive.

"It seems I judged you wrongly, Your Grace. No doubt you meant the introduction of Lady Allenbrook for the good of the girls, and I thank you."

"You are most welcome, and I hope she may prove a valuable friend to them."

"How do you come to be acquainted with her, my lord?" Relieved by his surprising graciousness, Roxanne could not suppress her curiosity on this point.

Rutledge regarded her with raised brows and an impish smile. "Do you think that a miserable sinner such as myself must entirely confine his acquaintance to those equally depraved? You forget, I sit in Parliament, where there is pressure building among many well-born people and others of consequence to reform the morals of this country, to end slavery, to succor the poor, and most of all, to convert the dissolute to their particular form of religion. Of course" — he folded his hands behind his back and strolled to the hearth — "the revolution in France has frightened many powerful people here. Thus, lest something similar occur in England, the real object of many of these well-meaning souls is to keep every man is his preordained place — you recall, 'Let every soul be subject unto the higher powers'? As a Duke, I am one of those powers, at least in an earthly sense. I would be foolish to interfere with the aims of these well-meaning Christians, would I not?"

Roxanne could not tell whether he mocked the reformers or himself, but there was a trace of bitterness in his tone. She did not know quite how to react. His aimless strolling about the room had brought him to her side again. He stood much closer to her now, and she felt a twinge of uneasiness in her stomach. She looked up and said briskly, "In any case, Lady Allenbrook should prove a valuable acquaintance for my sisters. Perhaps she may teach them to remember *their* proper place, at least in company."

"Your mind is very quick, Miss Winston, and your tongue only slightly less so. I admire that," he said absently. She could not see the look in his eyes, because she could not make herself meet his gaze. That his gaze was fixed intently on her face, however, she could not doubt. Her pulse had gradually quickened, and now that he stood so close to her, she could almost feel it jumping at her neck.

"Are you unaware that I have given you a compliment, Miss Winston?" He asked softly.

"N-no, Your Grace. I am perfectly aware . . ." She took a step back, just to reassure herself. He followed.

"Ah, but I forget that you hate me. How foolish of me." His voice was caressing, and he put out a hand to gently lift a curl that had fallen over her eyes. Roxanne held herself very still under the light touch. This time she would not retreat, as it only appeared to encourage him.

"When will you admit that you have misjudged me from the first, my dear Miss Winston—oh, but I forget, I am not permitted to thus address you. A pity."

Roxanne stirred herself to one more effort, though his nearness made her feel as though the very breath was being squeezed out of her. "I—I am not likely to admit anything of the kind, Your Grace. Your kind actions now can never erase the past. I am only sorry that we are such a trouble to you. I—

we had not meant, you know to bring ourselves to your attention. It is only that Lady Camberwick and the Duchess . . ."

The Duke stroked her cheek lightly, and this time Roxanne looked up, startled. The touch had been careless, but to her distress it had sparked a response in her of the sort that no man with Rutledge's history should ever be able to invoke. Not even Geoffrey at his most ardent had done more than press her hand to his lips. She scolded herself now for examining the Duke's sculpted lips with such interest, and she was thoroughly ashamed at enjoying the gentle expression in his eyes as he searched her face. Whatever he saw there, it appeared to please him, for he smiled.

"Yes, my dearest mama and your respected aunt. A fine plot they have gotten up between them, have they not? I had supposed you a party to it, Miss Winston, but now that I have come to know you I realize that you would never bend your rigid standards for the worldly purpose of securing a rich husband. That mortification must be reserved for your sisters. Since you have relieved my fears on that matter, let me reward you — No, I shall reward myself, for being clever enough to discover that you had no part in the insidious marriage plot."

With that he bent and pressed his mouth to hers. Roxanne, startled, would have stepped away, but he put a hand on her shoulder, and in an instant those lips that she had examined so minutely were exerting a magical effect on her will. They were warm and gentle, but evoked such feelings as she knew would disgrace her in the eyes of the world. Shame suffused her, but a secret wish that he would not withdraw his mouth from hers for a long time, and that he would embrace her more closely, crept into her heart.

The first wish granted, the second one soon followed. She stood very still in his arms, too frightened at her own awakening emotions to touch him in return, but his warmth spread through her and enveloped her wondering soul. How could she permit this to happen? Her mind asked this question over and over again, but her treacherous body ignored her brain's confusion and allowed the Duke to continue insulting her with his attentions. But they did not, she could not help but reflect, feel at all insulting. Perhaps she was too far gone in sin to recognize the insult.

Finally her conscience grew too restless, her lungs too short of breath, and she stirred in his arms. Rutledge let his lips linger a moment more on her mouth, and then lifted his head a little. He whispered something so surprising and so uncharacteristic of him that Roxanne almost disbelieved her ears, and then he released her. She was too ashamed to look at him, but she heard him step away to the door.

When he was gone, closing the door very softly behind him, Roxanne stood holding her fingertips against her lips. They seemed not at all the same lips she had begun the evening with. Her breath was soon steadied, but for a long time her heart refused to beat at its accustomed regular pace.

Roxanne was thoroughly disappointed in herself. Had she not betrayed herself, her brother's memory, and her faith?

If Melodie and Gemma could have heard the Duke's last whispered words, however, Roxanne thought that though they would have been shocked at her behavior, they might have taken some comfort in the result of the embrace. Perhaps their idea of using their sister's beauty to bring men to salvation had some merit. As evidence, she could inform the twins that the kiss seemed to have awakened His Grace's spiritual nature.

It had to be so, she told herself, for after releasing her, he had whispered into her neck, "You are like a prayer."

Chapter Seven

Fortunately for Roxanne's peace of mind, the Duke did not soon make an appearance in Upper Brook Street, nor did she encounter him in society. During the next week, she had plenty of time to consider how she ought to behave in his presence.

What had occurred between them seemed to make any casual relations impossible, but Roxanne was determined to at least *appear* unaffected by the experience. She had no idea how she would be able to face him, and it would not do to draw anyone's attention to her discomfort in his presence. Above all, she must strive to forget that for a few moments he had unleashed certain very dangerous feelings.

She could hardly ignore him. To be permitted to ignore him, however, was all she wished to do when she recalled the way she had utterly given herself up to his embrace.

If only she could confide in someone — but she could not discuss the Duke's kiss with anyone. Fanny would smile and tease, Lady Camberwick would pretend to be shocked but would begin to harbor foolish hopes, her father would be angry, and the twins . . . they would likely be horrified, or else tell her that she must use whatever strange and fleeting influence she had on the Duke to bring him to a sense of his own sin.

But Roxanne's most shameful recollection was that of her own complicity in the sudden embrace. She found herself wishing she could hug that moment to herself, ignoring its implications, to take it out and examine it again and again, like a child with a beloved bauble. Such thoughts tormented her far too often.

Fortunately, she was provided with plenty of material for distraction in the necessity of seeing the twins through the season, and managed now and again to forget this treacherous subject. The Sunday after the Duchess's eventful dinner party, the ladies of the family went to an early service at St. George's, Hanover Square. The twins were disappointed that they might not worship with a more like-minded congregation, and afterward loudly voiced their disapproval of the staring and whispering and subdued flirting that went on during the service.

"I'm sorry that there is no more suitable place for us to worship of a Sabbath, girls, but this is the church to which all the world goes, and it would look decidedly odd if I suddenly stopped attending, just because I had a pair of nieces who do not approve!"

Poor Lady Camberwick, Roxanne had observed, was more inclined to snap at the twins now than before. Her store of patience had been exhausted very quickly, and she seemed fatigued by the continual struggle to present the girls to society properly dressed and with their crusading instincts subdued.

After the twins took themselves off for private worship in their sitting room, Roxanne followed her aunt to her own room, where Lady Camberwick, waving her maid away, sat before her dressing table and sighed into the mirror at her tired reflection.

"I fear, dear Aunt Maria, that you are regretting the generous impulse that made you offer to sponsor the twins this season," said Roxanne, who stood beside her, absently unstopping scent bottles and fingering combs and brushes.

"Certainly not, my dear. I should be terribly remiss if I did not do as much as I could for you. It was only what your mother would have wished, and with no children of my own, I am glad of the occupation. But those girls!" Her ladyship sighed, and Roxanne tried to comfort her.

"It is by no means a hopeless endeavor, Aunt. Although my sisters have been busy offending as many people as possible, they have managed to acquire three admirers between them."

Lady Camberwick brightened. "That is true. Why, the Earl and Mr. Bentley called again yesterday, and even Lord Wynne became interested, after he had gotten over the shock of his public scolding. In fact," she said, looking increasingly cheerful, "I heard someone say after service this morning that gentlemen are talking about your sisters with great interest."

"No doubt they are talking," Roxanne replied, "but what they are saying may be nothing to my sisters' credit except that they are pretty. The girls must be made to behave themselves, or society will quickly develop a disgust of them." She sniffed at a crystal bottle of strong rose-scented cologne, stopped it up, and put it down reluctantly. "I will join them now, and try to make them see that I am on their side, else they will pay no heed to my next lecture."

The reminder of her nieces' unexpected success had made Lady Camberwick relent. "You need not be so stern with them, my dear, and it seems as though you shall not have to watch them so carefully in society, when the Duke of Rutledge is always there to settle their scrapes for them." She smiled slyly at her niece.

Roxanne felt her face growing warm. "Yes, but I am sure His Grace will be busy attending to his own affairs, and one cannot depend upon him to be at hand when next my sisters take it into their heads to cause a public scene."

Privately, Roxanne hoped that he would never again be so conveniently present should such mortifying scenes continue to occur. She did not believe for a moment that the twins had decided to entirely abandon their schemes for the salvation of London society, and she could not bear to have the Duke take charge again, making her appear incapable of watching over her own sisters.

But she did have cause to be grateful in the coming days for the Duke's introduction of Lady Allenbrook. Her ladyship called frequently in Upper Brook Street, and the twins often went to her house to assist her in various charitable projects, and to meet other like-minded individuals.

For several days all was peaceful, though the girls did complain of having to give up an afternoon or two at Lady Allenbrook's for drives in the Park with their now more or less constant attendants, Mr. Bentley and Lord Culverton, or of being detained at home by Lord Wynne's unexpected calls.

This gentleman's initial anger at the twins had

slowly turned to puzzlement, and had then been inexplicably transformed into admiration. So far, however, he had shown no signs of preference for one or the other of them. Lady Camberwick insisted his smile was broader when he looked at Melodie, but Sir James claimed that the fellow stared much harder at Gemma. Roxanne only wondered that such a man could care for either of them, after they had publicly reproved him.

On one occasion, when the girls were absent and his lordship called, Roxanne had to entertain him for a quarter of an hour, and the young man, much less surly than he had appeared upon first acquaintance, waxed enthusiastic about her sisters.

"Do you know, Miss Winston, what it is that makes 'em so fascinatin'? They don't just simper and fawn at one—they tell the truth, even if it is painful at first—just as though they weren't at all impressed by one's appearance or title or fortune."

Roxanne saw at once that the poor boy's arrogance was due to entirely too much flattery from the female sex, and that to Lord Wynne the scrupulously honest twins were different and refreshing. It was a pity that apart from himself and their two other victims, no other gentlemen seemed to feel the same.

But while her Aunt Maria fully expected that no more than another fortnight would pass without an offer from at least one of the three men, Roxanne was not so hopeful. After all, Lord Wynne, as the days passed, showed not the tiniest sign of a partiality for one of the girls—he seemed to regard them as a single being—while the two other young men behaved more like playmates than suitors.

Roxanne sometimes thought that her sisters' chief attraction for the Earl and Mr. Bentley was that there were two of them, conveniently identical. Thus the two friends could enter the realm of courtship without having to go their separate ways, and certainly without any danger of rivalry over the same lady. But their behavior toward the girls in society was not at all loverlike, and as the girls never danced, scarcely anyone noticed their friendship with these two eligible gentlemen.

A week of relative calm was all but shattered one morning by the nearly simultaneous arrival of three callers. The first was Geoffrey Pearson, who entered the morning room with a triumphant smile, scarcely limping, supported by the arm of his beaming sister Fanny.

Roxanne greeted him with an affection renewed by their separation and her concern over his wound, and he quickly went to her, catching her hand in both his own, demonstrating his ability to walk and stand unassisted.

"I'm happy to see you looking so well, Geoffrey. And Fanny, you slyboots, why did you not tell me that your brother was coming to town?"

Fanny favored her brother with a look of mock severity. "I did not know it myself until yesterday evening, when I came down to dinner and found him drinking Mr. Broughton's claret in the drawing room, as cool as you please. He arrived yesterday afternoon at our sister's house, without a word of warning."

Geoffrey ignored his sister and kissed Roxanne's hand. "As I learned in the army, surprise gives one an advantage. Margaret and her stuffy old Broughton

137

could not then refuse to take me in—"

"As if they would!" interrupted an indignant Fanny.

"And you, Roxanne, cannot refuse to go driving with me tomorrow. As you see, I am a whole creature once again, thanks to you. No, do not blush, I must give credit where it is due. And at the very next opportunity, I will claim that dance you promised me."

"Surely you ought not to be thinking of dancing so soon. But how long will you be in town? Will you stay with your sister all season, or will you take up your lodgings again? You must all dine here soon! I am sure Aunt Maria would—"

Fanny interrupted her with a laugh. "Slowly, Roxanne!"

"Yes, and you haven't said whether you will drive with me." He flexed his wrist. "My driving, thank heaven, cannot have been affected by that little accident."

"I trust you will not overturn us," replied Roxanne with a smile. "But you distract me—everyone will want to see you." She instructed a servant to tell her aunt, father, and sisters that they had callers, and begged Fanny and Geoffrey to sit down.

"And do you believe, my dear," said Fanny when they were all settled comfortably, Geoffrey, despite his protestations of health, with his leg stretched out before him, "that he has not yet told me how he came to be shot?"

"Why, did you not hear the ridiculous tale of a highwayman?" asked Roxanne. "Your brother had the impudence to suggest that I request further details from the Duke."

"And did you?" Geoffrey wanted to know, his blue

eyes gleaming with amusement.

Roxanne hesitated. She had not really wanted to bring Rutledge into the conversation, but somehow his name had crept into it, and it had been her own doing.

Before she could reply, Fanny cried, "Oh, but Harry is as bad as my brother. How he likes to tease! And Roxanne, he has charged me with a message for you. With all the excitement over Geoffrey's arrival I had almost forgotten."

"A message?" Roxanne stiffened, and suddenly found that the last breath she had taken was insufficient.

Fanny smiled wryly, and looked at her brother. "I suppose you have already discovered, Geoffrey, that Roxanne does not share our opinion of the Duke. No doubt that is why she looks so sour."

"Never mind, Fanny, she will come to realize one day that—"

Fanny flashed him a look that was incomprehensible to Roxanne, and hurriedly went on, "But the message—it was merely that he hopes you and your sisters will have no need of his intervention again, and he thanks you for your great generosity. An odd message, I thought, but there, I have delivered it faithfully." But her eyes plainly told Roxanne that she was curious about it.

Roxanne ignored the unspoken plea. "Thank you for delivering it, my dear. And here is my family at last. They will be glad to see you both."

Though her heart was only now beginning to return to its normal rhythm, she felt she was successful in keeping her expression neutral. Geoffrey—soon involved in teasing the twins, flattering Lady Camberwick, exchanging jests with Sir James, and eating large amounts of cake, for though the hour was early, a concession was made to his recent invalid state—plainly did not think the message at all interesting.

But Roxanne knew that her friend was not so easily distracted. At the first opportunity, Fanny whispered, "What is it about? You must tell me!"

Roxanne was fortunately saved from the immediate necessity of a reply by the twins' request that she inform Geoffrey that they were most emphatically *not* a pair of Friday-faced females, and from there she was drawn into the general conversation.

Lady Camberwick, looking swiftly from Geoffrey's glowing face to Roxanne's blushing one, wore an expression of happy speculation, and her niece perceived at once that she would have no peace from matchmaking while Geoffrey was in London.

Sir James then invited Geoffrey to join him at his club, for which they were about to depart, and the twins, already dressed for outdoors, were about to be dragged off by Lady Camberwick for an early appointment with a lady who had two unmarried sons to dispose of. Roxanne, who was to have gone with them, was beseeched by Fanny to give her company for the rest of the morning.

"Go along, dear, I shall manage without you," Lady Camberwick urged her.

Roxanne had no desire to be alone with her friend, who, she was sure, meant to discover the meaning of the Duke's message, and would no doubt observe that there was something troubling her besides her avowed dislike of him, but the plans for the day were settled in an instant and she had no recourse but to agree.

However, she was permitted a short reprieve as another caller was announced. Since it was still rather early in the day for calls, everyone was surprised and curious, but the twins were delighted, as the appearance of the new visitor delivered them, for the moment, from the humiliation of being paraded as eligible brides before a prospective mother-in-law.

"Mr. Driggs!" the girls cried as one. Roxanne was startled, Sir James disgusted, Lady Camberwick warily puzzled, as the pastor of the little flock at Westcombe was shown into the morning room.

A slim man of medium height, the clergyman had thin hair of an undistinguished shade of brown, sticking in shiny patches to his partially bald head.

"Dear ladies, and sisters in the Lord." He clasped the twins' hands and smiled affectionately at them. "How happy I am to see you in health, although" — he frowned — "your appearance suggests that you have become a little too at home in the world."

Melodie gestured deprecatingly at her simple, but very smart morning dress of white figured muslin and her deep blue pelisse. "Oh, it is all part of this wearying pursuit of husbands. We are made to dress quite contrary to our wishes."

"But we have not lapsed into any other worldly habits, Mr. Driggs, you may be certain of that," Gemma assured him.

Lady Camberwick, instantly perceiving that this was the instigator of her nieces' odd behaviors and beliefs, put on her haughtiest mien as he was presented to her and greeted Geoffrey and Fanny. She merely nodded to him, ignored his inquiry as to whether she had accepted the Lord as her Savior, and said, "Come along girls. We are expected in Grosvenor Square."

Sir James was in no way any more well disposed toward Mr. Driggs, as they had several heated disagreements behind them, the main one being that the man of God insisted Sir James had been struck down with paralysis as punishment for some sin committed in his wild youth, to which the hearty invalid invariably replied, "Rubbish!"

Geoffrey and Fanny seemed more inclined to laugh than disapprove of Driggs's solemn manner, and Roxanne herself, though mildly annoyed by his very fervent clasp of her hand and inquiries, made in an intimate tone, as to her health and state of mind, knew that she would giggle if she met her old friends' glances.

The twins, however, were full of protestations. "But Aunt Maria, we must not leave. Mr. Driggs has come all the way to London to give us guidance in this difficult time."

Lady Camberwick sniffed. "Then I am sure that it can wait until tomorrow. I doubt he came all the way to town meaning to return at once to Wiltshire."

Mr. Driggs gave his solemn, thin-lipped smile. "That is correct, my lady. I remain in town for a fortnight. I am lodging with a very pious landlady in Paternoster Row — so convenient for my visits of consolation to Newgate. She keeps a good table, with prayers morning, noon, and evening, a very modest household. . . . But of course I should not wish to encourage the young ladies to any disobedience toward their near relation and benefactor. If it will be more convenient, I will call again tomorrow."

Lady Camberwick relented a little. "Well then sir, I am sure you appreciate the difficulties of our situation, and that you will do your best to impress upon these children their duty. . . . I trust you will be a good influence." She fixed the minister with a forbidding look, and he quivered a little, but stood fast.

Her ladyship had long ago had her maid bring her own and the twins' bonnets and gloves downstairs, and now the twins groaned in protest at being requested to put them on. The bonnets in question had been a bone of contention between them and their aunt all week.

Melodie's was blue and Gemma's was rose, and both examples of the milliner's art were high-crowned, beribboned, becoming, and up-to-the-moment fashionable. The twins, of course, despised them. It was a pity, Roxanne thought, for they accented the girls' simple attire to perfection, and though they were not in any way severe, there was nothing really frivolous about the bonnets except that they were attractive.

"Come, girls, put them on and don't make such a great bustle over a trifle. The bonnets look delightful and there is nothing sinful, after all, in making the most of one's looks," Lady Camberwick told them.

The twins looked to Mr. Driggs for assistance, but though he gave them a sympathetic glance, Lady Camberwick's gimlet eye was upon him and, to Roxanne's amusement, he dared not speak. However, he looked at the airy creations as though he would gladly burn them.

With her reluctant but fashionably attired charges

143

in tow, Lady Camberwick prepared to leave. Geoffrey was ready to follow, wheeling Sir James in his chair with a last grin at Roxanne, when yet another caller was announced. Lady Camberwick was visibly restraining her exasperation, and was regretting aloud that she had not instructed her servants to deny her, but in a moment her expression changed, and she beamed with delight.

Roxanne did not know whether to be happy or sorry for the presence of so many other people in the room, for the caller was the Duke of Rutledge. Though he paid his respects first to her ladyship and then to Sir James, his glance seemed to find Roxanne immediately, and even in all the confusion of greetings and the introduction of Mr. Driggs to His Grace, she felt the Duke's attention centered upon herself.

After conversing for some minutes with the others, he turned toward Roxanne. Though she felt her aunt's eyes on herself and Rutledge, the others had for the most part turned away to their own talk and were out of hearing. Roxanne felt panic-stricken for a moment, as though her family and friends had abandoned her.

Rutledge approached and bowed over her hand, and she endeavored to send her heart back to its rightful place beneath her ribs, that her throat might be clear for its proper use, for she would certainly need to speak.

"I hope Miss Pearson conveyed my message to you, Miss Winston?" His voice was smooth, his tone without undercurrents of any kind.

For all of her good intentions, Roxanne could not look up and meet his glance. She only hoped no one else was observing her confusion, and that, holding her hand as he still did, Rutledge could not detect her tumultuous pulse. "Yes, Your Grace, she did. I, too, hope that my sisters and I will have no need of your intervention. Perhaps with their pastor, Mr. Driggs, now in town, they will be brought to behave sensibly, and curtail their activities."

The calm tones of her own voice gave her courage, and at length Roxanne looked up. His eyes were not laughing at her, as she had imagined. His face was somehow . . . *softer* than she remembered it, but there was nothing in his expression to embarrass her. What had happened between them might not have happened at all. She was conscious of a ridiculous twinge of disappointment.

"I hope so, too." He dropped her hand and stood straight again. "I confess I am hard pressed to predict what frolic they will attempt next, and how best to forestall it."

Roxanne could help laughing at hearing her sisters' religious activities referred to as a "frolic" and the sound made both Geoffrey and Fanny turn around and glance at her. She avoided their eyes. "As for the second part of your message—you owe me no thanks for any generosity. You know that your help with my sisters has more than recompensed the little time I spent nursing your wound." Roxanne felt that this was a great concession. This man was extracting entirely too much gratitude from her.

The Duke's eyes flickered with silver lights, and his lips curved. "That was not the generous act I meant to thank you for, Miss Winston," he said softly, so that only she could hear it.

Roxanne bit her lip and quickly looked down at her

hands in her lap. He had not neglected this opportunity to taunt her after all. Those strange whispered words after his kiss must have represented only a momentary lapse on his part. If she ever told her sisters the entire story, she would have to tell them that her spiritual influence had had only a temporary effect.

She forced herself to look up and keep her chin firm, her eyes cold, though she spoke softly, very aware of the curiosity of Fanny and Lady Camberwick. "I know exactly to what you refer, Your Grace, but I assumed that as a gentleman you would not wish to advertise your lapse, or to remind a lady that she had been subjected to such attentions."

"Subjected!" He raised his eyebrows, and his mouth was twisted in such a way that Roxanne could not tell whether he was angry or amused. "That was not the impression I received, though, to be sure, I thought your initial lack of response due merely to your . . . inexperience. Well, my dear Miss Winston" — his tone had changed to one with which she was more familiar — "if you had been subjected to such a disagreeable experience, I am surprised that you did not immediately inform everyone and insist that I be horsewhipped, or at least shunned by all respectable females forevermore."

Roxanne could not help blushing, for she knew that she could have told her aunt or her father that Rutledge had insulted her, and thereby relieve herself of the necessity of tolerating his company any longer. But her conscience told her she could not do such a thing. She had, after all, permitted his familiarity, and to her confusion, enjoyed it.

"I have mentioned it to no one. You should realize

that it is highly . . . distressing to me to even think of it. I could not allow anyone to know, to speculate . . ."

Rutledge smiled without humor. "To speculate that you might not be totally averse to kissing the man you regard as your brother's murderer? Yes, that would cause a stir, would it not? But of course, Miss Winston, I will respect your decision."

While this discussion had been taking place, Mr. Driggs had been advising the twins and arguing with Sir James, while Lady Camberwick, one eye on Roxanne and the Duke and the other on her younger charges, seemed to be torn between administering a set-down to the minister and eavesdropping on her niece's conversation.

Just before she managed to direct her full attention to the latter activity, Roxanne turned away, considering her conversation with Rutledge at an end, and Mr. Driggs signified that he was ready to take his leave. He had observed Roxanne's tête-à-tête with the Duke, and now favored her with a worried frown. "Will you join us tomorrow, Miss Winston? I am certain that you are as in need of comfort and guidance as your sisters, since you are subjected to the same temptations, nay, perhaps more . . ." He glanced at the Duke, who was talking to Geoffrey and Fanny.

"Thank you, Mr. Driggs. I will not join you, but I should like to discuss the twins with you before you see them," Roxanne told him, mentally assuring herself that she would not allow the clergyman to discover the turmoil of her mind. His admiration for her would certainly interfere with his giving her unprejudiced advice, and he would no doubt tell her it was all her own fault for associating with such a fallen creature as Rutledge.

When at last everyone had gone except Fanny, Roxanne felt as though she had narrowly skirted some dangerous precipice. But her ordeal was not over yet. As they drove out, changed their books at the circulating library, and looked at muslins, bonnets, ribbons, and fans, which for the most part neither one of them could afford, Fanny was relentless in her pursuit of the meaning of the Duke's message.

Roxanne insisted that it was nothing. "He simply wishes to taunt me over the twins' bad behavior," she told her friend, "and over the fact that he has always come to our rescue. And at the same time he wished to thank me for taking him in when he was shot. That is all."

Fanny had the use of her married sister's barouche for the afternoon, and late in the day, when the young ladies got back into it after they had left a milliner's in Picadilly, Fanny pondered this reply. "I suppose you must be right," she decided. "But I still think you do His Grace an injustice in supposing that he means to remind you of your difficulties in dealing with your sisters. He can be very kind, you know," she added seriously.

Roxanne looked away, not wanting her friend to see that she had found that the Duke could be occasionally kind, but also many other things that she once would not have believed.

"I am sufficiently aware of the gratitude I owe him for his help," she said stiffly, "and he need not remind me of it. Anyway—" She shook off her irritation, and smiled at her friend. "This is foolish. It is a lovely spring day, we are friends again, you have bought a length of gauze and I some pretty green ribbon, and later we can stop for some ices. What has the Duke to do with anything?"

"What indeed?" said Fanny, but she laughed and turned the conversation to other subjects. At that moment the ladies, after directing the coachman to take them to Pall Mall, where they intended to meander through aisles of silks, laces, gloves, fans, and perfumes at Schomberg House, were suddenly aware of a disturbance, seemingly emanating from the region of St. James' Street. This street, Roxanne, knew, was filled with the clubs and lodgings of gentlemen, and no respectable female ever allowed herself to be promenaded past the many masculine strongholds it contained, lest she be the target of some unwanted gallantry or insulting attention.

As they drove past the intersection of Picadilly and St. James', Roxanne could see, from her perch on the seat of the open carriage, that traffic, both horse-drawn and pedestrian, was stopped. In the middle of the street there was a crowd of people milling about. She and Fanny exchanged glances as the sound of shouts and masculine laughter traveled to their ears.

"Whatever—" began Fanny.

But at that moment, in the milling of what seemed a mob of elegantly dressed gentlemen and their less finely attired grooms, waiters, and coachmen, Roxanne caught sight of two bonnets, identical except as to color. She recognized them immediately.

"Coachman, turn down the street—no, nothing is moving, I must walk—oh, Fanny, it is Melodie and Gemma, and how they got where they are I don't know, but I must get them out again."

"Roxanne, no! You must not, I won't let you! Think of how scandalous—"

Roxanne was stubbornly climbing down from the carriage, without even waiting for the assistance of the sleepy coachman, who merely looked at her as if she had run mad.

"But I must—just think what a scrape they must be in this time!" Holding up her skirts in what she knew was a most improper fashion, Roxanne managed to leap down, thanking years of long country walks for her nimbleness, and only suffering a ragged tear in her hem for her pains. Then she straightened her bonnet, which had gone askew, and ignored by the gentlemen nearby whose attention was fixed on the altercation in the center of the street, she progressed as rapidly as possible toward those lovely nodding bonnets.

Some of the curious gentlemen crowding the street ignored her pleas to be let through, others said things that made Roxanne's ears burn, while some, in good-natured amusement, helped her to pass to the center of the disturbance. Now she could hear her sisters' voices.

"Gentlemen, idle not your hours away in these dens of sin, drink not of the brew of Satan, cease to waste your substance in wagering, and go burn your playing cards, lest ye burn in the fires of eternal damnation," Melodie cried over the rumbling laughter and shouts of the men.

Gemma picked up her plea. "Use your power and wealth to help those more unfortunate than yourselves—feed the hungry, clothe the naked—"

Here someone interjected a remark, mercifully unintelligible to Roxanne, and there were hoots of laughter.

"—help teach the ignorant the joys of submission unto the Lord—come, take up your Bibles again and drink from the fountain of wisdom."

"Help us end slavery, convert the heathen, and bring prisoners the joy of God's forgiveness," continued Melodie, and now that Roxanne was almost opposite her sisters, to her horror she saw Gemma holding open a large reticule, turning from one man to another in the crowd around them. For a moment her mortification was so great that she thought she might faint. But her sense of duty upheld her and she pushed through the last of the men to face her sisters.

They stood in the street between two clubs which Roxanne recognized, as they had been pointed out to her by her father on a drive one day. One was Boodle's, where Sir James, when in London, was generally to be found, the other, opposite, was Brooks's. She had a new terror that her father and Geoffrey might still be at Boodle's and might at any moment come out and witness the twins' disgrace, but none of the faces about her, fortunately, looked at all familiar.

Melodie looked glad to see her, but Gemma looked startled and a little guilty. Under Roxanne's gaze, she slowly drew the reticule closed, her face crimson.

"Sister!" cried Melodie. "Join us in trying to save these poor wasted lives."

"I'll thank you to go on your ways quietly, young ladies," said a tall, severe-looking gentleman who, by his dress, was undoubtedly a senior servant of one of the clubs along the street. "You can't obstruct business on this street. We shall call in the authorities!"

"Sir, we have obeyed your request in leaving the premises of your establishment, though we could have done great good amongst your members," Melodie told him, "but you have nothing to say about any activities conducted outside its doors."

Roxanne gasped at the thought that her sisters had actually entered a gentlemen's club, and did not know how Melodie could maintain her courage and dignity in the face of his anger. The crowd laughed and Melodie's red-faced attacker was taunted by the shouts of the men.

"She's not afraid of your bluster, man!"

"The lady's right, you can toss them out of Brooks's, but you can't throw 'em out of the street. You don't own it, you know."

But some other men took his side, and began to shout at the girls to leave. "No respectable woman comes here on purpose. Or perhaps these chits ain't respectable, eh? If so, they're fair game," suggested one man, who had been leering at them.

"Nonsense," said another, "what member of the muslin company with a jot of sense would come here and spout all this Bible-talk? You've got maggots in your head, my friend."

Nevertheless the leering man reached tentatively for Gemma's sleeve, and Roxanne, unable to bear the suggestions and the look of terror on her sisters' face, leaped to strike his hand away.

"Leave her alone, sir."

"Why?" he wanted to know, turning his greedy gaze on Roxanne, "are you jealous, my dear?"

Roxanne wished for a moment that she were a man,

for she felt as though to "plant him a facer," as in the boxing cant she had heard from Alfred and Geoffrey, would be the greatest pleasure of her life. But she ignored him and turned to her sisters. By now even Melodie had lost her bravado, and they were both white-lipped and trembling.

"Come, Fanny's carriage is waiting at the end of the street — hurry — " She began to pull them through the crowd, and on this occasion they willingly followed.

Some men let them go with a chuckle, some, perhaps realizing the youth of the offenders, and remembering spirited daughters and sisters at home, let them pass with a gentle remonstrance and halfhearted offers of assistance, but others plucked at their gowns, shouting remarks that turned Gemma's face almost scarlet and her eyes huge. Melodie stared down at her feet as they flew along.

Fear was leaping up in Roxanne's throat, but with a steely determination she pushed her way through and pulled her sisters along after her toward where she had left Fanny and the carriage. She felt tears of shame and vexation gathering in her eyes, but impatiently shook them aside.

For a seeming eternity they were surrounded by a wall of liquor-soaked and tobacco-smoked air, crowded by burly figures in coats of blue, brown, black, green, fabrics rough and smooth, faces both clean-shaven and hirsute, neckcloths white and snuff-stained, hats on heads and hats in hand, boots shiny and dull, breeches and pantaloons, men spitting and coughing and shouting and laughing — and then they were out of the worst of the crowd.

Roxanne turned around to see that many of the

men had dispersed and gone back to their clubs, or taken up their lounging positions along the street. But several, patently not gentlemen, were still following and making themselves as disagreeable as possible, and their way was still impeded.

"Courage, girls, we are almost there," Roxanne managed to gasp to her frightened sisters. They finally reached the end of the street, their stubborn pursuers all but surrounding them. Quite suddenly there was a murmur and they all fell away.

Roxanne, who had been looking at the ground to avoid the curious glances and insulting stares of the men, looked up. Fanny's carriage was nowhere to be seen.

Before her stood an elegant crested private drag, with a coachman in livery up on the box. A gentleman stood by the door. He was tall and dark and but for his dress, the confused Roxanne might have thought him a footman. But just in time she recognized the crest and realized that the strong hand held out to her, the hand she so eagerly grasped with a sob, the angry gray eyes fixed on her face, to which she raised her own tear-filled blue ones, belonged to the Duke of Rutledge.

Chapter Eight

"I will not ask you how you come to be here," said Henry Malverne grimly, after handing Roxanne and the twins into the carriage. He rapped a signal to the coachman, who immediately drove on. "I merely suggest that you never again attempt such an unwise thing."

Roxanne, torn between anger at his unspoken contempt and gratitude at his timely appearance, at first could hardly speak, but she managed to choke out, "If you think that it was by choice that I put myself in such an unpleasant situation, then you must be mad!"

For the first time since seeing her, the Duke actually fixed her with his full glance. Roxanne almost flinched, but pride upheld her. There was rage, and relief, and some other strong emotion she could not identify reflected in his gray eyes.

Melodie spoke, her voice shaking a little. She sounded not at all like the girl who had bravely harangued a crowd of gentlemen in St. James' Street just minutes before. "Roxanne, that was shockingly rude. You must apologize to the Duke."

"I have nothing to apologize for."

"—and Your Grace, you must apologize to Roxanne for being unfair."

"Impertinence!"

"Nevertheless, both of you are wrong to be angry with one another. I must tell you that . . . that . . ."

"It was our fault, my lord." Gemma took up the explanation when it became plain that her sister, under the seething glances of Roxanne and Rutledge, could not finish. "We thought that we could do good where it was most needed, and somehow Roxanne found us there and helped us get away, when the gentlemen—"

"—had had enough of being lectured by a pair of impudent chits just out of the schoolroom," finished the Duke, his tone almost indulgent, compared with the way he had spoken to Roxanne. But nevertheless she saw that he was angry indeed. "I have never encountered two such foolish young ladies."

"I will not have you speak to my sisters this way," cried Roxanne, feeling impotent and very confused. Somehow it had become her fault.

"Will you not, Miss Winston? But someone should have spoken to them in just such a way ere now. Perhaps I would not then be obliged to render assistance so often. No, do not thank me, for I know how much it galls you to do so. But what else can a sensible man do when he sees a female allow those in her charge to continually suffer from their own folly?"

Roxanne was speechless with rage for a moment. Her eyes spoke eloquently of a desire to throttle her opponent. The Duke glared back at her. The twins glanced at one another in fright.

"Oh, Roxanne, we are so sorry! And Your Grace, please do not blame her for all the trouble we have caused you—it is our fault alone," cried Gemma.

"Yes, Roxanne saved us from a most disagreeable experience, and she does try to stop us—it is only that

156

we are disobedient," said Melodie, and turned to her twin. "Sister, we have sinned in our pride and arrogance. We should endeavor to preach only by good example. It is apparently not meant for us to bring souls to God by public exhortation."

The Duke laughed briefly. "I should say not! And in St. James', of all places! It is a wonder you were not stoned in the street."

"Do you mean like the early Christian martyrs?" asked Melodie eagerly.

Gemma glowed. "Do you think it might have come to that? Think of the glorious example—"

Finally Roxanne laughed, with more than a slight note of hysteria. "Oh, you are both so absurd that I cannot even bring myself to scold you! But I do hope you have finally learned your lesson. You are fortunate that Fanny and I were driving past at the moment when you—Fanny! Where could she have gone? I climbed out of her carriage at the end of the street, and when I got back, she had disappeared, and you, sir, were there in her place."

The Duke had been about to say something, but now he looked at her in amazement. "You *climbed* out of the carriage?"

Roxanne looked down and shamefacedly twitched her torn skirt together. "Well, it was not a high-perch phaeton, you know, only a barouche! That stupid coachman was far too slow to help me, and I had to get to the twins quickly. But I confess I am angry with Fanny for driving off like that, when she might have been here to take us up—"

"And you would have thus been spared the evil of being indebted to me yet again," said His Grace, smiling wryly. This time Roxanne met his gaze without rancor.

"I should have preferred it," she said candidly. "But I forgive you for all the dreadful things you have said, and I thank you. I trust I will not find it necessary to do so again." Roxanne felt as though she was becoming as practiced at this sentence as she was in delivering thanks and apologies. It did not, however, become any easier with repetition.

"I trust not," replied the Duke, looking as though he, too, was becoming all too familiar with this type of exchange.

The twins appeared to have forgotten their fear, and smiled upon their two rescuers impartially.

There was silence all the way back to Upper Brook Street, and when they had been set down, the Duke, to Roxanne's dismay, ordered his coachman to wait and followed them into the house.

"There they are!" cried Lady Camberwick, who, as they entered the drawing room, was pacing and wringing her hands distractedly. "I was so worried . . . I could not think of what to do next, and poor Sir James not here to advise me! Where have these girls been?" she demanded of her eldest niece.

Roxanne thought it best to temporarily ignore this question. "However did they get away from you, Aunt Maria?"

Lady Camberwick turned her darkest glance upon the twins. "An excellent question, my dear. After our calls, I wished to stop at my modiste to discover if she would be able to finish my new walking dress by Thursday. I left the girls in the carriage, and by the time I came out, they were gone! I drove all about looking for them, until I decided to see if they had somehow come home."

Roxanne turned to her sisters, her anger with them renewed. "How could you do such a thing to poor Aunt Maria, who has been so kind? This is inexcusable. It is bad enough that I found you . . . where I did, but that without a word you left Aunt Maria worrying and wondering where you had gone . . ."

"I doubt her ladyship's anxiety would have been relieved by knowledge of your sisters' whereabouts, Miss Winston," said the Duke, and with all her will Roxanne wished him gone. But he stood relaxed, legs apart, arms crossed casually, looking as though he meant to make a long stay.

At this, Lady Camberwick was naturally reminded of her unanswered question, and turning to the twins said, "Yes, where *did* you go? Naturally, I was beside myself with worry, but I now see that you are quite unharmed, though Roxanne seems to have a disgraceful tear in her dress."

Roxanne flushed with annoyance, and saw that the Duke was grinning at her. She loftily ignored him.

Lady Maria sighed. "But let us sit down while you tell me. I am worn to death with worrying, and my feet hurt excessively from pacing."

Roxanne raised her eyebrows and looked at the Duke, hoping to signal by her glance that it was high time he made a polite exit. He looked back at her and calmly settled himself in a chair next to the sofa where she herself had taken a seat.

While their aunt's eyes grew wider and wider, the twins explained where they had gone, and for what purpose, and begged her ladyship's forgiveness very humbly.. "We did not wish to worry you, Aunt. In fact, we thought we would be back in the carriage before you came out, since you usually take a dreadfully long time when you are at the dressmaker's," said Gemma.

By now Lady Camberwick's face had turned a pasty white, and she uttered little choked cries until she could speak. "St. James' Street! How could you dare—and to think that I was not far away, and never thought to look for you there—well, of course, it would not have occurred to me that I might ever find you there! How could I have known that you girls would be so foolish . . ." She was overcome for some moments with the shock of this revelation, and Roxanne comforted her the best she could.

"It is all right, dear Aunt, I retrieved them in time, and no real harm was done. I doubt anyone even knew their names."

"And your father—he was there at his club today—"

Roxanne shook her head. "I saw neither him nor Geoffrey anywhere in that crowd, and of course they would have come to our aid if they were. I suppose they had left Boodle's by the time the twins descended on Brook's."

All were in agreement, and the Duke, too, was drawn into the plot, that Sir James should not know of the near disgrace of his daughters. Roxanne only prayed that no one had recognized the three of them and informed him of it.

"And I shall undertake to squelch any gossip that may come of it, Lady Camberwick," added Rutledge.

Her ladyship favored him with a bright smile dripping with gratitude. But Melodie's continuing attempt to explain her and her sisters' actions irritated their aunt's barely soothed nerves.

"You see, Aunt Maria, we thought we should go into Brooks's, because we had heard that there was an unconscionable amount of drinking and gambling going on there, and that it was a resort of those who were most in need of our help. But a very rude and unrepentant man made us leave, and that was why Roxanne found us preaching in the street. We did not know that it would take so long to get back—"

"Into Brooks's!" Poor Lady Camberwick was now totally distracted, and had pulled at her cap so many times that it was completely awry. "How in heaven's name did you get in? No ladies are ever admitted—oh, my poor dear girls, were they very rude to you?"

"It was not very pleasant," admitted Melodie with what Roxanne thought was a fine sense of understatement. "Especially when the crowd started to gather, and—"

"A crowd! Oh, dear, Roxanne, take me upstairs, I feel quite ill—and girls, we shall talk of this later, I don't think I can bear to hear any more right now! Your Grace, my sincere thanks, and if you will excuse me—"

Roxanne assisted her trembling aunt from the room, and called her maid to administer hartshorn, continually assuring her that no evil had befallen the girls. "I arrived in time, before any harm could come to them."

Though now ensconced in the comfort of her own chamber, lying on a daybed with her stays loosened and a handkerchief moistened with eau-de-cologne across her forehead, Lady Camberwick was agitated anew. She sat straight up and the handkerchief fell to her lap. "I had not thought of it, but you were there

161

too, Roxanne! The scandal! Now I shall never get any of you married." But suddenly her brow cleared. "Ah, I was forgetting—thank heaven for Rutledge." She sank back down against the cushions.

By now Roxanne's nerves were as irritated as her aunt's, though for different cause. "You might well thank *me,* my dear aunt, for it was *I* who brought the girls away from danger, not the Duke. He merely happened to be at the end of the street when we arrived, and took us up in his carriage."

"Yes, very kind of him, and how like him to be there when he is needed." Her ladyship sighed, closing her eyes. "Do leave me now, Roxanne, I must rest after this trying afternoon. Please thank His Grace for me again." She opened her eyes briefly. "And do smile at him a little; he obviously is doing this for your sake and if you would make the slightest push to engage his affections further, you could be a Duchess before year's end."

"That is something I have no desire to be," said Roxanne coldly, and left the room. As for her aunt's belief that all the favors done by the Duke were for her sake, it was too absurd to even consider. He had been quick enough to steal a kiss, but as for his harboring any real affection for her, it was simply unthinkable.

When she reached the drawing room, the twins were gone and the Duke stood sipping a glass of wine. As soon as she entered, he handed her a glass, already poured out.

Roxanne's nerves began to tingle with anxiety. Had he dismissed the twins from his presence, or had they had enough of his scolding and taken their leave of their own accord? Either way, it was wrong, and Roxanne knew she should not be alone with him. But she did feel rather shaky, and the thought of a few strengthening sips of wine after her ordeal was not unappealing, so without speaking, she took the glass and drank. The wine warmed and steadied her a bit, and she faced the Duke with renewed composure. Instantly he spoke.

"I realize that I owe you an apology; pray accept it."

For a moment Roxanne thought she had imagined this. The arrogant Duke of Rutledge apologizing to *her?* But she thought better of showing her surprise and only nodded coolly. "You confuse me, my lord. For which of your offenses do you apologize today?"

Immediately Roxanne thought she had gone too far, but after a moment, his face creased in a smile, and she relaxed.

"Let us simply say . . . for all my sins, Miss Winston. For being the man you blame for your brother's fate. For not giving you credit for at least trying—though not altogether succeeding—to deal with your troublesome sisters without my help. For being a friend to Geoffrey and Miss Pearson, when you would prefer I wasn't. Am I forgiven? Will you give me your hand?"

Roxanne could not help but relent, and even smile a little. Her grievances against him were certainly justified, but she felt that there was genuine contrition behind his wry demeanor. His sincerity merited nothing less than a Christian acceptance of his apology. But he would get no more than that from her, she told herself. Any real friendship between them was not to be thought of.

She gave him her hand, and it was immediately

enveloped in his own. His hand was smooth, his grip firm. Roxanne knew a moment of anxiety lest this lead to a repetition of a certain shocking scene, and she had an urge to withdraw her hand, but he went no further than to press it respectfully and release it. It was not until after he left her, which he did almost immediately, that she began to wonder what had prodded him to make this sudden apology. No reasonable explanation, however, came to mind.

On his heels arrived Fanny Pearson, looking more than usually windblown. "Thank goodness you are here! And the twins? Are they safe?" she was as breathless as if she had run all the way there.

"How kind of you to be concerned, my dear, considering that you drove off and left us in a most uncomfortable situation," replied Roxanne, but with a smile. It was obvious that Fanny's worry was genuine. But she was not quite ready to forgive her friend for abandoning her to her fate.

"Don't be cruel, Roxanne, I've been worried to death. You see, Margaret's stupid coachman was scandalized at your behavior, and refused to drive into St. James', so I was going to climb out and follow you, for you know that no paltry crowd of beaux and loungers could keep me from assisting you, but the wretched man drove off so fast that I was nearly knocked out of the barouche. He would not stop, and when I finally managed to get him to drive past St. James' again, the crowd was dispersed and you and the twins were nowhere to be seen. Luckily, I soon saw—" But at this point Fanny gasped and signified by a hand to her chest that she had run out of breath. She stopped talking for a moment and dropped herself into a chair.

Roxanne was instantly contrite. "You poor dear! I knew you wouldn't really desert us. But it was simply dreadful."

And she told her friend about their ordeal and timely rescue by the Duke, while Fanny reacted with amazement. "But why ever did it take so long for him to fetch you? As I was saying, it was not very long before I saw Rutledge stroll past, and when I told him of your situation, he said his carriage was not far away, and that he would—"

Roxanne felt a renewal of her annoyance with the Duke. "That is extremely odd. He said nothing to me about your having dispatched him to us. Hmmph! It appears His Grace would prefer to play the hero and seem to descend out of the clouds just in time, rather than admit to something as prosaic as being sent by you. A pretty piece of playacting!"

Fanny frowned. "You wrong him, Roxanne. I'm sure he must have meant to tell you that I sent him to you. Harry is not the kind of man who wishes to seem something he is not. And after all he has done to prove his goodwill, how can you persist in your dislike of him?"

Roxanne sniffed. The Duke's surprising apology was all but forgotten in this new burst of ill-feeling. "His unsolicited assistance changes nothing about his past behavior, Fanny. As for goodwill . . . he is always in the wrong place at the wrong time, making it appear that I am a simpering fool who can't control a pair of children like Melodie and Gemma."

"Oh, Rozzie," Fanny said sorrowfully. "Very well, I shan't mention him again, if it upsets you so."

"It is not of the slightest consequence to me, my

dear, should you mention His Grace an hundred times a day. It can have no possible affect on my state of mind."

Fanny merely rolled her eyes and began to speak of something less inflammatory.

The next morning brought the return of Mr. Driggs, and in private conference with him Roxanne told an unvarnished tale of all of the twins' misdeeds since their arrival in town. Although she could not exactly *like* the clergyman, she was relieved to have someone else to help her bear the burden of her sisters' misbehavior.

He clucked disapprovingly and murmured, "Indeed! Indeed!" at regular intervals, and at the end of her tale, he shook his head and said, "I am sure you will agree with me now, Miss Winston, that no good can come of mixing two worlds—those of the flesh and the spirit. Your sisters are of the spirit, and do not thrive in London, where the spirit is so grievously neglected for the sake of the flesh. The flesh abounds! Though they struggle against it, the flesh may yet overcome them."

All this talk of flesh made Roxanne feel as if she were in the presence of a butcher, but she managed to keep her composure. "No, sir, I still do not take your part, for it is their duty to obey their father and aunt, who have only their welfare in mind. The girls' fault is that do not obey wholeheartedly. They fail to see that they must, for the present, repress even such praiseworthy aims as theirs until the family's needs are met."

Mr. Driggs sighed and brushed aside a few greasy strands of hair, already disarranged by his hat, which was so tight that it had left a red line about his balding pate. "Ah, Miss Winston, I see that you too have been

166

contaminated by all of this worldliness." He regarded with disfavor her fashionable gown of embroidered white muslin. "And to think that once I had hopes that I could make you the companion of my life . . . but I am afraid you would not do, my dear, not now."

Roxanne felt a flash of anger, a symptom that was becoming more frequent in her lately, and which troubled her, but she could not refrain from a sharp rejoinder.

"What absurdity! I never encouraged you to believe that I would ever accept an offer of marriage, sir. And as for my faith, I am as steadfast as I ever was, and as vigilant over my conscience and behavior."

That this was not strictly true did not prevent Roxanne from saying it. She felt that the preacher was in dire need of a set-down for his impertinence, but in that moment she realized that he was right, at least in one respect. She *had* become more worldly.

Was it as a result of the contaminating companionship of worldly people, or was it merely the necessity of assuring security for her family that had brought about this change? She thought perhaps it was a little of both, but though she knew that her new "London" self had some grievous faults of temper, it was not such a bad change as Mr. Driggs seemed to think.

It was as though she was seeing the world much more clearly these days. At home she had often hidden herself from its realities, especially since the events of her last season. Now she saw the world as it was, and thus could better avoid its real pitfalls, without fogging her mind with prejudices against unimportant things like dancing, cards, and dress.

"In any case, Mr. Driggs, I should like you not to

encourage the twins to believe that they can convert the haut ton; it is unbecomingly arrogant of them to think that they could have such an influence, even should their preaching be desired. By all means, keep them strong in their faith, but do remind them of their duty."

Mr. Driggs silently bowed his head for a moment. Whether this was to indicate his assent or if he was simply praying over her, Roxanne could not tell. After a while he looked up and said, "I trust that your sisters may continue to assist me in my efforts to bring comfort to the unfortunate? We have an organization to supply Bibles to the heathen slaves, whose release from bondage we pray for, and to bring God's forgiveness to the condemned prisoners, and also to urge the many—"

"Certainly," Roxanne cut him short. "The girls may assist you in such endeavors, so long as it does not put them in any danger, or involve them in any scandals among the ton."

He bowed again and Roxanne decided it was time to let him talk to the twins alone, so she left him tsk-tsking behind her. She had an appointment to drive with Geoffrey that afternoon, and she found herself looking forward to it more eagerly than she would have believed possible a few weeks ago.

Perhaps, she thought, tying the yellow silk ribbons on her chip straw bonnet and tucking in her golden curls before her mirror, in her old friend's company she could recapture some of the carefree feelings of the distant past, and forget the tribulations of the present. Too late, she realized she was wrong. From the moment he took her arm to lead her out of the house and down to his curricle, Geoffrey was more the attentive suitor than the boyish companion.

"Now, my sweet Roxanne," he said when he had handed her up, given her hand a surreptitious squeeze, and taken the reins, "we shall display ourselves in the park for all the world to see, and I shall be the envy of all my acquaintance, for you are surely the most beautiful creature in London, and today you are mine."

Roxanne laughed lightly, but her tone was serious when she spoke. "Geoffrey, if I had known that you were planning to make love to me, I should never have accepted your invitation. I believed I had made it clear to you back at Westcombe Hall."

"Will you give me no hope?" His clear blue eyes, much like her own, fixed her with a glance full of unbridled longing, and though Roxanne's compassion was stirred, she was not sure she could ever love Geoffrey as she would wish to love a husband. But to spare him, she simply said, "You know it would not do, my dear friend. Why, between us we would bring the Pearsons and the Winstons to the workhouse! You know that you need a wife who can bring you at least some fortune, and I—"

"And you are on the lookout for a wealthy husband?" There was pain in his voice. The curricle was rolling through the park gates now.

"No, indeed not," said Roxanne firmly. "I must see the twins settled, and then there are the younger girls as well, and after that, Papa—"

"You will become his nursemaid, and a charming aunt, and eventually will decay into genteel spinsterhood," said Geoffrey, his eyes on the road, which was crowded with carriages and riders. "No, not you, Rozzie! You are too beautiful, and too full of life—"

"Do smile," Roxanne whispered. They were within sight of several acquaintances. "I should not wish people to think we were quarreling."

"Oh, my dear girl, could I ever quarrel with you?" Geoffrey was contrite and his voice was caressing. Roxanne knew a fleeting wish that circumstances were not so against this match. True, she was not in love, but perhaps it was more important that Geoffrey loved *her*. If there were enough money between them, she would not have to worry so about her family, and about a lonely spinsterhood—and in the next moment she scolded herself. Silly, as if I would ever be alone! Between Papa and Elizabeth and Dorothea and Miss Lynchard, who was like part of the family—

But Geoffrey broke into her thoughts. "I know what it is, Roxanne. You think me still a boy, but I am a man now, and I have grown to know my own mind. Oh, Rozzie, the places I have been, the things I have seen!" For a moment his voice broke, almost as if he were, despite his protestations, still a youth. "Through it all, the thought of you at home, lovely and sweet and calm, sustained me. And Alfred," he whispered, "you know he would have wanted—"

"Geoffrey, it is unfair of you to appeal to me thus." Roxanne had difficulty keeping her expression emotionless.

"Yes. I know. I am sorry." With that Geoffrey flicked his whip and, with a clear stretch ahead of them, sent his curricle moving briskly along. The breeze cooled Roxanne's cheeks, and dried the incipient tears in her eyes.

To divert him, Roxanne told her companion of her morning's adventure with the twins, and as she had expected, laughter was his reaction. "Oh, to have seen the faces of those fellows, especially at Brooks's, when those two young ladies appeared cloaked in all their righteous indignation, and capped with fetching bonnets."

Roxanne joined him in his laughter. Now that they were all safe, she could see the humor in the situation.

"Yes," Geoffrey went on, "I can imagine they were quite astounded to see Melodie and Gemma descend upon them with Bibles in hand, politely requesting that they put down their cards and glasses and attend to Scripture instead. Thank heaven that Sir James and I had gone before their arrival." At Roxanne's request, he readily agreed to keep the story from the Baronet.

"You needn't worry about your sisters, Roxanne," Geoffrey told her with a grin. "They are certainly Originals, if nothing else, and they will attract attention."

"But will it be attention of the right kind?" Roxanne told him of her sisters' three tentative suitors, and Geoffrey broke into renewed chuckles. "Tony and Cyril are mere babies, but good fellows, if one could ever get them to talk of anything sensible, and each has a tidy fortune. Now Wynne is another sort; he has a high opinion of himself, but with no real abilities to justify it. A fabulous fortune, and a title, of course, but" — he frowned — "I fear he takes up with your sisters out of boredom. I doubt he could ever be brought to the point."

"Just what I thought," Roxanne agreed, and for a while it was almost like old times as they talked over the twins' chances of matrimony, the entertainments planned for the coming weeks, and the world in general. It was refreshing to Roxanne to find a gentleman whose opinions on people agreed so well with her own, and they spent a merry quarter of an hour discussing Mr. Driggs and his influence, though Roxanne did feel a twinge of guilt for laughing at such a devout man. Still, she had separated herself from his congregation, and did not feel so much loyalty toward him as she once had.

It was only after they were back in Upper Brook Street that Geoffrey took up his courting theme again, and by then, Roxanne's pride, which had been so injured from battle with the Duke, had been salved somewhat by Geoffrey's warm admiration and pleasant company, so she did not scold him when he held her hand between his for a long time and pressed his lips against it.

"I will go now," he whispered, gazing into her eyes, "but only tell me that you are still my good friend."

"Silly," she scolded gently, "you know that my feelings toward you have not changed. But you must understand that I cannot have you proposing to me every time we meet. It is most unsuitable, and will only make you unhappy. And I don't," she added gently, "in spite of the necessity of refusing you, wish to make you unhappy."

Geoffrey smiled broadly. "I would have made almost any sacrifice to hear you say that! Imagine how I would sacrifice to have you as my wife."

"Geoffrey, it cannot be."

"Shhhh." He put a finger to her lips, smiled, and left her.

Although she had been diverted from her other worries by her drive with Geoffrey, Roxanne felt as though she had been thrust back into reality rather abruptly. If he continued to plague her . . . but she could not help feeling some pity for him, along with a little thrill of conquest, for which she chastised herself.

In the next few weeks Roxanne found her pity for Geoffrey increasing, for he was severely tried by her acquisition of several admirers. Whether these gentlemen were deceived as to the amount of her fortune, or simply, as they often told her in discreet compliments, overcome by her beauty of face and figure, she could not determine, but they did make the season much more pleasant than she had expected.

The Duke of Rutledge appeared not infrequently now in the same society as the Winstons. He did not accept Lady Camberwick's invitation to her rout, pleading another engagement, and the twins were disappointed. Roxanne knew a moment's irritation, too, at the news, though she hid it well.

At other parties His Grace never asked Roxanne to dance, which disappointed Lady Camberwick and the Duchess very much, and Roxanne not a little, despite her wish to be relieved of his alarming presence. However, the Duke always managed a wry smile or an amusing remark to her, especially when she seemed to be the object of some masculine attention. Often she saw him watching with an unscrutable expression as she danced with some young sprig of the nobility or received the attentions of her admirers.

He did call occasionally in Upper Brook Street to inquire after the ladies' health and their pleasure in the season, but during these times his conversation was impeccably polite, and Roxanne had not found herself alone with him for a very long time. She had the sensation that he was deliberately avoiding her, and told herself that it was exactly what she wanted.

But the memory of his embrace haunted her, and sometimes she felt she could not rest until she discovered what was behind it, or whether he had ever felt the urge to repeat it. However, she was usually able to distract herself from this unprofitable speculation by becoming very busy with amusing her father, who seemed to thrive in London, but who was increasingly impatient of his physical inabilities.

While the twins each spent one morning a week with Sir James, during which they delighted him with their curious theories on the proper way to conduct society, Roxanne appropriated at least two other mornings out of the week for private talk with him, and when they tired of exchanging gossip or discussing the family affairs, he would read aloud to her, the book propped up on his lap, turning the pages with his good hand while she plied her needle. On one such morning Roxanne was surprised by her father's asking, "What has happened to Rutledge lately, Rozzie? I made sure he was going to be one of your steadfast suitors, but perhaps young Pearson has frightened him off."

His eyes were twinkling but Roxanne was aware of a more serious intent despite his facetious manner. "Why, I don't suppose anything at all has *happened* to him, Papa. As for the Duke being one of my suitors . . . you know it is impossible, not only because of the past, but because . . . because . . ."

"Because?" Sir James tilted his head and looked at his eldest daughter inquiringly.

"Because he is wealthy and titled and I am not the sort of female a Duke would marry," she said quickly.

174

It was impossible to describe to her father the exact difficulty in her relations with the Duke, aside from her resentment of the part he had played in the loss of her brother. It was impossible because the feelings Rutledge aroused in her were so peculiar she could not adequately describe them even to herself.

"I take your meaning, but I think you underestimate yourself, my dear," he replied affectionately. "You are worthy of not only a Duke, but a King."

"Oh, Papa, you know you are unfairly prejudiced. But I doubt we shall have to put either of our theories to the test; His Grace gives no indication of wishing to join the ranks of my suitors, as you call them."

From there she went into a lively description of the absurdities of these gentlemen, of which there were not more than four or five in all, who left posies at the door with their cards, who danced with her at balls, and who called for her in their sporting carriages, until she was sure that her father was completely diverted from all thought of the Duke.

When she was not with Sir James, Roxanne was visiting among her growing acquaintance and attending social engagements, or accompanying the twins or her aunt or Fanny on various expeditions of shopping, pleasure, or duty.

Once she joined the twins, Lady Allenbrook, and Mr. Driggs to hear Wilberforce speak in Parliament, and sometimes she went with them to Lady Allenbrook's to help sort donations, copy letters, sew, or otherwise assist in the work of her Charitable Society. Mr. Driggs seemed to be making an indefinite stay in town, and was often there to lead Lady Allenbrook's particular friends in prayer, which was no surprise, but one day the Duke was there as well.

He sat in respectful silence during prayers, spent a good deal of time speaking apart with Lady Allenbrook, and paid no unusual attention to Roxanne, but many times she felt his gaze on her, especially during the singing of hymns when, to her surprise, he enthusiastically added his rich baritone. He obviously enjoyed the music, Roxanne thought as she played upon her hostess's elegant little pianoforte, even if he had not a great opinion of the words.

That afternoon Rutledge bade her good day in no different a manner than the others, and left. Roxanne's curiosity was so great that she could not resist saying to Lady Allenbrook, "I was surprised to see His Grace the Duke of Rutledge among us today."

"Surprised, my dear?" Lady Allenbrook smiled fondly at her. Though she was mainly the friend of the twins, she always had a moment and a kind word for Roxanne. "You would be even more surprised if you had visited when some other of your acquaintances are here." Before Roxanne could be distracted by this mystery, she continued, "But surely you remember that it was he who introduced me to your sisters?"

Roxanne blushed, recalling her own misinterpretation of that generous and astute action. "Of course, but I . . . I did not think to see him so comfortable in a gathering like this." She gestured at the serious little group, who now were exchanging confessions of their faults and reporting their attempts to reform.

Lady Allenbrook's smile grew wider. "Why, I do not think you precisely understand the nature of my friendship with His Grace." Seeing Roxanne's puzzled look, she gestured to a pair of empty chairs. "Sit down, my dear, and I shall explain it to you. You see, I have known Harry—yes, I call him that when we are alone—all of his life. I am his aunt."

"I did not know!" Roxanne cast her mind back over the past weeks, desperately trying to recall if she had made any imprudent comment about the Duke to this kind lady, then gave up the effort, knowing it was unworthy of her to think of such a thing now.

"Harry doesn't wish it widely known—" She stopped and shook her head at the sudden knowing look on Roxanne's face. "No, it is not what you think, my dear Miss Winston. He thinks that because of his father's evil reputation—my brother, the late Duke—that my work among the unfortunate will suffer if the connection was widely known."

"But surely it must be known that you are related?"

"Oh, yes, but people tend to forget such things once the gossip of the moment is past. When first my brother and I parted ways—it was even before his wife left him to live in London—it was talked of here and there. But the ensuing gossip over their separation drove it out of people's minds, and I'm afraid that ever since then it is poor Althea and Harry who have had to bear the punishment for my brother's sins. The one, for refusing to consider herself his wife any longer, and the other, for having had the misfortune to be raised by him."

Roxanne sat, open-mouthed, astounded, for she had not heard more than a vague reference to the Duchess's unfortunate marriage and she had never thought to wonder about what Rutledge's childhood might have been like.

Lady Allenbrook looked concerned. "Oh, dear, I am

afraid I spoke out of turn. Yet I thought that a worldly, modish miss like you would have long heard this old tale before now, and that *that* was why you were surprised to see my nephew here today."

Roxanne, crimson with embarrassment, could only say, "Modish miss? Is that me?"

"Why yes. Compared to your sisters you are much more . . . awake to the world. Though you are, I'm sure, devout in your own way, you have a much greater connection to secular life than those dreamy children."

Roxanne tucked this away to ponder later and began to apologize, though she did not know precisely what for. "I'm so sorry, I did not mean to seem . . . I meant no insult to His Grace by implying that one did not expect to see him among serious people, but . . ."

Now Lady Allenbrook laughed, and her laugh was as merry and trilling as a young girl's. "You need not say another word, my dear. I know exactly what you mean, and of course, to those who do not know him well, Harry seems too dashing a figure to be able to spare a half hour a week to his dull, doddering aunt and her hymn-singing friends, but he is a good boy, for all that. Do you know that he franks all our correspondence for us? He has saved the Society a good deal of money, and has made very generous contributions besides."

Roxanne's opinion of the Duke was beginning to rise, but at that moment she remembered his bitter assessment of the uses of Evangelical religion among the lower classes, and his implication that he, as a member of the ruling class, benefitted from having those below him encouraged to keep to their place.

But she said no more to Lady Allenbrook, and that

night, after she had chided herself for her impulsiveness and other faults, which seemed to be mounting daily, she thought a great deal about the Duke and his aunt and the story she had been told, until her head ached. She slept badly that night, and the next, until she was able to forcibly banish these contradictory opinions from her mind. The only way to get any rest, she found, was not to think of Rutledge at all. Fortunately, she now had some other gentlemen, not nearly so maddening, to think about.

Although she still considered herself a chaperone to the twins, Roxanne now found herself dancing instead of sitting, talking instead of watching over her sisters, and being treated as an eligible young lady rather than one past her prime. She even, to the horror of the twins, spent an evening at the theater with Lady Camberwick and her friends and her newest admirer, Mr. Yerton, the baby-faced heir to a sizable fortune, while the girls attended a meeting of a prison relief society under the watchful eye of Lady Allenbrook, and Sir James, having the house to himself, entertained a group of old cronies with port and cards.

The twins, however, were not the only ones to disapprove of this expedition. In a box across the theater, Roxanne saw Geoffrey and Fanny with their sister Margaret and her husband. Fanny smiled and waved as their glances met, but Geoffrey looked sulky. During the interval, the Pearson party made their way over to Lady Camberwick's box.

Margaret, an older Pearson daughter, was a stolid blonde who was exactly the opposite of the mercurial Fanny. Her husband, a plain Mr. Broughton, was her equal in phlegmatic temper and, though not extremely wealthy, had fortune enough as well as a distant connection to an Earl's family. This couple was left to the attentions of Lady Camberwick and her guests, while Roxanne and Mr. Yerton conversed apart with a mischievously smiling Fanny and a frowning Geoffrey.

"Delightful play, don't you think, Mr. Pearson?" offered Mr. Yerton.

"Delightful," said Geoffrey through his teeth.

"The actresses are very pretty, are they not?" asked Fanny.

"Ah," said Mr. Yerton, "but none so lovely and graceful as Miss Winston. Though, to be sure, one is very nearly as blonde."

"You insult Miss Winston, sir, to compare her to those creatures upon the stage." Geoffrey looked as though he might have drawn a sword upon poor honest Mr. Yerton, had he been wearing one.

"I—I meant no offense sir, I—I . . ."

Roxanne looked pleadingly at her friend, and Fanny, taking Mr. Yerton's arm, immediately desired him to escort her for a stroll before the interval ended, leaving her glaring brother and Roxanne nearly alone.

"Well, if Yerton is a specimen of the rich fellow you hope to catch, I can't say I approve," growled Geoffrey when the man was barely out of hearing.

Roxanne struggled to conceal her annoyance. "Please don't be hurt, and you certainly must not be rude. I am not pursuing a husband, you know, but gentlemen will call on one, and I see no reason to restrict my amusements to following my sisters about, simply because it is impossible for us to marry."

Geoffrey flushed, reproved. "Of course. I am being a graceless monkey, and I daresay Rutledge would tell me so. He often does."

Roxanne was suspicious. "Oh, have you discussed our situation with the Duke?"

Geoffrey stammered. "Not — not precisely. That is, back at Wiltshire I told him I intended to ask for your hand."

"And I am sure His Grace had an opinion," said Roxanne, though she knew it was wrong for her to press him.

"Yes. He said I ought to wait, give us time to learn to know one another again. Mayhap he was right."

Roxanne was both fascinated and repelled to learn that she had been a subject of discussion between Geoffrey and the Duke, but said only, "Neither of you is right, you know. Whether at present or in future, Geoffrey, I cannot accept your honorable offer."

Geoffrey's mouth was a thin line. "We shall see," he said grimly.

Fortunately, Lady Camberwick called upon her niece to give an opinion of Mrs. Broughton's evening cloak, which she admired excessively, and Roxanne turned to speak to the others. Their conversation ended with an invitation for the Pearsons to join Lady Camberwick's dinner party that Wednesday, after which they would all attend the assembly at Almack's.

On Wednesday Roxanne entered the morning room to find her aunt just ending a consultation with her cook about the menu for the evening.

"I daresay I have done no harm in inviting that Driggs person to dinner, though he will not, of course, accompany us to Almack's," said Lady Camberwick without preamble, searching about for her workbag. "We shall have a larger party than I thought. Not only

181

will the Pearsons be coming, but I sent a note yesterday to the dear Duchess and one to the Duke, and they have both accepted. As I had already planned, Lord Culverton and Mr. Kemperton will join us, and with the twins, that will make the numbers even."

Roxanne swallowed before she ventured to speak. "The Duke has accepted?"

Lady Camberwick looked up, having been successful in her search and in the process of stretching out on an embroidery frame a chair cover she meant to work. She attempted to hide her triumphant smile, with little success. "Certainly. Of course, Geoffrey will be there too, but I suppose there is nothing wrong in giving these gentlemen a little bit of competition."

"Aunt Maria, you are quite wrong. You know that it is impractical for Geoffrey and myself to marry, even if I had wished to, which I do not. As for the Duke—"

Lady Camberwick sighed. "A fine catch indeed. But I hold out no great hopes. His mother swears he is impossible. She thinks he will never marry. But there is nothing wrong with my throwing the two of you together."

Roxanne bit her lip, realizing that argument would be useless. It was as well, she thought, that she had some warning, so that she could prepare to spend an evening in Rutledge's company while those two eager matchmakers, the Duchess and Lady Camberwick, looked on.

To her surprise, Roxanne found it all went much smoother than she had supposed, at least with Rutledge. True, it was arranged that he would take her in to dinner, but she found his company not at all irksome. He made no references to any of their past experiences, and seemed only to wish to entertain her. Between him and Geoffrey, who sat at her other side, Roxanne, though at first reluctant to give the Duke the satisfaction, was well entertained indeed.

The two gentlemen competed in telling humorous stories, much to the disapproval of Mr. Driggs, who frowned across the table at Roxanne every time she laughed, which was often. She felt a childish impulse to put her tongue out at him. What right had he, she wondered, defiantly taking a second glass of wine, to decree what company she should keep and how she should amuse herself?

Roxanne was very pleased with Geoffrey. His behavior had undergone a great improvement in the company of his friend the Duke, and she felt that she owed something to that gentlemen, who, whatever his faults, seemed to have a talent for exercising restraint on impulsive young people. That it had had the opposite effect in her brother's case now began to seem odd to her.

When the gentlemen rejoined the ladies after lingering over their port, Roxanne found that the change in Geoffrey's behavior was only a temporary one. He arrived at her side and stuck there for the rest of the evening, easily fending off the interruptions of Mr. Driggs, and gradually growing more and more insistent, while Roxanne sat restlessly under the ironic gaze of Rutledge, who moved about the room with casual grace. She saw him go to his mother, and the Duchess, who had seemed disappointed to find Roxanne the object of Geoffrey's assidious attentions, smiled delightfully at something said to her by her son.

But Roxanne's attention was drawn away by Geoffrey. "Come now, Rozzie, isn't this pleasant? Think how many more pleasant evenings we could have together—I shouldn't be one of those husbands who deserts his wife to dine at his club every evening, or never dances with her in public. In fact, I would dote on you so much that I would no doubt be considered a laughingstock—but then we could creep back to Rosemark when we tired of London, and ride about the country as we used to do—why, think how happy your papa and the girls would be to have you living so close to them."

Roxanne strained to keep a smile on her face. "Of course it would be pleasant, Geoffrey, but when the time came to see our families settled in life, what would we do then? Would you wish to sell even an acre of Rosemark? Would you give up coming to London altogether? How could you afford to support a poor wife and send your little brothers to Eton? Do you think I want my sisters to grow up in poverty? Come, be reasonable, or I shall soon grow cross with you."

Geoffrey, despite her coaxing smile, did not smile in return, though he did leave off his pleading. Roxanne turned and began to speak to Margaret Broughton while her suitor sulked.

It was becoming clear to her that in some ways Geoffrey was not the man he claimed to be, and even less the carefree boy she had once known. There was a darker, stubborn side to him, and she regretted that she must be the person to bring it out.

A shadow crossed the polished floor before her. Roxanne looked up to see the Duke bending to talk quietly with Geoffrey, who was still at her side. For the first time, she saw Geoffrey darken with anger, and bite out a sharp but whispered retort to the older man. She tried not to be distracted by the scene, lest she draw unwanted attention to it, but she did witness the result, which was that Geoffrey finally left her side and Rutledge quietly took his place.

Mrs. Broughton seemed placidly unaware of anything untoward having taken place, but Roxanne was instantly cognizant of a change in the neighboring air. There was a quiet but inexorable presence beside her, and before long, she found that she had drifted out of one conversation and into another, with the Duke.

"I hope that puppy was not annoying you," he said.

"If you refer to Mr. Pearson, Your Grace, I beg you will speak of him more respectfully," she said.

He raised his eyebrows. "In that case I should have told my meddling mother that you needed no protection from any unwanted attentions."

"Geoffrey is my friend, and his . . . attentions . . . are not unwanted."

"Oh? Then am I to wish you happy?"

Roxanne blushed. "No, certainly not. Geoffrey ought not to have discussed the situation with you, but as he has already done so, I might as well tell you what I told him. It is impractical for us to marry."

"Impractical. Such a cold term. It leaves no room for emotion."

Roxanne grew more and more confused. "Our emotions are not your concern, my lord. And although I like and respect the Duchess a great deal, I think she has done me a disservice in dispatching you to my aid this evening. I can handle Geoffrey."

Rutledge, his face grim, bowed. "I am certain that you can, Miss Winston." With that he left her.

Roxanne found that she was trembling a little. Why must the man continue to meddle, if only at his mother's bidding? She blamed Geoffrey for making him a confidant, but perhaps, after tonight's sharp words, her old friend would not be so quick to sing the praises of the Duke.

The party, with the exception of Sir James and the disapproving Mr. Driggs, proceeded to Almack's without much more delay lest they arrive too late to be admitted, and though the twins had been brought there before, they protested nonetheless strenuously against it.

"Be still," Roxanne told them in the carriage, where she made sure she could sit alone with her sisters and aunt, out of hearing of their guests. "You never dance anyway, and what harm can it do you merely to sit and talk quietly with your friends, or walk about the room?"

"But Roxanne, think of the danger to our weak and sinful souls, being in the midst of all the gambling and dancing—" began Gemma, but Lady Maria snapped, "Oh, I beg of you, cease to plague us. I do believe the two of you could sit praying and sermonizing in the midst of Sodom and Gomorrah with the greatest of success! A bit of diversion at a highly respectable place like Almack's isn't likely to send you to eternal damnation."

At which the twins were so shocked and mortified that they fell into silence. Roxanne, however, laughed. "Aunt Maria, you are quite prickly this evening. I hope *I* do not have the misfortune to incur your displeasure tonight."

"You will please me very much, my dear, if you make

a greater effort toward getting a husband," replied her aunt promptly.

"But—"

"Yes, I know, the purpose of this season is to marry off our twin angels, but I have come to believe that it would require less effort to find a suitable match for you." She frowned at her younger nieces, who sat with eyes modestly downcast and hands clasped.

"Now, there is that nice Mr. Yerton for one, and there is Geoffrey, though to be sure, he has no fortune. Then there are those gentlemen who have taken you driving and danced with you more than once—oh, and if you tried, I'm sure you could manage to take that puppy Lord Wynne from your sisters, who don't seem to want him anyway. And of course, there is the Duke of Rutledge, if you would put your silly scruples behind you."

"Aunt Maria!" Roxanne was left with no suitable response to this unexpected attack. They were in King Street now, and the carriage was rolling to a stop behind a long line of others. "I can only repeat, ma'am, that I am not in search of a husband, and that in your comprehensive list, there is not a single person I would be tempted to pursue, or who would be seriously tempted to pursue me, except Geoffrey, and that is out of the question."

Melodie and Gemma were suspiciously silent as they ascended to the assembly rooms. As they were divesting themselves of their wraps, Roxanne took them aside. "Now, girls, you are not planning anything to-night, are you? Please do not leave me in wretched suspense this time. Tell me at once; should I call upon the Duke to be at hand this evening?"

The girls giggled in spite of their solemn countenances, and assured her that they had completely reformed their ideas of converting the ton. "Lady Allenbrook scolded us severely when she heard of the last incident," Gemma confided.

"And she said she would refuse to have us in her house if we ever did such a thing again," Melodie added.

Roxanne sent up a prayer of thanks for the good sense of that lady and her excellent effect on the girls, and set forth with spirits somewhat restored.

She had no lack of partners, for not only her own but her sisters' suitors wished to dance with her. The Earl of Culverton informed her that she was a pleasure to partner. "Pretty and sensible — and quiet," he said as they danced. "A fellow likes that in a woman now and then."

"Oh, has Melodie been plaguing you to repent again, my lord?" Roxanne inquired with a smile.

"Well, she needn't, for I'm not exactly a reprobate! And neither is Cyril, you know."

"Indeed not." Roxanne saw her sisters' chances of matrimony slipping away. "I shall speak to the girls again, my lord. They must not presume on your kindness any longer."

"Kindness . . . well, it's not such a hardship drinking tea with Lady Allenbrook once a week. She's a charming lady — makes a fellow feel welcome and comfortable. And I don't at all mind supporting these Bible societies — very useful book. Why, my nurse used to read it to me all the time when I was a little boy — but I'll not visit any prisons with that Driggs fellow — that's where I draw the line, and Cyril, too!"

Roxanne, but for the necessity of beginning a figure which would separate them, would have cried out in amazement. At the very next opportunity, she asked, "Can it be possible that Melodie and Gemma have drawn you into their activities?"

"Can be, and is," her partner replied shortly, and then they were separated again.

At last, they found themselves standing out at the foot of the set, and were obliged to wait until they could rejoin it.

Roxanne lost no time in interrogating her informant, and found, to her amazement, that the Earl and Mr. Bentley had become avid attendees at Lady Allenbrook's meetings, pillars of the Charitable Society, and had contributed generously to various worthy causes. And though their worldly situations did not meet with the approval of Mr. Driggs, who alas, lingered in London, they had been accepted into the fold.

Now they were being pressed to accompany the preacher on his prison visits.

"No, you certainly should not," agreed Roxanne. "I will speak sharply to my sisters, and to Mr. Driggs as well. One must have a real vocation for such activities, and it is no disgrace that you and Mr. Bentley have not. It is the twins' fault, they have dragged you in beyond your inclination, and I offer my sincere apologies to both you and Mr. Bentley."

They re-entered the set, but at the end of the dance, before he brought her back to Lady Camberwick, Lord Culverton said, "Don't be too hard on them, Miss Winston. It's not that I don't . . . that we . . . well, Cyril and I have a great admiration for your sisters. It's wonderful that they have so many ideas, and such strong convictions, but a fellow needs to follow his own mind, you know!"

"Of course, my lord. But please do not be fearful of offending my sisters by telling them that you will no longer be at their beck and call in these matters. They shall be made to realize that everyone cannot share their enthusiasm."

It was with a vengeful countenance that Roxanne at length descended on her unsuspecting siblings, who were sitting quietly and with perfect propriety beside their aunt among the chaperones and dowagers. But it was several minutes before she could take the girls aside and give them the benefit of her thoughts on the subject of dragooning two fashionable young gentlemen into the Charitable Society.

Melodie began the expected round of defense. "But Roxanne, they said they wished to know where we spent so many afternoons—"

"And so we asked Lady Allenbrook's permission, and she said she would be pleased to have them visit her," continued Gemma.

Now Roxanne recalled Lady Allenbrook's mysterious reference to others of her acquaintance whose presence at the Society would surprise her, but the girls went on.

"Really, they have never complained, and even seem to be enjoying themselves. And their deep voices are most useful in the hymns." Melodie's brown eyes were guileless and completely unconscious of any absurdity.

Roxanne stifled an impulse to laugh, and said, "Nevertheless, you must not press the gentlemen to visit prisons and that sort of thing. Goodness, is it not sufficient that you have extorted so many donations from them, and that they are squiring you about to what must be to them some very dull and unfashionable events?"

The twins looked at one another. "Very well, Roxanne, we shall not urge Lord Culverton and Mr. Bentley to make prison visits, but you cannot blame us for trying to encourage them to live better lives."

Roxanne sighed. "No, if you were at all sensible, and had any realization of the fine chances you have of making excellent matches, I would not blame you at all. But you are so very innocent, my poor dears."

For she had noted that during this conversation, the twins could not keep their glances from straying to the dancing.

A flutter near the floor told her that two identical feet were tapping in time to the music. At last, she thought, they were beginning to be normal young women and to feel the need of a little amusement. Solemnity, before the family tragedies had occurred, had never been part of their natures. The twins had been jolly little girls, and Roxanne knew that if they would allow themselves to dance, they would be light and graceful and a pleasure to watch.

But a silent colloquy between them ended, she saw, in a determined turning away from the dancers. Some convictions were apparently strong enough to overcome even nature.

Roxanne was cheered when the Earl of Culverton and Mr. Bentley joined them, and she saw her sisters' faces light up with pleasure. She watched them for a while and was glad to see that, despite all their talk of cultivating the gentlemen for their salvation's sake, the girls actually liked them and enjoyed their company.

When Mr. Bentley ventured a compliment, she even saw a blush creep up Gemma's face and a smile of pleasure curve her lips.

"So there is hope, is there not, my dear?" Lady Camberwick whispered to her eldest niece after observing the same scene.

"I believe there may be," Roxanne replied cautiously, for who knew what maggot would next enter the girls' unpredictable heads?

Geoffrey came then to claim her for a dance, and he seemed to have taken to heart what must have been a scolding from Rutledge. He did not plague Roxanne about marriage but, to her annoyance, talked almost exclusively of the Duke. Apparently Geoffrey's displeasure with his mentor had been short-lived.

From her position on the dance floor, she had seen them conversing, not quarreling, as she had thought they might after that evening's episode, but talking earnestly. Smiles had gradually erased Geoffrey's sulkiness, and in the end he had gripped the Duke's hand, as if strongly moved. An air of triumph hung over both of them, and now there was a palpable tension about Geoffrey, as if he had some news but was not permitted to share it. He danced energetically, his leg completely healed, and Roxanne was soon out of breath.

After their dance was over, they were both in need of a rest, and Roxanne readily agreed to sit down with him. At first she was afraid that he would return to his usual theme, but instead, he rambled on about what a capital fellow the Duke was, of how Roxanne ought not to resent his involvement with her family. "And if it had not been for Alfred, you know," he concluded, "I would not have minded seeing the Duke marry

Fanny—no, I should be proud!"

Roxanne's nerves, worn with the strain of trying to understand the changes in herself, tired of withstanding the pressure from her aunt, exhausted with predicting the next mess from which she would have to extricate her sisters, could take no more.

"And if it were not for your great friend the Duke of Rutledge, Alfred would still be with us, and very likely married to your sister as he had meant to be," she replied tartly.

"Roxanne!" Geoffrey looked down at her, shocked.

"Forgive me, Geoffrey, but I can't bear to hear you and everyone else telling me what a wonderful man the Duke is, not when I know, and you know, that he is the cause of—"

"Hush!" Geoffrey had never seemed so angry with her. "You must not—you don't know . . ." Geoffrey looked torn. He glanced over her shoulder, and Roxanne turned to see the Duke regarding them. He smiled, nodded, and walked on, but Roxanne was made even more annoyed by his untimely appearance.

"No doubt His Grace wished to know how you are progressing in your suit," she said. "Since you probably tell him everything already, you may tell him that his interference is uncalled for, and I would appreciate it if you would not discuss my personal affairs with him." She rose and went swiftly to the other end of the room, where her aunt sat chatting to the Duchess of Rutledge while the twins decorously promenaded with their two suitors under her not too watchful eye.

"Why, Roxanne, what has happened? You are quite red. Sit down, dear . . . no, go and bathe your face instead until you look more the thing. Shall I lend you my handkerchief?" Lady Camberwick was all concern.

"No thank you, Aunt Maria," said Roxanne stiffly, settling her skirts around her. "I am simply angry with Geoffrey. I shall be all right shortly."

"Oh, dear, have you quarreled again? I suppose it is too much to expect that people who have known each other all their lives should be able to get along without quarreling so regularly."

"Indeed," was all Roxanne would say, and observed gratefully that Fanny had just finished a dance and, recognizing her look of distress, was coming to her rescue.

Just then, the Duchess, whose sympathetic smiles Roxanne had felt unable to return, whispered a word to Lady Camberwick and left her chair. Fanny slid into it.

"What have you said to my brother to make him look like that?" she asked, directing Roxanne's attention to Geoffrey, who slouched against a wall, fixing a sullen gaze on the musicians as if he wished to wrap a bow about the violinist's neck.

"I only reminded him of some unpleasant truths, Fanny."

"I see," she replied with a knowing glance.

Roxanne's frustration made her sharp with her friend. "No, I don't think you do. No one else seems to realize that the Duke of Rutledge is not our benefactor, but our enemy. Even your brother, who was angry with him earlier, is eating out of his hand once more."

"My dear Roxanne, I wish —" Fanny was looking at her with eyes full of pity.

Roxanne was so annoyed that she did not even care that her friend did not continue. She had no desire to hear what Fanny wished. She stood up. "I must go — I should bathe my face, comb my hair—I probably look like an utter disgrace." She walked swiftly away from the assembly room, irritated more with herself, for so losing control, than with anyone, even Rutledge himself. But before she could reach the sanctuary of the ladies' retiring room, she was stopped short by the sound of two familiar voices.

Just outside the doorway stood the Duchess of Rutledge and her son. Roxanne did not wish to pass them, so she hovered out of their sight, waiting for them to move.

Mother and son were apparently arguing.

"It is quite clear, my dear mama, that the girl has not the slightest interest in me except to dislike me, though I am sure she admires my title and fortune. Do you know that she has turned down Pearson, who loves her to distraction, simply because he isn't rich enough? I am certainly not going to make a cake of myself for such a heartless creature."

"How can you say such a thing, Harry! Miss Winston is a sweet child, beautiful, clever, and good, and as I have said from the beginning, the perfect bride for you. And I think you are wrong about her disliking you, and about her being mercenary. She must be practical, since she does have a large family to see to."

"Indeed. I have spent much time during the past weeks seeing to it that some of that family do not disgrace themselves," muttered Rutledge.

"Good. Then she must be grateful, at least, and she has learned to appreciate your excellent qualities. Do ask her for a dance." Her Grace could be heard to sigh. "You would look so handsome together on the dance floor!"

The Duke snorted. "No doubt, Mama, and all eyes would be drawn to us. What joy for the gossips! The sister of the ill-fated Alfred Winston dancing in the arms of his old friend and enemy, reconciled, and so romantically. You have been reading far too many novels, Mama."

"And you are a disagreeable, disobedient son." Roxanne had never heard the Duchess speak so sharply.

"I'm sorry, dearest Mama, but I cannot humiliate myself so."

"Who speaks of humiliation? Do you think she would refuse you?"

The Duke's reply was uttered in a cynical tone. Although Roxanne could not see his face, she could picture that familiar twist to his lips and the expression in his eyes. "Certainly not, Mama. Dancing with me would add to her consequence and attract favorable attention to herself and her plight. Why, any number of eligible suitors might present themselves to Miss Winston once the Duke of Rutledge has been seen to show an interest in the little nobody from Wiltshire."

"Then do it, ask her to dance. For me?" The Duchess's voice took on a wheedling note.

Rutledge sighed deeply. "Very well. For you, Mama, I will go against my better judgment. I only hope it does not lead the chit to expect any further attentions."

Roxanne did not know where to turn. Was everyone conspiring to destroy her peace this evening? She was sorry for having eavesdropped, but it could not have been helped. It would have been more distressing if she, the subject of their talk, had passed through the doorway and interrupted it at such an embarrassing point.

Her cheeks burned with renewed anger. The little nobody from Wiltshire, indeed! How could he be so callous, so cruel, so hypocritical? He had seemed to find a stolen kiss very much to his liking, but Miss Roxanne Winston, with her troublesome family and mercenary tendencies, was apparently not good enough to receive His Grace's more respectable attentions at Almack's.

Fortunately the twins and their beaux were passing by, and Roxanne turned her back to the doorway and engaged them in conversation. She had no recollection later of what she had said, but only of that moment of relief when she realized that the Duke and his mother had safely passed without noticing her.

By the time she had escaped the assembly room and set herself to rights, Roxanne knew exactly what she was going to do. His Grace could not be allowed to cling to his belief that she would never turn down the chance to display herself with him before the ton. Did he think that she disliked him? Well, that opinion would be confirmed before the evening was over.

Roxanne was fully prepared when the moment came. It was the last dance, and though Geoffrey had asked her for it, she had declined, having already danced twice with him, and had not promised it to anyone. Now she saw that he, like a few other people, had already gone, either home or elsewhere to continue the evening's revels. She sat beside a yawning Lady Camberwick, ostensibly keeping an eye on the twins, but actually awaiting the Duke's approach.

It was not long in coming. Directly the musicians struck up the tune and the dance was announced, he was at her side, bowing. Roxanne looked up at him coolly, though she feared her traitorous hammering heart and the catch in her throat would betray her.

"Miss Winston, I have not yet had the pleasure of dancing with you this evening, and here is our last chance. Would you do me the honor, whilst we still have music?"

It was gracefully done, Roxanne had to admit. No one around them, and almost all of the remaining people were now clustered at this one end of the room, would have guessed from his voice or demeanor that His Grace was unwillingly bestowing a favor on the lady before him. But Roxanne did not waver in her resolve.

"You will forgive me, my lord, if I deny you that pleasure. Although your graciousness overwhelms me, I find myself quite capable of resisting the temptation to display myself with the Duke of Rutledge, though it may indeed be my last chance. In short, I would not dance with you, sir, were you the last man in London!"

The satisfaction these words gave to Roxanne was fleeting but delightful. It was wiped away in an instant, for the shock on the Duke's face was soon followed by a thundercloud of anger. Two red spots burned in his cheeks, his eyes glittered, and his mouth thinned to an implacable line. Around her Roxanne heard gasps and whispers and the immediate remonstrances and apologies of her aunt, but despite her knowledge that she had gone too far, she ignored them and her gaze bored into Rutledge's until he looked away. Finally he spoke in a low but perfectly audible voice.

"I understand you very well, Miss Winston. Indeed, who would not? Forgive my impulsive display of good manners. It was obviously wasted on an unappreciative object." He turned on his heel and walked away.

The murmurs grew louder. Roxanne's face burned. She was aware only of two things. One was the whispered scold of her Aunt Maria, who took her arm and, beckoning to the horrified twins, led her out of the room. The other was of an ache in the pit of her stomach. The ache spread upward to her very heart. She had been either very foolish or very brave. But there was one satisfaction she could muster. The Duke had not been able to look her in the eyes while he had said those words. She had won.

Chapter Nine

On a dismal wet evening in late June, Henry Malverne stood at one of the tall windows in the Subscription Room at Brooks's. In the light from a huge crystal chandelier he saw nothing but his own rain-dappled reflection, but he sought no more rewarding activity for several moments. Finally he let go of the heavy red damask drapery he had been holding back, and turned away as its gilt-trimmed hem brushed the toes of his shoes.

The Duke was magnificent in full dress, from black satin breeches and white silk stockings to spotless white neckcloth and embroidered satin waistcoat, but his countenance was not that of a man anticipating a festive evening. There were shadows under his eyes, and his face lacked its usual animation.

Around him the long, elegantly furnished room echoed with emptiness, except for the murmurs and occasional exclamations from a group of gentlemen playing whist at a baize-covered table in a corner.

Although it was past the fashionable dinner hour, it was still rather early for serious gambling; later, Rutledge knew, the Subscription Room would be full of noble gamesters playing at faro, macao, hazard, and the inevitable whist, for the highest stakes. Fortunes would be won and lost, but for now the room was innocent of any such excitement.

One of the whist players gathered up his winnings, left his chair, and approached the Duke. "Care to take my place, Rutledge? Promised m'wife I'd accompany her to some ball or other."

Rutledge declined, knowing that the ball was probably one of the events that he himself was promised to for the evening, but that he had no heart for. The ballgoer departed, and the three abandoned whist players called for a waiter to bring brandy. A good night for brandy, thought the Duke, but he did not accept an invitation to join the drinkers, fearing it would only intensify his mood.

It had been almost a month since that distressing scene at Almack's, and though Rutledge thought he had neatly bettered his fair opponent, it had not failed to shock him that such a scene could have taken place at all. His mother was quite chastened over it, and had apologized profusely for her demand that he invite Miss Winston to dance. Perhaps, he reflected, he had cured his irrepressible mother of matchmaking at last.

He had certainly cured himself, at least, of any foolish ideas he might once have harbored about Miss Roxanne Winston. Part of him had wanted to think that despite her need to blame him for her family's misfortune, Miss Winston was neither unaware nor unappreciative of his admiration. It was a startling and growing admiration which, after his regrettable lapses in gentlemanly behavior, he had decided to restrain.

In fact, all the nonsense he had spouted to his mother that night at Almack's had only been a sop to his pride. But how Miss Winston had lived up to it! He need not have bothered to rein himself in, the Duke thought bitterly. Had Miss Winston been acquainted with his real feelings, she would only have disillusioned him sooner, though perhaps not so cruelly.

Certainly, Rutledge had had the last word. But he had found it a hollow victory. Since that evening, pleasure had eluded him, and his soul was as dismal as the damp night outside. Even the satisfying reflection that the cause of Miss Winston's enmity would soon be safe in the bosom of his family once more brought him only momentary comfort.

By the time she knew the truth, it would be too late to convert Miss Winston's loathing to liking. Very likely it was already too late. It seemed irrelevant, for if rumor was correct, his friend Pearson had somehow managed to overcome the lady's resistance to his proposal.

The Duke was roused from his reverie by the sound of a familiar voice speaking his name. He turned swiftly to find Geoffrey Pearson standing before him. He had not heard the young man's footsteps, swallowed as they were by the thick patterned carpet. Pearson, he observed, wore an ecstatic smile and swayed slightly on his feet.

"So I've finally caught up to you, Harry! Been to your lodgings — servants couldn't tell me where to find you. Visited the Duchess in Albemarle Street, but she was out. Finally thought of your clubs — luckily this is the first one I looked into."

The Duke made an effort to appear interested. "Here I am, as you see. I apprehend that you have some news for me." He looked around to be certain that no others had wandered in and were within hearing distance. Perhaps there was more news from France . . . although it was usually he, not Pearson, who got word first.

Geoffrey understood. "Don't worry, my lord, no news that all of London won't know soon enough. But I've just come back from the country — wanted you to be the first outside the family to know — even before Roxanne . . ."

The Duke repressed a start at the sound of her name, said, "Come, then," and led Geoffrey to a sofa near the marble mantel. He felt a chill and wished, though it was nearly July, that a fire and not a huge bouquet of flowers filled the hearth. "I am honored," he said when they had seated themselves and ordered wine. "It must be very important news indeed."

The club waiter served the wine with silent swiftness. "The most important thing that has ever happened to me," replied Geoffrey solemnly after the servant had discreetly stepped away. "I am now a wealthy man. I have inherited an estate worth fifteen thousand a year, and properties in Bath and London. There is even a baronetcy to go along with them." Geoffrey's solemnity disappeared and he uttered the last with a childlike pleasure. "Now Roxanne will have no excuse to put me off any longer, and we can be married."

Rutledge thought his chair had given way beneath him. It was as though he dreamt of falling and was suddenly jolted awake. His face, however, did not betray anything but pleasure for his friend. He raised his glass. "To Sir Geoffrey — and his lady."

They drank. The exquisite wine could have been vinegar for all Rutledge knew. "You will forgive me, my dear fellow, if I ask how this came about. It is so sudden — I didn't know that you were in line for any sort of inheritance." Only now did he notice that the young man was all in black, unusual for the former soldier, with his fondness for colorful coats. Mourning, mused the Duke — and rejoicing.

Geoffrey's cheeks were flushed, his eyes glittered. "I had not thought it a possibility at all, Your Grace, and it would have been most unlikely until a recent chain of unfortunate events. My father's elder brother was the current baronet. Though he had married late, he seemed a healthy man, with a growing son and a young wife who would likely give him more heirs. Who would have imagined that his son would be fatally thrown from his horse, or that, weeks later, my uncle would succumb to a heart ailment no one knew he had?"

Geoffrey's voice was low and serious now, and despite his joy in his altered prospects, he seemed deeply affected by the tragedies.

He drank and continued. "And here" — he pointed to himself, sloshing his wine about in his glass — "you see the unexpected but grateful heir."

It was understandable, the Duke thought, that Geoffrey's happiness would not be dimmed for long, especially as lack of fortune had been all that had stood between him and the woman he loved.

The Duke expressed his sympathy for the family, and inquired if there was anything he could do to assist the widow in some official matter, or to help his friend during the transition, all the while wondering how soon the betrothal announcement would be made. The official announcement, that is . . .

Henry Malverne thought again of the rumors he had heard in the past few weeks of a secret engagement between Miss Winston and Geoffrey Pearson. His immediate response had been to shrug it off, as he had doubted that Geoffrey would keep such news from him. Now he wondered if perhaps the rumor had been started by Pearson himself, on expectation of the death of his uncle. He pushed the thought from his mind. Geoffrey was replying to his offer.

"You're very kind, but the widow is well provided for, and the solicitors and I have everything well in hand. If you will excuse me now . . ." Geoffrey rose unsteadily and put down his glass. "I must go. . . . I want to tell some of my friends and treat them to a little celebration. Will you join us?"

The Duke declined without pointing out that Geoffrey seemed to have done quite enough celebrating already. But he could not stop himself from saying suddenly, as the young man turned away, "And Miss Winston? When will . . . when will the betrothal be announced?"

Geoffrey grinned. "I'll call upon her first thing tomorrow—that is, as soon as I've recovered from tonight! Last outing, you know, mourning and all."

Geoffrey grew loquacious under the influence of wine, one of the reasons Rutledge had sometimes wondered if he was completely trustworthy.

"I daresay I shall be too bored to stay in town much longer. The season's nearly over, and anyway it's much easier to be in mourning in the country, don't you think? Perhaps I can persuade Roxanne to leave her sisters to Lady Camberwick and go back to Wiltshire until the wedding."

The Duke, who had barely touched his wine, raised his glass and took a long swallow. "To the wedding, then."

"I have no idea when His Grace means to honor us with his presence, Melodie, and I wish that you and Gemma would find some other subject to discuss," Roxanne said for the third time in as many weeks. Her patience was being sorely tried by her sisters, for the twins had never ceased wondering why the Duke did not visit. Still worse, they wanted Roxanne to apologize to him for her rudeness that night at Almack's.

In vain did she endeavor to make them understand that they must not expect Rutledge to appear, unless it was *he* who intended to make the apology. This, of course, she did not expect. His disdain and dislike had been all too plain. No doubt he was still boasting of the set-down he had given her. "People visit one to *make* apologies, not to receive them," she had told her sisters.

"Then you must go to him," Gemma insisted.

"Impossible."

"We will accompany you," Melodie offered. "It will be quite proper—besides, we wish to give His Grace a token of our gratitude."

Roxanne groaned. One sister coming to the Duke groveling in abject apology, the other two offering gifts and gratitude—His Grace would have his fill of laughter.

"Would you set him up higher in his own esteem than he already is? If you had a thought for his spiritual welfare, you would not. Besides, you owe His Grace no gifts. He has made no extraordinary exertions for your benefit."

"Oh, Roxanne," said Gemma sadly, "how can you say that? And it is quite a proper gift, look—" She

206

handed her sister a snuffbox, adorned with a Wedgewood cameo, the portrait of a suffering black slave. Underneath this figure were the words, "Am I not a man and a brother?"

"Isn't it touching?" asked Melodie. "We are distributing to our friends some snuffboxes, hairclasps, fans, and other things decorated with this design to aid in the struggle to end slavery. Lady Allenbrook has lately added this mission to the works of the Charitable Society."

Roxanne duly admired it, and found herself devoured with curiosity as to how Rutledge would receive this gift.

"I'm sure His Grace will be very affected and moved," said Gemma, admiring the box anew.

Aside from this preoccupation with the Duke, the girls had, after a brief period of calm, become troublesome again. Lady Allenbrook was absent from London for a fortnight, during which Roxanne had had to dissuade her sisters from inviting the public to a prayer service, to be conducted by Mr. Driggs in their aunt's drawing room. A few days later she discovered them to be soliciting donations during the rout at Mrs. Broughton's.

The phlegmatic Broughtons had been only mildly surprised when a few irate guests informed them that, while the footmen circulated with champagne, people were being asked by the Winston sisters to subscribe to the Charitable Society. Geoffrey had simply laughed, but Fanny had seen at once how the wind was blowing and had scurried about distracting and soothing ruffled guests while Roxanne put an immediate stop to her sisters' misplaced endeavors and issued them a lecture in Mr. Broughton's library. Even Melodie's protests that several people had been happy to contribute did not stop her from being severe with the girls.

Mr. Winston, too, was this time informed of his daughters' misdemeanors, and though he found it hard to be stern, Roxanne knew, while he was inwardly laughing at the way they confounded what he liked to call "the haughty ton," he made them aware of his displeasure that his daughters could not be relied upon to behave like ladies.

The girls promised good behavior, and their father dismissed them with kisses, telling Roxanne, "They'll do, my dear. I pity the unfortunate fellows who will eventually marry them, but they are good girls. Now you"—he placed his good hand on Roxanne's shoulder as she sat beside him—"you are a prize I shall be proud to bestow on some lucky man—"

Roxanne laughed. "Papa, these are not the Dark Ages, you know—I am not something to be awarded to the victor of a battle."

Sir James pretended to sigh with regret. "Alas, no, disposing of daughters is no longer such a simple matter. One must consider their feelings—"

Roxanne laughed a little grimly. "You needn't worry, Papa. Very likely you will not have to exert yourself to 'dispose' of me at all."

He looked surprised. "What? Is there an offer impending? Perhaps it is that gracious Duke—though I hear you gave his ears a scorching—and received one in return." His blue eyes, of the same shape and shade as Roxanne's were inquisitive.

Roxanne blushed. This was the first time her father had mentioned the debacle at Almack's, and though he had not been present, she knew it had been too much to hope for that someone had not informed him of the highly entertaining scene. But it was good of him not to have scolded her for it.

"No, Papa, you misunderstand me. I only meant that I should probably never leave you. I did not mean to imply that there had been an offer—and good heavens, certainly not from the Duke of Rutledge! How could you think I would marry such a—" She stopped lest she say too much. Her father was looking at her with sadness.

"Roxanne," he said softly, "Alfred was my son. Do you not realize that if there is any blame to be settled in that affair, I shall have the settling of it? And that I have not settled it on His Grace the Duke of Rutledge must tell you something."

"What should it tell me, Papa?" Roxanne looked down, unable to meet her father's gaze any longer.

"That no one was to blame. Alfred was a grown man who made his own decisions. Just as you are now a woman and will make yours. And that is all I will ever say to you on the subject. Now," he said in an ordinary tone, turning a page of his newspaper with his good hand, "if you have no offers of marriage to report to me, perhaps you will leave me to my paper, and go and see what deviltry your angelic sisters are getting up today. Although I think I have impressed on them the importance of curbing their zeal, and in the future we can rely on them to behave circumspectly."

But the fond father's hopes proved too ambitious, as it was only the day after that when, having not long ago seen her sisters safely off in two carriages, accompanied by their more or less faithful attendants, the Earl of Culverton and Mr. Bentley, Roxanne had to turn back from setting out for her own afternoon engagement because of their sudden, unlooked-for return.

The twins, their faces glowing with defiant martyrdom, were being brought back in apparent disgrace by these two gentlemen, who stiffly handed them down before the house in Upper Brook Street and requested permission to speak privately with Miss Winston.

The twins having been temporarily banished to their room with the promise that they would have a chance to tell their side of the story, Roxanne received the agitated gentlemen in the drawing room. At first they were reluctant to begin, but with the encouragement of a little Madeira they were persuaded to address the subject of the interview.

"Cyril and I have sustained a great shock, Miss Winston," began the more articulate Earl, while his companion swallowed and nodded agreement.

Roxanne expressed her regret, impatience vying with amusement at the forlorn expressions of the two gentlemen.

"As I told you once before, we—Cyril and I—admire your sisters very much."

"Charming girls—delightful," added his friend. "Especially Miss Gemma."

The Earl quelled his companion with a frown. "And we had thought—Cyril and I," he continued, "that our feelings were in some degree returned."

"I had reason to believe the same, my lord, or else I would not have let them take up so much of your time," said Roxanne.

The Earl looked gratified. "Do you see, Cyril, we were not wrong! Not if Miss Winston believed it too."

Cyril smiled and nodded.

"Unfortunately, Miss Winston, when we ventured — separately of course — to make clear our intentions, in short, asked permission to speak with your father with a view to requesting *his* permission . . ." The Earl stopped; either he was confused, or too choked with emotion to go on. Roxanne could not decide which it was.

She felt a giggle rising up in her throat at his sudden delicacy, but he was taking far too long.

"You wished to ascertain if they would react favorably to your offers of marriage," she prompted.

"Exactly!" cried Mr. Bentley, and nudged his friend. "See, Tony, you haven't told it right. Miss Winston's a clever 'un."

To end their misery, she concluded for the Earl, "I take it that Melodie and Gemma did not react as you expected. They gave you no reason to hope that your formal offers would be received in a favorable way." This was only what she had feared, though she had dared to hope otherwise.

The gentlemen sighed in unison. "If it were only that, Miss Winston," said the Earl.

Alarm now joined disappointment. "Tell me quickly, please. What have they done?"

"Do not be frightened, Miss Winston — it is nothing so dreadful." Mr. Bentley hastened to comfort her.

Lord Culverton scowled at him, and he subsided. "What I meant to say, Miss Winston, is that they received our confessions of . . . affection . . . in the most insulting manner!"

"Insulting?" Roxanne's heart sank further. The twins surely had no equal in thoroughness.

"Yes, they deplored our characters, told us that they could never unite themselves in the holy bond of matrimony with such dissipated creatures, and that, though we showed some promise of salvation, we should have to travel a long road of repentance before we could consider offering marriage." To do him credit, the Earl looked not angry at this outrage, but only sad.

"The arrogance and impertinence of those children!" cried Roxanne. It was only what she could have expected. Her fault had been in not warning the gentlemen, but how could she know that Melodie and Gemma would carry their prejudices so very far?

"I — I'm sorry that the girls insulted you, but it is too absurd! You mustn't pay the slightest heed to my foolish sisters, gentlemen. They will eventually apologize for such effrontery, and I advise you not to be too quick to forgive. Your offers of marriage do them much honor, and if they cannot see it, then they are not worthy of being your wives."

"Do you mean to say it is *they* who are unworthy of *us?*" asked a confused Mr. Bentley. "And we don't have to tithe, or to make public confession of our faults, or give up cards, drinking, and dancing, the theater—"

"Good heavens, did they demand that you do all of these things before they would marry you?" Laughter threatened, and Roxanne found herself wishing that the Duke had been there—only, of course, because he would appreciate, as few people could, the humor in the situation.

"Yes," admitted the Earl. "And we would have been fools enough to think about doing it, had they asked us from affection rather than pride. You see, Miss Winston . . ." He reddened, and could not meet her eyes.

212

"We are . . . our feelings . . . that is . . ."

"We're in love, ma'am," said Mr. Bentley in his ingenuous way.

Roxanne was touched, and once again angry with her sisters for toying with these honest, earnest boys.

"Gentlemen," she said, "I sincerely regret the pain these silly girls have caused you. I was right. At the moment, they are *not* worthy of you. All of their virtues have not yet taught them to consider the feelings of others. Not of slaves, or prisoners, or the vast unknown poor, but of their immediate neighbors. And though I still believe that they harbor some tender feelings for you, they are not yet ready to be married."

"What do you suggest we do, Miss Winston?" asked the Earl, who looked thoroughly miserable even down to his drooping collar.

"Forget them for a while. Show them that you are offended. Be cool—pay them no compliments, no distinguishing attentions. It will be as if your offers had never been made. After all"—she smiled at the sad faces before her—"you have never approached their father, only their sister, and very informally." She winked. "This conversation never took place."

The men looked at each other. "We'll do it," said Mr. Bentley. "Won't we, Tony?"

The Earl of Culverton sighed. "I see no other way. The young ladies—they *are* very young after all—do not know their own minds. We must leave them to decide—without any more urging from us. Thank you, Miss Winston. Come, Cyril, let's to White's."

Pondering this illuminating interview, Roxanne made her way upstairs to her sisters' chamber.

"Well?" was all she said after knocking and being

bidden to enter.

The girls were seated, Gemma at the dressing table, leaning her elbows on it, her chin propped up in her hands, and Melodie in a chair by the window, some sewing hanging listlessly between her fingers.

"We aren't sorry," said Melodie at once, her chin in the air.

Gemma seemed to gain strength from her twin's show of energy. She raised her head and turned to look at Roxanne, who sat on the edge of the bed.

"No, we are not. We could not possibly be expected to marry them unless they had completely reformed their ways."

Roxanne did not disagree. She knew that to offer opposition would only increase their stubbornness.

"Of course not," she replied quietly. The girls looked at one another in mute surprise.

"No one would expect anything of the kind," Roxanne continued. "Everyone knows that neither of you would be tempted to marry by mere good looks, wealth, and position. Your husbands' characters must of course come first with you. I am happy that you did not encourage those two gentlemen to make offers for you to Papa. He might not have understood as I do."

"But . . . Roxanne, we thought that you *liked* Lord Culverton and Mr. Bentley," said a puzzled Melodie.

"What has that to say to it?" she replied. "They are likable, ordinary young men of their class, but not suitable husbands for such as you, who can see through the civilized veneer to the unredeemed souls beneath."

She glanced up at them from beneath her lashes, hoping she had not gone too far, but the twins were seriously considering what she had said.

While they were digesting it, she continued. "Being the proud, worldly young men they are, they were offended at your making all those conditions, and I had to soothe them as best I could, but of course they could never change sufficiently to be satisfactory husbands for you. If change does not come from within, it means nothing. And within they are—" She stopped to gauge their response. Their gazes rested on her expectantly.

She prepared to deal the final blow. "Well, as you told them—they are all but depraved."

"Not depraved, sister," cried Gemma immediately, no doubt thinking of Mr. Bentley's innocent blue eyes.

"As near as makes no difference," Roxanne asserted. "Drinking, gaming, dancing, theater—who knows with what else they occupy their time? Activities unfit for us to contemplate, no doubt." She affected a slight shudder, and was amused to see that her sisters could contemplate her list of their suitors' sins without a single expression of disgust.

"I fear they have not a single good quality between them. No, you had best take them as they are or not take them at all, for they will always be the men they are now, no matter how many promises of reform you extract from them."

Melodie moved from the window to join her twin. Gemma made room for her on the little bench before the dressing table. "We certainly cannot take them as they are," she said thoughtfully, rubbing her hand gently against the bristles of a silver-backed hairbrush she had absently picked up.

"And Roxanne is right," mused Melodie. "Such confirmed sinners — though they do have many good qualities that you might not have noticed, Roxanne — cannot change simply because we have asked them to."

"No matter how strong their feelings for us," Gemma said in a low voice.

Roxanne pretended to be shocked. "Have they had the audacity to make love to you?"

"Oh, no," cried Gemma. "Though they have made it clear that they hold us in considerable esteem—"

"But they have never importuned us with words of love, Roxanne—"

"—nor attempted any undue familiarity."

Roxanne thought she detected a curious note of regret in these reports. "And of course you have not encouraged them?"

"Certainly not," said Melodie.

"We did not dream of it," added Gemma. For the first time since they had become young ladies, neither of them met their elder sister's glance.

They were all silent. Roxanne could feel the usual silent discussion taking place between them, and waited for the moment when it would be right to ask a delicate question.

"What about *your* feelings? These two gentlemen may be unworthy objects for the affections of young ladies like yourselves, but they are undoubtedly attractive. I would not wish you to suffer any heartache on their accounts."

Roxanne sensed a softening in their attitudes, but Melodie's response was, "We have not allowed ourselves to feel other than a—a sisterly affection for them. Isn't that right, Gemma?"

"Yes," her twin replied miserably.

Roxanne judged it time to become brisk. "Good," she said, getting up. "I am proud of both of you. You have done well." She went to the door, but before she opened it, she turned and said, "By the way, your suitors will trouble you no more. I knew that it would be too painful for you to have to keep repulsing their advances or watching their unsuccessful attempts to reform, so I hinted that they ought to leave you in peace."

The girls were silent, but two pairs of identical dark eyes were absorbing this information with obvious dismay. Roxanne went on, "After all, it is quite customary, when an offer of marriage is refused, to spare both parties the discomfort of any unnecessary intercourse," and left them to meditate on their actions.

She described these scenes in detail to Fanny as they sat working in the morning room in Upper Brook Street the next day, and such was her exasperation with her sisters that she was impelled to end her tale by saying, "And where is that wretched Duke when one needs him?"

Fanny chuckled as she smoothed out a seam. "You sent him off with a flea in his ear, or don't you recall? I'm sure everyone who was present at Almack's at the time could refresh your memory, my dear. They're still talking about it."

Roxanne picked up a bundle of her charity sewing from the little table she had drawn up to the sunny window and flung it at her friend, who caught it neatly. "Don't be impudent. I didn't mean that I had forgotten that awful evening."

"Of course not." Fanny put the bundle aside, tied a knot, and bit off her thread neatly, disdaining her little gold scissors. "What a triumph! The beautiful Miss Winston makes her presence felt by putting the Duke of Rutledge in his place before half the ton — and nearly getting her head bitten off for her pains. Who could forget it? But you don't seem the least bit repentant."

"Of course not. I have told you what I overheard your precious Rutledge tell the Duchess — would you be sorry for having returned the compliment?"

"Oh, Rozzie, I'm sure Harry didn't mean — "

"His meaning was perfectly clear, Fanny. And I have no regrets." She looked down at the coarse linen shirt she was making and found that she had sewn a sleeve upside down. She snatched up Fanny's scissors, cut a thread, and ruthlessly tore open the seams.

She had been dishonest with Fanny; if the truth were to be known, she had many regrets. The night after the scene at Almack's, Roxanne had lain in her bed stiff with nerves, wondering how she could have done such a thing, worrying that she had ruined her sisters' chances by creating a scandal worse than any they had been able to raise, and finding that her satisfaction in replying to the Duke's rudeness in kind had very soon trickled away. She ought to have known better. There was no profit in returning wrong for wrong. Would she never learn to turn the other cheek?

To her usual prayers for patience she now added one that she might one day be able to set down the burden of blame and resentment that she had carried about with her for three years. But this apparently called for more strength than she had.

At such moments Roxanne felt contempt for herself. Why, even the often silly and impractical twins had accepted the Duke, though Alfred was their brother, too. And Geoffrey and Fanny as well — were they all wrong?

Sometimes Rutledge's face swam in her dreams, and in her dreams, as in life, though she had struggled to forget it, his smile melted the stiffness in her spine and the sun itself seemed to stream through his gray eyes straight into her heart. But as in life, in her dreams she shut her eyes to these phenomena and cried, "No, no, murderer, blackguard!" And in these dreams the Duke's face frowned and withdrew, never to be seen again . . . as in life. She had not met him once since that night, though he was still in town.

"What would I say if we met? He would never apologize . . . and he would never forgive me," she murmured.

"Never is a strong word, Roxanne. I think you underestimate His Grace."

She started, having almost forgotten Fanny's presence.

"His Grace? Are you speaking of Rutledge?" Lady Camberwick swept into the room, casting aside her gloves and untying her bonnet. "We have not seen him for a long time, have we, Roxanne?" she said sharply to her niece, and gave the bell cord a fierce pull.

Roxanne looked down. Her aunt had not ceased to be angry with her, though she was nominally forgiven. Every time the twins had gotten into a scrape, her ladyship mourned the absence of the Duke's sobering influence on her two charges. Now she glanced significantly at Roxanne, settled herself in a chair, and put her feet up on a tapestry-worked footstool.

"It is not bad enough, my dear Miss Pearson, that

my niece has offended and driven away her most illustrious marriage prospect, but it seems that the rest of the gentlemen who once might have been brought to the point are gone, too. What have you to say to that, Roxanne?"

Roxanne had nothing to say, as it was unfortunately true. Although she had previously argued with her aunt that the defection by her few suitors had not taken place immediately after the public quarrel with the Duke, but almost two weeks later, she knew that Lady Camberwick would forever connect the two events in her mind.

"Yes," said Fanny with a forced smile, "where is that dear little Mr. Yerton, and the others I used to see squiring you about? Have they all deserted you? That is too bad." To Roxanne, who knew her as well as she knew her own sisters, her friend's teasing manner seemed a trifle artificial.

"Too bad, indeed, Fanny," she replied. As to the sudden loss of suitors, she really did not care, but had wondered about it nevertheless. "I would not have married any of them, you know —"

"No, you would have done nothing to oblige me. And your two foolish sisters have thrown away the very best matches they could possibly make. Have you heard of the absurd replies, my dear Miss Pearson, which my nieces gave to Lord Culverton and Mr. Bentley? What nonsense! To say that they would marry them only on condition of their good behavior!"

Fanny gently replied that Roxanne had told her the story, and she exchanged a look of sympathy with her friend.

Lady Camberwick wrung her hands and gazed heavenward. "Why must I, a decent, sensible woman, be plagued with such nieces?"

No answer was forthcoming, and Roxanne was exchanging a wry glance with Fanny when fortunately the arrival of her maid forced Lady Camberwick to cut short her lamentation. When the servant had collected her bonnet and gloves and had withdrawn, her ladyship turned apologetically to her niece. "I'm sorry, my dear, it's been such a difficult season, and you know how hard I have tried to present the three of you properly."

"Oh, Aunt Maria . . ." Roxanne rose and went to kneel at her aunt's chair. "I never meant to cause you any trouble, it is only that . . . the things I overheard the Duke say about me . . . I could never have danced with him, knowing that he thought he was conferring some great favor upon me, and that he imagined me eager for such attention."

Lady Maria smiled. "You are proud, my child, and I can't blame you for it, though perhaps your sisters would call it a sin. As for your disappearing suitors — well, there is still Geoffrey." She smiled at Fanny.

"Yes, don't forget, Roxanne, there is still Geoffrey." Fanny's smile was uneasy.

Lady Camberwick did not appear to notice. "Tell us, child, how does your poor aunt? Such a shocking story! First her son dead, then her husband taken ill."

Fanny said slowly, "We — we have heard that my uncle is no worse . . . but no better."

Roxanne again divined some awkwardness in her friend's manner, and intercepted a swift glance from her. Fanny looked away again immediately. What on earth was troubling her? Fanny, however, left soon after, so Roxanne had no opportunity for a private conversation with her friend.

Her puzzlement only increased in the next few days. Fanny seemed to be avoiding her, and Geoffrey, to her relief, no longer plagued her with a daily proposal. Instead he went about wearing a look she could only interpret as complacent. Her other acquaintances of the male sex, however, behaved in the oddest fashion.

She met Mr. Yerton one morning as she descended from her aunt's carriage in Bond Street. He uncovered his head, made his bow, and bade her good morning, but with nothing like his usual easy manner.

By this time Roxanne felt there was definitely a mystery afoot, and her impatience with it overcame her training. She said without preamble, "We haven't seen you for a long time, Mr. Yerton. Have you been away? I hope there is nothing amiss."

"Oh, no, Miss Winston . . . that is, I have been quite busy . . . looking to set up a new carriage and team, you know . . . meeting with coachmakers, looking over the stock at Tattersall's . . . I'm quite well, Miss Winston, very kind of you to ask . . ."

Roxanne smiled, attempting to put him at his ease. "Why kind? I thought we were friends, Mr. Yerton."

At this the young man's embarrassment only increased. He looked about him as if afraid of being overheard, and his face reddened. "You know, of course, Miss Winston, that you would have only had to say the word and . . . but now, you know . . ." He became incoherent, and all Roxanne could make out was a whispered ". . . very happy, I'm sure," before he bowed once more and left her.

The next few days brought no solution to this mystery. At a musicale none of her accustomed admirers so much as offered to find her a good seat from which to hear the performers. Fortunately Lord Wynne was capable of adequately attending to three ladies, and saw her to a comfortable seat with the twins, whose escort he was.

The girls had been persuaded with difficulty that listening to secular music was not sinful, and Lord Wynne, who seemed to have taken their original advice to heart, had left off much of his bad language and boasting and proved to be a most attentive, though not entertaining, companion.

Since the Earl of Culverton and his friend had immediately obeyed Roxanne's advice, Lord Wynne had stepped into the place vacated by the rejected pair. His main disadvantage, Roxanne thought wryly, was that there was only one of him, and neither twin seemed to regard him as anything but a useful object.

Roxanne duly noted how their eyes searched the room for a sight of their erstwhile suitors, and how, once these gentlemen were located, the girls hurriedly turned away. She hoped she had not put matters *too* strongly. Eventually her plan must work, if there was a grain of affection between either couple.

However, as the evening progressed from musical diversion to conversation and refreshments, her own odd situation began to trouble Roxanne more than the twins' dilemma.

Again, she found herself deserted by former admirers—greeted, but not otherwise noticed by gentlemen who once would have at least stopped to exchange a few pleasantries. Geoffrey himself had breezed in during the last performance, an aria by a large foreign lady with many quavering chins, and though his hostess had frowned at him, he had barely waited till the applause was ended before attaching himself to Roxanne.

But Geoffrey's presence at her side, she recalled, had never before stopped any of her admirers from addressing her. Perhaps, she thought, it was only that the truth about her lack of fortune had filtered down to them all at last. Not that anyone had thought her an heiress, but perhaps all the dismal details had not been public knowledge until now.

Could Geoffrey have . . . ? But in a second she dismissed the thought, ashamed. Geoffrey would not stoop to broadcasting the fact that she was penniless, simply to stop her from being courted by eligible gentlemen.

Still, she searched his face many times that evening, and weighed his lightest word. But he seemed just as usual, and treated her with only the familiarity and respect that their long intimacy justified. He did not appear to notice that he had no longer to compete for her attention with the other young men.

The next evening the Winstons and Lady Camberwick were all engaged for a large dinner party at the townhouse of the Countess of Culverton, the scene of the twins' first social disaster. The Earl and his friend were not present, his mother explaining that his lordship had been engaged to dine elsewhere.

Roxanne was encouraged to see her sisters' faces fall at this news. They had been unusually irritable all day, and had taken unaccustomed pains over their dress, a good sign, she thought. And it would be salutary for them to be balked a little. It was only now that their gallants were ignoring them had they learned to miss those attentions.

But Roxanne's own difficulties distracted her again, for tonight, as on other recent occasions, men whom she once had counted on as enjoyable companions did not do more than politely inquire after her health. She was startled by one young man, whose company she had enjoyed mainly because he was capable of talking nothing but nonsense, who this evening greeted her by whispering solemnly that he hoped she would be very happy.

"Well, I certainly hope to be," she replied. But before she could question him as to this sudden concern for her happiness he was gone to talk agreeable nonsense to some other young lady.

Geoffrey, meanwhile, was more like his old self than ever before. He gossiped comfortably with her, and amused her at dinner, during which he was seated at her side, by pithy critiques on the evening toilettes of the ladies seated opposite.

Roxanne, by way of experiment, looked up at him through her lashes as she sipped her wine. "And what have you to say, sir, about *my* gown?"

With a graceful gesture she indicated her white and gold sarcenet with its gathered overskirt and demure gold ruching. Her glance and voice were as flirtatious as she could make them, and for a moment she regretted her impulse, for a little flame kindled in Geoffrey's eyes, but he only smiled and said, "You look very well, my dear. You know I admire your taste. Such simplicity suits you." He uttered this, however, with an almost proprietary air.

It was very odd indeed, thought Roxanne.

She did not see Geoffrey again for a few days, and

neither did Fanny make an appearance. It had been raining all week, and Roxanne was kept at home tending to her father, who suffered a sudden bilious attack, but she prevailed upon her aunt to send a servant to call at the Broughtons' to inquire after her friends.

The footman returned, reporting that the house was shuttered and hung with black crepe and the family all gone off suddenly to a funeral in Hampshire two nights ago.

"Depend upon it," said Lady Camberwick, as she and Roxanne whiled away the wet June day with backgammon, letter writing, and embroidery, "it is some ancient relative whom no one has heard of these twenty years past, and they will curtail their mourning and be back in town tomorrow."

But Roxanne wondered, recalling that an uncle of Fanny's had been ill. The next day proved Lady Camberwick partially right, for though it was not a *distant* relative whose demise had called the Pearsons away from London, that very evening brought their return, as a note from Fanny, delivered after dinner, informed Roxanne.

It was cryptic, only informing her that there had been a sudden death in the family, and that though they would be in mourning, she and Geoffrey had decided to remain in town for the rest of the season and see only a few friends very quietly.

Therefore Roxanne was not at all surprised that an early caller had been announced in Upper Brook Street while she was finishing her breakfast the next day. Still sleepy, she only heard the name "Pearson" and, assuming it was Fanny, told the servant she would see the caller alone in the morning room.

She was the only occupant of the house able to receive callers, since her father was still feeling ill, the twins had not come down yet, and her aunt rarely left her chamber before noon. But she wished she had called one of the maids to sit with her, for the Pearson she found in the morning room was not Fanny, but Geoffrey.

His blond hair was carefully arranged, his suit of mourning perfectly fitted. His face was pale, solemn, and bore telltale signs of a night's overindulgence, but was lit from within by some strong emotion. All this Roxanne had barely taken in before he rushed to her and took both of her hands in his, pressing them against his chest.

"My darling, there is no reason to wait an instant longer. From this moment we can be considered betrothed, and the wedding will be as soon as we can decently manage it, considering my poor uncle's death—"

"Geoffrey, wait, please . . . I don't understand—"

He brought her hands to his lips and kissed them one at a time. "My poor dear, of course not—I have startled you, rattling on in this absurd fashion, but oh, Rozzie, we have waited so long, and we needn't wait any longer."

Finally Roxanne managed to withdraw her hands from his fervent grasp, to bring her own emotions under control, and to ask him quietly to sit down. She felt as though she had been thrust into the center of a whirlwind, and it was some time before Geoffrey could make her understand that he was now quite rich and that, therefore, they could be married.

"I—you never mentioned anything about the possibility of an inheritance," Roxanne said, forestalling the inevitable. For no sooner had his meaning become clear to her than some inner voice had told her what she must do.

"Because I wasn't my uncle's heir until my cousin died, my dear," he replied. "I understand your surprise — it's a very unexpected reversal of fortune — but it has made me the happiest man in the world — or will, when you name the day for our marriage."

Roxanne simply looked at him, wishing herself anywhere but where she was. It had not occurred to her that she would ever have to seriously consider marrying Geoffrey, and now that the moment had come, she could no longer take refuge in the plea of their mutual poverty. But though her heart told her that, fond as she was of him, she could not be his wife, she knew not how to give him his answer.

Seeing her uncertainty, Geoffrey grew puzzled. Slowly the joy faded from his face. "Roxanne," he said, "why do you hesitate? All along you have said — "

" — all along I have said that I could not marry you." She trembled a little under his unflinching gaze, though she knew that she was doing right. Her voice grew stronger. "Nothing has changed in that respect, Geoffrey. I shall always be grateful for the honor you — "

"Don't mouth that worn-out sentence to me, Roxanne!" Geoffrey had risen and now stood over her, his face distorted from its usual amiable expression. "How could you have deceived me like this? You are all I have ever wanted, and are all but promised to me."

Now it was Roxanne's turn to be angry. "You insult me, sir, by implying that I have been false to some promise which was never made! You have asked for my hand in marriage a hundred times since you returned to England and a hundred times I have declined. Although your lack of fortune was an impediment, I never once said that, immediately upon remedying that situation, I would be your wife."

Geoffrey sat down next to her on the sofa and took possession of her hands again. Now his manner was apologetic, but Roxanne shivered at the hardness behind his gaze. "I — I'm sorry, Roxanne, I didn't mean . . . but you always led me to believe that it was only fortune that prevented you from accepting me, and now I lay a fortune at your feet, and you refuse it! I always thought that you loved me."

Roxanne felt the heat rise to her face, and knew it was very pink. She evaded Geoffrey's gaze, but allowed him to retain hold of her hands. Indeed, she doubted whether he would let go of them without a struggle. "Although you are a dear friend, and I care a great deal for you, I do not . . . I have never said that I loved you, Geoffrey — not as a wife should love a husband."

For a second she thought he was going to crush her hands, but at her soft cry Geoffrey appeared to recollect himself. He let go of her, turned away, and rested his face in his own hands.

"I have been a fool," was the first thing he said after a long period of silence. Roxanne had sat very still, pained because she knew she had hurt him, but knowing in her heart that she had every right to refuse him. One could not break a promise that had never been made. An insistent voice within her cried out that she was not intended to marry Geoffrey Pearson.

"No, Geoffrey, you are not a fool. You are a very

charming, accomplished, and amiable young man, and you deserve every penny of your new fortune. I wish you — I *sincerely* wish you joy of it," said Roxanne, bending over him, touching his shoulder lightly. "However, though I hope we will always be friends, I could not be so dishonest as to share that fortune with you under false pretenses."

Geoffrey looked up. The dissipation of the night before was even more noticeable now in his angry dishevelment. The whites of his eyes were shot through with red, and dark circles ringed them. His neckcloth and collar were crumpled, and he swallowed as though his mouth was very dry. His voice, however, was now clear, and very cold.

"You do not understand, Roxanne. In the eyes of the world . . . that is, in the eyes of many of my friends and acquaintances, and many of yours . . . we are already betrothed." He ignored her outcry of astonishment and went on. "Oh, yes, it is true. Perhaps you wondered at your sudden dearth of admirers? I considered myself completely justified, based on your avowals of affection for me, my dear, to anticipate our betrothal when I learned that my uncle was dangerously ill and I stood a chance to inherit. I wanted to be certain of you, and to cut those other fellows out, just in case one of them might be on the way to capturing your heart. It was a reckless wager, now I know. Although I will have won the fortune, I will have forfeited the respect of everyone when it is known that you have broken our engagement."

Roxanne stood up, her eyes glittering with tears. "You have certainly forfeited my respect, sir, and any esteem I once had for you as well, by this shabby trick.

It is unworthy of you, Geoffrey! How could you have done such a thing?"

Geoffrey grew reckless. "You are angry because I chased away your rich suitors? Then come, recoup your losses and marry me, for I assure you, I am now quite as rich as your Mr. Yerton, or any of them!"

"I have every right to be angry, but it is not for the reason you believe. You have employed my name to tell a tremendous falsehood, and before you were even sure you would be offering for me. That is what I find unforgivable."

"I never thought you would refuse. I thought you loved me."

His tone was piteous now, but Roxanne did not relent. "And I thought you were my friend. It seems we were both deceived."

Geoffrey stared at her with all the rage of disappointed pride and love in his eyes, lunged for the door, and stalked out of the room, slamming the door with a resounding crash behind him.

Roxanne's legs suddenly felt too weak to support her, and she all but fell onto the sofa. How could Geoffrey, whom she had trusted, have descended to such dishonesty and trickery? His only excuse was that he loved her, but she could not honor his feelings if they affected his judgment so adversely.

She sat quietly and attempted to calm herself, examining her own part in the affair. It was not the loss of her suitors that enraged her; these, she knew, would soon have ceased to buzz about her once they learned of her poverty. And though Geoffrey, to be sure, would have willingly married her on his own slender income, he had no right to abuse her friendship by involving her in rumors of a betrothal when she had not consented to marry him.

She had just decided to dash off a note to Fanny, whose counsel she desperately craved, when she heard quick, decisive footsteps approaching the door. She turned, expecting to see one of her sisters or the housekeeper, perhaps, come to see what all the noise was about. Instead, she saw the Duke of Rutledge, and all her painfully acquired calm dissolved instantly.

He stood poised for a moment in the doorway, dressed in a well-tailored dark green riding costume, handsome but much bespattered with mud. He had removed his hat, and his dark hair, slightly rumpled, was pushed back from his broad forehead. His eyes shone, his cheeks were flushed from exercise.

Roxanne's impression was that his visit was an impulsive one, an impression that was proved true as he spoke with something less than his usual confidence and without so much as a "good morning."

"I've been riding, but I couldn't keep away—only tell me if Pearson has been to see you yet—if he has not, I will disturb you no longer."

Roxanne was too startled to speak for a moment. Finally she managed to say, "Your Grace—I do not know to what I owe the honor this visit, but please, sit down, and I shall ring for some refreshments."

Roxanne took refuge in the time-honored phrases of hospitality, lest he see how his sudden entrance had affected her. Then, too, she did not want to receive him alone.

He was beside her in a moment, staying her hand on the bell pull.

"No, thank you. I simply wish to know if

Geoffrey—" He stopped, took a breath, and continued speaking with somewhat less urgency. "—has Mr. Pearson paid you a visit yet this morning, Miss Winston?"

Finally Roxanne raised her glance to his. He was outwardly composed now, but there was a strange tension about him that she could not understand.

"Why, yes, Geoffrey left only a few minutes before you arrived. In fact, I am surprised you did not meet him at the door."

Once he heard her say that Geoffrey had been there, it seemed to Roxanne as though the Duke heard not another word.

"Pardon me if I seem to be prying into areas that are none of my concern, but as you will soon realize, it is of the greatest importance to me. Did he—has he once more asked you to be his wife?"

Roxanne flushed and looked away. "Your Grace! I really do not see that this is any—"

"I beg of you, Miss Winston, humor the fancy of a much-indulged aristocrat who is accustomed to having even his most absurd questions answered," she heard him say in a less serious tone.

Roxanne could almost imagine his smile. When he touched her shoulder and she turned to face him once more, she found that her imagination had been quite accurate. There was still a keen edge to him, but he had himself well under control now.

She drew a long, shaky breath. "Very well, my lord. Yes, Geoffrey did propose once again. I assume that you know he has inherited a substantial fortune."

"Yes, yes," he replied, waving away this inconsequential matter. "I have heard all about it. But only tell me—what was your answer this time?" His voice was gentle, as if he thought he might frighten her.

Roxanne was amazed at his sudden interest in her answer to Geoffrey, and her heart slowly picked up its pace at the very extraordinary look in his eyes. They seemed to be trying to see right through to her heart. She had meant to tell him roundly that it was none of his affair, but she simply could not.

"I—I have refused him."

He moved closer to her and instinctively she stepped back, frightened by the sudden change in his expression.

His Grace seemed not to notice her fear. "Then, my dear Miss Winston," he said softly, "I wish you would do me the honor of becoming *my* wife."

Roxanne thought for a moment that she must be going mad. It was simply not possible that the Duke of Rutledge, her old enemy, with whom she had exchanged bitter blows before a scandalized audience only a few weeks ago in Almack's assembly rooms, should now be offering for her!

But he was not waiting for her reply. Words tumbled out from between his lips while his glance remained fixed on her face. "If you should have accepted Geoffrey—and nothing would have been more natural, of course—I would have gone away and never referred to the matter again. Or if he had not yet had his chance—and the boy deserves it, after wooing you so persistently—I should have stepped aside and left him to his business. But since you have refused him, knowing that he can now offer you and your family a comfortable life—"

"I do not understand, my lord, not at all!" was all

Roxanne could say.

The sound of her voice seemed to break some kind of spell that had laid hold of the Duke, and some of the tension left his face. "Of course not, my dear, how could you? I have never led you to believe that you would ever hear a proposal of marriage from my lips, in spite of that kiss we once shared. Yet here I am."

He came closer still, and Roxanne, feeling the sofa against the back of her knees, could not retreat any further. He rested his hands gently on her shoulders. "Miss Winston — Roxanne —" He seemed to like the sound of her name on his lips, and repeated it softly while he gathered her trembling form into his arms. "I have been a damned fool, and perhaps I am still behaving like one, when for all I know you still hate me, and blame me. But my mother was right, you know, you are the perfect wife for me, and I am vain enough to suppose that I might be the perfect husband for you."

"And you always do as your mother suggests, do you not?" said Roxanne, with difficulty wriggling out of his arms. "First I am to dance with you, and now to marry you. It is a pity, Your Grace, that your mother did not teach you as pretty a speech on the second occasion as she apparently did on the first."

"Roxanne!" It was a cry from his heart, but it did not soften Roxanne. The arrogance of the man, blithely coming and informing her that he was fulfilling his mother's instructions, without a word of love! What she would have said if he had claimed to love her, Roxanne did not know. She only knew that he had managed to make her feel wretched once more.

The exact reason for her wretchedness she refused to contemplate. It was enough that he had offered her such a graceless proposal, and on the heels of her suffering over Geoffrey, it was too much to bear quietly.

This time she did manage to get to the bell pull and ring, but as she did so, the Duke swung about and caught her in his arms.

"You bear your grudges very prettily, my dear, but perhaps I can satisfy you that I mean to make full amends for those hurtful words of mine the night we almost danced together."

With that he pulled her closer and kissed her mouth, expertly and with the utmost persuasiveness, and while being subjected to these practiced delights Roxanne, in the intervals when she could think at all, only hoped that the servant would not answer her ring at this inopportune moment.

In her hurt and confusion she clung to Rutledge and was strangely comforted by the closeness of his strong warm body. Despite her determination not to give in to such inducements, she enjoyed the experience of being kissed with such thoroughness, but after he had slowly released her it was as if she stood alone in an icy wind.

Rutledge was looking down at her with satisfaction and triumph, assured of his answer, and Roxanne could not bear to let herself be subject to his pride again.

It was plain, despite his protestations, that he did not love her, that he was merely ready to marry and sought to please his mother and please himself by marrying the sister of the man he had offended, salving his conscience and making amends for his crimes to the Winston family.

As she searched for the proper words to rid him of

this delusion, Roxanne sternly ignored the turmoil in her breast, and put off any examination of her own feelings, so eager was she for him to be gone. She trembled inwardly lest he take her in his arms again.

Rutledge saw the unrelenting look on her face and stepped back. His disappointment was evident. For a moment he looked like a schoolboy deprived of some promised treat, and Roxanne felt a pang of remorse, but quickly strengthened herself.

"You know that I will not marry you, my lord, and you know very well why. You may make love like an angel, but to me you will always be as the—" She felt her color rise again and could not finish the sentence.

"Very well expressed, my dear, and thank you for the compliment. Said like a lady, although you almost allowed yourself to be carried away."

While Roxanne burned at having made such a fatal admission, she saw the strange manner that had possessed him disappear. Observing his sardonic smile and the new hardness in his gray eyes, she found it difficult to believe that Rutledge had actually meant seriously anything he had said to her during the interview. He bowed deeply, almost as one would to royalty, and swept up his hat.

Before he passed through the door, however, almost colliding with the tardy footman who was rushing in, he turned and said, "I thank you for a most illuminating conversation, Miss Winston. My compliments to Lady Camberwick and your father." And then he was gone, before Roxanne could even order the servant to show him out.

She brushed past the astonished footman and hurried up to her room, where she closeted herself for some hours, declining all offers of entertainment and fending off worried inquiries from her aunt and sisters. When she emerged, in time for her afternoon engagements, she had rigorously searched her soul and conscience, and was satisfied that she had been a complete fool.

She had had two unexceptionable offers, and had turned them both down, out of pique, or vanity, or girlish fancies. She had been selfish. She had not thought of her father, or her four sisters, or of anything except herself. Lady Maria would chastise her severely when she found out, as she eventually would. And how could she ever face Fanny again? Geoffrey would be sure to carry his resentment home, and she would lose two good friends.

As for the Duke, he would surely slight her and all her family. Perhaps it would even mean the end of his mother's friendship with Aunt Maria. Oh, you detestable, sinful, stupid creature, Roxanne scolded herself. Think of the people who would have been made happy by your acceptance of either offer.

But though she vowed, if given a chance, to make amends to Geoffrey somehow, she felt as though she had escaped a very dangerous fate by turning down the Duke of Rutledge's offer. His kisses were now so completely burned into her memory that for days afterward she could still feel the imprint of them on her lips.

Chapter Ten

Rutledge retrieved his reins from the urchins who had been holding his horse for him, tossed them a few more pennies, and swung into the saddle to resume his interrupted ride. But even as he headed for the park he knew he should not bother to attempt it. At this hour it would be impossible to find space for a good gallop, and no mere ambling among the fashionables would satisfy him now. He wished he had not let himself get so carried away as to actually present himself in Upper Brook Street, boots, mud, and all, for he might have known what reception he would get.

After Geoffrey Pearson had left him the evening before, the Duke had been tortured by regrets and odd impulses concerning Miss Winston. Her face haunted him all night. He moved like a sleepwalker through drawing rooms, ballrooms, and card rooms, and when he found himself back at his lodgings he could not remember whom he had met or what he had said.

Toward dawn he had found himself lying awake, picturing Roxanne as Geoffrey's bride, picturing Alfred Winstons's happy face when he came home to find his sister betrothed to his old friend. No doubt all concerned would rejoice at the marriage.

But Rutledge persisted in imagining that Roxanne would not be as happy as everyone else. To his knowledge, she had never expressed any real regret that circumstances prevented a marriage between herself and Geoffrey Pearson. Perhaps she would accept him only out of duty, or friendship.

Not that she could have been expected to confide such things to him — she had flatly told him not to interfere in the matter — but the Duke could not help feeling that Miss Winston did not love Geoffrey Pearson. This thought for some reason provoked him, and he bounded out of bed, bellowing for his valet. Shortly thereafter he was dressed in his riding clothes and on his way to the park.

But once there, his pleasure in the cool morning air, clear and sweet now after days of rain, dissolved. Mud flew up from the path, spotting his boots and breeches and his horse's legs and flanks. He rode just long enough for the animal to shake off its fidgets, and decided to go home, but on his way he recollected that at this very moment Geoffrey Pearson might be in Upper Brook Street making a formal offer for Roxanne.

Anxiety churned in his stomach. It was nonsensical, he told himself, but he could not forget the feel of her in his arms, even as he could not forget her accusing face as she tore into him at Almack's. The girl could not hate him forever, he knew, and once Alfred . . . but no, he could not take advantage of any change in her feelings when the truth about his dealings with her brother became known.

She must learn to judge him on his own merits. He had been at some pains to make these known to her ever since she had nursed him back to health in Wiltshire, but now he acknowledged with a rueful smile

240

that perhaps he had gone about it in the wrong way. Of course it was too soon to expect her to have changed her mind about him, but if he did not make the attempt now it might be forever too late.

Before he knew it, the Duke found that he had turned his horse toward Lady Camberwick's house. And having made a complete and utter fool of himself at the ensuing interview, he angrily betook himself home, glad that both the end of the season and the end of his pose as the instrument of Alfred Winston's ruin were fast approaching.

Though Roxanne said not a word to anyone, and naively assumed that Geoffrey and Rutledge would be equally reticent, it took no longer than twenty-four hours for her family and the rest of the world to become acquainted with the occurrences which had taken place in the morning room. She had hoped to be left at peace for some time longer, there having been no witnesses to the morning's adventure except for the servants, but the very next morning the twins burst into her room wearing accusatory faces.

"Roxanne, we must speak with you," said Melodie, fixing her with a solemn glance.

Roxanne raised her eyebrows to remind her sisters of the presence of Lady Camberwick's maid, who was engaged in dressing her hair, and the girls subsided until this operation was completed. The servant had scarcely left the room when Gemma burst out, "How could you refuse him, dear sister? Did you not think of your duty to the family?"

Not certain to which "him" her sister referred, Roxanne took advantage of the moment to remind the twins of their own dereliction of duty. "I suppose that though you two may turn down eligible offers, I have been too long on the shelf to be permitted such a privilege?"

Gemma murmured an apology, but Melodie said, "It is not at all the same thing, Roxanne. Why, you have said yourself that you are not as particular about character nor as devout as we are. Setting aside his lack of Christian faith and his lack of fortune, he was an unexceptionable suitor. And now he is very rich, so you ought to have accepted him, and by your example brought him to salvation."

Roxanne knew a moment of relief that it was not her *other* eligible suitor the twins had fixed on. Evidently they did not know of that much more advantageous offer. But though she had soon explained to them that her lack of proper feeling for Geoffrey made it unfair to him to accept his offer, and would not contribute to his happiness, she was brought up short by their next question.

"And what about the Duke?" Melodie wanted to know.

"Do you mean Rutledge?" she stalled, adjusting her already perfectly arranged gown.

"Really, Roxanne, with what other Duke are we intimately acquainted? Did he not also call yesterday morning? What did he say? Did he come to apologize after all this time?"

Now Roxanne could at least take satisfaction in knowing that Rutledge had not immediately announced his failed proposal to the world, as Geoffrey must have done. But then, she though wryly, His Grace was too proud to make such news public. Just as she was thinking how lucky she was that the twins did not know of the Duke's proposal, the door to her chamber flew open and an agitated Lady Camberwick rustled in.

"How could you have refused him, Roxanne? Have you no gratitude, no sense of—"

"Just what we were telling her, ma'am," sang Gemma, while Roxanne examined her aunt's countenance for a clue as to who the "him" was in this case. The extreme rage depicted there could only mean one thing.

"A *Duke,* of all things, and his mama one of my dearest friends! I hope, at least, that you did not insult him. In fact, with the way you have been treating him, I am shocked at his offering for you at all. You have bitterly disappointed me, my girl."

"I cannot imagine how it is that the entire house can know of these things, which took place in complete privacy," Roxanne cried, unable to tolerate a moment's more scolding. "And you need not worry, Aunt Maria, I did not insult the Duke. It was quite the other way around." She was instantly sorry she had said as much, for the twins looked shocked, while Lady Camberwick merely looked curious, and this mitigated her anger.

"There, now, my dear, do not upset yourself. I daresay it was not quite proper for him to approach you alone without first consulting your papa, but rank has its privileges, you know, and though Rutledge's character, despite what some people may think, is quite unimpeachable, he does have a tendency to dispense with the proprieties on rare occasions."

Roxanne was tempted to inform her aunt that these

243

occasions were not so rare as she might believe, but she knew she had already said too much.

"And as for Mr. Pearson," her aunt went on, while Roxanne groaned, realizing that Providence had entirely forsaken her, "now that he has a respectable fortune he would be an ideal husband, though I quite understand, my dear, if you feel that he is too close a friend to be a husband. That might be awkward," she admitted with a complete disregard for the younger generation's idea of connubial bliss. "No, my only real regret is for Rutledge, and I hope that when your family is bankrupt and the twins have to go out as governesses and the little girls are put in a charity school, you will be very sorry for what you have done! If I know the Duke, he will not ask twice."

"That is the difference between me and His Grace, Aunt Maria. Should he ask a second time, I would be very happy to give him the same answer!" Roxanne suddenly found herself fighting back tears, and her own refuge being occupied by three self-righteous and displeased females, she fled the room, seeking solace in a sunny window of the morning room, where she put pen to paper and begged Fanny to come to her. She would have gone to the Broughtons' herself, but she feared meeting Geoffrey there.

Lady Camberwick departed in a huff on a shopping expedition without another word to her niece, and Roxanne managed to avoid the twins until Fanny arrived. Then, over ratafia and sweet biscuits, she poured out her tale into the ears of her friend, who seemed strangely embarrassed and did not dispense her usual bracing advice.

When Roxanne reached the point of explaining the

deception of Geoffrey's which had rid her of her few suitors, Fanny's agitation increased, and finally she cried, "Please do not go on. I knew—or rather I suspected that he was up to some such rig, and I was afraid to question him about it. But I should have, for you sake. It was only that I hoped it wasn't true."

Roxanne was immediately enlightened on the subject of her friend's awkwardness at last meeting. "You are forgiven, Fanny, because it would not have made a difference. I might not have believed it of Geoffrey then, and you and I might have quarreled over it. And I am so sorry if I hurt him."

"But he should never have told such a lie," Fanny protested. "It was insufferable of him to expect you to fall into his arms just because he had acquired a fortune, as if you were some mercenary creature."

But Roxanne barely heard her. "Perhaps he will give me the chance to make it up to him," she mused. "But you see, Fanny, I realized I didn't love him. Once perhaps I thought I could, but there seemed no way we could ever be married, and I never allowed myself to feel more than I should."

"I quite understand, my dear," Fanny assured her in sympathetic tones. "I tried quite desperately not to fall in love with Alfred when I knew my parents would not consent to our marriage, but it happened anyway. Now *you* are a very different case—so careful, so determined to be good—it is no wonder that you simply could not love Geoffrey, after forbidding yourself for so long."

This odd philosophy somewhat comforted Roxanne, and she felt calm enough to move on to reporting the second interview of that fateful morning. Fanny listened in growing wonder.

"If I did not know you for a completely truthful girl, Roxanne Winston, I should not believe it! Harry to ask for your hand, after you had publicly refused to dance with him? And you allowed him to kiss you? At least one of you is mad, though I'm not sure to whom the honor should go."

"I didn't allow him to kiss me, Fanny," said Roxanne crossly and with little regard for truth, "he just did. And it was not the first time." Relieved at having such a matter-of-fact confidante, she revealed her previous amorous episode with the Duke.

Fanny smiled. "He must be in love with you."

"Nonsense." Roxanne was now sorry she had said anything.

"Well, though Rutledge has a reputation of sorts, he has never been known to trifle with an innocent girl's affections in that way. Therefore his heart must be seriously affected."

"He said nothing about love, Fanny. He simply said that his mother thought I would be a suitable wife and that he had begun to agree with her. Of course I said no, and he soon became his old self, bowing himself out in the haughtiest fashion."

"You were right to say no," Fanny remarked, to Roxanne's complete surprise. She had been prepared for some argument on her friend's part, as that young lady had spent many an hour defending the Duke to her.

"I am glad you think so, Fanny," she replied uncertainly.

"Of course. It is exactly the same case as with Geoffrey. You do not love Harry either, and your principles are far too high to allow you to accept him merely for material advantage, even if it would make you a Duchess and relieve your father of any anxiety about the future. You could not stoop so low as to marry your brother's murderer."

"No, certainly not," Roxanne said faintly. "Of course he is not really a murderer, though I may have said so when I was angry and grieving. He certainly has some deep character faults, and he did lead Alfred astray, but His Grace is not all bad. He is quite generous to the Charitable Society, you know, and Lady Allenbrook is his aunt and thinks highly of him."

She told the story of how His Grace would not advertise this connection, for fear his reputation as a man of the world would harm his aunt's religious enterprises. Fanny was delighted but, to Roxanne surprise, did not launch into further praise of the Duke, as she might once have done.

"You are right, perhaps you are no longer justified in thinking of him as a murderer," Fanny said. She gave Roxanne an inscrutable glance. "But as a possible husband —"

"We simply should not suit," Roxanne said quickly, blushing at the memory of how well suited she had felt when in his arms.

"You are very right to think so," Fanny assured her. "Now, before I forget, Margaret wants all of you to come and dine with us on Friday, just a small family dinner, because of the mourning, and you Winstons are almost part of the family — oh, I'm sorry, I shouldn't have —" She interrupted herself, seeing Roxanne's stricken look. "But you will have to face Geoffrey sooner or later, you know, and I shall see to it that

247

he behaves himself."

"Very well," said Roxanne reluctantly, "I shall ask my aunt. I do not think we are engaged for dinner, although we have a ball afterward."

"Oh, yes, Lady Marchison's, the last really exciting ball of the season," said Fanny regretfully. "Well, it is bound to be a shocking squeeze, and I daresay no one will miss Geoffrey and me. We're getting ready to leave for Wiltshire soon anyway. The family can't wait to hear what Geoffrey's plans are for improving Rosemark, and to know all the details of his inheritance. Will you be going home soon?"

"I suppose we will, not having accomplished what we came here to do." Gloom settled over Roxanne's features. "There isn't much more time to get the twins and their two admirers together, and I have been so overwhelmed by my own problems I have barely given a thought to them lately."

She explained what stratagems she had employed to change her sisters' minds about the "sinful" gentlemen who had offered for them.

"How clever." Fanny cast her an inscrutable glance. "I should never have thought of it. I daresay before you return home the girls will have thought better of refusing those offers, if only you can induce his lordship and Mr. Bentley to repeat them."

The next day, with this thought in mind, Roxanne dispatched notes to the gentlemen in question, asking them to come to see her in the afternoon. She knew that the twins would be busy at Lady Allenbrook's, and it was high time she made further plans for overcoming the girls' objections to their lovelorn beaux.

In order that she might have some evidence of a

change of heart to offer the two gentlemen, she gently interrogated her sisters that morning.

"I can hardly believe that the season is almost over, and none of us are going home successful," she remarked at breakfast, where the three of them were alone.

There was no response from the girls, although they exchanged a glance over their coffee cups.

"To be sure, we were all given the chance," Roxanne continued, selecting a roll. "It is a pity the offers were so unsuitable. But perhaps we are to blame as well. I do not think any of us tried hard enough," she said, trying to look guilty.

Melodie looked a little relieved, having apparently expected a scold. "You are right, Roxanne, and I have often prayed for forgiveness because in the past weeks, I have neglected the purpose for which I was sent here." She put down her cup with a little chatter.

Gemma hurriedly swallowed a bite of ham. "But sister, we have done God's work, you know, as best we could," she protested.

Melodie screwed up her pink mouth in a frown. "Of course we have, but in carrying out our heavenly Father's will, we have forgotten the task our earthly father had laid upon us and that, too, is God's will."

Roxanne could imagine her father's chuckles, had he been present, to learn that his paternal requests were regarded as the will of the Lord.

Gemma, whose face had worn a peevish look all morning, put down her fork with finality, and gave a haughty sniff. "Oh, stuff! It isn't as though we attracted no suitors at all, Melodie. Why, if you had not discouraged me I'm sure I could have induced Lord

Wynne to offer for me."

Melodie laughed a trifle bitterly. "Nonsense. You know that if he seemed to show any preference at all, it was for me. It was I who listened to his wretched poetry."

Gemma's cheeks turned bright pink, while Roxanne looked on in wonder and amusement. "Poetry! Then how could you scold me for allowing him to teach me that French song?"

"If you had paid more attention to Miss Lynchard during our French lessons, my dear little sister," said Melodie with all the superiority of one who was five minutes older, "you would have realized how shocking the lyrics were, and have refused to allow him to sing it with you!"

"Oh! You . . . you hypocrite!" Gemma's lips trembled in anger. The silverware rattled as she brought her small fist down on the table.

"My dear girls! Please do calm yourselves," Roxanne begged. She had never seen them suffer a moment's disagreement since their mother's death, and did not wish to encourage it, though the result was quite illuminating. She made an attempt to steer them toward the most important matter.

"I'm sure you both agree that Lord Wynne is hardly a worthy subject for such a heated argument. Why, if you thought Lord Culverton and Mr. Bentley sinful, I do not see how you can even consider Lord Wynne as a suitor, when he is much, much worse."

"*I* could never bring myself to marry him," said Melodie loftily, "it is Gemma who thinks that she could have enticed him, and she is certainly welcome to him, if she wishes to so degrade herself."

"For my part, Roxanne, I might have been persuaded to accept Cyril's offer," cried Gemma, looking daggers at her twin. "It was Melodie's idea that he was not good enough for me."

"My idea? It was you who suggested that we accept his lordship and Mr. Bentley only on condition that they reform their ways."

Gemma snorted. *"I?* Do not be so foolish, Melodie. You were the one who said from the beginning that they were unworthy, and that we must tolerate them for Aunt Maria's sake, so that she would see that we were not being uncooperative."

"But if you had not encouraged me to be so strict with them," said Melodie, tears shining in her eyes, "we might *both* have been betrothed by now."

"Would you indeed?" interjected Roxanne, fascinated. She was thrilled with the results of the discussion her simple remarks had provoked. "My dears, forgive me. I blame myself. I did not know—indeed, I could not suspect that you felt this way. Thinking that the gentlemen could never come up to your standards, I sent them away. How stupid of me! Can you ever forgive me?"

The twins forgot their grievances against one another and went to comfort their older sister, who was secretly planning what she would say that afternoon to Lord Culverton and Mr. Bentley.

"Oh, no, Roxanne, it is our fault. After what we said to them and to you there is no way you could have known," said Gemma.

"Although we regret being so presumptuous as to make all those foolish conditions, we still would not accept them without some indication of a willingness to consider our feelings," said Melodie with a return of her old firmness. "But we realize now that they are not the evil, fallen creatures we thought them," she admitted.

"Yes, there are men *much* worse than they!" cried Gemma. "Did you know, Roxanne, that some gentlemen never pay their bills, and are cruel to their servants, and cheat their friends, and drink until they collapse every night, and visit ladies . . . that is, females who . . ."

"But not Tony and Cyril," said Melodie proudly. In a moment, however, her lips drooped. "Little good it does us to know that now."

Roxanne cheered them as best she could, with the promise that once at home they would take a greater part in local entertainments and assemblies, that she would ask Fanny to help introduce them to more young men, and that they might have another chance in London next year, until they went off to Lady Allenbrook's, reconciled to one another but full of guilt at their failure.

Roxanne was eager to receive Lord Culverton and Mr. Bentley, and expected them at any moment, but to her dismay one of the Countess's servants arrived with a depressing communication from the young Earl. It stated that he and his friend regretted that they were unable to oblige Miss Winston with an interview, having already made plans to be out of town for the rest of the season, as they had found it painful to remain in proximity to the objects of their admiration in the face of so little encouragements from the young ladies. They were leaving this very day, hoped that in future they would all meet again, and were her obedient servants, etc. . . .

"Of all the infuriating things!" Roxanne was so irritated that she tore the letter in several pieces, crumpled the fragments in her hand, and aimed the little ball at the mantel, where it knocked over an especially ugly china ornament which she had long despised. Her wrath dissipated, she guiltily picked up the little figurine, which was miraculously unharmed, set it back in its place, gathered up the scraps of the letter, and wondered what to do next.

She had hoped to salvage something from this dreadful season, but owing to her own silly mismanagement, neither she nor the twins would return home betrothed. And soon she would have to face Geoffrey again, for they would be dining at the Broughtons' the night of Lady Marchison's ball.

She would not be at all surprised if Geoffrey cut her before everyone, or said something hurtful, or perhaps made another engagement when he found that she would be dining there that night. Roxanne racked her brains wondering what to say, how to behave, and finally decided that she must say as little as possible and pretend that nothing unusual had happened, difficult as this might be. So long as Geoffrey did the same and Fanny kept close by, everything would go smoothly, she told herself.

It was only the delightful fit and appearance of her new ball dress of seagreen taffeta, a last gift from Lady Camberwick, that lifted Roxanne's depression a tiny bit. Although this ball at Lady Marchison's was the finale of the season for most of the ton, for Roxanne it would be a sad anticlimax.

Her mind wandered to affairs at home. She wondered how Miss Lynchard was handling the latest round of Elizabeth's tantrums, or Dorothea's mischief in the larder, from which she would often steal treats. She thought about all the charitable duties she had had to abandon, and planned how she would take them up again and improve all her schemes of relief for the local poor. She wondered if the housekeeper missed her daily battles with Sir James's personal attendant.

But though she knew she would soon be immersed again in these homely matters, Roxanne had no hope that they could make her forget the troubles that her sojourn in town had brought her. If disturbing thoughts of the Duke of Rutledge pursued her even during the busy hours of the London season, however would she escape them in the country?

When Roxanne stepped into the Broughtons' drawing room, as timid as though she were at her first London party, she spied Geoffrey immediately. He appeared to occupy a fixed position in an unpopulated corner of the room, and was sulkily sipping wine. He glanced at her and looked away, his hurt evident in his eyes.

She pretended not to have seen him, and in a moment Fanny was at her side with words of welcome, drawing her away from Geoffrey's corner.

Soon Roxanne had spoken to every one in the room except her late suitor, and as yet he had not approached her. It would be highly irregular if they did not so much as greet one another, so she took her courage in her hands and went to him. She felt at least four pairs of eyes on her back as she faced her rejected suitor, and wished that her aunt, sisters, and Fanny would find something else to occupy themselves with. It was difficult enough to face Geoffrey without having an audience. Fortunately, no one was near enough to overhear anything.

"Good evening, Geoffrey." She held out her hand to him.

He looked at it and did not take it. "Good evening, Miss Winston."

Roxanne's heart fell. He was going to make it difficult. Well, it was no more than she deserved for making him so miserable. She tried again.

"It's good to see you. Fanny tells me that you're returning to Wiltshire soon, as we are. I expect my sisters and I will call at Rosemark upon our return."

He did not meet her glance. "I'm sure my family will be honored, Miss Winston."

Her patience snapped. "Oh, Geoffrey, do come down from your high ropes! One would almost think you were your friend the Duke, you are so stuffy."

Geoffrey finally looked at her. "It appears that stuffiness of that kind delights you, Roxanne. I heard that Rutledge lost no time in presenting himself to you upon my dismissal from Upper Brook Street last week."

Roxanne recoiled at this completely unexpected attack. "Does the whole world know of every caller I receive?"

"When the outcome of the interview is of interest to the whole world, yes," Geoffrey replied. His agitation betrayed itself in a trembling hand. He drained his glass and set it down.

Roxanne grew even more uncomfortable, if possible, than she had been. "The outcome of the interview, Geoffrey, is not the business of the world, or indeed of anyone but myself and His Grace. However, since you are an old friend, I will tell you—"

"—that Rutledge came to offer for you. I know." Geoffrey uttered a contemptuous sound. He stuffed his hands into his pockets, ruining the splendid cut of his coat, and turned a little away. "He knew I would propose that morning, and perhaps he thought to cut me out. Not that I blame him. You are worth ten of most of the other females that have flitted about him. And I suppose I ought not to blame you either, though I cannot help it. After all, a Duke of his magnificent wealth is a far greater prize than a paltry Baronet of fifteen thousand a year."

Roxanne was frankly bewildered. "Geoffrey, whatever do you mean? You cannot think that I would—"

He turned to her, his eyes blazing with hurt and jealousy. "Of course. That must have been your game all along, pretending to despise the Duke, all the while knowing that he likes nothing better than a challenge where ladies are concerned. I apologize if my pathetic little offer disrupted your plans. No doubt you were expecting only *him* that morning."

No, thought Roxanne, he must not think that of her. Her mind buzzed with confusion. Should she seek to bring about a repetition of his offer? She would only be sacrificing some unrealistic ideals, and her family would benefit immeasurably . . . Rutledge's face, his laugh, his lips . . . her thoughts were too muddled. She could not decide. But Geoffrey should be set straight.

"You could not be more wrong! I was completely surprised at his visit and at his offer. Although you did not witness it, I am sure you have heard from Fanny of the words His Grace and I exchanged at Almack's. You could not possibly believe that he meant to offer for me after that, or that I had any intention of accepting. I refused him as I had refused you." Her eyes pleaded with him. She could not bear for him to believe she had refused him in favor of a better offer.

"Did you really?" At last her protests seemed to be making some impression on him. He put down his glass, took her arm, and drew her even farther away than the rest of the guests. "Do not trifle with me, Roxanne, I implore you." He looked at her as if she had the power to save him from some terrible fate.

"I have no intention of trifling with you or anyone, Geoffrey," said Roxanne firmly. "I have not become engaged to the Duke of Rutledge. And I am sorry, very sorry for hurting you as I did that morning. I did not intend to."

They were interrupted, for everyone was beginning to move into the dining room, and Geoffrey, muttering, threw a last pleading look at Roxanne and hurried away to Lady Camberwick's side, as he was to take her in to dinner. Roxanne went in on Mr. Broughton's arm, and in his placid company was able to decide exactly how to continue that conversation with Geoffrey.

Her friend's accusation of mercenary motives had hurt her, but she had been a fool, and she had better do her duty while she still had the chance. The cause of Geoffrey's anger was his love of her, and her own anger with him at his deceit had faded. She knew that she should be satisfied that he loved her enough to do what he had done, no matter how cool her own feelings might be. They might warm in time. But she must speak to Geoffrey alone again soon, for they were expected at Lady Marchison's ball and she could not linger in the Broughtons' drawing room.

Accordingly, as the ladies rose from the table after dinner, she fixed Geoffrey with as meaningful a look as she could manage. He seemed startled, but gave her a slow nod. Upon leaving the dining room she dawdled in the hall before a mirror, and once the ladies were all safely within the drawing room again, Roxanne sat down in an alcove to await Geoffrey.

He emerged from the dining room only a few minutes later, shutting the door carefully behind him, looking up and down the hall. Roxanne beckoned to him, and he hurried over to her.

"Did you have something to say to me, my dear?" His tone was no longer so unfriendly. Apparently he had been thinking over what she had begun to say before dinner, and was anticipating her wish. Roxanne breathed a silent prayer of thanks.

"I want to apologize for being so abrupt with you when you . . . when you did me the great honor of asking me to be your wife. As I told Fanny, it had seemed so impossible that we could ever marry, that I had never allowed myself to feel . . . to hope . . ."

Roxanne could not go on without uttering a falsehood, but this was fortunately quite explicit enough for Geoffrey.

"My darling," he whispered, kneeling before her. He pressed kisses on her hands. "I did not realize . . . of course, being the practical little person you are, you would never indulge in daydreams as I have. But I can wait for your love to grow. We both know that it will. Only give me your promise now. Say that you will marry me."

"I will marry you, Geoffrey." The words sounded

strange to Roxanne's ears, as if someone else had said them. There was a sharp intake of breath from Geoffrey, and in a moment he had pulled her close to him and was kissing her.

Roxanne's heart beat quickly, but she recognized it as a symptom of anxiety and not the wicked excitement that had possessed her in Rutledge's embrace. Geoffrey's kiss was warm with gratitude and love, and although she felt no revulsion, she felt nothing else either. It seemed hardly to affect her at all, except for a strange sadness that swept over her when, with a whispered promise to speak to her father, Geoffrey left her.

Chapter Eleven

Lady Marchison's ballroom was crammed to capacity that evening. The luminaries of society were paying tribute to the end of the season before leaving to disport themselves in fashionable Brighton or to recover from their social exertions in the quiet of their country estates.

Among the crush of splendidly dressed persons gathered there was His Grace the Duke of Rutledge. He entered alone, and the grimness of his countenance very quickly discouraged some of his more timid acquaintance from greeting him. His mother, however, was not one of these poor-spirited creatures.

"Harry, come here," she said, beckoning imperiously, an ivory and painted silk fan clasped in her kid-gloved hand.

"Your servant, ma'am." He bowed.

Her Grace took in the sight of his face and sighed. "You don't look well, my dear boy. I suppose it is partly my fault, since it was my idea to marry you to Roxanne Winston. I never supposed she would be so foolish as to refuse you."

"But if you recall, Mama, *I* did suppose it. I only wish I had not let my judgment be so affected."

Her Grace fixed her son with a questioning glance. "Affected by what, Harry?"

For the moment the Duke was nonplussed. "Why

. . . by my desire to be an obedient son, ma'am," he said with a sudden grin.

The Duchess slapped his arm gently with her fan. "I am not such a gudgeon as to believe that you would offer for the girl simply to please me, Harry, although I had once hoped . . ."

"I am afraid your hopes are at an end, Mother. As I told you, she refused me most definitely."

"I am sorry, my dear boy," the Duchess said softly.

"And I, Mother," he replied. His face, however, betrayed no emotion.

The Winston party had arrived and was making its way about the room. Roxanne, her face serene, pushed her father in his Bath chair, the twins pranced along behind her in a state of unaccustomed excitement, and Lady Camberwick looked as though she was bursting with news. She soon approached her friend, her joy tinged slightly with embarrassment.

"My dearest Althea, you will never guess — " But before her friend could attempt to refute this statement, she went on, "Mr. Pearson has repeated his offer and Roxanne has accepted him!"

The Duchess murmured her congratulations, while her gaze traveled to her son, who stood near enough to hear but was unnoticed by the ecstatic Lady Camberwick. The Duke stiffened, and his mother saw him turn to the nearest available lady. With his most charming smile, he engaged her in light conversation.

By this maneuver Henry Malverne finally attracted Lady Camberwick's notice to himself, and her smile faded. She dropped her voice to a whisper. "Of course, my dear, I would have preferred to unite our two families, and I was quite vexed when you told me

261

Roxanne had refused His Grace, but Mr. Pearson—that is, Sir Geoffrey—is quite eligible now that he has inherited, and he and Roxanne have been friends since childhood. I only hope that His Grace . . ." She stole another look at the Duke, who was apparently unconcerned, delighting his female companion with his bon mots.

The Duchess forced a smile. "My son will recover from his disappointment, my dear. Perhaps, considering the past and that poor young Mr. Winston, it is better that Miss Winston refused him. And I am very happy for the two young people. They make a charming couple."

Only the stiffness of her lips betrayed Her Grace's effort; her tone was completely sincere. She darted another glance at her son, who was studiously ignoring the entire conversation. Lady Camberwick did not notice anything amiss.

"Why then, I hope you will tell Roxanne so, for I am sure she deeply regrets not being able to oblige you by marrying your son," her ladyship babbled in relief. She gestured to her niece, who approached warily.

"My dear child, I am so happy for you," began the Duchess.

"Thank you, ma'am. I know it is rather unexpected . . ." Roxanne trailed off, unsure of what to say. According to Aunt Maria, the Duke had immediately informed his mother of the failure of his suit, which, Roxanne thought, was not surprising, as she was the instigator of it. If Her Grace was disappointed, she was hiding it well. Roxanne felt a pang of regret. It would have been lovely to be able to please this kind and clever lady, who so eagerly wanted her as a daughter-in-law, but unfortunately her son was part of the bargain.

The Duchess was looking at her with complete sympathy, and it only made Roxanne feel more uncomfortable. "I know that Your Grace understands my dilemma. It would have been an honor, but . . . I found it not within my power to give your son a favorable reply."

"Do not disturb yourself, my dear." The Duchess pressed her hand and smiled.

"I only hope that His Grace will understand," Roxanne told her.

A deep voice in her ear said, "I assure you, Miss Winston, I understand perfectly. Come, will you dance?"

Roxanne turned and beheld the Duke offering his arm with perfect assurance. Upon entering the room she had at once seen him but had set out to ignore him, and so she had been unaware when he detached himself from his female companion. Before she could reply he had placed her hand on his arm and led her to where the sets were forming. She looked back, but the Duchess was already engaged in another conversation and seemed unconscious of anything else.

"That was high-handed, Your Grace. I had not yet accepted your invitation."

"Yes, I daresay it was high-handed," said Rutledge agreeably, "but that is one of my little faults. And perhaps, after the last occasion on which I asked you to dance, I did not wish to risk another blistering refusal, and so carried you off like this instead."

Roxanne was covered with confusion until the commencement of the music forced her to behave naturally. In the intervals between the figures that separated them, the Duke made a polite effort to engage her in conversation. However, she could do no more than reply numbly to his remarks. His nearness, and the touch of his hands as he guided her through the steps, had set her pulse racing and thoroughly distracted her. Her very nerves told her that his casual cordiality was superficial, but she wished she could imitate it.

His face barely masked some strain or tension. She realized that he must have heard the news of her betrothal, and that he was undoubtedly offended. Then why had he asked her to dance?

"Come, Miss Winston, away with that frown. You should at least appear to enjoy my company," he whispered. "And you must allow me to wish you happy."

"Must I?" she asked with something like her usual animation. She lifted her chin, determined not to let him disturb her hard-won composure.

The Duke blinked, but was otherwise unperturbed. "Certainly." He took hold of her hand and squeezed it as they passed each other across the set. He did not let go of it, however, until the lady of the couple next to them frowned and hissed at him. He was impeding their performance of the next figure.

Roxanne retrieved her hand, smothering a smile. The Duke looked discomfited. Apparently he was not accustomed to being rebuked for any errors he might make in the ballroom.

He recovered quickly, however. "I hope you will accept my good wishes. After all, Miss Winston, it was the terror of receiving my offer that sent you flying back to your first suitor."

"You are mistaken, sir," she replied coldly.

The dance was ended, and as he escorted her back to her aunt, he stopped suddenly. "Am I, Miss Winston?" he whispered.

Roxanne was conscious that their tête-à-tête could now be observed on all sides, and was frantic to get away. But he held his arm close to his side so that she could not withdraw her hand, and put his other hand over hers. "You are mistaken," she repeated. "Your offer had no effect on my decision to marry Geoffrey. I merely changed my mind."

He ignored this. "I frightened you, did I not?" he whispered, gazing down at her intently. "So you retreated to the safety offered you by your dear friend Geoffrey. I wager he has not the power to disturb all your chaste notions of courtship."

Roxanne flushed, recalling how little Geoffrey's kiss had affected her. How infuriating Rutledge was, behaving as though he knew every secret of her soul! That he could only suspect the confusion that filled her in his company was her only consolation.

"I am not so easily frightened, Your Grace," she said, putting as much contempt into her voice as she could.

"Shall we test your bravery again, my dear?" His eyes gleamed like silver in the candlelight. Roxanne inadvertently found her gaze traveling to his lips.

"I will thank you to remember that I am betrothed, my lord, and my fiancé might perhaps take exception to such an experiment."

The Duke removed his hand from hers. "You are deceiving yourself, Miss Winston." He stared at her silently, and took a long breath. "Now that you are betrothed, however, your self-deception is not my affair."

Without more ado he led her back to Lady Camberwick, whom he plied with congratulations, even delicately venturing to hope that her two other nieces would soon meet with as much happiness as their sister.

Roxanne bore all this with outward patience, while her aunt fluttered and smiled at this evidence of the rejected suitor's good breeding and gentlemanly conduct.

Lady Camberwick sighed after the Duke's retreating figure. "Ah, Roxanne, when I think of what might have been! But your Geoffrey is a fine young man, and only think, you will be Lady Pearson! What good you will be able to do for your sisters! Your papa, you know, is very happy. You will be so close that it will hardly seem as though he is losing a daughter at all."

With such things Roxanne had to content herself. It was true, Sir James had heartily congratulated his prospective son-in-law, thanked Lady Camberwick for all her care of his daughters, and told Roxanne that she was a sly puss to have so hidden her intentions from her old papa.

Roxanne felt the need to be entirely frank with someone, so she told him, "I want you to know, Papa, that I originally refused Geoffrey's offer. I did not think that I should accept him simply because his inheritance suddenly rendered him eligible."

But Sir James, for once, did not appear to understand her. "To be sure, my dear, it would not look well if you had taken him up immediately he inherits a fortune. But those who know you would realize that the fortune weighs very little with you, except for the help you can give your family." He pressed her hand and smiled at her warmly. "I know of your longstanding affection for the boy, and though your aunt seems to think that this mighty Duke of hers would have been a greater prize, I only want your happiness, my dear."

Roxanne knew then that she would have to carry this struggle within herself. No one understood what she was sacrificing by marrying Geoffrey — but this train of thought only confused her more. Since when had she a right to expect love to go along with marriage? Had they not all set out for London to find fortune, or at least comfort, and not romance? Besides, she told herself, love did not enter the picture at all. Though she was not in love with Geoffrey, she had no deeper feelings for anyone else, so it hardly mattered.

This sudden change in their sister's feelings had puzzled the twins for a little while, but they were too joyful at her engagement to care that only a few days before, Roxanne had told them she could not love Geoffrey. They simply assumed, for their own convenience, that their sister had decided she was in love with the handsome ex-officer after all.

"Of course," said Melodie, "you must endeavor to improve him spiritually. I fear the army must have coarsened his moral fiber, though of course, he is every inch a gentleman."

"And Roxanne," Gemma chimed in, "perhaps you can institute daily prayers when you are mistress at Rosemark. They are shockingly neglectful there since old Mr. Pearson's death."

"Perhaps," she replied absently. Though the family and servants of that house had known her all of her life, the idea of being mistress there frightened her.

And somehow she felt that, mistress or not, she ought not to presume to reinstate formal prayers there, or even attempt to make Geoffrey think more seriously of spiritual things. How he would laugh at her! Oddly, she found herself thinking of the Duke heartily singing hymns in Mrs. Allenbrook's drawing room.

The next week tried Roxanne's good humor severely, as she had to accept congratulations from everyone, and to endure Geoffrey's amorous company each day. Gradually his soft words and gentle kisses had begun to arouse more irritation than indifference. His attentions had become irksome. Roxanne could not decide whether this was because these attentions had changed the comfortable nature of their companionship, or because Geoffrey could no longer conceal his impatience for the further intimacies their wedding would bring.

She pushed these thoughts from her mind, busying herself in preparations for the return home, and with consoling the twins, for it became apparent that the earl and Mr. Bentley would make no early return to London. They wound up their religious activities under the eye of Lady Allenbrook with no further scandal, and with an uncharacteristic indifference. Roxanne heaved a sigh of relief when there was only one day left before their return home.

They were honored that day with a farewell call by the Duchess of Rutledge, who was retiring to what she called her "cottage" in the country, which was a pretty and commodious little estate she had purchased in Kent.

"I am getting up a party of pleasure seekers who are to come to me in about a fortnight, for though I enjoy the country in summer, I cannot bear to be lonely. I was hoping that I could count on you and your charming nieces, dear Maria, to join us. And of course"—she stopped to smile at Roxanne—"I shall invite Sir Geoffrey and his lovely sister. In spite of their mourning, no one could object to their joining our quiet little group. Do say you will come."

Lady Camberwick had no objection, and Roxanne thought it might be easier to handle Geoffrey's importunities in a large party than at home, where he would be riding over every day from Rosemark and wanting to see her alone. The twins were apathetic but thanked her ladyship and said they would be happy to come. Sir James, when applied to, gave his consent, but turned down an invitation to join them. After his sojourn in town he was eager to get home and see what the county had been up to in his absence.

"I shall bid you good-bye for now, then, and hurry off to make my cottage presentable for visitors," said the Duchess. Roxanne smiled at a mental picture of the Duchess, attired in apron and armed with a duster, readying her country home for guests, and almost did not hear Her Grace's parting remarks to her.

"But I hope, Miss Winston, this little visit will not interfere with your wedding preparations," the Duchess was saying.

"Wedding—oh, no, ma'am, there will be no wedding until the Pearsons are out of mourning, very likely," Roxanne told her, and she found it difficult to keep the relief out of her voice.

The Duchess only smiled, but Lady Camberwick looked at her strangely. From that moment on, Roxanne vowed to herself that no one, especially her intended husband, should ever again to able to suspect from her behavior that she looked forward to her wedding with anything but joy.

"Is it really true? Well done, then!" Sir Geoffrey Pearson laughed, while his companion, the Duke of Rutledge, only permitted himself a smile.

It was afternoon, and he was entertaining the new Sir Geoffrey in his lodgings off Bond Street. The four large, airy rooms were sparsely but elegantly decorated, and the simplicity of his life there with only two servants suited the Duke much better than did the imposing townhouse in Albemarle Street, which he left to his mother.

The Duke sat at a small satinwood table, writing long overdue letters to his steward and the other caretakers of his various properties, which persons had been without benefit of his instruction since the beginning of the season, an unusual occurrence. But then, he reflected, he had had much to occupy him this year. Why, the Winston family alone, in its various members, had taken up so much of his thought and time . . . he bent his head and wrote on, ignoring the full wineglass at his elbow.

His guest lounged against a carved white marble mantel, looking at his own flushed face in the small gilded mirror over it.

"By God, Harry," Geoffrey exclaimed, "I'd have let them shoot me in all four limbs if it would have brought Alfred home any sooner, but this is magnificent!" He slapped a palm down on the mantel and turned to face Rutledge. "The Frenchies have swallowed the bait. The fact that we put ourselves at such risk must have convinced them that the information you carried was the real thing."

The Duke scribbled his signature at the bottom of the sheet and picked up a penknife. "How generous of you, my dear fellow, to offer up your limbs for your country," he remarked, mending his pen, "but it was not intended that we be wounded at all, you know, merely robbed. I unfortunately miscalculated the brutality of the ruffians hired by the French. But of course it added a touch of verisimilitude, and the pain we suffered will be worthwhile if the false information helps our brave friend Winston get back safely."

"I'm sure it is an excellent plan, but you have never explained exactly how it will work," said Geoffrey.

The Duke dipped his pen in a bottle of ink and pulled a fresh piece of paper to him. He began another letter, but spoke while he wrote. "It made them think that he was still spying out French intentions regarding a possible English invasion, when in reality, he and we had long since discovered that the French hadn't the means to carry it out. By the time Boney's men had read those false documents, Alfred was already gone from Paris."

Geoffrey, restless, had sat down for a moment, but now leaped up and paced, stopping to clutch the curved back of the green silk-covered chair. "And all the while he was really hidden in the countryside, changing his identity yet again for the journey home."

"Yes, and by September he will be with us."

Geoffrey clasped his hands before him in satisfaction. "I cannot wait to tell Roxanne. She—"

Rutledge put down his pen. "Say nothing, Pearson,"

he said in his sternest voice. "The affair is not over until Winston sets foot on English soil."

"No, I — of course not. I was only imagining the look on her face when she sees her brother." Geoffrey grinned. "And then there will be another betrothal. If I know Alfred, he will race over to Rosemark and propose to Fanny again as soon as he has convinced his family that he really is alive."

Sir Geoffrey's engagement might well have been an awkward subject between the two men, but Providence had so arranged things that it was not. Although Geoffrey was fully aware that the Duke had, after his own failed first attempt, offered for Roxanne himself, he was not in possession of all the details of that interview and was satisfied with knowing that he, and not Rutledge, had won Roxanne.

Rutledge's proposal seemed surprising, but not shocking to him. Besides, Roxanne's refusal of the Duke and all his riches gave Geoffrey his first reason to feel superior to his older friend, and no man can long resent someone who provides him with such a golden opportunity.

As far as the Duke could tell, Geoffrey was so convinced of Roxanne's growing affection for him that the whole affair now caused him not the slightest pang of jealousy. And why should he not be sure of her, thought the Duke. They had known one another forever, he was now wealthy enough to suit Miss Winston, and it was in every way a most suitable match. Besides, the new Sir Geoffrey was the best friend of a beloved brother, soon to be returned to her.

Geoffrey's small part in this miracle could only render him more acceptable to Roxanne. In his heart

Henry Malverne persisted in believing that Miss Winston did not actually love her fiancée. He did not, of course, flatter himself that she loved him instead, but there was something in her eyes when she looked at him, some generous response when he had kissed her . . . these things had once given him grounds for hope. He resisted this train of thought as Geoffrey was now importuning him for details of Alfred Winston's return.

"It all hinges on his being able to travel without arousing suspicion. He is to go in the guise of a French merchant, ostensibly heading for Brussels. After a stop at Reims, where he changes his disguise, he then he makes a detour to Boulougne, where he goes into hiding and emerges as a common seaman — and sails in a small vessel whose crew is in our pay — carrying a cargo of brandy, by the way."

Geoffrey laughed. "I hope they let him have a few bottles — to drink your health with. I'll wager this whole idea is yours — just as the scheme to get him to France was yours."

The Duke admitted that he had had quite a say in how the departure of Alfred was to be managed. He did not say, however, how much he regretted the spurious quarrel and duel, or the later addition to the plan of Alfred's supposed death.

"And to think of Alfred involved in such playacting! Why, I suppose he has even grown a moustache for the occasion."

"Our friend's capacity for playacting will very likely save his life. But he is not out of danger yet."

Rutledge thought back to the time when, a restless youth himself, he had posed as a frivolous English

273

aristocrat, a dilettante blessed with unlimited funds, who had cut an elegant swath through Europe, buying paintings, sculpture, and jewels, when all the while he had been a conduit of information for his government. He had had some unlucky moments, but on the whole he had been fortunate, as he hoped his protégé Alfred Winston would be. "If his disguise fails for a moment — his mannerisms, his accent — "

"Not he," boasted Geoffrey. "When we shared a tutor years ago, it was he who insisted on learning not just Latin and Greek, but modern languages as well, and a French emigrée we once met told him that his accent could not be faulted."

Rutledge sighed, and picked up his long-abandoned wineglass. Geoffrey leaned over and reached for his own. They raised their glasses and toasted their friend in France, and then the Duke, meeting his companion's glance unflinchingly, said, "To your forthcoming marriage, sir." He drained his glass and set it down with a thump.

Geoffrey looked first proud, and then sheepish. He only sipped his wine before saying quietly, "I did not know that you cared for Roxanne, Your Grace. Though, of course, it would not have changed anything. She did refuse you, although I'd think any woman'd be proud . . . but Roxanne never understood you."

"I do not believe it is precisely accurate to say that I 'care for' Miss Winston," replied the Duke with perfect truth, "but as you once told me, it was time I set about finding a wife, and since my mother had recommended Miss Winston to my attention, and you had apparently not succeeded in your suit, I thought I should try my luck."

Geoffrey looked relieved, and the Duke saw that no matter how much his friend had enjoyed his amorous victory over him, he had been afraid of causing a strain in their association. "And you are quite right, Geoffrey. Miss Winston does not understand me at all. Perhaps one day she will, but of course, it will not matter."

Wiltshire welcomed the Winstons back with glorious summer weather. On their journey home the downs in the distance, covered in turf, seemed cloaked with soft green velvet. Barefoot children shouted and waved as their post chaise rocked through the narrow lanes of the village, passing thatched cottages, crossing a little bridge over a chalky stream, and setting them on the final road home.

Miss Lynchard, together with Elizabeth and Dorothea, stood before Westcombe Hall and awaited their alighting from the chaise with barely concealed impatience, and the servants quickly unloaded Sir James's Bath chair, carried him out, and wheeled him onto the ground floor of the house.

After joyous greetings, a riotous babble of conversation, congratulations for Roxanne, and prayers of thankfulness for a safe journey said by the twins, the travelers were allowed to retire to wash off the dust of the road before to partaking of a feast of tea, cream cakes, bread and butter, and jam tarts.

Little Dorothea greedily crammed cake into her mouth, unrebuked for once by Miss Lynchard, who was occupied in listening to the twins' report of their activities in London. Elizabeth sat next to her papa and buttered his bread, getting the butter mostly on her fingers, while Lady Camberwick looked about the comfortably shabby drawing room and lectured Sir James on the obvious shortcomings of his servants.

Roxanne listened happily to the family chatter and wondered how long it would be before her peace would be disturbed by Geoffrey. On her last day in London she had gone to the Broughtons' to pay a final call and he had bidden her a lingering farewell as they waited for Fanny to join them.

"In another week I shall be at Rosemark, and we can see each other every day," he said, obviously relishing the thought. They sat in Mrs. Broughton's morning room, alone and unobserved, and he had taken advantage of the moment to slip an arm around Roxanne's waist.

She had felt herself stiffen within the circle of his arm, and she did not know why but tears had sprung to her eyes and had to be hastily blinked back. But Geoffrey was absorbed in his plans for the next few months and did not notice. She also sensed that he was bursting with some news or other.

"Soon we'll be enjoying the Duchess's hospitality — the Duke tells me her cottage is delightful, and that you will particularly enjoy the gardens, Roxanne — and then home to Wiltshire again, where, I believe, there will be a very great surprise awaiting you." By the time he finished he was smiling.

This, then, was what he had been waiting to tell her, but he frustrated all her attempts to get more details. Roxanne had questioned him, even teased him, but all Geoffrey would do was smile and say, "You must wait,

I cannot tell you any more." He fairly glowed with happiness. "Oh, Rozzie, you cannot imagine how wonderful it will be—for you, for me, for both of our families."

At which Roxanne was stung with curiosity, but not another word could she get from him regarding this "surprise," and having so little information, she had thought it best not to mention it to anyone else, lest it be some reckless scheme she could not approve, for now that he had a fortune, Geoffrey had surprised her by admitting to the desire for all kinds of extravagance—he, who had lived on his lieutenant's pay and had scoffed at luxuries.

Or perhaps he planned to offer her some magnificent gift that she could not accept. For she had even, so far, refused an engagement ring. Something in her protested against being showered with gifts from Geoffrey's inherited store of riches; she felt it unjust, as if his own family had first call upon his generosity, and she could not become accustomed to thinking of herself as soon to be a part of that family.

Geoffrey and Fanny arrived at Rosemark three days after the Winstons' return to Westcombe, and Roxanne at least had enough time to see to various domestic crises that had cropped up in her absence before she received notice of their return. In fact, she was in the kitchen, wrapped in a big apron and helping the cook make plum jam when Miss Lynchard, the little girls trailing behind her, brought her the note.

"Now, Miss Dorothea! Miss Eliza, that'll do, you'll spoil your dinner," scolded Mrs. Preston as little fingers snatched some plums from a pile on the table.

Miss Lynchard's reproving glance was more effective

277

than the cook's remonstrances, for the latter female smiled all the while she scolded, and the girls knew her for their friend in their raids on the larder. "For that, young ladies, you must stay in the kitchen and help Mrs. Preston work, or you'll get none of those plum tarts I smell baking," the governess told them.

"What must we do?" Elizabeth asked the cook and housekeeper warily. She was known to go out of her way to avoid work in any of its forms.

"I'll set you to chopping some carrots, Miss Eliza."

"Oh," the little girl replied, relieved. "I can do that. So long as it isn't onions, or anything dirty."

Her sister, however, clapped her hands and cried, "I'll even dig weeds in the kitchen garden, so long as I can have plum tarts!" And she willingly set to work under Mrs. Preston's instruction.

Roxanne had discarded her apron, read the note, and retired with Miss Lynchard to the rear sitting room, which had the benefit of the afternoon sun.

"The twins and I will go and call on the Pearsons tomorrow morning," she told her former governess.

Miss Lynchard, who though relieved of her young charges for the time being, was never one to sit idle, picked up some work she had left on a little table and joined Roxanne by the window.

"Well, my dear, you certainly will not have to spend so much time about the housework when you are Lady Pearson, you know, and Elizabeth and Dorothea will soon consider themselves too fine to help in the kitchen, plum tarts or no. They're already clamoring to go to that fashionable boarding school where Mr. Pearson—Sir Geoffrey—has promised to send the little Pearson girls."

Roxanne had let the note slip from her fingers. She was gazing out at the garden. "Oh, but I should not let my household duties lapse, you know, even if I were a Duchess, and not only Lady Pearson." Her face flamed at that moment, and then her color subsided and she looked paler than ever.

Miss Lynchard pushed back the cap that covered her gray-tinged brown hair where it was falling over her eyes. Then she looked up at her former pupil. "Forgive me, dear, but I cannot help but notice that you look awfully sad for a bride-to-be. Is there anything you would like to tell me?"

Roxanne was sorely tempted, for she had often confided in her old governess, but she could not make sense enough of the tangle of her thoughts to tell them to anyone right now.

She straightened up and tried to pretend that nothing troubled her. "Really, I am quite all right. But the journey, and the twins moping about, and all the little household problems have tired me."

"Yes, the twins," murmured Miss Lynchard, distracted, as Roxanne intended, by this interesting observation. "It is a pity that those gentlemen gave up so easily."

"If only they had waited a few days before leaving London," said Roxanne. "I had those girls almost ready to accept their proposals." She made herself smile. "I should be grateful that Geoffrey was not so insulted by my first refusal as to run off somewhere, else the season would have passed without one engagement among us, and poor Aunt Maria would have been beside herself."

Just then that lady returned from a round of calls in

the neighborhood. She made at least two or three visits a year to her late sister's family, and had developed quite a large acquaintance of her own. "The neighbors are all so happy about Geoffrey's inheritance and your marriage," she reported somewhat breathlessly, and untying the ribbons of her bonnet, took a seat on the sofa opposite her niece. "And all of them have congratulated me."

Roxanne looked up. "Congratulated *you,* Aunt Maria! I suppose," she said with a smile, "you told them it was all your doing."

"Yes," said that lady, unabashed, "and I told some of my very particular friends—not boasting, of course—that if you had not been so stubborn you could have had a Duke, but that of course it was more suitable for you to marry Geoffrey. I could not," she informed her niece, "let them imagine that I was disappointed, you know."

"Is this true, Roxanne?" asked Miss Lynchard mildly.

Roxanne felt a bit guilty, for she had not troubled to tell her old governess about the other offer of marriage she had received, and apparently no one else had seen fit to inform her of it either.

"Yes, I did receive an offer from a Duke—you may recall the Duke of Rutledge?"

Miss Lynchard bent over her work again and Roxanne could not read her expression. "I recall him perfectly. A very intelligent gentleman, but no, I completely understand why you could not consider his proposal. In fact, in view of his past association with your brother, I am surprised that he bothered to try. However, it is regrettable. A Duke, you know . . ."

But Roxanne knew from the frown that creased the sides of her mouth that her former governess was more disappointed than she seemed. Of course, it would have added to the family's consequence to have its eldest child married to a Duke.

The next morning brought Roxanne and the twins to Rosemark. As it was a fine morning and the Pearsons were less than two miles away over the fields, they dispensed with the carriage. This country exercise was pleasant to them after their prolonged stay in town. As they walked up the graveled drive that led to the big brick house, Roxanne wondered if Fannny would welcome having her live there as its mistress.

In London, Fanny had seemed happy enough at the engagement of her brother to her best friend, but on their last visit together Roxanne had sensed some absence of mind in her friend. There was quiet happiness about her, and also an anxious expectation that Roxanne could not account for.

Today Fanny seemed the same, but more subdued than she had been in London. Now Roxanne wondered if it had anything to do with Geoffrey's "surprise," but when she mentioned it, her friend assumed a blank expression.

"No, I haven't the least idea of what he means, my dear. But let me call Mama and the others—they are thrilled about the betrothal and are dying to see you again."

Soon the drawing room was crowded with Pearsons, and Mrs. Pearson embraced her daughter-to-be kindly, while the little girls and boys crowded round begging to know what they would have to eat at the wedding breakfast. The twins were prodded by the next eldest

Pearson daughter, whom her brother had promised to bring out next season, to give details of London fashions. Melodie and Gemma interspersed their reports with warnings against vanity, and sad comments on the unreliability of a gentleman's admiration.

Roxanne knew she should have felt warm and comfortable being received as if she were already one of the family, but she only felt ashamed, as if she were there under false pretenses, when Mrs. Pearson offered to show her all the secrets of her housekeeping.

Then Geoffrey came in, and the youngsters all rolled their eyes as he bent low over Roxanne's hand and smiled sweetly up at her. Fanny looked on benevolently, Mrs. Pearson produced a handkerchief with which to wipe the mist from her eyes, and the twins smiled on their new brother.

It was only a few minutes later that Roxanne found herself and her fiancé shooed out to the gardens by an indulgent Mrs. Pearson, and when Roxanne would have asked Fanny to accompany them, that treacherous friend found that she had something else to do.

So she strolled with Geoffrey along the bricked and graveled paths of the neglected garden, while he told her of his plans to make Rosemark worthy of her. "It seems an eternity since we saw each other last, Roxanne," he told her when they had gone out of sight of the drawing room windows, and pulled her down onto a bench.

"It is barely a week, Geoffrey," she replied uncomfortably.

"Oh, but when one is in love, a week is an eternity." He pressed kisses onto her hands. Roxanne turned her head away and stared steadfastly at a straggling yellow rosebush. "Don't forget that we will be spending years together," she said with as much enthusiasm as she could.

"True, my dear, but not soon enough! I spoke to Mama, and she feels it won't be correct to leave off mourning until the spring. Will you marry me in May, then?"

"Whenever you wish."

Again, he did not notice her lack of enthusiasm, but took her in his arms.

Roxanne held still for his kisses until she could bear it no longer. She pulled gently away.

"Roxanne, what is wrong? Come, dear, I haven't frightened you, have I?"

She reflected bitterly that she knew what it was to be frightened by kisses, and that Geoffrey's did not have that power over her. Once again, the insufferable Rutledge had been right. "No, of course not, but . . . you must be patient with me, you know."

He withdrew from her a little. "Of course, I am an insensitive boor. And I know you are more concerned, my dear, with the spiritual than the physical. I like that in you. But don't let that ridiculous preacher fellow, or your prosing little sisters, tell you that this is wrong. It's perfectly natural . . ."

"I know." She could not bear to hear him persist in misunderstanding her so completely, especially when she could not set him straight. "But we must be patient. We have many months till the wedding—"

"Yes, I see exactly what you mean." Geoffrey was smiling again, confident once more of her affection. "We must not get ahead of ourselves. It would be too much to endure." With that he planted a chaste kiss on

283

her cheek, rose, and took her hand to help her up. "Let us go back to the house, my dear, where we can be adequately chaperoned," he said with a grin that disarmed her, and she smiled back.

Geoffrey was, after all, still Geoffrey, and perhaps they could be happy together. If only she could get rid of the nagging sensation that she was doing something terribly wrong. It was unfair, because after all of the mistakes she had made, she was desperately trying to do something right.

Chapter Twelve

The Duchess of Rutledge's "cottage" was a large, rambling white house with a steep slate roof, set in a pretty property of several acres. It was surrounded by orchards and situated near a village full of half-timbered houses in countryside dotted with hop gardens. Even the twins were roused from their state of apathy by the warm welcome of the Duchess and the charm of their surroundings. However, this did not stop them from closeting themselves in their room for an hour of prayer and self-criticism.

Roxanne frowned after them, but the Duchess smiled and said, "Do not be cross with your sisters, my dear. It is partly their age that makes them such avid devotees of spiritual matters. At eighteen, you know, one has a tendency to throw oneself wholeheartedly into whatever causes one's family the most trouble, and garners oneself the most attention."

Although she knew that her sisters' devotion was not a passing phase, and indicated a true and deep concern for serious things, Roxanne could not help but feel that the Duchess was right about their age being part of the trouble. Perhaps when they were older their passion would settle into a quiet piety, and surely when they were married . . . but it did not look as though that would happen, unless their suitors could be made to approach them once again.

"Come, my dear, I wish to show you the gardens." The Duchess took Roxanne's arm and led her out of the doors of the drawing room onto a terrace fringed with flower beds, from which they stepped out into lawns, shrubbery, and winding gravel paths.

"Generally, you know, I can accommodate twenty guests," Her Grace informed Roxanne as they strolled, "but everyone goes to Brighton nowadays, and I'm afraid we will be rather a small party after all. Which is just as well, you know, because Harry hates a crowd."

Roxanne was startled, having allowed her attention to wander as her gaze traveled over the variously hued roses in Her Grace's garden. Her heart began to thud against her white muslin bodice, and despite the shade of her parasol, her face felt as though the sun were full on it. The scent of honeysuckle made her dizzy.

"Does this mean that His Grace will be joining us?"

There was the slightest uneasiness in Her Grace's manner. "Why, yes, Harry generally spends a week or two with me here in summer, and when he heard that Sir Geoffrey was to be among my guests, he said that he would come and keep his friend company."

Roxanne was silent, and the Duchess stopped and looked at her young friend anxiously. "I do hope it will not make you uncomfortable, Miss Winston. I ventured to suppose that you and my son had decided to remain on cordial terms. When he suggested coming, and I warned him that you would be of the party, he told me it would make no difference."

Roxanne hastened to assure her hostess that the presence of the Duke would not cause her the slightest anxiety. She could do no less, since His Grace had not deigned to change his plans because of her presence. She could not, in truth, reassure his mother that they had parted on amicable terms, yet they had not exactly parted enemies. The heat was making her head swim, happy birds were making a positive din with their song, and Roxanne was glad when they came to a bench in the shade and the Duchess suggested they sit down.

"There is one affair, however, Miss Winston, in which I hope you will forgive my meddling," the Duchess confessed. "I have invited two other guests whose presence might prove troubling . . ."

Roxanne looked at her in surprise, unable to imagine of whom she spoke.

The Duchess poked the tip of her sunshade into the gravel at her feet, and peeked up at her companion from under a perhaps overly youthful but very pretty broad-brimmed bonnet. "I fear your sisters may be discomfitted at meeting the Earl of Culverton and Mr. Bentley again. Dear Maria, you see, has confided in me about the unfortunate results of their proposals. I'm afraid I grew a bit ambitious, and thought that perhaps if your sisters were to see the gentlemen again on neutral ground . . ." In her gray eyes danced an impish light that reminded Roxanne of the Duke.

"You are a genius, ma'am, and I cannot thank you enough." Roxanne was suddenly overcome with an impulse to hug the older lady.

"There now, my dear." The Duchess laughed and set her bonnet straight. "I am no such thing. It is simply common sense, you know."

"But I have been racking my brains to think of how to effect a reconciliation between them, and I could not even discover where the gentlemen had gone. How did you find them?"

The Duchess smiled. "I know those two boys fairly well, and I am also acquainted with their mothers. It was not too difficult to discover that the gentlemen had quit London early to go to Brighton. But I have lured them back somehow." She dimpled. "Perhaps it was because I happened to mention that the Misses Winston would be my guests."

Roxanne thanked her again. "Aunt Maria will be happy to hear that she may hope for another two betrothals. I only hope the twins have learned that they must not demand such perfection of everyone. In spite of the way they refused those offers, ma'am, I believe that my sisters are in love." Roxanne chuckled, recalling her sisters' reasons for dismissing their suitors. "I doubt, though, that they would ever admit that they could love men who drink, dance, and gamble."

The Duchess stood up and opened her sunshade. "Well, my dear, women are often surprised to discover what sort of men they are capable of loving. In my case, I was sadly mistaken in my choice of a husband. Like your sisters, I thought I could change his ways."

Roxanne was silent, a little embarrassed at receiving such a confidence.

"But regarding your sisters' case, and other cases as well," Her Grace continued with a sideways glance at her companion, "one may find that knowing the worst about a man before one marries him is far better than deceiving oneself as to his merits, only to have one's eyes opened too late. Your sisters' error was in expecting their lovers to change for their sakes." She sighed and shook her head. "No, my dear, a man is what he is, good or bad, and remains so unless he decides to change for himself."

The uncomfortable thoughts that this conversation provoked in Roxanne could not be quieted, but the arrival the next day of two more parties of guests left her little time to torment herself over how the Duchess's lessons could be applied in the case of her son.

That day first Fanny and Geoffrey, and then the Earl of Culverton and Mr. Bentley, presented themselves, the latter two accompanied by valets, handboxes, and trunks enough for an extended tour. The twins had been warned of their former suitors' arrival, but did not come in from their ramble in the garden until it was time to dress for dinner.

After spending the afternoon showing Fanny and Geoffrey about, Roxanne hurried into her own evening dress and went to the twins' chamber, wishing to discover something of their reaction to the arrival of their suitors.

"I hope you are not angry with the Duchess for inviting the Earl and Mr. Bentley. I assure you she did not mean to distress you," she began.

Gemma was suspiciously flushed and seemed to be dissatisfied with the way Lady Camberwick's maid had arranged her hair. She sat tucking in and pulling out strands of it while she waited for Melodie, who stood in a pile of discarded dresses, frowning at her reflection in a tall mirror. Roxanne was encouraged.

"We are not at all distressed, Roxanne," said Gemma. "If the two gentlemen are not too uncomfortable to stay in the same house with us for a fortnight, I am sure that *we* have no reason to be. After all, what passed between me and Cyril — and Melodie and the

Earl — was unfortunate, but not surprising."

"We never encouraged them to harbor any illusions about the acceptability of their habits," Melodie added, "but of course, if they have decided to improve themselves and repeat their proposals — why, we might be persuaded to consider the matter, would we not, sister?"

Gemma agreed with a calm that did not ring true, that there would be no harm in considering it.

Roxanne hid her smile, and patted Gemma's restless fingers. "There, my love, leave it alone," she said, smoothing her sister's coiffure, "else your hair will look as wild as Fanny's. And Melodie" — she prevented her other sister from unfastening the latest gown — "do leave on this rose-colored one. It flatters your complexion. Now as to the Earl and Mr. Bentley, pray do not think that you must sacrifice your moral convictions to please the family. Since I am betrothed, it is not at all urgent that you girls marry, unless it be for love."

She led them downstairs, and the thoughtful look that passed between them did not escape her.

Lord Culverton and Mr. Bentley had been languishing in the drawing room for a quarter of an hour, resplendently dressed, their locks curled and shining, and though there was a full decanter of Madeira ready to hand, they were both of them still nervously sipping the first glasses they had been handed. They rose with a jerk as the three young ladies entered the room. The twins held their heads high, but their sister noticed that their color was equally high, and the look in their eyes softened as they beheld the gentlemen.

Roxanne supervised the awkward meeting, and though all parties were stiff and embarrassed at first, she was eventually able to encourage everyone to speak, and once they had exchanged greetings, she guided their talk into neutral subjects until the rest of the guests had come in. By then the air had warmed a bit, and the gentlemen had just inquired as to how the ladies had left Lady Allenbrook, when Geoffrey and Fanny swooped down upon them and bore Roxanne away with them.

Gemma and Melodie cast one desperate glance at their sister, but she only smiled at them encouragingly and walked away on Geoffrey's arm. Fanny gave the girls a wink and followed her brother and his fiancée.

From across the room they watched the twins and their young men and speculated on the success of the reunion.

"As far as I can tell, Roxanne, the Duchess's scheme is going to succeed," said Geoffrey, watching as Gemma smiled at something Mr. Bentley said to her.

"I don't know," Fanny said, eyeing the couples with doubt. "Just because they are civil to one another doesn't mean they are going to end up being married."

Her brother laughed. "Certainly not, my dear, although mutual civility can be considered a basic requirement for marriage. At least Melodie and Gemma haven't dashed the wineglasses from their hands in a fit of piety." He tucked Roxanne's arm in his. "It is an improvement over the scolding they once gave poor Lord Wynne, is it not? I should be relieved that so far they have not attempted to reform *me*."

"You, Geoffrey!" Fanny chuckled. "They are clever girls, you know, and if they knew what a hardened reprobate you were, I doubt that they would be likely to waste their breath on you, or even permit you to marry

291

their sister."

Geoffrey looked at Roxanne in mock dismay. "It is too bad we may not marry quickly, my love. Between my sister's blackening of my character, and your sisters' disapproval of all the common gentlemanly vices, they may withdraw their blessing from our union, and you should have to marry Rutledge after all since, though he is no saint, they apparently dote on him. Oh, yes," he said as Roxanne colored up at his casual reference to the Duke's proposal, "I saw the princely gift they sent him. A snuffbox, adorned with a Wedgwood cameo! No, I am sure they would have preferred His Grace for a brother."

Roxanne forced a smile and patted his hand. "But they will have to be satisfied with you, and if you remain on your best behavior, perhaps you shall have one of those snuffboxes for a wedding present."

Roxanne knew that Geoffrey had not noticed her agitation at the mention of the Duke, but she could not hope that her jest had deceived Fanny. Her friend only gave her a sympathetic glance, and swiftly changed the subject.

The evening passed pleasantly, with music and duets after dinner, when the Duchess's guests were joined by a few of her young neighbors. An impromptu dance was got up, and Roxanne fully expected the suitors of the twins to dance with Fanny or one of the neighboring young ladies. Therefore she was shocked when she saw her sisters stand up with the gentlemen and, to the accompaniment of the Duchess's playing on the pianoforte, enter into the dance without the slightest awkwardness, as if they had been dancing all season.

"It appears that a miracle has been wrought, my

dear," Geoffrey commented, spying the surprising couples.

"I can hardly believe it," Roxanne replied. "Perhaps my sisters have come to decide that dancing is not sinful after all."

Roxanne was relieved that Geoffrey seemed to have himself well under control, for he had not tried to get her to himself since his arrival that morning, and had allowed Fanny to sit with them without a murmur of protest. Although she was sure her last talk with him had had some effect, Roxanne was still grateful for her friend's presence, for who knew when Geoffrey might again let his passions overwhelm him?

As the evening progressed, Roxanne also had cause to be obliged to one of the Duchess's young neighbors, a pretty little blonde, Miss Rogers, who flirted with quite openly with Sir Geoffrey, thus diverting much of his attention from his fiancée. It did not seem at all odd to Roxanne that the smiles and compliments he accorded this young lady ignited not a single spark of jealousy in her bosom. She was simply glad that Geoffrey would have a reason not to hang about her all evening, and that she could devote herself to watching over her sisters' progress with the Earl and Mr. Bentley.

After the neighbors had gone home, but before the guests retired to bed, she managed to have a few words with these two gentlemen.

"Miss Winston," cried Cyril Bentley, " 'twas the oddest thing, the Duchess's asking us here like this. My mother happened to tell Her Grace that I was at Brighton with his lordship, and Her Grace wrote directly and said she would be delighted to have our company for a fortnight."

"And when she told us who was staying here with her . . ." The Earl's handsome face flushed. "Well, we took it as a sign that the young ladies would not be averse to meeting us again."

Roxanne blessed the Duchess for her benevolent interference. "What I wish to know, gentlemen, is if you are both still of the same mind that you were before you left London."

Both gentlemen assured her that their feelings for Gemma and Melodie had not changed.

"I am happy to hear it, for I believe that time and the absence of your attentions, which they had certainly come to expect and enjoy, has worked its changes upon their feelings." Roxanne smiled at the sudden lightening of their expressions. "Witness their dancing with you this evening."

"Most extraordinary considering how dead set against it they were in London," Mr. Bentley commented.

"Indeed, and I hope it may point to other changes, too." Roxanne swiftly gave them her impressions of her sisters' current mood, adding, "I do not wish to give you false hope, but you have some cause, I believe, for optimism. Tread carefully, gentlemen, and you may yet succeed."

They pressed her hand in gratitude and went up to bed, the Earl smiling wistfully while his friend whistled until sharply reminded by his lordship that he would wake the house with his noise.

While Roxanne was preparing for bed the twins came to say goodnight to her. But when Roxanne bid them sleep well, they still stood about awkwardly until Melodie blurted out, "I suppose you noticed that we danced tonight, Roxanne."

"Yes, and I thought you danced very well," she told them blandly.

The girls met her glance briefly and then looked away. Gemma spoke. "We have decided that an occasional quadrille or country dance could not be considered a danger to us, so long as we remind ourselves that amusement is not the primary aim of our lives."

"And in a small, private family party such as this," Melodie continued, "it was perfectly acceptable and appropriate for us to dance."

"And it is not as though your partners were unknown to you or your family," Roxanne commented, brushing out her hair but watching the girls in her mirror. She saw them smile reminiscently.

"After all," she went on in a casual tone, "a man from whom one has elicited an offer of marriage may be said to be an intimate acquaintance, and is an acceptable partner, I should think, even for those who do not generally dance. Especially as such a gentleman must have dispensed by now with the notion of paying his addresses, and only asks you to dance out of common courtesy."

Gemma looked as though she were about to protest Roxanne's last statement but Melodie spoke first. "Of course it is perfectly harmless for us to dance with them . . . although I am not certain it was only courtesy that motivated them."

"Certainly not," said Gemma with a telltale gleam in her eye. "In fact, Cyril gave me to believe that they were glad the Duchess happened to invite them while we were here." She smiled. "How upright of them, Mel, not to avoid our society simply because we could not marry them! I am sure no harm was done by our dancing with them. After all, we must not let our own beliefs hinder us from being polite to others."

Roxanne hid her smile and was careful not to reveal her own excitement at these revelations. She wanted to give them time to make up their own minds, and the best way was to let events take their course without any further interference. But she could only consider the Duchess's "meddling" a true act of charity.

The next day brought the arrival of the Duke. Until he actually appeared, Roxanne had hoped that he would stay away, but no sooner had she returned with her aunt and the Duchess after paying a call on the Rogers family, to whose flirtatious daughter she had such reason to be grateful, than she saw Rutledge's carriage being driven to the stables, and footmen carrying in his bags. She resigned herself to an end of the peaceful pleasures she had so far enjoyed, and girded herself for battle.

However, nothing could have been more amiable than the Duke's demeanor toward her when they met. He was going up the stairs as she entered the hall behind his mother, and when he heard the noise of their arrival he made his way back down, greeting the Duchess with genuine affection that Roxanne could not help but notice. Lady Camberwick received his best bow, and he greeted Roxanne as if he were greeting an old friend.

"How do you do, Miss Winston? I hope you are enjoying the country. It appears to agree with you."

There was frank admiration in his eyes, but Roxanne detected an air of strain behind the careless compliment. Each time she saw him she could not help renewing her memory of his face and figure in a long glance. Finally she realized that she had not answered him, because his face began to betray his amusement at her mute stare. "Yes, the country has agreed with me remarkably, Your Grace . . . so far," she replied.

"Ah, you reserve judgment until you should have finished your visit! Let us hope, then, that my arrival does nothing to change your opinion," was the Duke's riposte. He was smiling straight into her eyes.

Roxanne assumed an air of nonchalance, though her pulse was drumming in her ears. "I doubt that you hold it in your power to disturb the charm of the countryside, my lord, unless you have a talent for blighting the grass and flowers, or filling the sunny skies with clouds, or the fresh air with soot."

Now he took up her hand and bowed over it, so close to brushing it with his lips that Roxanne could feel the soft warmth of his breath on her skin. "If I had such powers I would instantly relinquish them to oblige you, Miss Winston. After all, I would not wish to be responsible for banishing that becoming pink in your cheeks, which I suppose is brought on by this healthy country atmosphere."

Lady Camberwick looked from the Duke to her niece and gave Roxanne a speaking glance, embellished with a sigh. The Duchess was conferring with one of her servants, and did not appear to notice.

The pink that Rutledge had commented on became more marked, and Roxanne had to abandon her pose of unconcern, for she could not help but take his meaning. She ought to have known that she could not fool him for a moment, for he saw through her every pose. It was ungentlemanly of him to tease her before such witnesses as her aunt and his mother. She pulled her hand away. "I—I am glad to hear it, my lord." Making some excuse, she fled upstairs.

That night Rutledge took Roxanne in to dinner, and though she felt her hand tremble a bit on his arm, she steadied herself. Geoffrey caught her eye across the table, and she summoned up a smile for him. It was not to him that she could look for protection from Rutledge. Why, her fiancé was no longer the least bit disturbed that the Duke had been hard on his heels in offering for her! She doubted he would show any jealousy even if he should find her in Rutledge's arms, at which thought confusion overcame her. She felt the Duke's glance on her, and hurriedly fastened her attention on her plate.

While she was thus occupied, the Duke talked in a lazy drawl of the fine weather, of the scenic drives in the neighborhood, and of the desolation of London, whence he had just come. It was as though he had nothing else on his mind but a repairing lease in the country, and the company of his mother and his friends. But Roxanne felt that behind his every remark was a deliberate reminder of what had happened between them, and in each one of his innocent smiles was a hint that it could very easily happen again.

When the ladies left the gentlemen to their port, she wore herself out wondering to what she owed this subtle change in his manner toward her, and decided, when he and Geoffrey joined her after dinner, conversing easily, that it was her betrothal that accounted for it. Geoffrey was, of course, unconscious of it, but His Grace appeared to accept the fact of her engagement to his friend as a license to remind her of what she had refused, and to belatedly play the gallant.

Roxanne received all his remarks as if they were double-edged, although she knew she was reacting out of fear. His glances at her held nothing of the restrained admiration which other gentlemen accorded a lady who was already spoken for, but were unabashedly provocative. Did he actually believe that she might change her mind and cry off, hoping he would renew his proposal? No doubt he would then exact his revenge by refusing to do anything of the sort.

Roxanne decided that he would not get the opportunity to practice any such sport upon her. How insufferable he was to assume that by a bit of shabby flattery and a few languishing looks that would shame a third-rate actor, he could induce her to believe that he loved her, or any such nonsense!

So she steeled herself not to rise to his bait, but her chilly demeanor only made His Grace smile. Roxanne was further annoyed by the fact that Geoffrey noticed none of the undercurrents of the situation. Eventually the Duke was called away by Fanny, and while she gave them some songs, Rutledge hung over the pianoforte turning her music for her.

Roxanne watched them a while, noticed their easy comradeship, and found herself recalling that Rutledge had once sought to make Fanny his wife. How odd that there were two women in the room who had refused his offer, and the two women bosom friends! It ought to have been an embarrassing situation. But Fanny smiled up at Rutledge, utterly unconscious of any of the discomfort that Roxanne knew in his presence.

Roxanne felt a flash of anger, which troubled her the

more because it was so unreasonable. How could her friend so forget herself and her love for Alfred? Fanny obviously considered the Duke a close friend, although he had, even if only inadvertently, caused the death of her first love. Some imp then implanted the notion in Roxanne's head that perhaps Fanny was even now reconsidering her refusal of Rutledge's offer.

The more Roxanne brooded on it, as she listened to her friend's sweet soprano mingling with Rutledge's baritone, the more sense it made. Perhaps his proposal to her friend had startled Fanny out of her dream, and having refused the Duke once, she saw that his intention to marry must be strong indeed as he had offered for a woman who barely tolerated him. Why, Fanny might even now be intending to bring on a return of his addresses.

It was unworthy of her, and quite ridiculous, Roxanne knew, but a fit of jealousy engulfed her. Not, she told herself, that she had welcomed or encouraged the Duke's dubious attentions toward herself, but that he could so easily take his dismissal, and snatch a kiss from her lips only to fly to Fanny's side again, piqued her. Still she watched them, and it seemed to her that by now they were most unequivocally flirting.

"Roxanne, I do believe you haven't heard a word I've said to you in the past five minutes," Geoffrey complained, tugging at her arm.

She flushed. "I'm sorry, Geoffrey. I was watching Fanny, and thinking about her and . . . Alfred."

He mumbled something that she did not catch, and then said, "It's time my sister married. But I was asking you if you had given Miss Rogers an answer about the picnic on Tuesday."

Roxanne had hardly recalled it, but the petite, green-eyed Miss Rogers, along with her mama and brother, had proposed a picnic luncheon at a local beauty spot not far away, and had invited the Duchess and her guests. "Why, yes, when we called on them this morning we told them that we would be happy to go. You do wish to go, do you not?"

"Oh — of course." Geoffrey appeared abstracted for a moment. "It is only . . . I thought perhaps you were displeased with me."

"Displeased with you!" She finally looked at him, tearing her gaze away from Fanny and the Duke, whose heads were bent over the music. Why, Geoffrey was blushing!

"You know . . . because of Miss Rogers flirting with me so persistently." He laughed nervously. "Would you believe that she is quite an heiress? Why, last year such a girl would not have looked twice at me. How things have changed! But I did not encourage her, and I'm sorry if it seemed as though I neglected you." In spite of his words, he looked more proud than abashed.

Roxanne realized that he was expecting her to make some kind of objection to his devoting himself so thoroughly to another young lady, and for the sake of his confidence in her affection for him, she assumed a suitable frown.

"Why, I thought Miss Rogers a little forward, and surely you might have found a kind way to dissuade her from hanging on your sleeve, but you must not think I am jealous, my dear."

It was enough to satisfy him without telling a falsehood, for she could not pretend to be jealous. Roxanne reflected bitterly on the extremity to which she had arrived, having to dissemble so with her old friend. If only he could remain simply her friend, and not become her husband. But she had given him her answer, and could not, in honor, go back on it now.

Roxanne saw the Duke watching them from across the room, and before she knew it, though he could in no way be said to have hurried, he was with them again. To her dismay, at that moment Fanny called her brother to her and with a quick, "Forgive me a moment, my dear," Geoffrey left her side, and she and Rutledge were to all intents and purposes alone.

Alone, but not unobserved, for Lady Camberwick, who was keeping a hopeful eye on the twins and their swains, yet had another to spare for her elder niece, and although the Duchess seemed occupied in talking to the local squire and his wife, who had been invited to form a table for whist, Roxanne knew that she was at every moment aware of what her son was doing. She even smiled encouragingly at Roxanne, who hastily looked down and folded her hands in her lap.

"What is this I hear about plans for a picnic?" the Duke inquired, seating himself beside her on the sofa where Geoffrey had just rested. But the sofa, Roxanne thought, had not seemed so small then, nor Geoffrey so close as Rutledge was now. With difficulty she formed a reply, and to her relief they simply discussed the picnic and the possibilities of the good weather continuing. Just as Roxanne was allowing herself to relax her guard, the Duke said, "Fanny tells me that you let your fiancé flirt with another woman last night, and completely gave him up to her. Is that the way one retains a man's affections, Miss Winston?"

She stared at him coldly. "Apparently it is, my lord,

for Geoffrey has apologized for neglecting me, and I am sure it will not happen again."

A slow smile spread over the Duke's face. "Come now, my dear, although you have made your choice, you must be careful it does not prove to be the wrong one. I have not met the young lady, but my mother tells me Miss Rogers is a confirmed flirt, as well as a considerable heiress. If I were you, I would watch young Geoffrey closely at this picnic affair, and see that he does not stray too far from your side."

"I am surprised, sir, that you can imply to me, his fiancée, that your friend might prove to be untrue. Besides, Geoffrey is not a child or a lapdog, to be restrained by my side. He may speak to any lady he chooses."

"I beg your pardon, Miss Winston," he said, though he did not look at all repentant. On the contrary, his smile was as insufferable as ever. Roxanne looked away, but his voice would not leave her in peace. "But you see, since I am the rejected suitor, and Geoffrey is my friend, I feel a certain responsibility to see that nothing occurs to disturb this betrothal."

"You may consider yourself relieved of that responsibility, Your Grace," Roxanne retorted, turning back to him with flashing eyes, "and to be plain, I consider that excuse to be a lot of humbug!"

The lazy look was gone from his face. Though still smiling, he was all attention. "Oh, and why might that be, my dear?"

But Roxanne could not possibly tell him that by paying her so much attention, and in a manner so particular, he could not be considered to be contributing to the stability of his friend's betrothal. How could she accuse him of flirting with her when she had been loftily pretending not to recognize it?

Perhaps the Duke did, after all, possess some power to make the country a less salubrious place, for the day after his arrival it rained and the picnic had to be put off until later in the week, since the ground was soaked and muddy. In that period the young people fully exhausted the pleasures of books, music, and cards, and only longed to be out of doors.

When it began to rain, Roxanne had been afraid that she might be trapped too often in the Duke's company, but after paying his respects to the ladies in the morning, he had gone to entertain Geoffrey, the Earl, and Mr. Bentley with conversation or cards, or shut himself up with the caretaker of the place and discussed the management of his mother's little orchard, or even walked out in the downpour.

In the evening Rutledge devoted himself to his mother, sitting on a footstool at her knee, sorting her silks while they talked in low voices, or else he read to her from works of her choice. He initiated no more troublesome conversations with Roxanne, although the look in his eyes that had set her nerves fluttering did not disappear. Indeed, he looked at her often, and though he did not say anything, she thought his eyes promised that she was not safe yet.

In fact, she felt the thrill of danger in his company, yet as she sat with her own work between Fanny and Lady Camberwick after dinner, she could not help admiring Rutledge's artless and engaging conduct with his mother. In the soft blue drawing room, sitting in a pool of lamp light, with the sound of the rain beating on the windowpanes and the fragrance of the

Duchess's china bowls of potpourri lulling her into drowsiness, the Duke seemed to Roxanne a comfortable, domestic figure, not at all out of place in his elegant town-made clothes.

She could hardly believe it, but it looked as though this pleasure-loving man of fashion was apparently just as happy sitting quietly in a nearly empty country drawing room and entertaining his mother as he was frequenting the clubs of St. James' or the ballrooms of Mayfair. His serenity was in sharp contrast, she found, to the behavior of Geoffrey, who cursed the weather and was at the window a hundred times that night, speculating aloud about whether the rain would stop before full dark or if he would be able to see the moon through the dense clouds.

Obtaining no encouragement in these conjectures from any one, Geoffrey seated himself near Roxanne and sought to entertain her with local gossip, plans for their wedding journey, and numerous other subjects, none of which evoked much of a response, for Roxanne was dreamy and abstracted. Neither his sister nor Lady Camberwick listened to Sir Geoffrey with more than a polite ear; each seemed wrapped in her own thoughts.

He got up then and wandered restlessly about the room, lighting now near his fiancée, now near the twins and their admirers, standing over them to comment on the twins' progress in learning backgammon, which, after much deliberation, they had judged harmless.

Finally the Duchess noticed and took pity on the restive young man. "Dear Sir Geoffrey, would you please ring the bell? I'm sure it is time for the tea to be brought in," she said, although it was a bit early for that evening ritual.

Geoffrey obeyed and before long the guests put down their various occupations and gathered around the tea tray.

"Will you pour, Miss Winston?" asked the Duchess.

Roxanne stationed herself behind the pot and performed this ceremony with her usual competence, only faltering for a moment when she recognized one of the hands that took a cup from her as that of the Duke. The cup shook, a little tea spilled into the saucer, and Rutledge took it from her with both hands, his fingers brushing hers.

Roxanne swallowed and glanced up at him. His eyes were in shadow, and had not that customary silver gleam that so disturbed her. His lips were curved, but not yet smiling.

"I'm sorry. How clumsy of me." She endeavored to speak coolly, but her voice shook almost as her hand had done. Fortunately, his was the last cup she had to pour, and she was able to rest her hands on the white cloth that covered the tray until they stopped trembling.

"You are forgiven, Miss Winston. Yes, thank you, some sugar. It is a pleasure to receive this cup from you, after the bitter cup you have often handed me in the past." His voice was soft, and Roxanne saw her Aunt Maria, sipping her tea a few feet away, straining to hear.

"I—I thought we were not going to talk about the past anymore, my lord."

The Duke took a sip, returned his cup to its saucer, and looked at her inquiringly. "Oh? Have we made an agreement on that subject? I must have forgotten it.

You shall refresh my memory, my dear Miss Winston."

Roxanne flushed in annoyance. "No, we had no agreement. But I thought that you would have the sense and delicacy to refrain from bringing up the matter."

"You honor me, madam. I had not thought that you gave me credit for either. But I find that I really cannot oblige you by agreeing not to mention the past. The past, you see, occupies me, especially *our* past, and what might have been our future if you had not been so stubborn."

"How can you—" Roxanne saw some heads raised from teacups; apparently she was talking too loudly. She lowered her voice. "How can you make such remarks when the man I am about to marry is in this very room, sir, and you call yourself his friend?"

The Duke smiled pleasantly. "Come, sit down, Miss Winston, and drink your tea before it gets cold." He took her cup from her, placed it with his on a little table near a sofa, and indicated that she was to sit.

Roxanne knew a moment of defiance, but again her aunt was staring and the twins were beginning to be distracted from their endless and somewhat pointless philosophical discussions with Mr. Bentley and the Earl, so she simply did as he bade her and sat down. He placed himself next to her and took up his teacup again.

"Now, you ask me how I can refer to our past—and the future that you have refused—when you are engaged to my friend here?" He indicated Geoffrey, whose irritability had found some release in the time-honored solution of arguing spiritedly with his sister.

"It is because I am his friend that I continue to annoy

you, Miss Winston. In fact, I would like to be your friend too . . . much more than your friend, and I will keep on annoying you until I make you see how unhappy both of you will be if you marry Geoffrey."

Roxanne's throat was parched and the tea she drank seemed to do nothing to remedy the matter. It was best, she thought quickly, not react too strongly to these ridiculous statements. It would only encourage him. "Why then, sir, when I refused did you seem to take the failure of your suit so calmly?"

"Ah, that was when I thought that you had also refused our mutual friend. No, my dear, that little demonstration of my esteem I presented you with that morning would have been enough, I thought, to show you what might have been . . . after that, I would have left you in peace — had you not changed your mind and become engaged to Sir Geoffrey."

Roxanne felt as though her face must be fiery crimson, and she bent her head, hoping to hide it from his observance. Her teacup clattered on the saucer.

"But when I discovered that you had changed your mind," he continued, "I knew that somehow I must convince you that you were making a mistake. And somehow," he said, glancing at Geoffrey, who had stalked away from his argument with Fanny and haunted the windows again, "somehow I think that my presence here will not even be necessary. All it needed was for you and your betrothed to be shut away in a country house together for a fortnight for you to discover that, friends though you are, you would not suit."

"Whatever do you mean? Geoffrey and I have not quarreled."

"Yes, but have you noticed—do not say that you haven't—the variability of his temper, his impatience, his vulnerability to flattery—the little Rogers heiress? You see, my dear Miss Winston"—he leaned closer,—"You are very well acquainted with the man, and though he is a good fellow, he is worldly in ways you would not understand, and is not the husband for a lady who is, as your sisters would say, devoted to a serious life."

Roxanne had to laugh. "Then you consider yourself less worldly, sir? And do you really think that I expect to marry a paragon of virtue? Although I may be only a bumpkin from the country and conduct my life along different lines than most of the ladies of your acquaintance, I am not ignorant of the world, my lord. And I am not like Melodie and Gemma, who, as you know, set out to reform the gentlemen of the ton and ended up, as you may not know, refusing the offers of the only two men who actually care for them because they refused to be reformed."

For a moment he was diverted. "Have they? Then I suppose this is my mother's attempt to mend the situation." He seemed to forget Roxanne and observed the other two couples for a moment. "I wish them luck," he murmured, though Roxanne did not know if he meant the wish for the twins or their lovers.

"In any case, as I once told you, my lord, I do not wish you to concern yourself in this affair." Roxanne seemed to gain strength when his attention was diverted from her. When it was fixed on her, when she was under siege from those brilliant eyes, her strength seemed to drain out of her, leaving her vulnerable to his insistent suggestions, making her think of the most shocking things, things that she had put to the back of her mind so that they might not disturb her.

"It is too late for that, my dear," he said softly, putting his hand over hers. "I am concerned in it, very concerned, more than you know." His gaze burned into her for a moment, as if he sought to tell her something without the aid of words. Then he rose and went to the Duchess again.

He left Roxanne feeling that she was on the verge of some great discovery, but that she must resist it because it would shatter the structure of everything she knew.

The next day dawned fine and looked to remain so for the picnic, and the Duchess's guests, inclined to be snappish after being confined for two days with so little variation in their entertainment, gladly emerged into the sun. The ladies, bonneted and carrying sunshades, piled into open carriages, while the men, in boots and breeches, chose to ride. The servants were dispatched ahead with a cart bearing rugs, hampers of food, and bottles of wine.

The destination of this pleasure party was a gently sloping hillside a few miles from the Duchess's cottage, where they were to be met by the Rogers family and several others who ranked high in the society of the neighborhood. A rather deep and rushing stream served the locale, with trees along its banks, under which the rugs were spread. For the older members of the party, a table and chairs were clothed and laid as if in her Grace's dining room, instead of under the blue sky.

The men on horseback had passed the carriages along the way, except for Geoffrey, who rode at the side of the Duchess's barouche, in which Roxanne was a passenger. His spirits, Roxanne noted, were high once more, and she attributed it to the end of his very understandable disgust with the bad weather. He kept her and the Duchess laughing at his town anecdotes, but as they climbed the hill and came within sight of the picnic ground, he fell silent.

Roxanne saw that Rutledge had arrived before them, and had dismounted, and that the Rogers family had already taken possession of the ground. In fact, His Grace was in the process of strolling with Miss Rogers over the grass, selecting the most advantageous spot for her rug to be laid and, from the sound of his chuckles, enjoying her artless prattle. Roxanne noticed Geoffrey's face tense, and when the carriage had stopped, he simply rode off toward them, instead of giving his horse to a groom and dismounting to help the ladies down from the carriage.

The Duchess raised her eyebrows at this ill-mannered behavior, but Roxanne affected to ignore it, though in truth she was a little annoyed. Her Grace set about supervising what little remained of the preparations, for the servants had done their work well, and iced wine and lemonade were ready for the thirsty travelers. Lady Camberwick had bustled over to Mrs. Rogers to exchange greetings and to estimate the cost of her and her daughter's bonnets.

Roxanne was left to chaperone the twins and their two gentlemen, who stood on the bank of the stream talking desultorily. Although they now seemed comfortable with one another, they had plainly reached an impasse. The gentlemen would not offer marriage again, and the ladies had not as yet given strong enough hints that they would like to

311

be offered for again.

On the ladies' part there had been no accusations of moral depravity, no promises of good behavior extracted, but on the gentlemen's part, there had been no return of those proposals which had formerly broken up their happy foursome. But Roxanne was well informed, being in daily communication with all parties concerned, and could not help believing that eventually the gentlemen would feel bold enough to assay the matter once again. By that time the twins, who looked less solemn every day though they prayed as constantly as ever, must certainly have come to realize that if they accepted the offers of marriage, they would have husbands of whom they could be proud, and not the careless dandies they had spurned.

They stood now in awkward silence until Mr. Bentley, who had been watching the sparkling waters as they rushed over the shining rocks, was taken with the bright idea of trying to cross the stream by stepping on these stones, with which it was liberally supplied.

"I'll bet you a pony that I can get across and back without spilling myself in," he cried to his friend, who replied, "Done!" and was about to give his hand on it.

Roxanne saw the frowns building on the twins' faces at this casual wagering on such a ridiculous feat, and shot a meaningful glance at the Earl. He withdrew his hand. "But then again, Cyril, it ain't as though I have any doubts that you can do it. No need to bet on a silly thing like that . . . in fact, there's far too much nonsensical wagering going on. I shall give it up, that's what!"

Mr. Bentley, poised to cross the stream, looked blank for a moment. His friend silently indicated the twins, who stood wearing the faces of martyrdom, patiently awaiting the outcome. "I believe you have the right of it, Tony. No reason for the wager. Doubtless I'll do it . . . or perhaps I may not. The bet is off, and tell you what, I won't bother to attempt it at all."

"Gentlemen, please, do not deprive yourselves of your customary amusements on *our* account, I implore you," said Melodie in a voice of doom.

"Yes, pray do not let us prevent you from wagering upon any trivial thing that strikes your fancy," said Gemma. Her mouth began to tremble, and her brown eyes looked at Mr. Bentley with great sadness. "It appears to be second nature to you, sir, and I would not wish to . . . oh, go right ahead and wager your *soul* if you like!" She turned away with a sob, and her twin, with a black look at the gentlemen, withdrew to attend to her.

Roxanne summoned the two transgressors. "It appears, gentlemen, that once again your timing has been faulty. I daresay these two girls have been waiting for you to propose again for the past three days, and their nerves are frayed. Pray, do it today!"

Lord Culverton looked sheepish. "We would have, honestly, Miss Winston, but every time I try to approach the subject with Miss Melodie, she gets that *look*—" Whereupon he demonstrated a certain forbidding expression of Melodie's that her sister knew very well, and Roxanne could hardly keep her countenance, the contrast between the Earl's distress and his comical impersonation was so great.

"Yes," Mr. Bentley chimed in, "and I have circled most carefully about the matter with Miss Gemma—after the last reply she gave me, I wasn't about to be less than careful, you know—but she freezes up and once

313

she even took out her Bible and began readin' it right in front of me!"

"Oh, dear." Roxanne sighed. "If only . . ." But she was about to wish that her sisters had never grown so devout, and that would never do. The comfort and guidance they had found in their faith was worth all the trouble it made for the family. But surely if they were more like other young ladies of their class they would know how to accept a gentleman's attentions more gracefully!

A sudden thought occurred to her. "Cross the stream, please, Mr. Bentley," she ordered.

"What? I . . . but . . ."

"Just cross the stream, sir." Then she gave him a little push. He cried out and, to keep his balance, put one foot on the first stone, and then a foot on the next, and so on, until he was doing a jerky shuffle across that rushing, bubbling body of water. By now the twins had returned their attention to the gentlemen, and Gemma cried out in alarm at the way her swain flung his arms up and out and around and danced a ludicrous ballet along the slippery stones. Disaster was imminent; at any moment it seemed Cyril would be lying senseless among the rocks and rushing waters.

"Save him," Roxanne hissed at the Earl.

"Do what?" He looked at her in wide-eyed astonishment.

"Save him. Do you wish to marry my sister or not, my lord?"

Lord Culverton instantly caught her meaning, and crying, "Wait old fellow, hand on, I'm coming to rescue you!" he made a bold dash into the stream, slipping in his highly polished boots, water splashing onto his white duck breeches (a concession to the country), arms flapping with great energy as he strove to maintain his balance on the slippery stones.

Now there were two young sprigs of fashion in the midst of the flowing waters, at one moment poised in a heroic attitude, then next swaying wildly and forced to continue to the next rock or fall in and sacrifice expensive boots, tailored coats, and starched neckcloths. As for their lives, these were not in danger, for to be honest, the stream was only two feet deep.

The twins were not the only spectators lined along the banks of these treacherous rapids, although perhaps they were the most affected. While the other young men of the combined picnic party, now all arrived, laughed and hooted and called out hilarious and useless advice to the two intrepid adventurers, the two girls clutched at each other and prayed for the safety of their lovers.

"Oh, how brave and good his lordship is," cried Melodie, tears in her eyes as she observed the Earl, momentarily at rest on a large rock in the middle of the stream, offering his hand to his companion, who teetered on a loose stone next to him. "How he puts himself in danger to help his friend. He is at heart, I am sure, a true Christian. No one could act thus if he were not."

But at the next moment it was Mr. Bentley who was in a position to assist the Earl, for though the former had gained, by his friend's assistance, a place on the big rock, there was not room for two, and after the girls had observed some little argument between the men as to who was to make the dangerous pass across the abyss and foaming torrent, namely, to step over a space of three feet to the next rock, Cyril shook his head angrily at his friend and ventured to be the one to take the first desperate step toward getting safely back to the bank, where two very tender young hearts awaited their victory over cruel nature.

"Oh, and dear Cyril is just as brave, sister. Look how he would not let the Earl risk danger again — he is gone ahead, and holds out his hand to him . . . oh, Mel, how could we ever have doubted their fitness? I am sure in the eyes of the Lord they are worthy."

Roxanne looked about for Geoffrey, wanting to share her triumph with him, but she found him only with difficulty, for he was attending Miss Rogers and, having taken her arm, was assisting her in wandering toward the stream to see what all the noise was about. But they were negotiating this rough terrain of tenacious turf and soft ground very slowly, and Geoffrey was at that moment engaged in seeing that his fair companion did not set her foot into a cavernous depression some three inches deep that had suddenly appeared before them, barring their way to the banks of the stream.

Roxanne clicked her tongue in impatience. The others who were watching were still laughing, and could not appreciate the sanctity of this moment. The twins had eyes only for their struggling heroes and, of course, would not understand Roxanne's feelings. Fanny was attending Lady Camberwick, who, unconscious of the hubbub, had discovered that she must have some lemonade immediately. Roxanne's spirits fell as she realized that there was no one there who could witness her triumph and recognize it as such.

"Congratulations, Miss Winston. It seems that you

have been successful. My mother herself could not have done it more neatly, and with so much consideration for the entertainment of the company." Rutledge was at her side, applauding with soft little claps and smiling in sincere appreciation.

"Thank you, my lord," she said, and felt her own smile escape all her efforts to suppress it. It was too hard that she should not be allowed to gloat, even if it must be to Rutledge! "It occurred to me that the twins needed to see some kind of heroic gesture, to make his lordship and Mr. Bentley seem something above the ordinary class of privileged young men, whom they cannot help but despise."

"And at this great peril to their pride and risk to their apparel, they obeyed you and crossed this treacherous torrent." He sighed. "How easy it is to please some ladies."

She laughed. "I think my sisters were disposed to be pleased. I simply supplied them with a reason."

"And are you, too, disposed to be pleased? If so, I can give you a reason to be very pleased with me, Miss Winston, but I will not, for it would give me an unfair advantage, and I should not like to employ it except in the direst necessity." He took her arm and slowly propelled her along the bank.

"Whatever are you talking about?" Roxanne had been listening with only half an ear, and quite forgot to be either distant or annoyed with the Duke. She was concentrating on her sisters and did not notice his grin at her natural tone and her lack of resistance to continuing in his company.

The two heroes were safely on the bank again, none the worse for a slight wetting — and infinitely the happier, for they were greeted with affectionate and admiring concern by the objects of their devotion, and Roxanne watched with contentment as her sisters clucked and fussed and led the performers away in search of seats in the sunshine.

"Never mind, my dear," said the Duke.

Roxanne, satisfied, now turned her attention back to him but before she could tartly request, once again, that he refrain from addressing her as his "dear," he was going on.

"The food will not be served for another half hour. At these affairs it is customary to allow the guests to work up an appetite by rambling about and admiring nature. You are a country girl, you must like a good walk. Come, there is a path I know here, it is a bit difficult, but I shall help you. The view is worth the effort."

Roxanne hesitated. He sounded so matter-of-fact. His flirtatiousness had dissolved, and he was even comradely. Perhaps he really did appreciate her adroit scheme for getting the twins together with their suitors. Perhaps he would not trouble her, but simply show her a pretty view.

She looked back at the picnic site. Geoffrey and Fanny sat on the ground with Miss Rogers, who was daintily twining wildflowers together while gazing soulfully at Sir Geoffrey. Roxanne's betrothed was offering fresh flowers to the heiress with a worshipful countenance, whenever he was not scowling at his sister with a look that plainly ordered her to be gone.

But Fanny stubbornly stuck by them, and when she caught sight of Roxanne and the Duke, she called and waved urgently, but Rutledge pulled his companion along, and the last thing Roxanne saw was Geoffrey's guilty face glancing up at her while Miss Rogers continued to prattle at him.

They moved farther along the banks of the stream, without speaking, and gradually the trees grew thicker, the slope steeper. The voices of the picnickers faded away, and Roxanne found herself alone with Rutledge in cool green shade, walking on a soft carpet of turf, hearing only the tinkling of the stream, no longer the rushing water that had threatened the boots of two London gentlemen but a clear steady flow over small polished stones and pebbles.

Strangely, she felt relaxed in his company for the first time. She admired his long strides when he went ahead to hold back a branch for her, appreciated his strong arm helping her over some obstacle, and enjoyed the silence that lay between them, not fraught with tension, but a friendly silence, such as she had never know even with Geoffrey.

The trees began to thin out again, and after a few more minutes' walk, with only necessary words spoken between them, they emerged onto the hilltop, with a view of the Kent countryside spread out before them. There were the oasts, or hop kilns, poking up cone-shaped and topped with white chimneys like funny hats, in between the cherry and apple orchards, fields and houses and gardens and lanes, and a church steeple. All these lay spread beneath them, and for a while Roxanne simply looked and almost forgot her companion.

But in a moment he had made it impossible to do so, for he took her in his arms, there in full view of the sky and the birds and the small white wisps of cloud, and kissed her for the third time. Roxanne was taken off guard, startled both by his gentleness and his urgency, sensing his restraint and knowing a thrill of power at the hunger she had made him feel. She found herself returning his kiss in full measure.

A thought of Geoffrey passed through her mind, but she saw him accepting the homage of Miss Rogers, the heiress. A thought of her dead brother likewise was driven away by the sudden realization that this man who made so plain his eagerness for her, and at the same time his willingness to check it for her sake, was a man who was no murderer.

Then she simply gave herself up to the feelings that swept through her, and allowed herself to respond to the question of his lips and his arms, and she did not think rationally again for quite a while.

Chapter Thirteen

The sounds of quick breathing and footsteps crunching on fallen twigs alerted Roxanne to danger. Then she heard her name.

"Roxanne! Where are you?" It was Fanny's voice.

Roxanne broke away quickly from the Duke's embrace, and he did not protest but only looked at her ruefully. "It seems we are followed, my dear. Perhaps it is as well . . ." He pressed a quick kiss upon her hand and then moved apart from her.

There were so many things she wanted to say to him! This time Roxanne had been determined not to let such an event pass unnoticed. But there was no time. His eyes flashed a warning, and she quickly turned aside and gazed again at the view, trying to focus her disordered thoughts and steady her pulses.

Fanny was upon them.

"There you are! I saw you wander away and told your sisters I would find you for them. Did you know that Lord Culverton and Mr. Bentley almost fell into the water trying to cross the stream? I cannot imagine what they were thinking of." Fanny's bonnet was askew, her face was flushed, and her words followed quickly upon one another as she glanced back and forth from her friend to the Duke.

Roxanne, too, looked at Rutledge, and his ready smile warmed her just as his assurance gave her confidence. Forcing herself to ignore the confusion in her breast and hoping Fanny did not notice anything unusual in her demeanor, she replied, "His Grace wanted to show me the view."

Fanny looked down briefly. "It is very nice. But what a long walk! You must be tired, my dear. Come, let's go back. The food is being served, and I'm sure His Grace would not want you to miss your luncheon for the sake of a view."

The glance she gave the Duke, Roxanne noted, was quizzical. Could it be that her absurd idea of Fanny reconsidering the Duke's proposal was correct? After all, there was no real reason for her to follow them up the hill.

Roxanne looked at her friend's face as they made their way down, preceded by the Duke, who calmly helped them both down the path. Fanny's color was still unusually high, although that might have been a result of her vigorous walk. But her eyes glittered suspiciously, and Roxanne's worry grew stronger.

Roxanne tried to convince herself that her friend was not jealous, but she could not otherwise account for her behavior. She could at least be grateful that Fanny had not seen her and the Duke locked in each other's arms.

Roxanne trembled when she thought of it. How could she have allowed weakness to overcome her so quickly? She had not been vigilant. It did occur to her that the explanation for her strange readiness to disgrace herself might be love. Although she tried to disregard it, her heart whispered the word to her again and again, until she felt she could barely breathe.

Her behavior had been improper, even, the twins would say, sinful, but if it had been love that provoked it, it was excusable. With Rutledge, of all men! But was he or was he not the man she had hated for so long?

For the sake of her sanity, she hoped that she did not love him, but each time the Duke turned to help her, Roxanne avoided meeting his eyes, for that simple act sent such a tremor through her that it was as though they were linked mouth to mouth once more.

She hoped for a word with him before they joined the others, but Fanny stuck to them and would not leave Roxanne's side. Eventually the Duke was called away by Lord Culverton, who was beaming and obviously wishing to tell him of his success with Melodie. Rutledge favored Roxanne with one last look, unsmiling but holding out a promise, and then he was gone.

In a few minutes Roxanne was surrounded by all the ladies of the party. Only now did Fanny relax her vigilance and leave Roxanne with her aunt. Lady Camberwick placed a trembling hand on her niece's arm.

"My love, it appears . . . though I could not swear to it, but . . . oh, look at them! If those two girls are not betrothed, I will eat this grass in lieu of my roast chicken!"

Roxanne turned to see her sisters coming toward them, arm in arm, their faces glowing.

"Oh, dear Aunt Maria! Dear Roxanne! We have —"

"— decided that we made a grievous error back in London."

"And the Lord has seen fit to open our eyes to the

truth. That two beings so generous and of such pure hearts despite their trifling faults—"

"—should honor us with their love . . ." Gemma was the last to speak in this partnership of communication, and only because Lady Camberwick interrupted.

"I hope, girls, all of this nonsense means that you are betrothed to those two fine young men."

"Oh, yes!" they cried in unison.

The four ladies drew apart from the others, unwilling to attract their attention, as a formal announcement could not yet be made without Sir James's approval.

With scarcely any prompting, the twins eagerly explained how they had begun to be convinced of the worthy natures of their suitors.

"First, it was because they gave up that foolish wager. We realize that it was not an easy thing for those so accustomed to gamble upon every uncertainty of life," said Gemma, her browns eyes misty with emotion.

"But mostly, of course, it was because they behaved so splendidly in crossing the stream" Melodie continued, equally moved.

"How the water rushed!" said Gemma in awe. "I was quite terrified, and expected to see Cyril lying with his brains dashed against the rocks at any moment. And how awful if his boots had been ruined."

Roxanne met her aunt's glance and hastily looked away again. It would not do to let their amusement spoil this affecting story.

"And only think, how Tony—" Melodie stopped and blushed. "—how brave his lordship was in venturing into the torrent to help his friend."

"But do not forget, sister, that they were both in danger, and Cyril risked himself so that his lordship could get safely back to shore."

"It was after that that they asked us again if we could consider marrying them," said Melodie, gazing starry-eyed at her love.

Lady Maria's joy was slightly tempered with irritation by now, but Roxanne was enjoying these outpourings of love quite thoroughly. Her gaze wandered about and lighted on the Duke, who was not far off, watching them. No doubt he had heard every excited word, for he was grinning. She gave him a shy smile and turned back to her sisters.

Lady maria was saying, "For heaven's sake, girls, you are as ridiculous as ever! Apparently, though you have done the first sensible thing in your lives, it has had only a temporary effect. All I know is that you are going to make quite exceptional matches, for which I can take all the credit, and poor Sir James will be rid of you and your prosing." But she was embracing them warmly as she said this, and they did not seem disturbed at her words.

Geoffrey finally joined his fiancée, leaving some other young man to attend to Miss Rogers's appetite and luncheon, and to Roxanne's surprise and relief, he did not seem to have noticed that she had been missing. She felt awkward with him under Fanny's intent observation, and also guilty. Fanny was obviously expecting her to say something about his wandering away with Miss Rogers, but she could not very well scold him for neglecting her when she had been, only minutes before, in the arms of his friend.

Roxanne silently prayed for forgiveness and guidance, but none seemed immediately forthcoming, so she could only pretend for now that nothing was amiss. In truth, Geoffrey seemed more careless of her than before, and when Fanny left them alone he did not resume the ardent gallantries which had formerly elicited her disapproval. Though he remembered his position enough to bring her a glass of wine and a plate of lobster salad, and listened to the story of how she had induced the twins to approve at last of their suitors, he seemed distracted.

At times Roxanne definitely saw his glance straying toward Miss Rogers, who was holding court under a tree and whose silvery laugh drifted over to them from time to time. One of her courtiers was the Duke himself, and at the sight of him Geoffrey frowned. Roxanne felt a surprising twinge of annoyance herself until she noticed His Grace's satirical look. Apparently he was only amusing himself. In how short a time had she found herself able to interpret his every expression, she thought wonderingly. Was that love?

After the luncheon had been consumed, the older members of the party settled themselves to sit and digest and talk, Lady Camberwick drifting off into a contented doze which everyone pretended not to notice. The young people were getting up an exploration party, and Geoffrey stood up, holding out his hand to Roxanne.

"Shall we go, Roxanne? I heard there is a tremendous view to be seen if only one will walk uphill a bit."

Fanny, who had eaten with them and had almost lost her strangeness of manner at hearing the happy news about the twins, now frowned at her brother. "Roxanne must be tired, Geoffrey. She has already been up the hill and seen the view. His Grace took her up there before luncheon."

"Oh!" Geoffrey seemed surprised but not unduly disturbed by this information. "Well, then I shall leave you two ladies to gossip. I'm going to stretch my legs a bit."

"But Geoffrey—" his sister began, but he was gone. It was not long before he had joined the energetic group of explorers, which included Miss Rogers. Armed with her lace-trimmed sunshade, she had difficulty making her way along the path in her tiny kid boots, and so required Sir Geoffrey's assistance. They trailed along behind the rest, and the sound of their laughter traveled back to Sir Geoffrey's fiancée and sister.

"I want to talk to you, Roxanne," Fanny said, almost sternly. "How could you have left Geoffrey to that silly little creature's machinations this morning? And now, though I tried to keep him here for your sake, since you wouldn't make the effort, he has gone off with her again."

Roxanne was startled. "I can hardly keep him my prisoner, Fanny. He is a grown man and must do as he likes."

Fanny sniffed. "How cold you are! You accepted my brother's offer of marriage, and yet you don't lift a finger to prevent him from drifting away from you."

Roxanne blushed. "I never pretended to feel as he does, Fanny. I did refuse him the first time, you know that. But he was so disappointed . . . and I am very

327

fond of him, Fanny, truly I am, even though he pulled that shabby trick of telling everyone we were betrothed when we weren't."

Now it was Fanny's turn to blush, as she had known of this and had not mentioned a word to her friend. "All right then. But I must warn you not to keep Geoffrey on such a loose rein if you ever want to be his wife. Now that he is a Baronet, the title and fortune have gone to his head, and a little flattery from an heiress like Miss Rogers might—"

"I don't think I have to worry about Geoffrey's constancy, Fanny," Roxanne interrupted her, although she was not at all sure of it.

"And I do not think it wise for you to go off alone with Rutledge in that manner," Fanny went on, her face tight with disapproval.

"In what manner?" asked Roxanne indignantly, hoping that the brim of her bonnet would hide her guilty face.

But Fanny ignored her. "I think it very odd of you, too, since you have made no pretense of your feelings toward the Duke, and though I have not told you this before, you have been very unjust in disliking him, but of course you could not know . . ." Fanny's face wrinkled up and unexpectedly she burst into tears.

Roxanne, horrified, comforted her as best she could, feeling helpless and bewildered. For a few minutes she could not get her friend to tell her what was the matter, but after a while, Fanny calmed herself and turned to Roxanne, her eyes reddened.

"I—I'm sorry I have been so troublesome. It is simply that . . . I am suffering from a great deal of anxiety just now over a certain matter. And I am worried, too, about Geoffrey. After pursuing you so energetically, he is making a cake of himself over that Rogers chit. And I was left all alone this morning, and went to look for you, and found you with the Duke . . ." She gave a last sob, but smiled a little. "Please forgive me for being so emotional. I shall not plague you anymore. And if you decide that you cannot marry Geoffrey — for which I would not blame you, now that you have seen what he can be like — I will never hold it against you."

Roxanne had been thinking carefully, and despite her friend's words, she had drawn her own conclusions about this outburst. More and more it looked as though Fanny was cherishing some regrets over having once refused Rutledge, and she must be worried about recapturing his affection.

Unless the Duke was much worse than Roxanne now thought him, he was not giving Fanny any encouragement, and her friend must have been hurt at finding them alone together. As for the Duke's attentions to herself . . . but no matter what feelings he aroused in her, they were unsuitable. Even though she no longer blamed him directly for Alfred's loss, she could not marry him. He did not love her, or he would have told her so. The Duke was not a man to mince words. No, if Fanny wanted him, then she must have him, for Roxanne could not.

Still, it cost her a pang to say, "No more should I hold it against you, dear Fanny, if you decided to marry. You have been faithful to poor Alfred's memory long enough, and if you may be regretting now having once refused . . ." After a glance at Fanny's startled face, she looked down. "Then I wish you success and happiness. Though I once might have thought him unworthy, after much reflection I have changed my opinion of His Grace. There, you have my blessing." She was very proud of herself for being able to say those words.

She kissed her friend's cheek, rose from the rug spread out on the ground, and went to join her aunt and the older ladies, leaving Fanny looking after her with an incredulous mile.

It was a tired, sated, but not altogether happy party that returned home after the picnic. The Duke rode alone, and while Geoffrey tore himself away from Miss Rogers and rode next to the carriage that held Roxanne and Fanny, he almost ignored his fiancée and began to bicker with his sister over trifles, which led to his riding away. The older ladies and the twins, however, were in alt, and urged Lord Culverton and Mr. Bentley to ride off at once to see Sir James, so they set off almost immediately for Westcombe Hall, not even waiting for dinner.

The twins were desolate at even temporarily losing, for the sake of mere convention, what had suddenly become so dear to them. No one could doubt Sir James's reaction to the offers, yet his consent had to be obtained. They were of a mind to accompany their suitors back to Westcombe and begged Lady Chamberwick to chaperone them, but she and Roxanne strongly impressed upon the eager girls that this would seem like ungracious behavior, especially as their hostess was the cause of their present happy state.

If the others were excited, Fanny, Geoffrey, and Roxanne were brooding and silent that evening. Brother and sister did not appear to be on more than the most superficial speaking terms, for which Roxanne felt a twinge of guilt. If only Fanny had not interfered when Geoffrey seemed to be paying too much attention to Miss Rogers, she thought, they would not have quarreled. As for she herself, she felt awkward with Fanny and avoided a tête-à-tête with her, although her friend approached her several times during the evening.

As defense against this, Roxanne stayed by Geoffrey's side, a tactic that Rutledge, himself the only seemingly unmoved one in the group, regarded with a knowing smile. Roxanne was beginning to be glad she had given up her silly dreams of love, for he had not attempted to speak to her privately that evening. Instead, he sat talking quietly to Fanny, and she saw him several times press her hand as Fanny looked up at him with shining eyes. How quickly he could forget what had passed between them! Clearly it had meant little to him. Yet Roxanne burned for the touch of his lips again and hurriedly looked away from temptation, chastising herself.

An early bedtime was urged upon everyone by Lady Chamberwick. "All of that fresh air, my dears, makes one so tired" — she hid a yawn behind her hand — "and we have had such excitement today." Passing by the twins, she pinched their cheeks. "We all need our rest. Tomorrow I shall begin planning the weddings," she said, blithely disregarding whatever might be her brother-in-law's or nieces' wishes on the subject.

Roxanne was at the foot of the stairs, taking her lit candle from Geoffrey, and was about to ascend to her

331

bedchamber, but he detained her. "I must speak to you, Roxanne. Please, only for a moment," he said as she hesitated. The older ladies had gone up already, and she knew it to be improper, but she could sense that her fiancé had no intention of pressing any unwelcome attentions on her tonight.

"All right, Geoffrey, for a moment."

The Duke, who was the only one who lingered, was staring at her, but Roxanne resolutely refused to return his glance. They had shared a magical few moments, she thought, but it was not to be. She must give him up to Fanny. He must have loved Fanny once, and he would do so again. About his feelings for herself she knew nothing, except that some pride or arrogance made him continue in his attempts to court her without a word of love passing his lips. Kisses, she told herself sternly, were not, to a man like the Duke, necessarily tokens of love. And so she followed Geoffrey back into the drawing room, knowing that Rutledge was still watching them.

As they entered the room, they heard a pounding on the front door, and a footman hurrying to answer it. Through the open door of the drawing room, they heard the Duke's footsteps fade away in that direction, too. Geoffrey ignored the disturbance and began at once.

"I — I want to apologize to you, my dear," he stammered, not meeting her glance. "I behaved very badly today, leaving you alone, while I gallanted Miss Rogers, but she is very persistent, you know. She is beautiful and an heiress and highly connected, and very used to getting her own way, though I did remind her several times that I was a betrothed man." He paced about the room, never looking at Roxanne.

"But I should have had more self-control, I know. It was unpardonable of me to treat you that way. Fanny tells me I risk losing you, and although we are not agreeing lately over many things, her saying that does not surprise me. Under the circumstances, I . . ."

He finally stopped pacing and glanced up at Roxanne. She was dismayed to discover the look of calculation in his eyes, quickly gone. "I have insulted you by paying so much attention to another woman and it is only right that I offer you your freedom from me, if you wish to take it."

Roxanne was too shocked to say a word, and only stared at him in amazement. So this was Geoffrey, this was the man she had known all her life, to whose entreaties she had succumbed, after he had already made free with her name in public, for the sake of their friendship and his supposed love of her! When she realized what he meant, her anger flamed high.

"Indeed! How gracious of you, Sir Geoffrey. Did I utter a word of reproach to you? Have I led you to believe that I was insulted? I thought it was a only a casual flirtation, that you were pleased by that sly little thing's flattery, and although I thought it ill done of you, I had no mind to interfere with your amusement, since I had been told that I was the one woman to whom you could give your heart. I paid you the compliment of trusting you, and now I see how wrong I was."

Geoffrey was startled, and had clearly not been expecting such an attack. His brows drew together, and his fair skin reddened. "I see it clearly now, Roxanne. It was not that you trusted me, but that my behavior was beneath your notice, as has been my affection for you. Do you think I was flattered that I had to beg for your hand, and you a nobody with hardly a cent to her name? If it were not for the sake of your brother, who is my dear friend—"

"I believe you forget yourself, Pearson. You will apologize to Miss Winston at once for such intemperate language."

Neither of the combatants had heard him approach, but now Rutledge was in the room with them. His face was white with anger, his voice hard. Roxanne had never seen him other than friendly toward Geoffrey, and she could see that Geoffrey himself was taken aback.

"I—I—" Suddenly Geoffrey clapped a hand over his mouth.

"Exactly," said the Duke incomprehensibly.

But now Geoffrey was apologizing, stiffly, and Roxanne was sure, not altogether sincerely. "I—I should not have said what I did to you, Roxanne. But I do mean what I said about my behavior today, despite what you may suspect. You may have your freedom if you wish." He glared at the Duke.

"Is that satisfactory, Your Grace?" he inquired icily.

Rutledge nodded. "And now I wish you will do me the favor of leaving me alone for a moment with Miss Winston."

Geoffrey's eyes were filled with suspicion.

"I'm not sure if I should do that. Miss Winston is still my fiancée, and there's something deuced odd about your wanting to be alone with her." His voice taunted the Duke.

Roxanne was further dismayed, as Rutledge had always been so kind to Geoffrey. She intervened. "It's all right, Geoffrey. I feel perfectly safe with the Duke," she said with somewhat less than perfect truth. She held our her hand to him. "We will speak again tomorrow," she said gently.

Geoffrey looked into her eyes keenly for a moment, took her hand and grunted his assent. "Very well, Roxanne."

"And before you go, Sir Geoffrey, if you will be so good, there is a matter of business I must discuss with you before you retire," said Rutledge mildly.

Geoffrey glanced at Roxanne and then at the Duke. But Roxanne made her face a careful blank, though her heart was thudding wildly at the idea of being alone once again with Rutledge. He nodded stiffly. "I await your pleasure, my lord, in my room." He left them, shutting the door heavily behind him.

Rutledge drew Roxanne at once into his arms, so quickly that she had no time to breathe or anticipate what would come next. "The insolent puppy," he murmured into her hair. "I shall thrash him, if you will but say the word."

Breathless with surprise, Roxanne pulled away with difficulty. It had been so wonderful simply to feel his arms about her and rest her head against his chest, feeling his heart beat in time with her own. He let her go reluctantly.

"Thank you for the offer, sir. I am so angry with him I should like to do it myself, but I fear it is neither

Christian nor ladylike to administer a thrashing to one's fiancé."

Rutledge laughed but there was a shadow in his eyes. "Do you mean you are still going to marry him?"

Roxanne hesitated. "It appears he no longer wants me, because I am no longer a good enough match for him. To think how he plagued me over this betrothal, only to surrender to the first pretty heiress that he came across! I am very disappointed in his character. But I said I will marry him, and unless he breaks the engagement himself, I will. Although," she whispered, her lips trembling, "I think we have small chance for happiness." This admission was hard for her to make, to the Duke of all people, and she could not look at him. But she heard him sigh.

"I will be honest and tell you that it is unlikely this Miss Rogers will take him. Her papa, according to the Duchess, has his eye on a bigger title for her, and she is a mercenary little puss, as far as I can tell," he said.

"And I thought that you too, Your Grace, had succumbed to her charms!"

The Duke smiled. "Certainly not. She is not my type."

"I'm very glad to hear it. You would not suit, you know. I hear she did not make it up to see that lovely view. You must marry a strong walker, Your Grace." Roxanne was smiling now too.

He drew closer. "You don't hate me anymore, do you, my dear?" he said softly.

Shyness and a silly but insistent hope filled her. "No, I have never precisely hated you . . . let us simply say that I feel you are no longer in need of so much prayer as you once were."

Rutledge laughed. "I am not so black as you once painted me, eh? But it is touching to think that I have been prayed for."

"Oh, not by me, sir, but my sisters grew quite fond of you, and prayed for you every day. I, however, had long since given you up for a lost soul."

"How sweet you are when you smile at me thus."

He bent and kissed her, and though it was a brief kiss, it brought back to Roxanne all the turbulent emotion of those other ecstatic moments she had spent in his arms, and she allowed herself to enjoy it, for after all, this must be good-bye. She hoped that he would not insult Fanny, if he married her, by going about kissing other women, just as she hoped that Geoffrey, once she married him . . .

She broke away. The kiss seemed to have brushed the cobwebs from her mind. How could she marry Geoffrey, after what he had done? The insult, of course, was not in his ignoring her to flirt with Miss Rogers; in was in his thinly disguised attempt to be rid of her so that he might court the heiress. Could his love, which he had proclaimed loud and long, have been so shallow and false? A deep sadness overcame her, and she was filled with doubt. What had gone wrong, that her judgment of people had proved to be so false? The Duke was not so bad as she had thought him; Geoffrey, meanwhile, was much worse.

The impulse to cling to the man at her side grew, and she knew he was observing her silent struggle. Suppose she did give up Geoffrey and, disregarding Fanny's hopes, accepted whatever the future might bring with

Rutledge, only to have her judgment proved false yet again? "Oh," she cried, "I simply do not know what is right anymore."

Rutledge reached for her again, and she went to him instinctively.

"I know that I have confused you, my dear, and that I have caused you grief, but I wanted you to have the chance to see how wrong you were about me — and about this engagement to Pearson. I knew, my sweet stubborn one, that you would not take on faith what I had to tell you, that you must discover it on your own, in your own time."

"Yes," Roxanne murmured, with a little smile, "I thought you a monster, and nothing, even all the kind things you did, and all the ways you showed me how good you were, would make me change my mind until I was ready to do so."

Rutledge pressed her close. "I, too, my dear, was stubborn and arrogant. I wanted to believe you were cold and mercenary, and when I ceased to believe it, you accepted Geoffrey and overturned my beliefs again. But" — he gently lifted her chin so that he could look into her eyes — "I loved you all the time. I hardly knew how much until now."

Roxanne's eyes brimmed with tears of joy. She had not been wrong. Her own tangled emotions smoothed themselves in that moment, and all the pain and confusion of the last months culminated in this present delight as she beheld the adoration in his eyes and answered his unspoken question with her own eyes.

When they had celebrated this moment in the best way they knew, they drew apart a little, and Roxanne gave voice to the one doubt that was left in her heart. "What about Fanny?"

Rutledge repeated, "Fanny?" as if he had never heard the name.

Roxanne wondered if she had imagined everything. "Yes. You did love her once, and lately it seemed . . ." but under his amused observation she could not go on.

"It seemed?"

"As though she regretted rejecting your offer. The two of you seem to be great friends."

"I am glad to see that you are human and not perfect, my love, but jealousy is an emotion I will not allow you to suffer for a moment. Yes, Fanny and I are great friends, but no, I do not love her, if I ever did, and she had no designs of me. In fact," he said, laughing, "she talked about you a great deal, and led me to believe that if you did not marry Geoffrey, she would be very happy if I would assume that honor."

Roxanne was amazed at her own ignorance and blindness, but she saw the humor in it, and in laughter her last doubt was washed away.

But their happiness was brief, for very soon the Duke said, "I have many other things to say to you, my darling, but I must leave you now, and I fear I may not see you again for a few months."

"Months!" Roxanne thought her heart had stopped.

"A urgent message arrived from London tonight. I am going away—I cannot tell you where, but you must trust me. I will return, I promise you that, my love."

Roxanne felt her joy crumble into dust. Had she been deceived again? She recalled the pounding at the door, and wondered who this mysterious messenger was. "I don't understand. Why can't you tell me?"

Rutledge's eyes clouded. "You are already withdrawing from me, and I cannot blame you. You have been disappointed before. But please believe me, what I must do is for your sake as well as mine. I only ask you to give me your promise, and to accept this."

He drew a ring from his waistcoat pocket and slipped it onto her finger before she could prevent him. "I have been carrying it about with me since London, Roxanne, hardly daring to hope that you would one day wear it. Tell me, will you?"

His eyes laid his entire soul open to her, and she searched in their silvery depths, seeing no deceit, no pride, only deep love and hope.

She looked down at her hand. The ring was a slim gold circlet set with sapphires and diamonds. It was unimpressive compared to the riches she had seen adorning the women in London, but to Roxanne it seemed the most beautiful piece of jewelry in the world.

"I — must I promise now?" she asked. She could not bear to risk her heart this way. But had she not been taught to have faith? There were so many things she accepted on that basis alone. Could she not now accept his professed sincerity?

"I ask it of you only because, if my mission is successful, you will have other reasons to love me, and I want you to love me now, only for myself."

Her curiosity was wildly aroused by this talk of a "mission," but she kept her mind on what seemed most important.

"I do love you, and I will accept this ring and give

whatever promise you wish," she said firmly. Her voice rang with faith, her glance did not falter.

His smile rewarded her, and he kissed both of her hands passionately. "Then only promise to free yourself from Geoffrey, and wait for me. The only thing that can keep me from you is death, and in that case . . ." He kissed her mouth again. "I want you to know that you have already made me happier than I have ever been, just by being yourself. But I fully intend to come to you, and I hope, to bring with me a gift which will make our happiness complete. One more kiss, and then I must go. I must speak to Geoffrey before I change my clothes and ride away."

The kiss performed, Roxanne asked, "Will you not tell me where?"

"I cannot. I can only tell you our government sends me, as it has sent me before, and that must satisfy you."

"The government! I never suspected that you could be involved in anything so . . . so serious."

Rutledge smiled at her surprise. "Yes, I am not always the careless man of pleasure that I seem. But you know that already, Roxanne."

She laughed, in spite of her sorrow. "Yes, I have discovered it. And yet, regarding this trip . . . Geoffrey knows all about it, does he not?"

He hesitated. "Yes. But do not ask him. He is weak. Besides, he is going to London. I know I ask you to believe in mysteries and secrets and promises, my own sweet love, but there is no other way."

Roxanne smiled and stroked his face. It was rough with dark stubble this late in the evening, but it was dear to her, more dear than she could have believed possible, stubble and all. "I am quite accustomed to believing in what seem to many people to be promises, mysteries, and secrets, my love. May the Lord guide your steps."

And then she turned and ran from the room, unable to hide her tears. She could not have endured to linger any longer. In her room later, she touched the ring on her finger, and prayed for the Duke's safety, and for strength to carry her until she could see him again.

As for his mission and his intention of bringing back something that would make her happiness complete, she entirely disregarded these things as utterly unimportant. He loved her, and that was all that mattered.

Chapter Fourteen

"And to what do I owe the honor of this visit, Your Grace?" Geoffrey's voice, cold and angry, came from a dim corner of the room, where he sat drinking by the light of a single candle. Apparently the Baronet had been consoling himself with brandy while he awaited his late caller.

"It's not an honor, Sir Geoffrey, but merely a business call. I have something important to tell you," said the Duke placidly, drawing up a chair to the small desk opposite Geoffrey's seat.

"As important as what you had to say to Roxanne?" Geoffrey thrust aside his empty glass, and it rang against the bottle. "I was wrong about you, Harry. I thought you were my friend and could be trusted. It's plain now that no sooner had I told you about Roxanne than you began working your tricks on her. By God, if you have compromised her . . ." He half rose from his chair.

The Duke chuckled. "How can you be such a fiery defender of Miss Winston's virtue, Geoffrey, when just a little while ago you were trying to rid yourself of her so that you could court an heiress? And that lady, by the way, would not have you unless you were at least a Marquess."

"How dare you speak of Miss Rogers that way!"

Rutledge clicked his tongue and drummed his fingers on the desk. "First Miss Winston, now the Rogers chit. Come Geoffrey, which one will it be? You need not decide, however. Roxanne has decided for you. But she will tell you that herself. What I have to tell you now is more urgent."

Geoffrey's face was suffused with crimson. But the Duke did not flinch before the younger man's rage. "I am leaving for France tomorrow, and there are dispatches for you to take to London."

Geoffrey paled suddenly. "France! Has something gone wrong? Why do they not send me?" He seemed to have forgotten his antagonism in his present fear.

"Unfortunately, there are difficulties. They will not send you because there is no time for you to learn the necessary techniques which, though a trifle rusted, are already at my command," replied the Duke coolly. He chose a pen and inkwell, and searched the drawers of the desk for paper. But before he began writing he turned to Geoffrey, his face very grave.

"We have word that Alfred has been captured." Ignoring Geoffrey's gasp of horror and a barrage of questions, he continued, "He arrived safely at Reims, where he was to change disguises and proceed to Boulogne. It was south of there that he was to disappear and be smuggled home. But in Reims, he was taken by an agent of Napoleon's secret police, according to one of our paid observers, who, being French and a secret Royalist, was powerless to do more than warn us. Moreover, Alfred was badly wounded, and since they wanted to keep him alive for questioning, he

344

could not be moved to Paris. That is why I am leaving tonight for Folkestone and from there to France—disguised, of course. I must get to him before they carry him away to Paris."

"Let me help," pleaded Geoffrey. "I swear to you, I did not mean the things I said . . . it is just that since this damnable inheritance I've been so confused—everyone treats me differently, even my own family. I hardly know who I am anymore . . . don't punish me for it by making me wait here, wondering what has become of Alfred."

His real suffering was obvious, but though the Duke pitied him, he held out no hope. "It is impossible. I have my orders and"—he drew a packet out of his coat and handed it to Geoffrey—"you have yours." Then he bent to his task and began writing quickly.

"I have already given orders for a bag to be packed and a horse made ready. I suggest you do the same and make some excuse to go quietly tomorrow morning, so as not to alarm the ladies. I am informing my mother that I have gone to inspect my Scottish estates, but you can tell her that you and I have quarreled and that we find this house too small to contain both of us. I'm sure Miss Winston will confirm it. Fortunately, the ladies have other things to think of, as the younger Winston girls have become engaged, and no one will wonder about us for long. You may tell Fanny, of course, at your discretion."

Geoffrey frowned. "I don't think I will, sir. She has been practically insane with worry ever since we heard that Alfred was going to try to come home, although for a long time she hid it well. If she knew his danger . . . no, I will keep it from her."

The Duke nodded. "As you wish. But Roxanne — she knows only that I must go away, though not where, and that it is at the government's behest."

He finished writing and looked at Geoffrey sternly. "I hope I can rely on you to keep it that way. I do not want her put into danger."

Geoffrey stared back at him. "You love her, don't you?"

"With all my heart," replied the Duke simply. He pushed his chair back and rose. "Which, judging by your behavior to her this evening, I'll venture you cannot claim to do."

Geoffrey looked sheepish, but did not evade Rutledge's stern gaze. "No. I thought I did, but I realize that I was wrong. She represented something unattainable to me. When I finally won her, I also had a title and a fortune, and found that I wanted all the other things I thought I'd never have. I know I'm not good enough for her, fortune or no. But I would never hurt her. I knew that she did not really love me, that she accepted me in the end because of our long friendship, and because she needed to marry well. Believe me, I would never have done what I did tonight if I had believed that I had the power to make her unhappy. I'm only sorry I did not have the courage to be honest with her. I hope that you — and she — will forgive me." He stuck out his hand awkwardly, and after a moment the Duke took it.

Then His Grace left, accepting his friend's wishes

346

for success and a safe return, and Geoffrey retired to bed to pass a restless night.

The Duke, as he passed his mother's door, slipped under it the note he had written, and hoped that when she knew all she would forgive his disrupting her peaceful fortnight in the country.

Roxanne rose the next morning with the feeling that she awoke to a different world from the one she had inhabited the previous day. The reason for this became obvious when she recalled the events of the night before. She smiled at herself while she dressed, slipping the ring on a chain and hanging it hidden beneath her gown, having refused the services of a maid. It would be better if she gave herself time to control her emotions and present a bland face to the world before anyone saw her.

She went down to breakfast in some trepidation, to find the Duchess up unusually early, and quite agitated. The twins were with her but were calmly eating breakfast, and Geoffrey, pale and aloof, was helping himself to eggs at the sideboard. He looked up when Roxanne came in, but she was immediately accosted by the Duchess.

"My dear Miss Winston, you will forgive me if I do not wait even to wish you good morning, but I am very concerned about Harry. He left me this ridiculous note"—she waved a piece of paper at Roxanne—"and says that he must leave, as 'urgent business calls me to our long-neglected Scottish estates,' she read from the

347

note. "That could be part of the reason, because he hasn't been up there in years, but I would hardly call it urgent! Sir Geoffrey seems to think that it is because of a silly quarrel they had last night, but Harry would not . . . that is, I do not doubt your word, Sir Geoffrey, but you have been such good friends. Does it not sound very odd to you, Miss Winston?"

Roxanne wished she could tell the Duchess everything that was in her heart, but she had promised. . . . She tried to keep her voice calm and hoped her looks would not betray her. "I am sorry to disappoint Your Grace, but there truly was a quarrel. I cannot give you any other explanation."

The Duchess looked crestfallen, but on Geoffrey's face, strangely enough, Roxanne perceived a look of approval.

"And I am afraid, my dear Duchess, that I must leave as well," he said. "I hope that you and the ladies will forgive me, but a message arrived last night and I must take myself to London to deal with some rather pressing personal matters."

The Duchess sniffed. "Well, if all you young men are determined to leave us, I do not see what we can do about it. But if your fiancée will forgive you for deserting her, sir, I am sure I will not be the one to scold you."

Sir Geoffrey looked at Roxanne. "Will you forgive me, Roxanne?"

She gave him a reassuring smile. "Yes, Geoffrey, I have forgiven you already."

He pressed a quick kiss upon her hand and left the room. The Duchess looked at Roxanne oddly, but made no comment, and soon after, proclaiming the onset of a headache from having risen too early, she retired again to her bedchamber.

Roxanne partook of her breakfast quietly, listening to the twins' talk of wedding vows and eternal faithfulness. Now that she knew at least something of the happiness they must feel, she wondered they could talk at all. She herself would rather be silent and think about her absent lover, and wonder, though she scolded herself for doubting, if he would return and if his words had been sincere.

Though she had placed her trust in Rutledge the night before, the light of morning brought with it uncertainties that she could not keep at bay. Fanny's entrance into the breakfast parlor troubled her even more when she remembered what traitorous thoughts she had been harboring about her friend. But when they were left alone, for the twins took themselves away to walk in the garden and lament the absence of their loved ones, and Lady Camberwick was still abed, there was no awkwardness between them, which was due entirely to Fanny's easy manner.

"I hope I may be allowed to wish you happy, my dear," said Fanny, as relaxed now as she had been agitated the day before. "I always thought you would come to see how wrong you have been about Harry, though, I confess, I never thought your opinion would improve quite so much as it has!" She laughed at Roxanne's amazement.

"But how did you know?"

"Geoffrey told me what passed between you last

night and I gathered that your betrothal is at an end. He also told me that you had a private interview with His Grace, and I drew my own conclusions." Fanny's eyes were alight with mischief.

"Fanny Pearson, what has come over you? Yesterday you were scolding me for letting your brother flirt with another woman and for taking a walk with the Duke, and today you are delighted at the prospect of my leaving Geoffrey for Rutledge!" But Roxanne laughed with her friend and confessed that her assumptions were right. She slipped the ring on its chain from beneath her bodice, and Fanny admired it.

"I do not wish it to be known yet," Roxanne cautioned her. "There will be no announcement until Rutledge returns."

Fanny looked serious. "You are wise, but not, my dear, for the reason you think. You may place your trust in the Duke, I assure you. But if you tell everyone he has offered for you when he is not beside you, you put yourself in an awkward position, especially as all your acquaintance believes you engaged to Geoffrey, and there has been no word from him about the ending of that betrothal."

"My goodness, I let him go without telling him — I shall write to him in London . . . but he knows, he must know how I feel." She described to her friend Geoffrey's shocking attempt to induce her to cry off.

Fanny did not defend her brother's behavior. "He has changed since the inheritance, Roxanne, and that is one of the reasons we quarreled. But we made it up early this morning, before anyone else was awake, when he came to tell me he had to leave for London — I know it wasn't because he quarreled with Rutledge but because he got a letter from an old friend who was in trouble and needed him. Which is strange," she said, wrinkling her forehead, "because when he told me Rutledge had to leave too, for a moment I was afraid that . . ."

Roxanne looked at her friend expectantly. Whenever she spoke to Geoffrey, Fanny, or the Duke, she had the feeling that they were enmeshed in a conspiracy of some sort. Geoffrey and the Duke had both spoken of a surprise. This was certainly part of the mystery.

"What were you afraid of, Fanny?" she asked, hoping for enlightenment.

Fanny's face grew wary. "Nothing, my dear, nothing at all. Anyway I know that Geoffrey is very sorry for what he said to you. He had not the courage, he told me, to break the engagement himself, but hoped you would do it for him. He knew, you see, that you did not love him as he had loved you."

"As he had loved you." Those were very sad words, and to Roxanne they meant the end of something that, though she had tossed it away, had always made her feel safe. Now she had let go of that rope and was drifting — clinging to the thread of a promise. But the thread, which she imagined as being spun of the silver of Rutledge's eyes, must hold her love fast to her until he returned.

The precipitous departure of all the gentlemen left the house very dull indeed. The Duchess seemed to have lost her heart for entertaining, although she made a valiant effort for two more nights, even to the extent of inviting every family of any consequence in the neighborhood to dinner and a dance. Miss Rogers, though devastated to find Sir Geoffrey gone, consoled herself with her other admirers, and Fanny and Roxanne exchanged knowing glances at the sight of her vigorous flirtations.

But although Roxanne forced herself to dance and Fanny, too, went through the motions of being happy with a prepared smile and a kind word for everyone, the twins were almost as morose as they had been before the tender emotion had first touched their lives, for they had not yet heard from their father or their suitors, and refused to dance with anyone.

Lady Maria was impatient because Geoffrey had gone away just when she wanted to win his cooperation with her plans for his wedding, for she had made short work of the twins' nuptials, the essence of which celebration now reposed in a small leather pocketbook in her writing case. Now she was ready to tackle the hymeneal rites of her elder niece and Sir Geoffrey. This intention the Baronet had frustrated by his departure. To poor Lady Camberwick's increasing irritation, Roxanne refused to discuss the matter, saying it was far too early.

No one was much surprised or dismayed when, after a quiet conference one morning with her dear friend the Duchess, Lady Camberwick informed the girls that owing to her Grace's sudden decline in health, she must go to Tunbridge Wells for a cure, and therefore they were all going home tomorrow.

The twins taking "home" to mean Westcombe and not London, were delighted, for by that morning's post they had received letters from Sir James, Mr. Bentley, and Lord Culverton announcing that all was well regarding the betrothals, and that the gentlemen would be returning to Kent soon. The girls begged leave to send an express to forestall this departure, and after it had been dispatched, they ran upstairs to pack and piously bully the maids.

Fanny took the news in stride, and went into the morning room to write a note to her mother about her unexpected return. Lady Maria expressed her eagerness to return to Upper Brook Street and discover by how much her servants had cheated her in her absence. But Roxanne found that she could not look forward to the prospect of returning home with any pleasure. Her friends and family would be sure to plague her about her marriage to Geoffrey, and even when he himself arrived and they could announce the dissolution of their engagement, it would be most awkward and she wanted to put off the difficult moment of revelation.

Miss Lynchard, she was sure, would have her secret out of her in a trice, and even to her Roxanne did not wish to talk about the Duke. Besides, she still could not be sure . . . she scolded herself for cowardice and doubt, and had to keep reminding herself that at last she had seen Henry Malverne as he really was, and not as the monster she had thought him. But it still amazed her that she had traveled so far from her original feelings about him that she could contemplate with delight the prospect of being his wife.

353

A Duchess, thought Roxanne. I shall be a Duchess. She simply could not take it in, it seemed so preposterous. She struggled to conjure up the face of her beloved and succeeded, but it only flashed before her eyes for a moment and was gone. Yet so close did she feel to him that she was sure that if any misfortune befell him she would know of it instantly.

Where had he gone? Had he really gone to Scotland? There seemed no reason for the government to send him there. And his last words to her had carried a warning of danger. She thought of the war raging on the Continent. "Oh, no, not to France," she whispered.

"Well, Roxanne, I suppose you are daydreaming again, like all young ladies in love," Lady Maria chided her. "I have spoken to you twice."

"Oh! I'm so sorry, Aunt Maria. I'm afraid my thoughts were wandering." Roxanne tried to keep her expression neutral. Lady Camberwick had a very sharp eye, and she must be on her guard, unless she wanted to find herself in a muddle of premature explanation.

"Never mind, dear. I simply wanted to know if you would like to come back to London with me for a bit. We must buy your bride clothes, you know, and I'm sure your Papa won't begrudge me your company until Christmas. He'll have you almost next door once you're married." But in the next breath her ladyship said, "Oh, I am a selfish old woman. I am forgetting Sir Geoffrey. I am sure the two of you were longing to spend some time near one another at your own homes."

Roxanne, delighted by the invitation and grasping

354

for an excuse to accept it, managed to imply that Sir Geoffrey planned to spend some time in town on business this autumn and perhaps they could have him to dinner, at which Lady Camberwick brightened and said, "Of course, my dear. And why don't you invite Miss Pearson to stay with us? She will be a companion for you."

Roxanne thanked her, happy to know that she would have an ally against Lady Maria's determined wedding arrangements, and went off to write to her father and to tell Fanny of the invitation.

Her friend accepted happily and rewrote her letter home to inform her mother of the change of plan. By the next day all five ladies were bidding good-bye to the Duchess, whose own traveling carriage was ready to take them to Maidstone, whence they would travel post to London. From there the twins, attended by two of their aunt's servants, would make a daring journey to Westcome Hall.

"I must thank you, ma'am, not only for this lovely visit," Roxanne told her hostess, "but for your invaluable help in managing my sisters' muddled affairs. They would thank you too, I'm sure, except that they don't quite realize how much they owe to your intervention."

The Duchess smiled and permitted Roxanne to plant a kiss on her soft cheek. "Nonsense, my child, it was nothing at all. I like to see young people happy. And I hope, my dear," she said, her smile fading a bit, "although the wishes I once had have not come true, that you and Sir Geoffrey will be very happy."

355

Roxanne thanked her, unable to meet her hostess's glance. She burned to tell her the truth, but she was sworn. If the Duke had wanted his mother to know, he would have told her himself. After expressing her hopes that the Duchess's health would be restored in Tunbridge Wells, she got into the carriage with Fanny, her aunt, and her sisters. Her Ladyship's maid and manservant traveled with the baggage, and altogether they made an impressive train as they set off with a great creaking of wheels and stamping of hooves.

The journey to London was accomplished without much delay, the month being September and the weather therefore finer than many of the days in August. The twins remained in Upper Brook Street for a few days, during which Lady Camberwick escorted them on numerous shopping expeditions and gifted them with a complete set of bride clothes each. Then the impatient girls, who wrote twice a day to the loved ones who awaited them at Westcombe, where they were arranging the marriage settlements with Sir James, were tenderly seen off on their second journey. They went in the care of a stern matronly housemaid who, to their delight, was of a Methodistical bent, and under the protection of a giant footman who was to ride behind and see to the baggage. At their departure they pressed Roxanne not to forget to pray for their safe deliverance into the bosom of their family, and departed London without a backward glance.

The next few weeks were outwardly peaceful for the three ladies remaining in Upper Brook Street. There was not a great deal of society to be found in London, and so they lived very quietly, attending only a few small parties and visiting those of Lady Camberwick's friends who were resident year-round in town. Roxanne was felicitated upon her betrothal to Sir Geoffrey again and again, so that despite her discomfort she acquired the ability to thank everyone gracefully, without wondering what they would say when they knew the truth.

Fanny, too, seemed serene, but under the surface Roxanne felt that her friend was as agitated as she was herself. Miss Pearson fell in obediently with all Lady Camberwick's plans, and was pleasant to what few young men they met, for that lady, now that her nieces' futures were assured, had decided that Miss Pearson was in urgent need of a husband, which situation her mother and elder sister seemed to have shamefully neglected, her ladyship said indignantly.

However, Roxanne noticed when Fanny thought herself unobserved, she sometimes sat alone with her embroidery undone in her hands, staring into space, or looking out of an upstairs window at the treetops in the square a few streets away. What her friend's thoughts were, she could not determine and Fanny, when asked, always denied that anything was wrong. But she grew listless, her pretty pointed face looked tired, and even her lively hair seemed limp these days. Roxanne worried about her health, but after her first attempt at solicitude met with a gentle rebuff, she left her in peace.

Roxanne's spirits were no higher than Fanny's. She had not had so much as a word from the Duke. Not that he had given her any reason to expect a letter, but she had hoped at least to hear something of his safe arrival at his destination, whatever that might be. Geoffrey was back at Rosemark, indeed, he had left London quickly, even before the party from Kent had arrived, and had written to both his sister and Roxanne, saying little. However, he and Roxanne quickly came to an agreement by letter to end their engagement, the announcement now to be postponed, not till Roxanne's return to Westcombe but until the Duke's return. Geoffrey, too, Roxanne mused, had no stomach for telling the tale without His Grace's support.

The days dragged. Roxanne exhausted her small store of pin money in the shops, sending presents home to Miss Lynchard, Elizabeth, and Dorothea, and suffering many pangs of guilt at not being with them. But in her present state she felt she could not have borne their excitement at her betrothal to Geoffrey. She read every bit of printed matter in the house, which, now that the twins were gone, was now restored to its status as a repository of novels, popular weekly papers, and ladies' journals. She walked in the park with Fanny, and once or twice a week they hired hacks and rode together attended by a groom, but between her and her friend stood an invisible barrier. Even though they took comfort in one another's company, Roxanne found it difficult to draw Fanny out regarding what was troubling her, and Fanny knew that to mention Rutledge to her friend brought an anxious look to her blue eyes, and so desisted.

Slowly, the flame of Roxanne's love faded to a gentle, steady glow like the embers of a fire. She thought of Rutledge, went over in her mind every moment they had spent together, from his invalid days in Wiltshire to their last kiss, criticizing her behavior rigorously, pointing out to herself her faults and realizing belatedly how she should have appreciated His Grace's warmth, tenderness, and sense of justice from the very beginning. She, however, had been too blinded by unreasonable anger and grief to admit that he could possess any such qualities. She had wasted so much precious time!

Sometimes terror gripped her. Suppose he was not to come back? Then it would be her own fault, she told herself, if she had so few happy memories of him. A shining afternoon under the trees with the world spread out beneath their feet, a darkened drawing room in a sleeping house—these were very nearly all she could conjure up to fortify herself against loneliness.

Just as she thought she would go mad with worry, doubt, and unhappiness, Geoffrey arrived in town for a few days and came to dinner in Upper Brook Street. The ladies cried out upon beholding his countenance, which was somewhat swollen about the jaw and adorned with a piece of sticking plaster over his right eyebrow.

"Good gracious, what has happened?" cried Fanny, turning white. Her face looked very thin, her eyes huge.

"It is nothing," Geoffrey assured his sister. "I— I met with a slight accident on the road, but as you see, I am uninjured."

Lady Camberwick sniffed, disdaining this explanation. "If you do not call that dreadful bruise on your chin and a large cut over your eye injuries, sir, I don't know what they might be." She was about to ring for her maid, but Geoffrey stopped her.

"Really ma'am, it is nothing of consequence. I have already been attended to at my lodgings. The cut hardly bled," he lied gallantly, "and as for the bruise, it will disappear in a few days."

The younger ladies pressed him for details, which he was loath to give, finally saying, "A man stopped me on the road and demanded the right to relieve me of a few belongings. It was all over very quickly, I assure you, and the scoundrel went away looking much worse than I do."

He would not discuss it further, but as she was on her way to change for dinner, Roxanne heard Fanny accost her brother in the corridor behind her. They were apparently unaware that she was close enough to overhear them, and when she heard Fanny say, "You must tell me, Geoffrey. Was this attack related to the one you suffered in the spring?" she did not feel at all guilty about stopping to eavesdrop.

"Sometimes you are too curious for your own good, Fan," he grumbled. "Yes, I think it was, but you must not worry."

"Of course I'm worried. I thought he'd be home by now, but there's been no word . . . and what about Harry? Why isn't he with poor Roxanne? I'm not such a gudgeon as to believe that tale of his going to Scotland. Tell me the truth, Geoffrey, or I shall go mad."

Fanny's voice carried a note of hysteria, and Roxanne heard her brother trying to calm her. "Sshhh, the whole house will hear you. Don't go all vaporish on me, Fan. Must I call the maid to dose you with hartshorn?"

There came the sound of two deep long breaths. "No," Fanny said, under control. "I'm sorry. But please . . ."

"Oh, all right. You are correct. Rutledge did not go to Scotland. He received word that he was wanted in France. More I cannot tell you. But you must not worry."

Roxanne thought she heard a half-sob. Then Fanny said quietly, "I know we can trust him. But I had thought it was almost over."

"And so it is," her brother assured her.

"But what about what happened to you today?"

"I recognized the fellow. One of the same band who were employed to intercept us in the spring. But this time he wanted me to talk. Where is your friend, he wanted to know. What port was he to sail from? I knew, of course, and the wretch even offered me money to betray him — imagine, to betray my friend! But until I could get my hands free—"

"Geoffrey!" came Fanny's cry of surprise.

"—which didn't take very long, I told him a lot of nonsense, and then I paid him back. By God, Harry would've been proud of me, with all the sparring he's given me at Jackson's. I drew the fellow's cork very neatly, and drove off. So no harm was done," he concluded.

Fanny laughed. "Oh, my dear, no harm indeed. And now I hope they have learned to leave you alone."

"They'll get nothing from me," Geoffrey boasted. And then the brother and sister began walking and Roxanne had to hurry on lest they discover her lurking round the bend.

In her room she pondered this extremely odd and disturbing conversation. Why should Rutledge go to France? Why would a highwayman, or whatever he might be, want to know where the Duke was and from what port he was leaving?

Now that she knew how great her lover's danger was, however, she was not surprised at not having heard from him, and it made the prospect of his safe return all the more remote. She shivered, and a sudden realization filled her with fear. The man she loved must be a spy. Was that the reason for his worldly reputation, the arrogant pose that had so blinded her to his virtues? If he did return safely this time, would he give up such activities after their marriage? Here was another anxiety to add to her list.

Roxanne tried to put all the bits of the puzzle together, and though this activity made her head ache, she persisted. Again, she felt that she was in the presence of an impenetrable conspiracy. And there seemed to be a "he" unaccounted for in the affair. Her cogitations gave birth to a sudden stunning insight, which she quickly discounted. It could not be. Alfred was certainly dead, the government itself had informed them. . . . Her head spun, her heart began to pound, and she grew so faint that she had to lie upon her bed. Could it be possible?

Roxanne made up her mind that she would not mention her suspicion to Fanny and Geoffrey. If it was not true, and there was an excellent chance it was not, they would think her insane. However, if she was not simply imagining everything, Henry Malverne might even be Alfred Winston's savior, and not his murderer.

She went down to dinner with a keen sense of awareness. Before this she had allowed a lot of inconsistencies and oddities to pass unobserved, but now she noticed how deftly Fanny directed the conversation away from Geoffrey's journey and his injuries, and the looks that passed between brother and sister when Lady Camberwick inquired if they had heard from the Duke. Geoffrey also shot a warning glance at Roxanne, before he answered quickly, "Yes, he has written to me from Scotland, and charged me to convey to you his respects."

Her ladyship frowned. "That is odd. The Duchess wrote to me saying that she was worried because she had not heard from him."

"I'm sure the Duke has written to his mother," Fanny interjected. "Perhaps the letter went astray."

"Perhaps," Geoffrey agreed before Lady Camberwick could comment. "Or perhaps His Grace is simply a poor correspondent, like many other disappointing sons, myself included." He quickly diverted any further discussion of the matter by launching into a description of how his mother despaired of him and his sketchy correspondence, and dinner ended without any other comment on the Duke's whereabouts.

After dinner some of Lady Camberwick's cronies arrived to make up a table for whist with her ladyship. Roxanne and Fanny had no heart for music making, their usual evening occupation, so the three young people walked up and down the room together for a few minutes. Sir Geoffrey, a young lady on each arm, seemed restless. His arm was tense beneath Roxanne's hand, and she exchanged a glance with Fanny, but her friend's expression told her nothing. As they passed a window Geoffrey paused, something below having apparently caught his eye.

Roxanne peered around behind him and saw, in the late September dusk, a shadowy figure across the street. The man was staring at Lady Camberwick's house very hard. She heard Geoffrey make a sound of impatience and annoyance, and then he drew her away from the window. Fanny, however, lingered, and she, too, seemed disturbed.

"What is it?"

"Nothing, my dear. Probably only a dun waiting for one of the poor fellows a few doors away to come home so that he can press his bills upon him."

Roxanne was certainly not satisfied with this explanation, for Geoffrey's immediate reaction had signified some personal irritation at the sight of the man.

Then he begged her to excuse him for a moment, and Roxanne turned to Fanny, but her friend had left the window and was now softly picking out a mournful ballad on the pianoforte. Roxanne stayed at the window, and before Geoffrey returned to the drawing room, she saw one of Lady Camberwick's footmen emerge and approach the loiterer across the street. The servant gesticulated and seemed to be threatening to call the watch, and after a while, the man went away. By then Geoffrey was back, and forestalling her questions, he drew Roxanne away and engaged her in conversation.

To Roxanne's relief, Lady Camberwick, with a wink, left the betrothed couple alone and occupied herself with the card players in a distant corner of the drawing room, where even her sharp ears could not distinguish a word of their conversation.

Despite Rutledge's request that she not ask Geoffrey anything about the duty which took him away, Roxanne could not help herself. Armed with her new suspicions, she sought for a way to induce him to talk about it. He obligingly, though unconsciously, gave her the opening she sought.

"You look a bit out of twig, Roxanne, and so does Fanny. Have the two of you quarreled?" he asked.

"Not at all, Geoffrey. I am worried about Fanny. . . . Something seems to be troubling her and she will not tell me what it is."

Geoffrey was silent.

"And I'm worried too, about the Duke. Can't you tell me anything? At least tell me where he's gone, if you can't tell me why. I must know . . . will he ever come back? I only hope . . ." She stopped and swallowed. "I hope I haven't been a fool about him."

Geoffrey's face grew serious. "You mustn't think that, Rozzie," he said, taking her hand in his. "He loves you with all his heart, he told me so, and you couldn't find a better man than Rutledge. He stands by his friends. He will come back to you, and when he does . . ."

"Yes, I know, he will bring me something that will make my happiness complete," said Roxanne, snatching back her hand angrily. "Well, I am tired of promises. You, too, once promised me some great surprise. I do not want any surprises. I want the man I love returned to me."

Geoffrey smiled slowly. "Harry would be glad to hear you say that, Roxanne, you don't know how glad. You see, he always thought you hated him because of Alfred, and he wanted you to love him for himself, and not for . . ." He stopped, uncertain.

For a moment Roxanne felt he was on the verge of confirming her wild suspicions and hopes, telling her everything, but he continued carefully, "He did not want you to love him only for what he could bring you."

That, Roxanne thought, disappointed, might just as well refer to the wealth and position that would be hers as Duchess of Rutledge. Geoffrey then turned their conversation to reports of her family, and the messages they had charged him with. Roxanne felt that she had held the truth in her hands for a moment and let it slip through her fingers.

Geoffrey finished his business in London and went home, but not without first leaving Roxanne with a curious warning. "I know this may sound silly to you, my dear, but I wish that you and Fanny would let Lady

Camberwick's groom ride with you when you are in the Park."

Roxanne looked at him with surprise. "But of course we take him with us. Aunt Maria would never hear of us riding out alone."

"Come now, I know when you're telling a bouncer. I caught you in your first when you were eight years old, Rozzie," Geoffrey replied with a grin. But his eyes were worried. "Besides, I have heard otherwise from the groom himself."

"Odious spy," said Fanny, who had tired of her gloomy music and joined them.

"Very well, then," Roxanne admitted, "we do take him, but he does not exactly ride with us. He is rather old, you see, and riding is hard on his rheumatism, so when we want a good canter, we tell him to wait for us, and we ride as far as we want and then go back, and he escorts us home. It is all very proper, Geoffrey."

Geoffrey grinned. "Knowing you and my hoyden of a sister, I have my doubts about that, my dear. But do be careful, promise me."

"Nonsense," said Roxanne stoutly, "what could happen?"

"Well . . . one of you could take a fall."

Fanny chuckled and Roxanne made a wry face at him. He had helped teach both girls to ride, and knew full well the extent of their abilities.

"Or some gentleman could accost you and . . . and be unpleasant to you."

Roxanne laughed outright. "While we are cantering through the Park?" She called upon Fanny to take note of her brother's absurdity.

"You certainly are becoming an old woman, Sir Geoffrey." But at the look in her brother's eyes Fanny grew serious. "However, if Lady Camberwick will send a younger servant with us, one who can take a good gallop, we will gladly let him keep us in sight."

Roxanne agreed, and with this Geoffrey had to be contented. A few days after his departure, the young ladies, attired in their riding habits, went out to mount their hacks and found a different servant holding the stirrups for them. He was a young, burly groom, with a face reminiscent of a prizefighter Roxanne had once had pointed out to her by her brother.

During her first season, they had driven past some sporting swells, devotees of the Fancy, who had taken up one of these rough gentlemen, and made a sort of pet of him, something which her brother, though he enjoyed a good mill himself, had deplored. This man had the same build, the same distorted features, the same surprising quickness and agility as he tossed them up into their saddles.

That, however, was not the only thing that was odd about this groom. He looked very familiar, but Roxanne could not place him. Although she recalled having seen him in a different livery, she could not remember to what family it belonged. She questioned the man, and all he would say was that Lady Camberwick had just hired him, and that he had come recommended by Sir Geoffrey Pearson. With this explanation satisfying them somewhat, the girls set off on their ride.

The day was slightly overcast, but both young ladies were glad to be out of the house, and out from under Lady Camberwick's observation. Since Geoffrey's visit she had begun to hint that they really must get on with ordering Roxanne's bride clothes, and chided her niece for falling behind with the embroidery she was supposed to be doing for her trousseau. "For we can't have you coming as mistress to a fine house like Rosemark without a stitch of new clothes and only a dozen sets of sheets. How shabby that would look!"

Roxanne had been rather miserably and ineptly embroidering monograms on a few handkerchiefs. To cheer her, Fanny had whispered, "Don't worry, you can put those aside soon and start embroidering coronets on your pillow slips," but Roxanne wondered if that day would ever come. Meanwhile, a few fittings for new gowns had served to quiet Lady Camberwick temporarily, but the girls breathed a sigh of relief when they were in sight of the park, and could look forward to an hour free from her ladyship's wedding mania.

They saw hardly anyone they knew, and so it was not very long before they were able to urge their mounts into a smooth canter. The new groom, to the girls' surprise, was obviously not an accomplished equestrian.

"Wherever did Geoffrey find this fellow?" Fanny whispered to her friend. "He can barely keep his seat."

He followed uneasily on a horse that looked, to Roxanne's knowing eye, far too good to be entrusted to a servant. In fact, it was a mettlesome beast, and in a few minutes the girls saw that the groom was in difficulties.

The two of them had slowed, but the groom, red-faced and to their shocked amusement, muttering curses at the horse, soon outdistanced them, apparently unable to check the animal's pace. Fanny said breathlessly, "It looks as though our attendant's horse is in want of more restraint than he is capable of giving it. What on earth does Geoffrey mean by recommending such a fellow to watch over us?"

"That animal is far too good for him," Roxanne told her. "I don't think he's used to such high-bred horse-flesh."

"Not to any horseflesh, apparently. Do you know," she said, staring after the animal as it carried its unwilling rider away from them, "it reminds me very much of a horse that Rutledge purchased not long ago," Fanny mused.

They walked their horses for a few moments, hoping the groom would manage to turn his mount around and come back to them, but he did not appear, so after some discussion they decided to go after him. The afternoon was drawing to a close, the cloudy sky threatened rain, and they could not return to Upper Brook Street unescorted.

As they picked up their pace, a rustle at the side of the path alerted them, and they thought to see their unfortunate servant emerge at any moment. The fellow who did emerge, however, though built along the same lines, was most decidedly not their pugilistic groom. Although dressed in an approximation of gentleman's attire, so that from a distance his presence among the riders in the Park would excite no curiosity, he had a brutish face, roughly shaven and pale in the lower half, as though he had been bearded until recently. He was mounted on a large but inferior animal, such as no fashionable frequenter of the Park would be seen riding in public.

They exchanged a startled glance, but before the young ladies could hurry past him, he turned his big horse and blocked their way.

"What is the meaning of this?" demanded Fanny. Roxanne admired her friend's bravery, but noted that Fanny was pale and her lips trembled. Roxanne had not at once realized that they ought to be afraid, for their groom surely could not be far off, and she had no proof, for the man had not spoken a word, that he meant them any real harm.

There was a look of recognition in his mean little eyes, however, as he fastened them on Fanny. "I'll not hurt ye, miss, so long as you tell me what I want to know. Your brother thought he was a clever cove, I don't doubt, but I have a notion that you was dealt the real brains in the family." His voice was half threatening, half wheedling, and Roxanne felt chills run up her spine.

She now noticed his swollen nose, and other signs of a recent encounter with another man's fists. His reference to Geoffrey, and Fanny's expression of fear, seemed to confirm that this was one of the men who had attacked him on his trip to London.

The fellow edged his horse closer. It was impossible

for the girls, riding beside one another, to turn around i 1 the narrow path. Roxanne, whose mind was whirling with the implications of this scene, was seriously frightened, and caught Fanny's eye, as she started to back her horse, hoping her friend would follow her example and that they could quickly turn and ride away.

Before she could retreat more than a step, out came a pistol from within the fellow's coat. It was pointed at her heart. Roxanne immediately stilled her horse, repressing a cry of fear.

"I sh'll 'ave need of yer company as well, miss. I've watched you both, ridin' alone these past weeks, and foolish I thought you, but till today I never found you disposed to receive me, as they say." He laughed harshly, and his eyes were icy. Then the man turned again to Fanny, but his pistol did not waver. "Come now, tell me what you know about your friend who went overseas all sudden-like. Rumor 'as it that the fellers who run all that brandy and silk to sell to the gentry carried a passenger not long ago. I'm sure a clever mort like yerself, no offense meant, has something interestin' to say on that subject."

"I don't know what you're talking about. You are drunk, or mad, and have no right to accost respectable females this way," Fanny said with contempt, though she eyed the gun warily.

But now the man was staring at Roxanne, as if attempting to identify her. Seeing this, Fanny cried, "Get out of our way, you detestable creature!" To Roxanne's surprise, Fanny pulled her horse in front of her friend's, so that the man's view of Roxanne was blocked. She raised her crop to him, as if she would strike him with it.

"No, Fanny!" Roxanne reached over and restrained her friend. "He will shoot us," she whispered in terror.

He ignored all of this and moved his horse so that he could continue to stare at Roxanne. "And who might be yer companion, missy? It don't seem like you're quick with an introduction. Mayhap she's some other friend of one of the bold gentlemen, and knows something worth money to an interested party?"

Roxanne searched her mind for a way out of their deadly predicament, but before she could even form the bare skeleton of a plan, their delinquent groom suddenly emerged, from where he had apparently been hiding in the trees.

He rode up on the young ladies' captor and flung himself upon the man's arm, wrestling the pistol from him. The man was so surprised that the pistol was easily wrenched from his hand. Roxanne and Fanny had already backed off and turned, urging their horses between the trees so that they might be out of range of any sudden shot.

They huddled together well away from the path, listening to the sounds of a battle. Finally there was a thud, the sound of a horse neighing, and of someone dragging something. Fanny whispered urgently that they must fly, but Roxanne's intuition told her that the burly groom was most practiced in rendering his opponents senseless, and prodded her horse forward a few steps so that she could peer out along the path.

373

Sure enough, the man who had accosted them lay under the trees, and their groom was looking about him frantically, and began to call their names.

"Come, Fanny, it's all right now," Roxanne called to her friend.

"Are you certain?" Fanny and her horse emerged.

"The dreadful man is unconscious, and the groom is looking for us," she reported.

"Suppose he is one of them," Fanny whispered.

Roxanne smiled. "I think we can be confident that, though he disappeared at such an unfortunate moment, he is not in league with that fellow. First of all, Geoffrey recommended him to my aunt. Secondly, you recognized his horse as one belonging to the Duke. And now I have remembered what livery I once saw him wear."

Fanny looked at the man again. He was frantically searching along the path. "Rutledge's!" Fanny cried.

The ladies put an end to the poor servant's distress by appearing before him safe and sound, whereupon he was so apologetic for his clumsy riding and for not being able to get to them in time to prevent the man from accosting them that they felt sorry for him, and assured him he would not be turned off without a character.

He thanked them, and tugged at his hat. "Bless you, young ladies. Else I'd 'ave to go back into the ring, just where 'is Grace found me. I'd rather work for 'im than go up against the Champion again and 'ave me face beat to a pulp till I'm so ugly me own mother'd be afeard of me."

"His Grace! Do you mean the Duke of Rutledge?" Roxanne asked. "We understood that you were now employed by Lady Camberwick."

The man turned beet red. "I guess I can't rightly keep me trap shut, but now that I've let the cat out, 'tis true enough. The Duke keeps me in 'is employ for special siterations, on account of me perticular skills, miss."

Roxanne and Fanny exchanged a glance, and though they both smiled at the man's barely concealed pride in his position, to Roxanne this added another thread to the tapestry of deception and mystery that surrounded the Duke's sudden departure, and her suspicions of its cause.

They rode home without further incident, and made a pact not to mention their recent peril to Lady Camberwick or to anyone, commanding the groom to abide by it as well, which, for fear of losing his position, he was very glad to do. Roxanne tried to discuss with her friend what had happened, but Fanny evaded her by pleading a headache. However, she made the mistake of coming down to dinner, and though in Lady Camberwick's presence not a word could be said, that night Roxanne knocked at Fanny's door, ready to demand an explanation.

"Fanny, you must tell me if I am going mad, or perhaps just letting my imagination run wild," Roxanne began firmly, wrapping her dressing gown around her and curling up in an armchair. Fanny sat in bed with her knees hunched up under the blankets, her hair poking out every which way from beneath her nightcap. She looked very young and rather startled when she was thus accosted, but Roxanne persisted.

"It is obvious that you and Geoffrey, and Harry too, are keeping something very important from me, and I believe it is time that you told me what it was. First the attack on the Duke and Geoffrey, then Rutledge's sudden departure, a second attack on your brother, the man watching the house that evening, and today—"

"Roxanne, after what happened to us today, you should realize that you are safer if you remain ignorant."

Roxanne made an impatient sound. "Safer? I had a pistol pointed at me today and being ignorant was no protection from *that*, silly!"

Fanny conceded that she had a point. She plucked at her sheets, tucked in her wayward locks, and finally looked at Roxanne. "Very well, I will tell you as much as I can, but . . . I hope this does not change your opinion of Rutledge, or shock you too much."

"I don't see how it can, unless you are going to tell me that I have been right, and that the Duke is as bad as I once thought he was, but somehow I do not think that is what you are going to say."

"All right, then, listen carefully. The reason you have been kept in the dark is because it was feared that you and your family would be in danger if you knew the truth about a certain matter, and *that* was proved today. The man with the pistol was very curious about you, and if you think you were frightened this afternoon, you had better be grateful that he did not know who you were, for he would have carried you off in hopes that you could give him more information about the real identity of a man who is suspected of being a spy for our country against the French." She paused, watching to gauge her friend's reaction, but so far Roxanne showed no sign of going off into a swoon, so she continued.

"This . . . spy . . . has passed extremely valuable information from France to our government, information very damaging to Napoleon and his ambitions. As far as anyone here knows, the man is presumed dead, and we must not allow the French to think otherwise, else they will hunt him down like an animal and . . ." Her voice broke; she could not go on, but by now Roxanne, who had been listening spellbound, had flown from her chair to Fanny's bed and taken her by the shoulders.

Her heart was pounding in her throat and she stared incredulously at her friend. "Is it . . . then I am not insane . . . it is Alfred! He is alive!"

For several minutes there were indiscriminate tears and laughter, exclamations and questions. When both young ladies were calm enough, Fanny blew her nose and wiped her eyes, offering her store of clean handkerchiefs to her friend, who was in a similar state of emotion, and began to explain more intelligibly the mystery that had been plaguing Roxanne for months.

"Geoffrey and I knew, you see, because Geoffrey was involved in helping get Alfred out of the country. Of course the Duke, who had spent much time in France before the war, helped prepare your brother for his new role, and though I was heartbroken when Alfred told me what he planned to do, I knew my parents would not consent to our wedding for years, and I supposed, like a fool" — she blew her nose vigorously — "that it was no worse than his joining the army, which he had promised your mother he would never do."

"And so that silly duel with Rutledge was a pretext to get Alfred over to France before war broke out again . . ." Roxanne surmised.

"Yes." Fanny nodded. "And then he assumed a false identity, which his excellent command of French made practically impenetrable, and the story of his death was made public."

"But to us, his family! How could the government be so cruel as not to tell us the truth!" Roxanne was enraged, and had any representative of the government, her beloved Rutledge included, come within a foot of her she would cheerfully have throttled him.

"I'm sorry, Roxanne. It was judged safer, and it was your brother's own wish," Fanny said softly. "You see he knew that if he ever came under suspicion of being an Englishman in disguise, the French would soon realize that he and their English visitor Alfred Winston, whose body had never been recovered, were one and the same. If Alfred Winston's family knew that he was still alive in France, Napoleon's spies here would not rest until they had extracted whatever information they could from that family. As it was, when the French did begin to suspect the truth, Geoffrey and the Duke were in danger because they were known to have been Alfred's friends. Fortunately for me, the French did not know that Alfred and I considered ourselves betrothed. But his father and sisters would not have been safe in the knowledge of his continued existence as a spy in France."

All at once everything fell into place. Rutledge's hurt at her previous contempt of him, his and Geoffrey's mysterious robbery on the way to Rosemark in the spring, and now, Rutledge's sudden departure from England. "The Duke is in France then, is he not?" she asked with renewed agitation. "And Alfred . . ."

But Fanny only shook her head. "That is just what I do not know. The last thing I was told was that he was on his way home—a difficult proposition if you remember his need for disguise. But I think that they—Geoffrey and Harry—have been keeping things from me lately. I think something has happened to Alfred . . ." Her tears threatened to flow again, and Roxanne pressed her hand.

"I only know that I have a terrible feeling, here"—Fanny pressed a hand to the center of her chest—"as though I'll never see Alfred again. And I have waited so long . . ."

"You have been very brave, and faithful and clever," Roxanne told her. "I could never have borne half of what you have borne in the past three years!"

Fanny smiled. "But you have endured something almost as bad. You believed your brother dead. But somehow, you still fell in love with the man you believed the indirect cause of his death."

Roxanne smiled, and her eyes shone. "I suppose that is one of the miracles of love," she said. "It manages to find its way over such obstacles. Somehow my pain and revenge became much less important than the way I feel when he is with me."

"The twins would very likely read us a psalm, or sing us a hymn at this sacred moment," Fanny said, putting on a solemn expression reminiscent of Melodie at her most dignified.

They giggled until they were weak, from sheer relief and exhaustion, and finally they were serious again.

"I must write to Papa right away," Roxanne told her friend.

Fanny looked horrified. "Oh, no, you cannot tell anyone. Why, I was not supposed to tell you, only I was sure you had guessed already."

None of Roxanne's arguments would sway Fanny, and after her danger that afternoon, Roxanne did see the wisdom of keeping the family in ignorance for a little while longer. If the girls and her father knew that Alfred lived, they would be unable to contain their joy, and the story would be bound to get out to everyone, and eventually to the French spies. Could she be responsible for some ruffian one day holding a gun to her poor invalid father, or the twins, or even to little Elizabeth or Dorothea? Roxanne shuddered at the thought, though she had a moment's amused curiosity as to how Miss Lynchard would have handled the scoundrel. However, she promised to keep the secret, as Fanny had kept it for three long years. It could not be much longer, she told herself. Soon they would know the outcome, good or bad.

With many expressions of gratitude and sympathy, Roxanne left her friend amid a pile of used handkerchiefs, recommending her with a smile to read a few pages of the Bible, and sought her own troubled bed.

Roxanne did not take her own advice, leaving her own well-thumbed leather covered Bible on the nightstand. Her feelings fluctuated between joy and terror.

Now there were two of her loved ones in danger. She was positive that Fanny was right. Something must have gone wrong with the plans to bring Alfred home, and the Duke had gone to his assistance. Love swelled her heart and she shed a few more tears, whether of joy or anxiety even Roxanne herself could not tell.

"Bring him home safe to me, please bring him home," she whispered. And though the news of her brother filled her mind, her heart was full of her lover, and it was for him she prayed.

Chapter Fifteen

On a crisp morning in late October a carriage emblazoned with a ducal crest pulled into the yard of the Angel in Westcombe. The proprietor, Mr. Muggins, was informed by his sharp-eyed servants of this important event, and tore himself away from majestically surveying the taproom to greet his noble guest in person.

"Welcome, Your Grace, I've not seen you since the spring, when you were here with Mr. Geoffrey — your pardon, Sir Geoffrey now." The landlord peered as keenly at His Grace as was compatible with his inferior position. "May I take the liberty of inquiring after Your Grace's health?"

The Duke of Rutledge, looking drawn and somewhat thinner than he had in the spring, his coat hanging on his shoulders in a way that would have induced his fashionable tailor to contemplate suicide, had to admit that he had not been well, though he was much better now. "My appetite, however, is unimpaired," said the Duke with a smile.

"Ah, luncheon, my lord! Certainly," said Mr. Muggins, relieved to find that his culinary services were still wanted.

"Oh, and Muggins, I have an ailing gentleman with me, and will require a private bedroom for him. He cannot sit up too long, and he will be here at least until this evening."

"Of course, Your Grace," replied Mr. Muggins, obviously consumed with curiosity. "And will Your Grace be requiring a room as well?"

"No, I shall be returning to London after I make some calls in the neighborhood."

"Very good, my lord." And the mystified landlord went off to do the Duke's bidding, without even the satisfaction of a peek at the unknown invalid, who had not yet emerged from the carriage. However, he promised himself that at luncheon he would bring in the wine with his own hands and thus look his fill upon that gentleman.

But he was to be disappointed, for the unnamed invalid was quickly muffled in blankets and carried up to the bedroom by the Duke's man, and once there, only the Duke attended him until he was summoned to the table. His Grace dined alone in a private room, leaving his man in attendance and apparently on guard in the bedchamber, for when a tray of food was sent up, this servant took it and quickly shut the door without vouchsafing the curious landlord or his maid a glimpse into the dim, shuttered interior.

Having made a hearty meal, the Duke ascended to his companion's room. There, Mr. Alfred Winston, looking pale, lined, and much older than any of his family would remember him, sat up in bed, not precisely at death's door, but certainly not the vital young man he had been three years before.

He was lanky and sinewy, with dark hair and eyes, a

383

bold chin, and an assertive, aquiline nose. These features were emphasized by his extreme thinness, but hwas still handsome in a roguish way. Altogether therwas nothing in his build or countenance to remind thDuke of Roxanne, yet His Grace felt a pang of recollection while looking at him all the same. Soon, he tolhimself. His only desire was to see her face when hebrother was carried into the house, and then, after theincredible fact of Alfred's existence had been digestedto get her alone somewhere and assure her of his devotion. Surely, he thought, after all he had gone throughhe deserved at least that.

Alfred, wounded and weakened from loss of bloodand his French captors' indifferent treatment, hadbeen rescued and smuggled home after a great deal ofdanger and hardship. In the process the identities ofboth men had been discovered, and so they would be ofno further use to their country in these matters.Rutledge could only be glad.

Although it would have been quicker for the twogentlemen to go straight to London, where several interested parties awaited Mr. Winston's return and reports of the conditions in France, Winston haddemanded to be taken directly to Westcombe Hall. TheForeign Office, he had told the Duke, could deucedwell wait. His family came first.

Rutledge had agreed. Although he had not discussedRoxanne with her brother, he assumed she would be athome by now and imagined her delight when both ofthem appeared at the hall. He, too, had had no desireto go to London first.

When they were unloaded from a smugglers' vessel somewhere near Hastings over a week ago, the two men had rested from their ordeal while hidden in a sympathetic fisherman's cottage. The Duke sent a letter to Sir Geoffrey Pearson, and instructions to his steward at Rutledge to send his carriage, some clothes, money, and other necessities to them. These things, under the care of the brawny manservant who now nursed Mr. Winston, had arrived promptly, along with Sir Geoffrey himself, joyful and eager to see Alfred. The Duke was expecting an emotional scene, but he was disappointed.

With the characteristic restraint of an English gentleman whose feelings are deeply stirred, Sir Geoffrey merely said, "High time you showed your face on this side of the Channel again, my fine fellow. Paris get too dull for you?"

To which Alfred replied, "I heard that you couldn't accomplish anything here without me, so I thought I'd better come to your assistance."

But the two friends were grinning from ear to ear and in a moment they indulged in a hearty embrace, until the Duke intervened. "Easy, Pearson, Winston'll be smothered and you'll have undone all my careful nursing."

There was not much time to catch up with all the changes the past three years had brought, except that Alfred whistled when he heard of the turn in his friend's fortunes.

"A Baronet, eh? Fifteen thousand pounds? Congratulations. I suppose the next thing is you'll find a wife — a good one won't be hard to come by now, I daresay."

The Duke watched with amusement as Sir Geoffrey quickly changed the subject, volunteering to relieve Alfred of the written reports that had to be brought to London. That was when Rutledge had discovered from him that Roxanne was not at home, but had returned to London with Lady Camberwick.

Taking advantage of a moment when Alfred drifted off to sleep, the Duke said, "I'll take those papers myself then, Geoffrey, and bring Miss Winston home with me."

Geoffrey smiled. "Then you'll be saddled with my sister, too, sir. She's staying with her ladyship as well."

"Good God! Do you mean that I have spent the most wretched two months of my life saving Winston's skin, only to find that the two females who love him most in the world won't be here to see his triumphant return?"

Geoffrey laughed and said he was afraid it was so, but it couldn't be helped. "You can take comfort in the fact that neither one of them knows anything about this yet," he offered.

Rutledge was by now regretting his promise to Alfred to bring him to Wiltshire, but he must deliver his charge, and there was nothing for it but to put off the reunion with his beloved. He had tortured himself for the last several weeks, wondering if her faith in him would endure such a long and silent separation, and he could hardly wait to take her in his arms and prove to her that his love had only grown since their leave-taking.

He was disappointed, too, that their reunion would be considerably less dramatic than he had supposed. He had planned to present Alfred to her as an offering of his love, but this would hardly be possible if the offering was at Westcombe Hall being pampered and overfed by his other sisters.

Then again in London he could have the pleasure of a private interview in order to inform Roxanne of the joyous circumstance that would add the final polish to their happiness, and of escorting her home himself. With these modified plans His Grace had to be satisfied.

When he and Alfred had made plans to set off on their journey into Wiltshire, Geoffrey had offered to travel with them, but the Duke thought he could make himself more useful by going ahead of them to prepare the Winstons for their son's arrival.

"It will be better coming from you, Pearson, since you are an old friend of the family."

"You must not tell them I am ill, you know," said Alfred. "Only explain how I happened to be reported dead, and say that Harry has rescued me from France and is escorting me home. And mind you be tactful, Geoffrey. You have told me that my father's an invalid now, so take care you don't send him into a fit by bursting in on him at dinner with the news of my resurrection."

Sir Geoffrey laughed. "I'm not a schoolboy, Alfred. I can delivery the message like a gentleman. Have no fears for Sir James, or for your sisters either, although the twins, I am sure, would love to hear me speak of resurrection. I am afraid, Alfred, that your temporary death sparked a sort of religious conversion in them."

"Did it indeed? I recall they always had a tendency to throw themselves wholeheartedly into things. They must be quite insufferable." Alfred laughed weakly, coughed, and tried to sit up higher. The Duke's manservant had placed another pillow behind his shoulders, and Geoffrey had regaled his friend with tales of his sisters' adventures in London, reserving the news of their betrothal for the girls themselves to tell their brother.

Alfred listened with pleasure, and his expression grew softer. "Ah, the girls. How the little ones must have grown, and Roxanne — is she a beauty now? I own I always thought she'd be one someday. Has she any suitors, Geoffrey?"

He had reacted to his friend's obvious discomfort at this question with a laugh. "I'd swear you're blushing. Come, am I to wish you happy? It's all right; I shall gladly entrust my favorite sister to you, old fellow."

Geoffrey muttered, "No, we are not . . . that is we were, but . . ."

Alfred, having fully expected to hear of a betrothal, looked disturbed, and the Duke hastened to say that although they were the best of friends, Miss Winston and Sir Geoffrey had mutually agreed that they would not suit.

Alfred's illness had by no means dulled his wits. He took one look at Rutledge's face as the Duke reverently uttered his sister's name and drew his own conclusions.

"It is you then, my lord?"

"Although at present it is a secret between your sister and myself, I have the honor of hoping to be your brother-in-law, should Sir James give his consent to the scheme," the Duke admitted modestly.

Alfred's face lighted with pleasure, though he expressed his regrets to Geoffrey, adding with a grin, "No offense meant, my friend, but I have a fancy to see Roxanne as a Duchess."

Then he had demanded an explanation of how it all came about, but Geoffrey, more and more embarrassed, said sternly that Alfred must rest for the journey, and that he himself must set off for Westcombe, and the Duke promised to tell Alfred the story on the way if he would promise to sleep now. Geoffrey left after his friend obediently fell asleep, having received assurances from Rutledge that he would not let Alfred know what a fool he had been over his brief betrothal to Roxanne.

That reunion in the fisherman's cottage had been a week ago, and now the journey was all but over, and they were only a dozen miles from Westcombe Hall. The Duke was impatient to press on, deliver his friend, and hurry to London and the arms of his love, but Alfred had had a bad night and could travel no farther today. His Grace's plan was to visit Sir James Winston and his family to carefully explain that Alfred, though not dead after all, had not returned to England in that prime condition in which he had left it. Then he would help them bring Alfred, still incognito, home to be nursed, and the Winstons themselves could have the pleasure of informing their friends and neighbors of

389

the miracle.

Seeing his charge settled comfortable, the manservant watching over him, the Duke hired the best horse in the Angel's stables and rode the twelve miles to the Winston's. He found upon his arrival that the servants remembered him and asked with respect after the wound that had once made him an enforced guest there, a wound which he had almost forgotten.

He was shown into the drawing room by a nervous maid, brought tea by a beaming footman, and was told that Sir James was out for his airing, the young ladies and the two gentlemen accompanying him, but that they would be back at any moment.

Rutledge puzzled over this while he drank his tea, but though he assumed that the young ladies referred to must be Gemma and Melodie, he was at a loss to discover the identity of the two gentlemen, his ordeals in France having swept from his mind the affair of his young friends Tony Culverton and Cyril Bentley.

In a few minutes a great deal of chatter and noise heralded the arrival of Miss Elizabeth and Miss Dorothea, accompanied by Miss Lynchard, whom the Duke recalled quite well. The little girls squawked and then quieted when they saw him, but Miss Lynchard showed no surprise, only a warm welcome in her hazel eyes.

"What a pleasure to see you again, my lord," she said calmly. Her glance, he felt, saw right through him, and though he was taken aback, he knew that here was a possible ally in breaking the news of Alfred's sickly condition to Sir James without ill effect, and to the young ladies without a single case of the vapors. The girls would not dare be vaporish, he sincerely believed, in the presence of Miss Lynchard's unrelenting common sense.

"I am glad to see you, too, Miss Lynchard. I shall never forget your kindness to me when I was a poor invalid here."

Miss Lynchard demurred. "I only did my duty, Your Grace. It was Roxanne who took it upon herself to amuse both you and Sir Geoffrey."

Not knowing how much his love might have told her former governess, the Duke grasped at Geoffrey's name to lead her away from the all too seductive topic of Roxanne. "He has been here, has he not?"

Miss Lynchard smiled broadly, replied in the affirmative, and the little girls broke out of their governess's spell of good behavior to cry, "Oh, yes, my lord, Geoffrey came yesterday and told us that our brother Alfred has come back from the dead!"

"Gemma and Melodie have been praying and crying all day," reported Dorothea with disgust. "They are worse than ever since they got betrothed."

"But we like Lord Culverton and Mr. Bentley, don't we?" asked little Lizzie, at which her sister nodded and said that they were not at all stuffy like the twins.

"You may go to the nursery and ask Nurse to give you your supper now, girls," said Miss Lynchard in unquestionable tones of dismissal.

"They seem to be more excited about the betrothals of their sisters than about Mr. Winston's return," the Duke could not help remarking as he watched them go.

Miss Lynchard was not at all offended. "Of course. They were so young when they were told Mr. Alfred was dead, they hardly knew what it meant. They remembered him, of course, but his much greater age and the fact that he spent little time at home with them make him a sort of legendary figure, rather than a real sibling. Of course, they are thrilled to have a big brother again, and they have been plaguing me since Sir Geoffrey came yesterday about when he will arrive."

"So Sir Geoffrey was only one day ahead of us? I'd not thought him so slow, but it is just as well. I did not wish to keep the family in suspense any longer than I had to. And as you no doubt surmise by my presence, Alfred is here, but I was not able to bring him with me. He is very ill, and I was hoping that I could count on you to see that the family do not experience too much of a shock at seeing him. I have left him resting at the Angel, under the care of a very trustworthy servant."

Miss Lynchard smiled, and the Duke wondered how her face could be wise and mischievous as the same time. "I have endured three years of suspense, though I had every confidence in you and Mr. Winston. Another day would not have hurt me. As for the family, just knowing that Mr. Winston is alive is enough to hold them until he comes. You may count on me to cushion the shock of his illness."

It took him some time, but the Duke eventually absorbed the salient point of her speech. "You—you *knew?*"

For a moment he was horror struck at what must be

the carelessness of someone, for how else could this simple governess, living in the country, knowing no one, have discovered one of the darkest secrets it had ever been his privilege to have shared?

"Sit down, my lord, and let me give you some more tea. You do not look at all well. I daresay the French made it difficult for you. Yes, of course I know all about it. I have suspected ever since that ridiculous duel that something was not quite as it seemed. However, I was well aware of the necessity of keeping it a secret from the family."

"Perhaps," the Duke said, recovered now and ready to be amused by Miss Lynchard's explanation of her surprising knowledge, "you will tell me exactly where the gaps in our deception first appeared."

"A simple matter," said Miss Lynchard, taking a seat opposite the Duke, which forced him to sit down as well. "I knew Mr. Alfred's character very well, and I knew that while his mother lived he would keep his agreement with her to the letter, though joining the army was his heart's desire. However, after she died, I was expecting any day to discover that his ambition and energy had found another outlet. When you took him under your wing, Your Grace, I wondered whether he would take up the career from which you had so recently retired."

"Good God," cried the Duke, forgetting his manners in his astonishment, "do you know every secret I have, Miss Lynchard?"

She smiled sweetly and poured him the glass of brandy, as he was beginning to look as though he was in need of stronger sustenance than tea. "Certainly not, Your Grace, though I trust that all is well now between you and Miss Winston? She, of course, told me she had declined your offer, but she and Sir Geoffrey looked anything but betrothed when they were together. I really think your wedding will have to wait until we have rid ourselves of the twins. They are bound to make much more of a fuss over their weddings than Roxanne will about hers. Besides, I'm sure we can leave a great many details to be seen to by Lady Camberwick and the Duchess, who, though I have never met her, I am sure will be delighted."

Rutledge nearly choked on the brandy, but recovered, and with an appreciative smile, said that as far as he knew, Miss Winston was ready to name the day upon which she would make him the happiest of men. "Just as soon," he added, "as I can finish all this business, which you, my dear clever Miss Lynchard, are making extremely difficult."

"Oh, I am so sorry, my lord! But since it will be some minutes before Sir James and the others return, I may as well relieve your mind by explaining that I have an uncle who is employed in the office of the Foreign Secretary. Since he knows of my intense interest in events abroad, and of a silly little talent I happen to have for ciphers, he has occasionally employed me — with the full agreement of his superiors, of course — to assist in decoding reports from our agents in France. Some of yours were quite interesting, Your Grace," she said, pausing to sip her tea, "though sadly lacking in details of what the ladies of the Directorate were wearing."

"I assure you, my dear Miss Lynchard," the Duke burst out, totally exasperated, "that they were wearing precious little at the time, and I'm deuced glad I said nothing about it, for no one troubled to tell me that a lady would be reading every word I sent back!" His face was crimson with astonishment and laughter.

Miss Lynchard's eyes sparkled but she pursed her lips. "Really, my lord, I know it is not my place, but I hope you will remember to watch your language when Melodie and Gemma come in."

"I am sure, my dear lady, that if I do suffer such a lapse they will not hesitate to remind me," he retorted.

When they had finished laughing at one another, the Duke said, "And now you must tell me how you knew about Roxanne—Miss Winston and myself."

Miss Lynchard looked upon him with mildly contemptuous amusement. "It was quite obvious from the very beginning, my lord, when you were here with your shoulder wound, that she absolutely despised you, so of course I knew."

This cryptic explanation was all they had time for, as a noise in the corridor told them that their surprising and rewarding tête-à-tête was about to be interrupted. In another moment Sir James was wheeled in, followed by his twin daughters and their attendant swains.

There was utter confusion for several moments, as some members of the family rejoiced and others cried, and all tried to thank the Duke and demanded to know when they would see Alfred. Rutledge began to wonder what story Geoffrey had told them all, when that gentleman himself strolled in, and the Duke demanded, "What have you done, Pearson? These good people seem to think I am a hero!"

"Oh, but Your Grace, you are!" cried Gemma. "You have brought our beloved brother back from the dead."

"You have brought the lost sheep back into the fold," added Melodie solemnly.

"I say, Rutledge, I must shake your hand. Never knew that you were running such a deep game," said Lord Culverton, suiting the action to the word. Mr. Bentley merely stared at the Duke in awe, as if he really had resuscitated a corpse.

For the first time in many, many years, Henry Malverne was embarrassed. He counteracted this uncomfortable emotion by inquiring in an icy voice if he might speak with Sir James alone for a few moments. This fooled no one, but the delighted father called for his attendant to wheel him into his study, and beckoned to his honored guest.

There Rutledge endeavored to inform Sir James that his son, though alive, was by no means ready to partake of any violent celebration. "He is weak, sir, in fact, he has not yet walked a step on his own since I smuggled him out of France, and he needs quiet, darkness, and nourishing food, but he is eager to come home, and if you will give the orders, I will take your carriage and fetch him for you."

Sir James straightened up in his Bath chair, and put out his good hand for the Duke to take. "I owe you — my family owes you — more than I can ever repay, my lord. If you do not mind, I will go myself to fetch my boy home . . ." His voice broke for a moment, and after a small struggle, he smiled.

"He shall have all the rest and nourishment he needs, you need not worry, sir. We shall postpone the killing of the fatted calf until he can come downstairs and celebrate with us. His sisters will wait upon him hand and foot, and I shall probably be neglected, but I shan't mind a bit." He rang for his servant and immediately ordered his carriage to be prepared.

The Baronet's pleasure encouraged Rutledge to consult him about another matter relating to one of his children, and although at first Sir James was extremely puzzled and kept asking, "But what about the Pearson boy?" eventually His Grace managed to convey to the old gentleman that his daughter Roxanne had already signified her willingness to become the Duchess of Rutledge.

"What a sly puss!" was Sir James's only comment, and he assured the Duke that he was doubly glad to have him in the family. "But I don't quite understand. . . . You must promise me that we will have a long talk later and tell me exactly how it all came about — Alfred and Roxanne and you."

At Sir James's request, the Duke then left the father of his friend and of his bride to be alone for a few moments, and returned to the drawing room, where Melodie was saying, "Do you think we shall hear from Roxanne? I suppose she will start for home as soon as she gets your letter, Miss Lynchard."

The Duke looked at the governess, startled. He had

so counted on being the one to give her the glad news. . . .

Miss Lynchard shot a speaking glance at the Duke, which he was unable to interpret. Sighing at his obtuseness, she explained that she had taken it upon herself to write to Roxanne and gently break the joyous news to her, for the girls did now quite know how to do it properly and Sir James was much too overcome to think of writing. "I'm sure it was posted yesterday, girls, just after Sir Geoffrey left us, for I was writing it while he was here, was I not? I suppose she will get it very soon." With this there was a repetition of the look that had so puzzled Rutledge, and which was no more successful in conveying its meaning than it had been the first time.

After a few more minutes in which the family deluged him with questions about Alfred and he answered all that he could, the Duke referred the rest to Alfred himself, who, he assured them, would be with them that very evening. Then he took his leave, and to his surprise Miss Lynchard got up to see him out.

"Don't worry, Your Grace," she said softly as they emerged into the corridor. "The letter was never posted. Go to Roxanne, tell her your news, and bring her back. And do not forget poor Miss Pearson. I'm afraid that she has had to wait for the news as well, and it really isn't fair."

The strange looks sent his way in the drawing room being thus explained, on impulse Rutledge grabbed her hand and kissed it. "Bless you, my dear, very dear, Miss Lynchard. I hope that when your services are no longer required here, we can make a place for you in the nurseries at Rutledge."

"Oh, my! Thank you, Your Grace, but I cannot quite feel that I am qualified to instruct the daughters of a Duke!"

"Nonsense, Miss Lynchard. You have, after all, unusual talents. And I shall particularly want all my daughters instructed in the art of the cipher. It is so useful and ladylike, you know."

If the Duke had been a boy she would doubtless have tapped him lightly on the cheek for his impertinence, but as he was not, Miss Lynchard merely smiled.

Chapter Sixteen

London was celebrating. London was mourning. Lord Nelson had soundly whipped the French fleet at Trafalgar on October the twenty-first. Lord Nelson was also, alas, dead. Roxanne and Lady Camberwick had driven out to pay a call the day the news came to London, and the streets were crowded with English men and women talking excitedly, waving little flags and reading broadsheets posted up everywhere, giving vivid descriptions of the battle.

The church bells rang, the newspapers deplored the death of Nelson, and England breathed a collective sigh of relief that a large part of the French menace was no more. Roxanne was as unaffected as a patriotic citizen could be, and wondered vaguely if Miss Lynchard had heard the news yet, since she always took such a minute interest in every item relating to the war.

The news was the only interesting point of what had been a dismal week. Lady Camberwick had demanded to know what Roxanne intended to do about her wedding, and had threatened to write to Sir Geoffrey herself about it, until Roxanne gave up and told her that she was no longer betrothed to Sir Geoffrey. At this her aunt muttered dark warnings about not tolerating any niece of hers becoming an ape-leader, and sulked for three full days.

Fanny had talked of going home soon, but now that

her sister Mrs. Broughton was back in town, she spent a great deal of time with her discussing a certain interesting event due to take place in that household soon. Roxanne felt unwanted and did not trouble to accompany her friend on these visits very often.

She was bored, frightened, and miserable, and had almost determined to go home herself. Oddly, she had not had her usual spate of letters from her sisters and Miss Lynchard that week, and wondered if something was wrong at home.

Just as she was determined to bring up with her still silent aunt the subject of going home, the Duchess of Rutledge returned to London after a presumably successful cure at Tunbridge Wells.

The Duchess greeted Roxanne warmly when the ladies of Upper Brook Street visited in Albemarle Street on that noisy celebratory day, but as they were not alone, Roxanne could not do what she had determined to do the moment she saw her, that is, tell her that she and the Duke were secretly betrothed. Having so little joy in her life at present, Roxanne hoped to manufacture some for someone else, but in another moment she realized that her inability to explain fully where the Duke had gone would only bring the Duchess more worry.

Fortunately, the three ladies had not been seated long in the Duchess's pretty green sitting room when that lady informed them that she had heard at last from her wayward son.

Roxanne sat bolt upright and listened intently, hoping that her eagerness and misery would not show on her face.

"That troublesome boy of mine has written at last,

from Wiltshire, of all places, to say that after Scotland he had traveled a great deal visiting friends, and now was come to stay at Rosemark with Sir Geoffrey Pearson. He says that I can expect him soon in London, however."

Fanny retained sufficient presence of mind to say, "I had no idea that the Duke was visiting Geoffrey. However, I must admit that my brother has been remiss in his correspondence lately." She exchanged a brief glance with Roxanne, whose heart was in turmoil, and who could barely speak. He was in England, he was alive . . . and he would soon be in London. Had he brought Alfred back? When would he come to her?

The visit at the Duchess's house brought no further enlightenment, and this disappointment and the incessant bell ringing gave Roxanne a dreadful headache, so that she could not even bear to share the suspense with Fanny, but retired to her room as soon as they managed to wend their way home through the excited crowds.

Roxanne rested with a handkerchief soaked in eau-de-cologne spread out on her forehead, and though she was agitated by the Duchess's news, she was so worn from lack of rest that she soon fell into a healing sleep, only to be interrupted by a violent knocking at her door. She groaned, and the knocker apparently took the sound as an invitation to enter, for Fanny burst into the room.

"Roxanne, you must come quickly. There is someone here to see you," she said. Her eyes were bright, her cheeks were rosy, and her thin face looked suddenly plumper.

Roxanne sat up and struggled to put on her shoes, still half-asleep. "Who is it? What has happened,

Fanny, you look so strange, so feverish . . ."

"Never mind that." Fanny tugged at her friend's arm as she paused by the dressing table to take a brush to her disarranged hair. "He is waiting—there, now I've said what I wasn't supposed to . . . oh, do hurry."

With that she forcibly pulled the slightly disheveled Roxanne from her room, led her down the stairs, and opening the door to the morning room, thrust her inside. It must be Alfred, Roxanne thought, or else Fanny would hardly look like that. Then a second thought told her that if Alfred was in the morning room Fanny would not have left him for a second, but sent a servant to call her.

She had no time to think of any other possibility, for the one possibility that held any meaning for her was apparently true. Upon stumbling into the room she was caught in a pair of strong arms and kissed quite mercilessly. Finally she found it necessary to breathe and the Duke released her, only to hold her face in his hands and drink in the sight of it.

"My darling, my darling," he whispered, and buried his face in her neck. It took no more than a second for all of Roxanne's doubt and misery to dissolve and for complete and utter joy to wash over her.

"It is really you . . . I am not dreaming, am I?" she asked, raising her head suddenly from its comfortable resting place on his chest, as she recalled that the last thing she had been doing was sleeping.

For an answer Rutledge kissed her again, and satisfied at last that this was real, Roxanne pulled away and made him sit down next to her. As he was still able to keep his arms around her the Duke did not complain, and Roxanne had an opportunity to note the changes in her love, his weariness and thinness, and it made her only the more grateful to have her beside him once again.

"Now you must tell me at once. Is Alfred with you? Fanny looked so happy that—"

She stopped, for she saw his face fall in extreme disappointment. "Why, what is wrong?"

"First Miss Lynchard, and now even you have betrayed me. A curse upon you clever females! Can I keep nothing from you?" demanded the Duke.

Roxanne laughed at his anguished look. "I suppose not. But aside from myself, who are all of these clever females?"

He ignored her except to hold her tighter. "I have labored for three years, my dear, to keep this secret from the world, and for several months to keep it from you, which was much the more difficult thing, I assure you. At Westcombe Hall your former governess coolly informed me that not only had she thought all along that your brother was not dead, and had with no apparent difficulty kept her suspicions from your entire family, but also that she knew from your first unkind word to me that we would shortly be married. And after all of my efforts you simply demand to know if I have brought you your dead brother!"

Roxanne began to understand and was quite ashamed for having disappointed him, he looked so unhappy. "Of course, you could not know that Fanny and I . . . that is, I guessed, and Fanny had to tell me. It was all because of that dreadful man in the park, and that groom of yours that Geoffrey made my aunt hire—is he paid two salaries, by the way?"

"What man in the park? And what the devil does

Pearson mean by hiring away my groom?"

Roxanne explained as best she could, which did not mollify the Duke very much.

"That, my dear, is why you were not to know," he said. "I would not have put you in such danger. But I cannot blame anyone. Pearson tried to protect you by sending my sturdiest servant to guard you, forgetting that the poor fellow was not really a groom and unaccustomed to horses."

Roxanne assured him that she and Fanny had not been harmed, only frightened, and then began to ask him again about Alfred, but he stopped her.

"Please! Allow me to fulfill what has been one of my heart's wishes ever since I first knew that I loved you, Roxanne."

The Duke rose from the sofa, went to the door, and pretended to enter the room, bowing deeply before her.

"My dear Miss Winston," he said solemnly, "I hope you will not be too shocked, but I have some wonderful news for you. Prepare yourself, my dear," and amid Roxanne's giggles, he sat down beside her again and took her hands in his, gazing into her eyes in a way that, despite her laughter, made Roxanne glad that she was already sitting down, for her legs suddenly felt as though they were of the consistency of jelly.

"Your brother is not dead, my love. He has been a spy in France for three years, and as it was through my influence that he attained that position, you were correct in blaming me for his fate. He has lately been in great peril. But I have gone to France and, against tremendous odds, have brought him back to you. Although he is ill, he is alive and on the mend, and he awaits you at home with the rest of your family. May I have the honor and pleasure of escorting you to him, as soon as you are ready?"

"Oh, my dearest, most absurd Harry!" Roxanne cried. "Fanny and I were right, then. You should not be disappointed, for I did not know everything. It was only after you were gone so long that I had time to think over all the strange things that had happened, and even then I thought I was imagining it. Fanny did not know that you had gone to France to rescue Alfred, though she guessed that something had gone wrong."

Roxanne leaped up. "I will go and pack, which I am sure Fanny is doing already. May we leave right away? I do not care if we drive all night. I must see Alfred. How long has he been home? Why did no one write to me?"

The Duke was ignoring this and chuckling to himself. "You called me Harry. I had always wondered if I would ever hear you speak my name. Curiously, you say it in exactly the same tone as my mother."

"Very likely I learned it from her," said Roxanne, blushing a little. "I have been wanting to be able to say it for weeks."

He stood up and scooped her into his arms again. "And I can think of no one who has a better right. But as to your negligent family, all I can say is that it was left to the cunning Miss Lynchard to inform you of the happy news, and she was, thankfully, too sympathetic to me, unlike yourself, to let you hear the news from any other source but my lips."

"Oh, I'm so sorry, Harry, that I quite spoiled what was meant to be a beautiful gift, the surprise that was to make our happiness complete," said Roxanne, and in penance she planted a kiss upon his cheek, shyly, for she had never yet initiated any such gesture with her beloved, though she had dreamed of doing this and more a thousand times.

His Grace took it well and like a true Christian, for he turned the other cheek in order that the salute could be repeated, and finally Roxanne, glowing with pleasure at the success of this maneuver, closed her eyes and placed her lips on his. The Duke murmured against her mouth encouragingly and if it were not for Fanny's interruption the two lovers would no doubt have pursued this experiment for several hours.

"Have you settled it all between you yet?" she demanded.

Roxanne broke away from her betrothed guiltily, but he put his arm around her waist and said, "As you see, my dear, we were still negotiating some final details."

Fanny made an impatient face. "Lady Maria is agog to know what you have been doing so long in here with His Grace, Roxanne. I think she suspects. Will you hurry and tell her so that we can all go home? I have told the maids to pack for all three of us." She stared at the Duke in a desperate plea, and he sprung into action.

"Of course, poor Fanny, you have waited long enough and the situation is indeed urgent. There is a very impatient young man awaiting you in a sickbed at Westcombe Hall right now, and although Miss Lynchard and his younger sisters are exhausting themselves to amuse him, no doubt he is tired of prayers and nursery prattle, and is pining for your tender care." He led Roxanne to the door. "I shall speak — no, my dear *we* shall speak to Lady Camberwick, and then to my poor neglected mama, and I shall escort you all into Wiltshire."

The Duke was as good as his word. The interview with her ladyship took only a few minutes, with time set aside for her incredulous silence, tears of joy, and finally laughter at the thought of how easily she had been fooled about such important and familiar matters as death and marriage.

His Grace then whisked Roxanne and her ladyship away to Albermarle Street, where an amazed and delighted Duchess was more than ready to welcome her dear young friend Miss Winston as a future daughter, and to scold her undutiful son for having risked his life without having first asked her permission.

After many promises by both Rutledge and Roxanne to write long letters to Her Grace, soon to be the Dowager, the betrothed couple and Lady Camberwick flew back home as quickly as the crowded streets would allow. By now Roxanne was as ready to celebrate as any of the roisterers reeling from the taverns, but Fanny was waiting, and she only made the Duke stop so that she could buy a flag to wave.

In what seemed to Roxanne like a miraculously short time, but which Fanny declared was actually an eternity, the entire party was in the Duke's carriage and on its way to Westcombe.

Upon their arrival, which was greeted by a great noise of confusion and delight, Roxanne took pity on Fanny and let her go to Alfred first, but her own impatience, despite her understanding of the lovers' dilemma, made her too eager to give them more than ten minutes alone. The reunion between Roxanne and her brother was as was to be expected, emotional and tiring, and after as much had been said that could be said through tears of joy, she left Alfred to his rest,

Fanny sitting quietly by his side, happy just to be in the same room with him.

The old house seemed full of people. Neighbors and the neighbors' servants came in and out bearing gifts of flowers, wine, and cakes for the family, jellies and broths and other nourishing trifles for the invalid. Roxanne held many an illuminating conversation with Miss Lynchard, and Lady Camberwick overbore Sir James in every particular of planning his eldest daughter's wedding, though he valiantly tried to carry his point that it should not take place in London. Fortunately, he gained some ground by reminding her that the Duke and his mother might also have something to say about the matter, and there her ladyship let the matter rest for the time being, until she could consult with her dear friend Althea.

The Duke had his promised long talk with Sir James, who now wanted to have every circumstance, both of his son's long absence and falsely reported death and his daughter's sudden change in wedding plans, explained to him, and when he was thoroughly satisfied in all these minutiae Roxanne went to him.

"Well, my dear, we have come a long way, a long way indeed. And so you will be a Duchess." He sounded subdued, and Roxanne searched his face anxiously.

"You are not disappointed, Papa, are you?"

"No indeed. But I am puzzled. I thought you despised the Duke. Tell me the truth, my dear. I know you are sincere, but search your conscience, as I know you often do. Do you love Rutledge now for the fact that he has brought back your brother?"

"Oh, no, Papa, I would never want you to think that. You see, I loved him in spite of believing that he had all but murdered Alfred," she explained.

She told her father how she had broken off the engagement with Geoffrey, how she had resisted this decision, for she did not wish to cause trouble between the two families, but how Geoffrey had sought to make her break with him so he could pursue an heiress.

When he had heard of the secret joys and sorrows with which his daughter had been burdened, Sir James drew her to him with his good arm and held her close. "My poor dear. You have had a great trial, greater than all of us. But you have come through it like a champion. I give you my blessing, my child. I have always liked Rutledge, and he has assured me he will do all in his power to make you happy."

Lord Culverton and Mr. Bentley had deserted their loved ones briefly, returning to London only to assure their parents that they still lived and to collect newer and more impressive costumes. Though their men of business had long since settled the issue of marriage settlements, and they knew that until the wedding their presence in Wiltshire was unnecessary, they had set up headquarters at the Angel, so as not to be a burden on the family, but were constantly at the Winston's, fascinated by the drama unfolding before them. They looked upon Alfred Winston with awe, as though he were indeed risen from the dead, and greatly assisted his recovery by telling him all the most amusing bits of London gossip.

The twins were, to Roxanne and Miss Lynchard's surprise, gentle with Alfred, neither annoying him with constant prayers nor encouraging him to read improving works. They seemed to respect his ordeal as though it had been a spiritual transformation of the kind they understood. Indeed, Alfred seemed a different man from the one who had left them three years before. Roxanne often wondered as she sat with her brother and watched him improve in strength and health day by day, if perhaps no one had really known him then.

On Sunday there was a special service of thanksgiving in the village church, and for the occasion the twins even deserted Mr. Driggs and his chapel, for love and happiness had made them tolerant. The family and their guests, excluding Alfred and Sir James, filled the Winston family pews and the voices of the three promised husbands of the Winston daughters soared to the rafters of the old church as they sang a hymn of thanksgiving.

Roxanne shared a prayer book with her Harry, exchanged smiles with him when their hands met as if by accident, and gloried in his presence next to her, dreaming of the day when, no matter what Lady Camberwick said, she would be united to her Duke in this little church with all her friends and neighbors about her.

But first the twins had to be settled. After the service the three betrothed couples stood in the sun outside the church, the object of their neighbors' curiosity. When they had gratified all of their acquaintance by introducing them to a Duke, an Earl, and a gentleman one day to be a Baronet, they made their way home.

In the garden before dinner the twins startled Roxanne and Harry by announcing that their marriages, far from distracting them from their Christian duty, would only extend the sphere of their influence, and that with the assistance and advice of Lady Allenbrook, they and their husbands would embark on a new project to benefit the unfortunate.

"It is to be called S-A-V-E," Melodie announced, pronouncing each letter. "Is it not clever? It was his lordship's idea." She smiled at her promised husband and he beamed with pride.

"What exactly is it that you are saving?" Roxanne wanted to know.

The Earl of Culverton looked with affection upon his betrothed. "Souls, Miss Winston. It is to be the Society for the Abolition of Vice in England. S.A.V.E., you see?"

"Very amusing,"·approved the Duke. "And my aunt put you up to this, you say? I shall have to have a talk with her," he murmured to Roxanne.

"Oh, is Lady Allenbrook your aunt, Your Grace?" Gemma asked, wide-eyed. "How curious that she never mentioned it. But to answer your question, she had nothing to do with it. It is our own idea."

"Yes," Melodie said proudly, "we have decided that since our solitary efforts to reform morals and induce the ton to think of serious matters were only partially successful, we must form a society. That is the only way we will have an impact, you see. Everyone respects an organized society."

Roxanne wondered at her sisters' capacity for self-deception after all the lessons they ought to have learned in London, but only sighed.

The Duke looked incredulous. "And do you gentlemen approve of this?" he asked his friends.

"Oh, certainly," said Cyril Bentley, though he did not really look certain. "Tony will be the patron — because he's an Earl, you know, and it will look well on our letters, and as I've not yet come into my title, I shall simply be an administrator, although of course our men of business will see to all that."

The Earl took his fiancée's hand and patted it. "Our wives will do the rest. They know about these things, you see."

Roxanne exchanged a look with her betrothed and forced herself not to respond to the invitation to laughter she saw in his eyes. "Indeed, I do, and I am sure it will be quite a successful venture." She looked at the Duke, willing him to say something encouraging.

"Yes," added Rutledge, thus prodded, "A worthy aim for a man of your position, Culverton."

"Well," said the Earl, "one can't have people forgetting the importance of good behavior, you know. Too much of this drinking and gaming going on about us."

Gemma was obviously impatient for him to finish, so obviously was she bursting with a good idea. "Suppose we make the Duke an honorary sponsor of our society? After all, he has done so much good for our family that we really ought to repay him."

Roxanne was about to speak, but Rutledge forestalled her. "It is too great an honor for a humble sinner such as myself," he said without a trace of mockery. "But may I suggest that you appoint to some position of high visibility one of your earliest successes in moral reform, Miss Gemma?"

Roxanne took his meaning immediately. "Yes, why not ask Lord Wynne? He seemed to take your instructions to heart, and I'm sure he would carry the word into the fashionable world."

"Even," added the Duke darkly, "into the clubs of St. James'."

Roxanne and Rutledge left the foursome pondering this advice, and strolled farther into the chill autumna garden. Roxanne shivered, and the Duke pulled he close.

"Harry, we are in full sight of the drawing roon windows, and my Aunt Maria is probably watching u right now," Roxanne scolded.

But he did not let her go. "Your sisters said I de served a reward, my dear, and I'm sure your aunt won' begrudge me a moment's impropriety. For services ren dered to the Winston family, I hereby declare mysel amply recompensed by the hand of the fair Roxanne,' he intoned.

And then, to the great satisfaction and amusement not only of Lady Camberwick but also of Fanny and Alfred, who had left his room for the first time, and of Sir James, who at his son's urging had had his chair rolled to the drawing room window, the Duke once more practiced bestowing kisses upon his future Duchess, though after the first three she assured him that in that exercise he had had enough practice and was now quite perfect.

EXPERIENCE THE SENSUOUS MAGIC OF JANELLE TAYLOR!

FORTUNE'S FLAMES (2250, $3.95)

Lovely Maren James' angry impatience turned to raging desire when the notorious Captain Hawk boarded her ship and strode confidently into her cabin. And before she could consider the consequences, the ebon-haired beauty was succumbing to the bold pirate's masterful touch!

SWEET SAVAGE HEART (1900, $3.95)

Kidnapped when just a child, seventeen-year-old Rana Williams adored her carefree existence among the Sioux. But then the frighteningly handsome white man Travis Kincade appeared in her camp . . . and Rana's peace was shattered forever!

DESTINY'S TEMPTRESS (1761, $3.95)

Crossing enemy lines to help save her beloved South, Shannon Greenleaf found herself in the bedroom of Blane Stevens, the most handsome man she'd ever seen. Though burning for his touch, the defiant belle vowed never to reveal her mission—nor let the virile Yankee capture her heart!

SAVAGE CONQUEST (1533, $3.75)

Heeding the call of her passionate nature, Miranda stole away from her Virginia plantation to the rugged plains of South Dakota. But captured by a handsome Indian warrior, the headstrong beauty felt her defiance melting away with the hot-blooded savage's sensual caress!

STOLEN ECSTASY (1621, $3.95)

With his bronze stature and ebony black hair, the banished Sioux brave Bright Arrow was all Rebecca Kenny ever wanted. She would defy her family and face society's scorn to savor the forbidden rapture she found in her handsome warrior's embrace!

Available wherever paperbacks are sold, or order direct from the Publisher. Send cover price plus 50¢ per copy for mailing and handling to Zebra Books, Dept. 2431, 475 Park Avenue South, New York, N.Y. 10016. Residents of New York, New Jersey and Pennsylvania must include sales tax. DO NOT SEND CASH.